CONTRAVENE

FIFTH STORY FROM
SPACE FLEET SAGAS

DON FOXE

CABALLUS
PRESS™

Written by Don Foxe. donfoxe.com

Produced by Caballus Press, USA Division
www.caballuspress.comm

Stock images are used for illustrative purposes only.
Some stock imagery from Pixabay.com, Pexels.com and Stock-adobe.com

ISBN: 9781732103658
9781732103665 (e)

Library of Congress Control Number: TBD

Acknowledgments

Thanks to Nancy Thurmond for continuing to expertly edit my manuscripts. Her hard work makes me appear a much better writer than I truly am.

Author's back cover photograph courtesy of Abri Kruger Photography, South Africa.

Cover graphics are mine, for better or worse. I do use others with more experience and better talent. I have a vision, so I go with it. Some graphics provided by pixabay.com, pexels.com, and unspash.com.

Every book is dedicated to Sarah because without her I would have no reason to write. She makes it possible for me to spend the time required to create, edit, and publish. During the months this story developed it was an especially stressful time. Her continued love and support, as always, kept me positive and on track. Everyone should have a Sarah in their life.

When Alexander the Great invaded India he used a group of special operators to scout ahead and prepare the way for his army. They looked and operated much like US Navy Seals.

Throughout history, small teams of brave men and women have performed the precision insertion, recon, and guerrilla tactics necessary to achieve goals a larger force would be unable to accomplish without high casualty rates and loss of lives.

Special Operation Teams have been an essential element of military forces since the first rock was thrown. I see no reason this will not be true long into the future, as long as anyone thinks they have good cause to toss rocks.

CONTRAVENE is dedicated to Special Operators across the world.

THE SPACE FLEET SAGAS

CONTACT AND CONFLICT
Aliens and Humans.
Book One in the Space Fleet Sagas.
The Launch of the PT-109, John F. Kennedy

CONFRONTATION
Aliens and Humans. Allies and Enemies
Book Two in the Space Fleet Sagas.

SPACE FLEET SAGAS
A Collection of Adventures.
Backstories Prior to the Launch of PT-109
Four Short Stories and Two Novelettes

CONFLUENCE
Book Three in the Space Fleet Sagas.

CONNEXIONS
The Fourth Story from the Space Fleet Sagas.

CONTRAVENE
Book 5 in the continuing adventures of Space Fleet.

In **CONTACT & CONFLICT . . .**

First contact is made by Captain Daniel Cooper, commanding officer of the SFPT-109, John F. Kennedy; Earth's first space-worthy battleship of the newly sanctioned Space Fleet.

In **CONFRONTATION . . .**

A trip to the planet Rys is needed to acquire power crystals to maintain and build more ships based on the Martian technology. During the visit, Coop and the JFK once more encounter Zenge invaders, this time saving Rys.

We discover the Zenge are pawns of a race called the Mischene. Mischene supremacists are convinced they should rule the galaxy. A confrontation with the Mischene, and their Zenge army is inevitable.

While these events occur in space, a secret society of influential and powerful people conspire to dissolve the UEC on Earth, returning our planet to regional rule.

In **CONFLUENCE . . .**

A group of unexpected allies work to save the United Earth from a conspiracy to dissolve the central government.

Space Fleet Battle Group sails to a dangerous region in space to face the forces behind the galactic conflict.

In **CONNEXIONS . . .**

Daniel Cooper is kidnapped by pirates and taken across the galaxy in a desperate bid to rescue two princesses and save a confederation of peaceful planets. In payment for services he is promised answers to the secrets of the Martians . . . and the origins of humans.

The targeted fire from the three Space Fleet flyers ripped into the Zenge, killing several. Those wounded, saved by their protective armor and thick skin, ignored the pain and the danger. Adding war cries to the ack-thack of laser fire, they charged forward with those uninjured. They overran Storm's position first.

The Fellen fired point-blank into an elongated snout filled with razor-sharp teeth before two others tackled her. The extended talons of the Zenge ripped at the METS. Rows of jagged teeth snapped at the woman as they attempted to bite down on her arms or legs.

Storm fought with the strength and skill of the residents of Fell. Her right hand smashing into the scaly enemy while her right slashed with her combat knife. It was quicker to retrieve the knife than draw her sidearm.

The blade gashed the throat of one. The other got his mouth around her wrist and bit down. The suit prevented the teeth from penetrating, but the immense pressure trapped her arm. The mortally wounded Zenge continued to rip at her as blood loss from the mortal wound weakened it. Claw tips caught a minuscule seam where the helmet integrated with the bodysuit, ripping it open and scratching the blue skin beneath.

She drove the knife beneath the chin of the bleeding Zenge, finishing it. When she attempted to recover the blade and hammer it into the one biting her wrist, another joined the fray in time to snare her free arm.

The Zenge with his teeth latched to Storm's wrist dug the claws of his free hand into the opening below her neck. He threw a muscled leg across her lower body to control her. The other Zenge continued to hold her other arm. The enemy trooper dropped to its knees, landing atop and penning Storm's left leg.

Talons capable of ripping sheet steel began to peel the METS away, tearing skin and spraying blood as the claws raked down and over her chest. The blood-lust washed over the two in anticipation of feeding on the woman while she still lived.

Elie laid down withering fire but could not prevent three of the Marauders reaching Storm's position. Incoming laser fire laced the pile of debris she used for cover. Refusing to hide while Storm and Jon-Jon were under immediate threat, her METS saved her four times when hits landed. The latest version of the tactical suit deflected the lasers, but could not stop the force of the impacts. Each hit landed like a blow from a sledgehammer. The fourth glanced off her helmet, rattling her already tender brain.

She brushed aside the cobwebs. She had to help Jon-Jon by taking out the Marauders advancing on his position. Then she needed to hot-foot it to Storm. As she raised her rifle, a thick mus-cled arm of green scale snaked around her throat and lifted her off the ground. One of the Marauders, the only one to not make the mistake of bunching with the others, had made her way around the conflict. She moved in from behind Elie. Foggy from the laser impacting her head, and not fully recovered from the crash, the Ranger did not notice the proximity alert on her heads-up display.

Jon-Jon stood in the doorway. Feet braced and rifle up with sights linked to his helmet optics. Twenty of the Marauders were down. Killed by Storm, Elie, and his weapons. Three reached Storm. Elie quit firing, but the Zenge had not advanced on her po-sition. She must have taken a hit. Six of the twenty dead lay on the ground in front of his position. Another half-dozen remained ac-tive, following behind those dead or dying, using the initial wave as fodder. He took out two more with clean head shots before an-other barreled through the opening. Three others followed. The structure, once used to protect him from enemy fire, now prevent-ed Storm or Elie, if either still lived, from targeting the Zenge in-side with him.

Storm's tears were not the result of pain. They were anger-dri-ven. Angry she would not be able to help Elie and Jon-Jon. Angry she would never know what became of Daniel Cooper.

Prelim

"Down! Down! Down!" Lt. Cardona ordered.

Incoming laser fire plowed into his line of Marines as they topped the ridge. Marines went down with broken bones and bruised organs. The wounded dropped, outer uniforms smoldering from the intense heat of the lasers. The Multi-Environment Tactical Suits (METS), worn beneath the cammo, deflected some of the energy. The force delivered by the high-velocity directed particles of light still resulted in physical trauma.

Three unconscious soldiers tumbled down the steep slope. Four others crumpled into tight balls.

Four Space Marines and an interpreter remained to face the enemy.

"Suppressive fire," Cardona called. He and the other four sprayed laser beams from shoulder-fired rifles to keep the ambushers away from the ridge-line. The lip of the ravine provided their only cover.

Sergeant Lewis, on the lieutenant's left, ceased fire to lob an optic-orb between the Marines and the enemy. The video from the orb's multiple lenses fed into his METS' faceplate.

"Video is screwy because of their jammers," he informed the others. "Looks like two to three-dozen operators with laser rifles. They are behind debris and burned-out vehicles on the roadway twenty-yards from our position."

The suppressive fire from the Marine squad did not suppress the enemy for very long. Laser beams blazed through the ozone overhead and bolts from less-contained strikes blasted the hard ground throwing up molten pieces of gravel and lighting small fires in the short grasses.

"Stay focused," Cardona ordered. "The ravine runs for miles in both directions, so they can't flank us without coming into the open. They may have thick scales and body armor, but our lasers can punch through while their's are less effective."

"Tell that to the wounded," Corporal Hanson whispered before ducking when a blast sent hot rocks and dirt at his head. The shielded helmet he wore would protect him, but the response was automatic.

Two of the Marines injured but conscious pulled themselves back into the firefight. Pieces of cloth glowed red around burned uniform material. Pain made it difficult to concentrate, but the drive to join their teammates pushed them to add their weapons to the defensive line.

A group of green-scaled reptilian aliens rushed them. They came from behind a shell that once was a commercial bus. The high-pitched screams issued from their elongated snouts joined the ack-thack of lasers criss-crossing the kill-zone between the two forces.

The seven Marines did not need to communicate to recognize the threat and react. Weapons in the hands of experienced fighters cut the charge into a retreat before the Zenge warriors made it off the asphalt road. Of the eight attempting to overrun their position, only three made it back to cover.

The freedom fighter acting as interpreter for the squad took a beam across her forehead. The female's fur could deflect laser's nearly as well as a METS. But not quite as good. The beam seared her and the force of the impact knocked her unconscious.

"She's alive but out," Corporal Hanson called, using the break in action to check on the fallen interpreter.

"Kous, have you gotten anything from hq?" Cardona asked.

Sgt. Kousa carried a transceiver with a more powerful battery than the crystal slivers used to power METS comms. The enemy jammers and the forcefield protecting the city played hell with communications. As soon as the North African could, he began sending distress signals toward a repeater station set miles away from the city limits. The repeater, with a much more powerful signal amplification capability, would rebound incoming messages to the surface command center and the battleship orbiting overhead.

"Nothing," he answered. "Our calls could be garbled or not getting out," he added. "If hq is trying to reply, incoming messages might be jammed."

Cardona lay prone, his feet on the slope and his head and shoulders just below the rim of the ravine. He did not lift up to peek over the edge, letting Sgt. Lewis keep him informed by monitoring the optic-orb. At the moment, neither side engaged.

The squad leader had three wounded scattered on the slope beneath him. They could be dead or dying. Two more out-of-action just behind the scrimmage line. Two working-wounded who could pass out at any moment, and a local unconscious with a head wound. Eight of twelve team members who could not escape if he called a retreat. A retreat that would leave them open on the side of a hill running toward a dirty stream they would have to cross only to run up the other side.

"Single fire," he called to the five remaining active operators. "Select your targets and conserve your power."

"If they charge?" Hanson asked.

"Aim like it's important," the Colombian commander answered.

The members of the team could assess their situation the same as the lieutenant. When the enemy decided they were tired of waiting, or if they called for more soldiers and bigger weapons, the small band of Marines would fight. They would not win, but they would fight.

"Surface Command believes they have Marines under fire southeast of the city," Storm reported from the comm-tac station. Elena Casalobos piloted Angel 7 through the alien troposphere. Jonathan Johnson, Jon-Jon, sat in the co-pilot's seat. He recently joined the forces on Phisor.

"Send me the coordinates," Casalobos ordered. "I'll slide across the top of the forcefield and drop in behind the Marauders. Jon-Jon can target them with laser fire. Watch for any sign of the Mischene dropping their shield," she warned the Fellen. "Their plasma cannon could turn us to ashes."

"Aye," Storm replied. The blue-skinned female from the planet Fell picked up military jargon while serving with Earth's Space Fleet over the past two years.

The Phisoran metropolis appeared on the eastern horizon as Loba (Casalobos' callsign) leveled the fighter below the cloud cover. At Mach 3 the distance separating them disappeared. The fields below turned to abandoned suburbs. The rubble they flew over next once a thriving business district on the fringe of a major city.

The invasion of Phisor left their metropolitan areas wasted. The result of the second incursion by Zenge troops led by Mischene military officers against a peaceful species. A field test of their combat abilities against a civilization without interstellar capability. A tune-up before the Mischene launched a war against partners in the Trade Alliance[1].

"I can't believe they destroyed this place," Jon-Jon remarked. The cockpit canopy rendered a view of the surface as they crossed. "It reminds me of Earth. It looks like someone took a flamethrower to the entire planet."

"They used it for practice," Storm said. "After they destroyed the few military bases and sank their naval ships from space, invasion troops swarmed the urban areas. The Mischene used the incursion to test the shock collars placed on the Zenge. They needed to make sure they could control the beasts when they went into blood-craze."

"Looks like it didn't work," Jon-Jon responded.

"The shock collars did work," Loba said. "The first planet they invaded ended in total genocide. Following the initial surface attacks here, the Mischene used the collars to pull the Zenge back. They turned Phisor into a training ground, sending units down to track and destroy resistance groups. After the Prophet's defeat in the Aster System some of his miscreant military officers, with thousands of the more vicious Zenge, retreated here. They planned to make Phisor their new base of operations while they continued the Prophet's dream of a Mischene conquest of the galaxy. Coming up on the forcefield," she alerted them.

"No drop in shield power," Storm called. "We are being scanned. They will alert the Marauders."

---

1 Trade Alliance Worlds: Loose amalgamation of systems which bartered goods and services through wormhole connections.

"Too late," Loba whispered. Angel 7 topped the forcefield at its apex above the center of the city. The ship raced downward, skimming the shield as it flew toward the embattled Marines.

"Lasers," Jon-Jon said aloud, his hands working two joysticks. From beneath the wings, four cannons fired ranged-bursts of deadly light. Locked to the coordinates provided by comm-tac, the lasers slammed into Zenge troopers hidden behind the remains of buildings and discarded transports littering the four-lane road-way.

The Marauders, the Phisoran designation for the Mischene-Zenge invaders, ambushed the Marines as they crossed a ravine. Space Fleet personnel adopted the term after arriving to prove not every alien meant them harm.

The squad under duress had been dispatched to scout for tunnels that might provide access into the city. Command hoped to discover a passageway beneath the surface not obstructed by the shielding.

The ambushers held every advantage. They outnumbered the twelve-person team three-to-one, held the high ground, and used cover to remain safe from return fire. The Marines were stuck on a hillside with open ground behind them. The ridge of the ravine the only protection from incoming rounds.

Angel 7's lasers changed the odds in seconds. Bursts rocked debris, reduced flammable rubble to ashes, and tore through the lizard-like skin of the Zenge.

"The Marines are crossing the ridge to engage the remaining Marauders," Storm reported. "The signal is garbled, but the team leader sends his thanks."

"Tell them . . ."

Casalobos never completed her sentence. Angel 7 reeled as if slammed by a titan's foot kicking the shit out of the ship.

"Angel 7 hit by a pulse wave," Lt. Izabella 'Izzy' Dominczyk reported. The communications specialist monitored comms and surface scans from a console on the bridge of the PT-109, John F. Kennedy.

"Did the Mischene lower the forcefield?" First Officer Genna Bouvier asked.

"Negative," Izzy replied. "The beam came from outside the shielded zone. I had no idea the Marauders had a pulse cannon."

"No one did," Bouvier said. "Contact Angel 7 for a sit-rep[2]. Weapons, fire on the coordinates for the pulse cannon."

"Tachyon burst fired," Lt.JG Lesego Ndaba reported. Ndaba, normally a pilot, currently acted as the 109's Tactical Officer.

"No response from Angel 7," Izzy said. "She's off-line and headed toward the eastern edge of the shield zone. They're going in hard, First."

"Tachyon destroyed two blocks," Ndaba said. "No sign of pulse cannon debris. The weapon must be mobile. Scans?"

"Energy signature before and after the pulse cannon discharged," Izzy reported, eyes jumping between data reports. "Likely the power source for the cannon. Nothing now. It's either cloaked or underground."

"Angel 7?" Genna demanded.

"Down," Izzy responded. "They crashed too close to the forcefield for a reliable scan. They are also inside the range of the communication jammers the Mischene use. General Gregory is aware and is in contact with Colonel Duval on the surface."

First Officer Genna Bouvier, in command with ship's Captain Casalobos away, sat motionless in the Command Chair. Her only outward appearance of emotion were the white-knuckles caused by balling her fingers into fists.

"Their ship crashed on the far side of the city."

Precisely because of situations like this, Anton Gregory regretted accepting his promotion. General Gregory paced the war room aboard the PT-109. Former *Colonel* Gregory, the Space Ranger, would already be on a shuttle headed for the surface.

"Contact?" he asked.

---

[2] sit-rep: Situation Report

"Nothing since the Mayday," the corporal monitoring surface communications answered.

"I had them on my display until the ship was hit," the telemetry specialist chimed in. "The image dissolved. I haven't located Angel 7's signature since."

"The Mayday came after the image faded," comms added. "Whatever took the fighter down didn't destroy it. The HATCH[3] captured the message, not short-range systems. The loop-return indicates an echo continued until it faded away on the Eastern side of the cosmopolitan area."

Calling the burned out urban center a cosmopolitan area constituted a reach. Following the invasion by the Zenge, the inhabitants became prisoners, hid, or escaped into the countryside.

"How near to the Mischene fortifications?" Gregory asked.

"An echo isn't going to give me an exact location," the corporal began, took note of the Russian's scowl, and said, "Three-to-ten miles. Marauder-held territory. Inside the city limits, but outside the shielded zone."

"General Gregory." The voice emanated from embedded speakers within the room.

"Yes, Kennedy?"

"The shield-arrays the Mischene use to protect their bases hamper scans."

"I am aware, Kennedy." Frustration seeped into his tone.

"Hampers, but does not prevent me from patching together data from multiple sources on board and from the surface of the planet," the artificial intelligence continued, unaffected by the General's sour mood. "I cannot pinpoint Angel 7, but there is increased activity within the enemy encampment. The Mischene are deploying assets toward the crash site."

The John F. Kennedy, PT-109, Space Fleet's first operational interstellar warship, maintained a stationary position above the

---

[3] HATCH - Hernadez-ASparquilla Tachyon Communications Housing. External-mounted array used to capture or dispatch communications via tachyon streams.

razed city. The Phisoran metropolis converted into a Revolution-ary Mischene Military (RMM) fortification. RMM became the new designation assumed by those Mischene formerly loyal to the Prophet. They planned to continue his vision to rule the galaxy.

The Patrol-Torpedo Boat maintained a high altitude in defer-ence to a plasma cannon protecting the enemy encampment. The ship needed the extra time the higher elevation provided to evade plasma bursts fired by the gunners below. An incoming load ar-rived in seconds. The threat required the crew and the AI to re-main on constant alert. The ship's sonic shields held up against the super-heated toroid[4], but the impact knocked her out of kilter. Internal systems and people took a beating each time the crew did not react in time.

"Comms, contact Colonel Duval. Maybe ground troops saw where Angel landed," Gregory ordered.

"Anton, it's Genna," the voice arrived via a subdural trans-comm[5] chip located beneath his right ear.

He hummed a "humph" to answer. Using the private channel meant she did not wish others to hear.

"Give the order and I will put us on the surface," she said.

"Continue," Anton ordered the personnel in the war room. He exited into the corridor before responding. "Genna, I'm not giving that order. You will not take this ship anywhere," he said as soon as the door closed behind him.

"Elie, Storm, and Jon-Jon are down there," Genna replied.

---

[4] Plasma Cannons fire toroids, a coiled material that revolves as it su-perheats and becomes plasma. The toroid has a hole in the middle. The weapon is doubly dangerous: the plasma load can disintegrate a target and the extreme velocity can cause devastating results from the force generated at impact. Extra-atmospheric plasma loads have extreme range.

[5] trans-comm: Translation and Communications system created and im-proved upon by engineers from the planet Fell. Provided instant transla-tion for known alien languages and translated speech into the alien's language. Short-range communications could be access. Long-range available if linked with a stronger communication array. Certain trans-comm chips included private channel access among a few trusted friends and allies.

"Three people who are trained to take care of themselves until we get troops to them," Gregory countered. "Remember the effort required for Elie and Admiral Patterson to get you approved as First Officer. You cannot do anything to make their decision look wrong, Genna."

No reply came from the avatar of the ship's AI. The Russian considered bulling his way to the bridge to make sure she did not jeopardize her status, the ship, or the overall mission. Instead, he calmed down and used a less-natural, softer approach.

"Genna, I'm their friend, too. I've known Elie over thirty-years. She is more my sister than friend. I want to take the 109 down there and bring them home. We can't. If we cause the loss of this ship, for any reason, but especially for a personal crusade, the mission to recover this world will become a defeat."

The big former Spetsnaz special operator leaned his wide back against the bulkhead. He understood now the full weight of accepting the promotion to General. As a Space Ranger Colonel, he could charge into any situation and worry about consequences later. Now an entire world relied on his judgement.

"Our mission is to remove the Prophet's Mischene leftovers, and the Zenge who remained loyal to them from this world. Return it to the Phisorans. We want to accomplish this without killing the civilian hostages they hide behind. The PT-109's job is support the ground forces and protect them against any attacks from space. Your job, Commander Bouvier, is command this ship until Captain Casalobos returns. Understood?"

"Understood. Genna, out."

Gregory sighed then returned to the war room.

"Colonel Duval waiting," the corporal on comms informed him.

"Duval, it's Gregory. Do you have anything on our lost sheep?"

"General vicinity of the crash is all I have," the officer in charge of the surface mission answered. "The pulse cannon used to shoot them down wasn't a known placement. The Mischene saved it for a surprise, and they have it on a mobile platform."

"They have a plasma cannon and a pulse cannon," Gregory said. "Any other heavy artillery I should know about?"

"None I know of," Duval answered. "But I didn't know about the pulse cannon."

"Colonel, can you think of any reason the Mischene are working this hard to hold their position? We have them surrounded. They have no air support. The Prophet is dead. The majority of Zenge abandoned them. The planet has no strategic value. What am I missing?"

"Fanaticism," the other officer suggested. "I can't imagine any other reason. Of course, it is also the worst possible answer. If they are truly fanatics . . . "

"They will fight until they die," Gregory completed Duval's response. "Can the squad Angel 7 flew in to support reach the crash site?"

"Communications are sketchy because of their jammers, but I believe the squad had too many injured to stay in the field. As much as they want to help, they need to get their people back for medical treatment."

"Can you get a team to the crash site?"

"Prepping to dispatch. However, no way they can get around the forcefield and to the location faster than the Marauders," he warned. "I also have reports the Marauders are massing troops on this side of the city. They probably hope we send a substantial force to rescue our downed crew, leaving our position vulnerable. It's why I decided on a six-person team and not a larger squad. I hope I made the proper call."

"We're talking about Elie Casalobos, Colonel." Gregory spoke with conviction. "Only one other Space Ranger could compete with her as the deadliest asset you could set against a superior force in a ground war."

"Do you think we will ever find out what happened to Captain Cooper?" Duval asked.

"I don't know. I do know Elie will make the assholes who come after her crew sorry. Your team might get there in time to save them from her."

"She's out," Jon-Jon said to Storm. "I think she slammed her head against the yoke."

Elie Casalobos lay inert on the galley deck. Jon-Jon knelt beside her.

"I can't get anything through the jammers," Storm said. She slammed a blue fist against the console. "Best communications expert in Space Fleet. Did you know Admiral Patterson said that about me at the Academy? My sister Stacey was in the audience. I've never been as proud of anything in my life. And I can't send a fucking message because of Mischene tech they originally bought from my own planet."

"Storm, I'm more concerned about Elie," Jon-Jon said. He kept his voice neutral, trying to calm the Fellen.

"I am too, Jon-Jon," Storm said. "How could she hit her head? She wore her harness."

"Safety lag," he replied. "The shockwaves hit fast and hard. She probably pitched forward, slammed her head, and then the restraints clicked in to pull her back. The same thing almost happened to me. She got it worse because the pulse hit her side."

"Get the grav-sled from storage," Storm said, forgetting her frustration and taking command. "We have to get her out of here."

"Manual says stay with your craft when you crash," the Space Fleet officer responded.

"Not when you crash where a few hundred enemy soldiers will find and eat you," she replied. The Zenge were known to devour fallen enemy. "I'll get the crystal out of the space-fold array and wipe the computers. Grab whatever weapons we can carry or place on the sled with Elie. We need to find a defensible location higher than the surrounding terrain."

"You sound like him," Jon-Jon said.

"Who?"

"Coop. Everything you said, I could hear him saying the exact same words."

"Then it must be the right thing to do," Storm responded. Her golden eyes faded to dark copper with red specs as her anger mounted. The color of her skin changing from light blue to a dark cerulean as her blood pressure rose. The physical responses to a combination of their perilous situation and being reminded Coop was not there. He would not be coming to save them.

The two exited through the ship's rear hatch. Elie lashed to the grav-sled between them. Two laser rifles secured beside her and her personal weapon belt placed beneath her legs. Her combat knife and laser pistol in their holsters.

Storm led the way, a third laser rifle in hand. She wore a holster with a laser pistol. A short, sharp tango-style knife rested on her left hip. A backpack carried emergency provisions, medical supplies, and the ship's most valuable item, a specially cut crystal. The crystal, when struck precisely by multiple lasers, created space-fold drive. The ability to travel by manipulating time-space was Earth's most important advantage. A secret they could not afford to lose.

Jon-Jon pushed the sled, He also wore a laser pistol. His backpack contained three Multi-Environmental Tactical Skin-Suits (METS).

Storm quick-footed through rubble and debris littered across an avenue where local residents once walked to schools and local shops. The shops now higher mounds of rubble on either side. She used one hand to help pull the sled over a major section of wall that fell across the roadway years earlier. Jon-Jon pushed until they topped the obstacle and bobbed down the far side.

Neither spoke after departing the ship. They did not know what tech the Mischene might use, and did not take a chance of being picked up on audio sensors.

At the base of the toppled wall, Storm hesitated. She pointed down the avenue. Jon-Jon would continue pushing the grav-sled with its precious cargo in that direction. She would remain and use the wall for cover.

Without argument, he followed orders. With Elie out of commission, Storm held rank.

She climbed the edifice, found a depression between jagged sections of stone, and waited.

A single star lit the Phisor System. The locals named it Spirius. A red dwarf with consistent flares which appeared as tails along the top and bottom of the corona. The spiral appearance of the flares engendered the name.

Spirius began to settle over the horizon, the waning light bright enough to force Storm to put on shades as beams crossed over the city behind Angel 7. The squad of Marauders went undetected until they converged on the crashed fighter. She lifted the tinted glasses and settled them atop her auburn hair. Two lizard-looking aliens advanced and entered the ship's open cargo bay. Two minutes later one emerged and waved. A Mischene officer and three additional Zenge entered the crash zone. The Zenge took up sentry points front, center, and rear of the ship. The officer walked up the ramp and into the spaceship.

Angel 7 was the first Earth spaceship she experienced. She made love to Daniel Cooper for the first time aboard the fighter. On Angel 7 she discovered jerky and coffee. The ship stood against a Zenge armada sent to destroy the Osperantue refugee ship, Star Gazer. Alongside Coop and her cousin, ASkillamentrae, they fought the enemy until Angel 7's sister ship, Demon, arrived to help.

Elie piloted Demon with her co-pilot, Mags. One year later Storm was on board Demon with Elie and Mags when the Mischene shot them down while fighting to save her home world, Fell, from the same Zenge-Mischene invaders. To prevent the Mischene from gathering any intelligence or technical secrets, Elie destroyed her beloved Demon before enemy ground forces arrived.

She loved Angel 7. She knew Elie loved the ship as much as she had Demon. Since the disappearance of Daniel Cooper, Angel 7 provided a tangible connection to the man.

A tear fell and rolled down the smooth blue skin beneath her eye. The salty taste caught on the edge of her mouth. She pressed the remote detonator and watched the result. The fireball rose into the darkening sky as Spirius, in tribute, disappeared over the Western horizon.

Storm scrambled down the rubble and hurried to catch Jon-Jon. Sad, but proud Angel's final act provided them extra time to escape.

PART 1

con·tra·vene

käntrə'vēn

violate the prohibition or order of (a law, treaty, or code of conduct).
synonyms: break, breach, violate, infringe;

conflict with (a right, principle, etc.), especially to its detriment.
synonyms: conflict with, be in conflict with, be at odds with, be at variance with, run counter to

Chapter 1

Earth: Space Fleet H.Q. / Toronto

"Why the hell was Angel 7 the only fighter-class ship on Phisor?" Fleet Admiral Pamela Patterson demanded. The five-two blue-eyed blonde in her fifties stared down the much taller Rear Admiral Terrance Singletary.

"The Phisor Operation advanced to the point Mischene and Zenge forces were reduced to a single fortified position," the lean Afro-American officer replied. His tone dignified and neutral. "Surface forces no longer required close air support. Spirit Wing fighters are not designed for in-atmosphere engagements, and could not be used against enemy sites regardless. The repurposed forcefield generator from the Mischene's spacecraft blanketed the inner city. Even if a fighter could penetrate the shield, Phisoran hostages were placed in positions to guarantee massive collateral damage."

"I saw the reports," Patterson admitted. She was angry over friends being shot down and their uncertain fate. Taking it out on Singletary would accomplish nothing.

"Admiral Kebede has a difficult job maintaining order in the Aster System," Singletary continued. "I ordered the Spirit ships back to Aster Farum 3."

"Proper thing to do," Patterson replied, letting her emotions subside. "Kebede needed them and they were of minimal value on Phisor. I'm just sick about Angel 7."

"Understandable," the Rear Admiral said. "I can order Spirit Wing back to Phisor."

"Don't. Your analysis was correct before. Spirit fighters aren't going to complete the mission on Phisor. It's a ground game now."

"General Gregory and Colonel Duval will do everything possible to recover the downed crew," Singletary added. "In six months the Space Fleet Marines have reduced the Revolutionary Mischene Military presence on Phisor to less than twenty-percent of their original numbers. The PT-109 destroyed two Mischene spacecraft and a third retreated via wormhole."

"Our scientists still have not discovered a way to overcome the forcefield?" Patterson asked.

"An EMT explosion followed by a massive assault," Singletary replied. "It would kill a lot of civilians. Other than that, no other options have been discovered. We are in siege-mode, Admiral. Our forces cannot enter, but neither can the Marauders escape, and they cannot receive supplies. Time is on our side."

"Not on the side of the hostages," Patterson said. "They will suffer from a lack of supplies first, and the Zenge are known to eat their enemies. We can't sit on our hands, Terrance."

"General Gregory is not known for patience," the tall officer reminded his superior.

"True," she agreed. "He'll get Angel 7's crew out, and he'll find a way under or around the Mischene's shield. Anything new from Aster System?"

"Admiral Kebede is keeping the other planets from retribution on the Mischene, as well as helping the other races on Aster Farum 3 recover from years of oppression. The planetary guilds are excellent ship builders. Work of the carrier to replace the Fairchild is ahead of schedule," he answered, relieved to report on something positive.

"The Destroyer Pegasus and the PT-99, Roosevelt, remain in the system under Admiral Kebede's command. Without a functioning carrier, Spirit Wing fighters are based on the surface of AF3 under Captain Noa Tal."

"Which leaves our only other battleship, the PT-89 on watch here," Patterson interjected. "Keep me informed of any changes," she directed her second in command, and added, "Good job, Terrance."

Singletary departed, leaving Patterson to her private thoughts. Her concern for Elie, Storm, and Jon-Jon ate at her soul, but she recognized she could do nothing for them than being done by others who cared as deeply.

On the other hand, events on Earth which threatened the fragile unification could be affected by her. Space Fleet did not have a mandate to operate on the planet, but did have a primary mission statement to protect Earth, the people of Earth, and the solar system from enemies. If some of those enemies happened to be humans, then taking action fell within her job description.

Earth: Fort Belvoir, Virginia

Col. Titus Andronicus Barnwell, Jr. normally operated from an office in the bowels of the Pentagon. Today he sat at a table overlooking the Potomac River from the northern Virginia side. A glass of iced sweet tea in hand and a view of Fort Belvoir's North Area. The scene from the river to the West encompassed dozens of buildings where thousands of people worked.

Major Amanda Black sat to his right, chin in hand as she read the report he received from the Geospatial-Intelligence Agency analyst. He read it first and presented it to her. GEOINT's offices were located in the same building as the cafeteria. Because they did not allow Level 1 classified material to leave the building, Barnwell and Black made the trip from D.C. to Fort Belvoir.

Finished, the slender woman rolled the data sheet into a tube shape. She banged it against the edge of the table, resulting in ashes floating to the floor.

"Some poor civilian is going to have to sweep that up," Tab said.

"In this place, I'm sure it's a daily requirement," she replied. "I take it you believe the construction in the Saudi desert is al-Rashid."

"He has a history of using extremists to push his personal agenda," Barnwell said. "The construction in the Turbah area is supposedly a Salafi development. They are about as extreme as you get."

"I thought the Wahhabi represented the extreme branch of Islam in Saudi Arabia."

"Wahhabism is what outsiders call the ultra-conservative doctrine. The people who practice it prefer Salafism. The unification of the planet required a lot of religious groups to swallow some pride and accept certain world-wide laws like equality, tolerance, and giving up private militia. The latest Salafi movement in opposition to centralized governing began the same time al-Rashid became a representative on the United Earth Council."

"The construction is a front for Camarilla Dissolvere. A new center of operations," Amanda surmised. "Getting kicked out of Mississippi slowed them, but it didn't shut them down."

"Key members were captured, but important players are still free. I can't see them giving up their vision of dissolving the United Earth Council and returning the planet to regional rule following one setback. I can see the strategy changing from one massive attack to a combination of localized revolts and media outrage when Big Brother steps in."

"Like the hundreds of martial law states that sprang up during the Pandemic?" she asked.

"Similar, but more organized and better funded," he responded.

"The Camarilla placed agents inside the UEC, including political representatives and military officers," Amanda said. "They turned a Space Ranger."

"Benny wasn't turned," Tab countered. "He was always a mercenary. al-Rashid waved money and power under his nose to persuade him to join. It didn't require a major effort. Getting people like Dr. Reinhardt, the head of Space Fleet's genetic research, took a lot more effort."

"What's our play?"

"The leaders of the Camarilla are known and the UEC issued a formal request for them to appear before a committee investigating dissidents. We escort them here."

Major Black studied her friend and superior's face, looking for any tell the answer was one of his understated jokes. Deciding the Colonel was serious, she assumed her role as the voice of reason.

"If we kidnap al-Rashid out of a religious sanctuary in the middle of the Middle East, it will start another faith-based war pitting the Near East against the West. The last one nearly destroyed the planet before the Pandemic took center stage," she said.

"The media moguls in the conspiracy have dropped out of sight, but you can bet they pull the strings for their outlets," she continued. "Every misstep by the UEC or Space Fleet or anyone tangentially connected is already blown out of proportion. If we invade an Islamic site, what do you think those hacks will say?"

"Tangentially?"

"I am an educated person, Tab," Amanda replied. "I can use big words. But maybe I should dumb this down for you. Going after any of the Camarilla will cause a shit storm. Going after al-Rashid in the middle of the Arabian desert will cause a fucking war."

"Not going allows them time to rebuild, hire reinforcements, and resume their efforts to segment the planet into fiefdoms," he said.

"Damned if we do and damned if we don't," she replied.

"Not if we do and don't get seen," he countered. "Arresting these people doesn't mean showing up with a piece of paper and a pair of handcuffs."

"Fine. Covert. We know they have spies inside the UEC and Space Fleet, and probably every other branch of service. Whatever move we make, regardless of where you pull assets for the mission, a warning will be sent."

"True," he agreed, but then added, "if we recruit from normal channels."

Amanda Black lay her forehead flat against the table top and said, "Shit storm dead ahead."

Chapter 2

Phisor

Temperatures dropped with the arrival of night. Jon-Jon located a building atop a hill. Windows and doors long gone, but four walls remained.

It required two-minutes to recon the interior. One-story with a single area separated from the main room made it easier. The roof, while missing sections, did not appear in imminent peril of complete collapse. From the look and the smell, the added section served as a restroom. The common area provided no clues as to the building's original purpose. Likely a retail store, but nothing remained on the walls, the ceiling, or the floor. Correction; dust, dirt, and pieces of roof occupied much of the floorspace.

The walls and partial ceiling would keep the inside warmer than setting up outside, and while it placed them in a box, it provided cover. He pushed the sled inside and into a rear corner. He disengaged the hovers to allow the sled to rest on the floor. With flight-suit on, the thermal blanket covering her, and walls protecting two sides, the cold should not bother her. He considered the METS skin-suit, but the thought of undressing his commander and then trying to redress her in the form-fitted outfit seemed less appealing than he would have otherwise imagined. If she woke with him undressing her, she might kill him before waiting on an explanation.

The explosion, coming on the heels of the mental image of Casalobos without clothes, made the Lieutenant jump.

The sky to his west flashed orange and yellow. He hoped Storm caused the blast, and was not something she might be caught within. He attached an optics package to the barrel of the laser rifle. Aiming the weapon now provided an enhanced night-vision view of the street.

"Looking for Storm?"

Jon-Jon jumped, emitted a muted squeal, and came within a hair of pulling the trigger. He spun to find Casalobos standing there.

"Sorry," she said. "I guess I'm not thinking too clearly to sneak up on you like that. What happened?" she asked.

"You hit your head when a pulse beam knocked us out of the air," he said. His heart continued runaway pumping, but breathing returned to normal. "We crashed outside the shield perimeter. I grabbed gear and loaded you on a sled. Storm stayed behind to make sure the Mischene didn't recover anything from Angel 7."

"The space-fold array?"

"I have the crystal," he replied.

"The rest of the tech?"

"I think Storm blew it to hell," he answered.

"I did."

Jon-Jon whirled, the laser rising as fast as his heart rate.

Storm caught the barrel before he brought it around.

"That's what you get for talking and not paying attention," she said. She released the weapon, passed him, and hugged Casalobos. "Glad to see you up and moving."

"Hell of a headache," Elie replied as she stepped back. "Angel 7 is gone?"

"Took out a Mischene officer and a squad of Marauders," Storm answered. "Cried like a baby."

"I'll cry later," Elie said. "You had to do it. Happy to know her last act accomplished something worthwhile. I'm not completely with it yet, Storm. You give the orders until my head clears."

"Anton and Duval will send a team to find us," the Fellen said. "They need to go around the forcefield to get here. Can't risk a shuttle because of the plasma and pulse cannons. Jon-Jon found us a nice spot to wait. I say we get into the METS, get comfortable, and see who arrives first."

"Sounds like a plan," Elie agreed.

"Jon-Jon, keep watch while we change," Storm said. She flicked on a mini-torch to locate the satchel with the armored skin-suits. Jon-Jon turned to the doorway a second after Storm's top started over her head. He caught site of Casalobos in his peripheral vision as her top opened and slipped over her shoulders. What he did not see was Storm's wink to Elie. It was nice to cause a bit of mischief to lighten the situation. Even if it was at Jon-Jon's expense.

Major Duval sent for six operators to join him in the building converted into his command headquarters. Four Space Fleet Marines with six-months experience fighting the enemy on the surface of Phisor and two non-humans.

"There was an explosion on the eastern side of RMM controlled space," he said. "It came as the sun set, and after Angel 7 went down. I assume the ship was blown by Captain Casalobos to prevent classified material getting into enemy hands."

Duval stood before the six and said, "You're going after them. Captain Elena Casalobos, Communications Contract Specialist, Storm, and Lt. Jonathan Johnson. All three are experienced fighters. Casalobos and Storm fought with some of you on Fell before Phisor. Many of you know Lt. Johnson from the battle in Aster Farum system. These are our people and they will be expecting us to find and extract them."

Duval directed the team to a portable field operations worktable and initiated a holographic-topography. The 3-d diagram displayed the city and outskirts. He circled a section. It expanded to replace the wider view.

"This is the area. Location was formerly a mix of homes and businesses on the southeastern rim of the city. Mostly rubble and wastelands now. Casalobos will seek high ground. A place she can fortify against Marauders and provide a three-sixty angle of fire. There are four hills within two miles of the crash which fit the bill. I doubt she would go further with darkness closing. You will take a surface transport vehicle to the edge of the zone. The STV[6] will be too big a target for the Mischene to miss. Leave it and proceed on foot. Locate each hill, clear it, move on until you find them."

---

[6] STV: Surface Transport Vehicle

"If they aren't on any of the four hills?" Corporal Khaled Hafez, the Egyptian, asked.

"Sergeant?" Duval addressed Master Sergeant (MSgt) Abigail "Abbie" Palmer, the Brit who would be team leader.

"Depends on the situation," she answered. "If we're under duress, we bug it home. If we remain covert, we keep looking until we find them."

"If we find them dead?" C.C. Galetti, Staff Sergeant (SSgt), asked. She was Can-Am, but never talked about exactly what area she came from.

"Don't," Duval answered.

"Captured?" Haz Tankian, the stocky Lebanese sergeant nicknamed Tank, asked.

"Confirm it," Duval answered. "If you can provide intel on their location, great. If you can shadow them without being seen, go for it. If Sgt. Palmer decides to break you into smaller teams; her call. What I do not need is more people captured. Or killed. Peter, anything you want to add about the location?"

"I'm not from this part of my planet, Major," the Phisoran responded. His alpaca-like ears and deep brown eyes drooped to show his displeasure at failing to know more. "The city and the surrounding area are as alien to me as they are to you."

"Understood," the Marine officer said. "Your main job is to make contact with natives. If the team stumbles on Phisoran survivors or resistance you're the liaison."

"Yessir," the slender, fur-covered alien answered. His black nose twitched, which is why the first group of Marines to meet him nicknamed him Peter. And the fact translators found it difficult to pronounce Phisoran names.

While the young Phisoran appeared harmless, he was a fierce fighter and a member of a resistance group conducting a guerilla-style war against the Zenge invaders and their Mischene commanders. His ability to handle a laser rifle and follow orders counted when Duval assembled the search and rescue squad.

"Anything you would like to ask or add?" he directed at the final member of the unit.

A negative shake of the head was all he got in return.

The STV could transport twelve fully equipped soldiers into combat. With Cpl. Hafez driving and MSgt. Palmer riding shotgun, the space behind them seemed cavernous with only four people.

It required a fifteen-mile trip to reach the spot designated as the edge of the search zone. The southern side of the city once provided wide lanes, mass transit rails, and bridges used to cross a scenic river. The multi-track all-terrain vehicle would be required to cross roads pock-marked from explosions, and littered with abandoned vehicles and destroyed buildings. Overhead rails more often lay twisted on the ground. Transit tunnels were booby-trapped and places Marauders and wild animals hid. Bridges no longer existed, and the once scenic river ran muddy brown with a sheen of chemicals across its surface.

The ravine where the Marines rescued by Angel 7 were ambushed proved how dangerous the local terrain could be for ground forces.

Before the invasion a surface transport would require thirty-minutes to cover the distance. With the sun down, the need to remain under the enemy's scans, and the current conditions, Palmer estimated a three-hour trip . . . minimum.

Tank took advantage of the space and time to stretch across a wide bench. The Lebanese Marine deeply asleep in seconds.

The recalcitrant alien sat on the rear seat near the drop-ramp exit. The team would likely exit the transport via the side door, the way they entered, but if an emergency occurred, the drop-ramp could be used for a quick escape.

Peter sat in a forward seat. The position allowed him to look out through a one-way portal. No ambient light escaped from the interior to alert watchers. The opti-film blocked light escaping. It also provided anyone inside enhancements to discern details of the landscape, even in darkness. Hafez used low-spectrum lights, visible only through the STV's treated windshield, to navigate around or over obstacles.

"If this isn't your part of the planet, why fight here?" C.C. asked, taking the seat beside the Phisoran. "If you don't mind me asking."

"I do not mind," Peter replied, turning from the apocalyptic view to the dark-haired, dark-eyed Marine. "Nothing remains of my home. I am positive my family is gone, and I do not have many friends," he confided. "When I met the first group of humans from Earth I was fighting with a resistance group of eight. Marauders had us cornered. They played with us, firing to keep us pinned down, but not trying to advance and finish us off. A ship, shaped like a quarter moon, flew in and cut through their lines."

"Spirit fighter," C.C. said.

"Followed by Marines on foot," he continued. "The Zenge were already confused by the air attack. They hardly fired a shot before the Marines cleaned them out. They took us to their camp, cared for our wounded, fed us, and allowed us to join them."

"Something we learned on Fell, and again in the Aster Farum system," C.C. said. "People want to fight for their home. If someone invaded Earth, I'd stand with anyone who came to help."

"I never thought we would actually be free of the Marauders. Fighting with the Marines, with Space Fleet ships overhead, was a dream. When the invaders retreated into cities, more Phisorans came out of hiding."

"I understand the Mischene were training the Zenge in combat tactics by hunting your race," the young sergeant said. "Brutal."

"We were not a warrior-species," Peter said. "Those who survived the initial attacks learned how to hide. When we realized we were prey, we learned how to fight back. I'm here, in a part of the planet I have never visited, because the fight is here. Colonel Duval asked for a volunteer. I came."

"We're about to get wet," Palmer called from the front. "Khaled is converting to hover-mode to cross the river. We'll be in the open. Everyone get ready in case we need to act fast. Somebody wake up Tank."

Storm took the first watch. Elie was no longer unconscious, but not fully recovered. Considering her regenerative capabilities as a Space Ranger, the hit to her head must have been nearly fatal. She slept on the sled, the METS environmental systems kept her warm and snug. The telemetry in the suit would warn Storm if anything unusual happened to her physiology.

Jon-Jon, no longer red-faced, and in his METS, slept sitting up. His back supported by a wall and his laser rifle across his lap.

Without the integrated helmet with enhanced optics Storm would not have seen the lights playing across the buildings in the distance. The lights, moving toward their location, came from the direction of the crash. A second team of Marauders following up on the first group eradicated by Angel's destruction. She debated waking Elie and Jon-Jon, considering the enemy might stop short of their location or pass by. Fearing the need to wake them at the last moment, she opted for a less stressful disturbance now.

"Elie. Jon-Jon. I have movement," she said, using the private channel within her trams-comm chip. Using a nickname directed the message to the person or people named.

Sleeping light was required for anyone operating where a deep sleep could become endless. Casalobos arrived by her side first. Jon-Jon a step behind.

"Mile west, along the path we used to get here," she said.

"Infrared torches," Elie confirmed. "They may have more sophisticated tracking gear as well."

"Pretty ballsy to be out from under the shield," Jon-Jon muttered. "They must know the area is free of Fleet assets. If they can see that, they may have seen us."

"They wouldn't be wasting time checking every structure and potential hiding place if they knew for sure," Elie replied. "I see a skirmish line three blocks wide. They're playing the odds we came this way, but they don't know which street or how far we might have gone."

"Should we move?" Jon-Jon asked.

"We have high ground and four walls," Elie said aloud. "They could stop looking and give up before they reach us. They could pass by. If we start bumping around in the darkness, something will pick up our signatures. METS or not."

"If they reach us they won't pass by," Storm interjected. "They are searching places completely destroyed. They will not pass by a nearly whole building. We need to be prepared to fight."

"Anton and Duval will have a team on the way," Elie added. "If we must fight, the noise should bring them in quicker."

"The 109 will be watching," Jon-Jon said. "If they see laser fire being exchanged, they could target the area from space."

"Genna won't fire," Elie responded. "The same reason we don't light up their headquarters. They use hostages as buffers. Out here, we could be mixed in with the bad guys. Urban combat is never clean and simple. If the Mischene jammers are up, and they will be, the ship can't hone in on our ident signals. She won't take the chance of hitting us with friendly fire."

"Another reason to not stay bunched," Storm said, voicing a private thought. "You and Jon-Jon stay here. I'll find a cross-fire position on the other side of the street. They have us outnumbered, but I bet we have better weapons. We only need to hold them off until help arrives."

"I don't like splitting our forces," Jon-Jon said.

"Nothing we do is going to be anything anyone likes," Storm answered. "This is simply the best we can do with what we have. I'll call on the private channel when I find a place to set up."

The Fellen melted into the darkness beyond the doorway.

The currents from the water crossing swept them a mile downriver before the STV reached a location where the driver could pull the craft onto a beach wide enough to redeploy the tracks. As the vehicle climbed a gentle rise, those aboard realized the beach connected to a public park. They watched in silence as playground equipment and overgrown shrubs passed by the view ports. Reminders this world once teemed with happy families.

"There may not be enough of us left to recover the planet," Peter said.

"One step at a time," C.C. said. "Getting the Mischene ships out of the system is done. We'll soon remove those left on the surface. Then you can start rebuilding. We'll help."

"More Phisorans survived than you may realize, Peter," Palmer said from the front seat. "The Marauders confined their forces to three cities and a dozen teams patrolling the countryside. Since the Marines arrived and the Mischene and Zenge fell back to a single fortified location, more and more natives have come out of concealment. I saw a report of hundreds of towns and villages beginning to show signs of life."

"I pray you are correct, Top," he replied.

The STV exited the park and turned north, toward the city limits. Hafez pushed the speed to recover time lost on the river. The roadway remained clear of obstructions until they reached the first business district.

"We're near the edge of the danger zone," Palmer called out. "After Khaled finds us a nice hole to hide the STV we begin walking. Start prepping your personal gear and someone wake Tank."

Hafez backed the vehicle beneath a large signboard leaning against the wall of a three-story office building. He placed the big rig far enough back to hide in shadows when the sun rose. They hoped to be back before then.

"We're going to break into two squads," Palmer said. She had her team assembled at the rear of the STV, beneath the toppled sign, and hidden should the Mischene decide to send a drone overhead. "Peter and Khaled with me. High spot number one is one-mile north. We'll stay east of center line. C.C. is in command of team two. Stay west of center line. Everyone give me a click with your comm."

She waited until she counted five single clicks from the chips integrated with the battle METS. Everyone but Peter wore a suit beneath BDUs[7]. Phisoran fur and the high-tech material in the suits did not get along. Anyone scanning for communications would disregard the clicks as background noise.

---

[7] BDU: Battle Dress Uniform

"We stay off all channels unless it's an emergency. The Misch-ene use Fellen equipment. With tech as good as it gets, they may be able to hack our transmissions. If you hear a single click, it's me checking status. C.C. gives one click back for a-ok. Two clicks means you have a problem. If either of us sends three clicks it means we have eyes on our targets."

"Or a serious case of TMJ," Tank said.

"If we see Marauders?" C.C. asked, ignoring Tank's lame joke.

"Two clicks, hesitate, and two more," Palmer answered.

"Or the sound of laser fire," Hafez muttered.

Chapter 3

Phisor - RMM H.Q.

"Have you found your answers?" General Ovan Vínier asked.

"Almost, General. Almost," the thin woman in black replied. She worked with her back to the rebel Mischene officer.

"The same answer you have given for over a week," he complained. Slender, though not as spindly as the Devee, the General's uniform hung loose over narrow hips, and a touch baggy across the shoulders.

"Alchemy. Science. Magic. Research is always the same, General Vínier." She gave a look over one shoulder. Her long nose bridged small eyes; the white shot with red veins. Her pinched lips displayed a distaste for life. "Almost is where you are before you are where you need to be."

She turned back to the operating room table. A dead Phisor female lay atop the cold metal. Her upper torso partially skinned.

"The Devee promised great rewards if we kept the Phisor under control," the officer said. "We have accomplished that. The arrival of the Earth forces cost me countless soldiers and the loss of equipment I cannot replace. I continue to hold up my part of the bargain, Chimia[8] Scalah. I expect the Devee to do the same."

Chimia Scalah scraped tissue from the inside of the Phisoran hide onto a glass slide. She handed the sample to another Devee female who bowed before accepting the specimen.

"Mix this with formula eighty-two," Scalah directed her assistant. "Centrifuge and return with the result."

The black clothing the Devee scientist-witch wore combined a dress with billowing sleeves and a cloak. Trimmed in dark gold, the outfit appeared to move when she did not. Her pale face and pale hands with red nails floated among the folds of black.

"The Devee always keep our promises, General," she said. With the aide and the sample gone, Vínier received her complete

---

[8] Chimia: Title for Devee Chemists and Alchemist with exceptional talent.

attention. "I believe you were a captain when I first approached you. Team leader for a squad of Zenge chasing Phisoran civilians like hounds after vermin. Now you wear the previous commander's uniform, and command the Revolutionary Mischene Military forces on Phisor."

"It will do me little good dead or in a prison," Vínier responded. The sorceress appearance of Chimia Scalah once frightened him. Following months of close contact with the Devee chemist, her looks no longer caused him concern. He found the female ugly outside, and equally ugly inside. He watched her slaughter, mutilate, and experiment on dozens of Phisoran. Male, female, young, and old came under her knife.

His own black skin showed signs of premature aging, and his white hair no longer appeared full and healthy. Stress and poor nutrition turned the under-thirty officer into a wrinkled, bitter, aged version of himself.

"The cruiser from Devisator arrived in the system, General. The time agreed upon before my arrival, and nothing has changed."

"Nothing? An Earth warship orbits the planet. Their troops and sky-fighters drove us out of every corner of this planet except this shielded city. We keep them at bay, but we are running out of food and other supplies. I believe those represent significant changes, Scalah," the haggard man responded.

"My mission is to discover the secret of Phisoran fur," she replied. Her calm tone matched by the languid movement of her body. She plucked a scrap of skin and fur from the table top. "It keeps them warm or cool. It sheds precipitation. It is nearly invulnerable to non-energy-based weapons. It produces pheromones capable of enhancing sexual desire. If the Devee can replicate the qualities of the fur, it will be a valuable new trade item. I was given a time limit, and the limit ends in two days. As I said, nothing has changed."

"And when the Devee cruiser arrives and the Earth ship intercepts?" Vínier asked.

"The Captain will destroy the Earth craft. Their military units on the surface will be dealt with, and you, General, and I, will be taken off of this world," Scalah answered. "You will receive the funds and support required for the RMM to continue the Prophet's dream of conquest."

"As long as we continue to work for the Devee," he added.

"Our paths parallel, General," the hag responded. "Your war against the Trade Alliance provides a distraction the Devee can use to our advantage. The same as your invasion of Phisor opened the way for my experiments. The Mischene are welcome to rule the galaxy. The Devee will control trading and take a healthy percentage from every transaction. Both of our races win."

"Two days?"

"Two days to complete my work, and another more for the cruiser to journey from the gate," she answered. "Keep the shield up, make sure the humans are reminded you have hostages within this building, and begin deciding who will accompany you when we depart."

Vínier nodded without further comment. He exited as the Aide reentered the morbid laboratory.

"He's weak," the assistant, Portence, said after the door closed.

"As were Amos Soren, and his son, Atticus Soren, The Prophet." Chimia Scalah replied. "Sepha[9] Chai kept them pointed in the proper direction for over one-hundred-years. Manipulating lesser beings is quite simple when you know the formula."

"Speaking of formula," Portence interjected and handed her superior a simple one-page report. "Formula eighty-two and the skin cells provided the same result as Formulas seventy-eight through eighty-one. You have solved the riddle of the fur. Five positive results. We can synthesize the properties of Phisoran fur."

"Timing is everything, Portence," the older woman said.

She slipped her hand through a slit hidden within the folds of her garment. On a belt beneath she tapped a sequence against a flat metal sensor. Golden filaments and sparks enveloped her head. When they dissipated, the ugly crone became a beautiful raven-haired woman.

---

[9] Sepha: Title of Devee Master Mixers. Brewers who blend mixtures from medical potions to poisons.

"I believe I deserve a reward for my hard work," she said.

Portence accessed her own glamour-shield generator. Her ugliness evaporated and a young woman with short black hair and ruby lips appeared. She deftly released sashes and ties, allowing the billowy black cloak-dress to fall away. Pale skin covered a luscious body of curves and fine lines.

"Will this do?" she asked.

Chapter 4

Earth

"The concept of a truly united planet is impossible," Col. Adekola said. A graduate of the University of Ibadan in Nigeria, Adekola continued his computer science post-graduate studies at the United Earth Naval Academy in Maryland. "That our world operates under a centralized government is a miracle in itself."

"The miracle required half the population to be wiped out first," Amanda said. She walked abreast the lean officer dressed in casual uniform. The blend of professorial demeanor and military bearing set well upon the UEC Marine Corps' Commanding Officer for Media Research.

"True," he agreed. "The needs of those remaining required more than any local government could provide. Hence, the Canadian-American Alliance rise to power, and the evolution to the United Earth Council. But nations and regions remain. It allows those less enamored with being governed by outsiders the ability to retain a colloquial identity."

"Nations which would have been ruled by military dictators and warlords if Can-Am had not taken charge," Tab interjected. He walked on Amanda's other side. The wide corridors inside the Marine Intelligence Operations Building provided ample space for the three to walk side-by-side as Adekola led them from his office to the section dedicated to his research team.

"No one disputes the benefits of life under the UEC versus life under military juntas," the African said. "But with time, people tend to forget details as they focus on ideology. The UEC needs to exist. The global application of laws, the oversight of trade, the removal of corruption between benefactors and recipients are valuable. The UEC maintains military forces under one banner. Anyone from anywhere on the planet can apply, but they join a transnational assembly. Army, Marines, Navy, Air Force, Coast Guard, and Space Fleet answer to the UEC. No one else may maintain a military. Only police are localized."

"Which, to some, appears as if the UEC is making sure no one can oppose the centralization of government," Amanda said.

"It isn't an appearance Major," Adekola responded. "The UEC will not allow a martial challenge to its power. As every dominant ruler in history learned, you must consolidate strength and vigorously deny others the ability to contest your sovereignty."

"Doesn't sound democratic," Tab said.

"Democracy is the next step," Adekola replied. "Until then there is the appearance of democracy. The United Earth Council consists of representative from the remaining post-pandemic nations. These representatives vote on issues from budgets to laws."

"The real power lies with the Board of Governors," Tab added. "They actually decide what will be brought to a vote, and what will be done regardless of opinion."

"Partially true," the other Colonel said. "The real power is still Can-Am. The Prime Minister, who is also Chairman of the UEC Board of Governors, pulls everyone's string. Granted, his actions are taken to protect the fledgling UEC from falling apart, and to keep the population of Earth safe and secure. If a true democracy is destined for our world, we must survive the transition."

"Which is why the Camarilla Dissolvere is dangerous," Amanda said. "They want to see the UEC brought down and regional rule restored. Without a military to fight with, they use public opinion. They sow discord by distributing lies and half-truths about the UEC's use of the military and institutions like Space Fleet. They frighten people by portraying aliens as demons sent to eradicate faith. "

"They are driven by two deadly motives; personal greed and national pride," Adekola said. "With their access to multi-platform media outlets, they disguise their personal agendas by espousing the failures of a centralized government to understand the needs of distant lands."

"They claim the loss of nationalism is the same as losing one's heritage. It is turning your back on your ancestors, your history, and your uniqueness by allowing UEC to control your laws, budgets, and militaries," Tab added.

Adekola stopped before metal double-doors. He placed his forehead against a rest on an eye-scan security panel. The doors separated and slid silently into the walls on either side.

"Fighting propaganda and discouraging false narratives were not the original reasons the Media Research unit began," he said, ushering them into the vast space on the other side of the opening. "With new threats, we adjust and proceed."

The space beyond combined the layout for an open-office suite, the multi-media haven of a teenage gamer, and, yes, believe it, a gourmet kitchen.

Two-dozen people of mixed races and a couple of aliens were scattered around the area. Some uniformed personnel, and others in street clothes, worked, played, cooked, or ate. No one noticed the three uniformed officers enter, or no one cared.

"We're less formal than most military units," the Nigerian said, answering the unasked query. "Left is the platform blender. Social and professional media feeds from around the world are dropped into a hopper, searched for relevant words or hidden codes, and anything found suspicious is shunted to a personal monitor. My people do cursory analysis, and if they see something interesting, bump it to a specialist for further analysis."

"You have a Fellen and a Posine," Tab noted.

"The arrival of non-terrestrials means there are aliens accessing and using the same platforms humans use. Earth now has a couple of platforms built by and for non-humans adding to the noise. I recruited TRshpor, the Fell, and Conitsch, the Posine, from Space Fleet Academy. Both were working toward communications certifications."

"Smart," Tab said, approving the forethought and the take-action attitude Col. Adekola displayed by adding aliens to his unit.

"Center stage are video feeds. We pay the most attention to the platforms and personalities with the highest subscriptions. We also pay a great deal of attention to those with narrow agendas and a more specific audience."

"National pride and government ineptitude," Amanda said.

Adekola smiled as a response. "Plus violence as a solution," he added. "On your immediate right is a rec-research area. Games.

Both for relaxation and because a lot of subversive ideas can be encoded into strategies, character profiles, and multi-player inter-actions. Besides looking for potential threats, our team personas are making friends in cyber space."

"The kitchen?" Tab asked.

"People gotta eat," the obvious answer. "This is one-third of my total personnel. We spend a lot of time here, and having good food, fresh and properly prepared makes for happy workers."

"Keeps them segregated from other personnel in the cafeterias," Amanda noted.

"Partly security, but mostly because they don't mix well with muggles."

Tab chuckled at the reference. Amanda Black, more a modern woman and less a student of literature, did not understand the reference. She let it go, making a mental note to look the word up later.

"None of this actually helps me go undercover," Amanda said. "I can get immersion into cyber-communications and esoteric protocols, but it isn't going to get me close to the Camarilla."

"There's one more studio," the unit commander said. He went right, taking a moment to say something to the Fellen, and continuing to a door. He tapped a circuit beneath a button glowing red. Waited, tapped it twice more, and waited again. The red button dimmed and the electronic lock disengaged.

The cramped studio behind the door consisted of a comfortable chair, an ottoman, dim lighting, and a young woman. "Session over," she said aloud.

"Col. Barnwell. Major Black, I'd like to introduce Miranda Muse," Adekola said.

"No way," Amanda said. "The Immortal Muse. The Voice of Sanity. Miranda's Rights. That Miranda Muse?"

The woman stood. Five-five, one-twenty-five, brunette, but nothing extraordinary in her looks. The type of face described as pleasant.

"The current edition," she said.

"Miranda Muse is the title of the most famous, longest running stream-cast commentary on social justice issues," Barnwell said.

"Began in the mid-twenty-first century. Miranda Muse is a mantle handed down through the years to make sure the voice of reason is always heard."

"You know your history," the woman said. "My name is actually Veronica Santenelli. Lieutenant, First Class, UEC Marine Corps. I've been the voice of the Muse for three-years-two-months."

"Miranda Muse is a product of the military?" Amanda's question came out closer in tone to an accusation. "If the world discovers you stole Miranda Muse and used her for propaganda, the backlash could shake the UEC apart quicker than the Camarilla. Shit, quicker than a photon-bomb on a nuclear missile."

"Which is why you are in the government's most secret studio on the planet," Adekola said. "The people in the other room believe Veronica analyzes tachyon communications between Earth, space ships, and alien planets. She's supposedly searching for personal messages hidden within official communiques."

"Accessed by tapping on a door?" Amanda queried.

"Because her cover isn't top secret work. We act as if it's only a bit different from the majority of our mission parameters and she prefers a quiet space. I allow others use of the room when she isn't recording a stream-cast."

"Making it less likely to arouse the curiosity of the rest of your team," Tab concluded.

"Exactly," Adekola said. "We didn't steal Miranda Muse, Major Black. The United States of America, specifically, the US Marine Corps Office of Intelligence, created Miranda Muse."

"I may need to sit," Amanda replied. "You're telling me Miranda Muse has always been a government operative. The Voice of Reason. The tip of the spear for holding governments to a higher standard. The person described as *the Beacon* for shining a light on over-reach, fraud, waste, lies, and corruption. Please, tell me the story."

"In the early twenty-first century access to social media platforms and control of the majority of social content on the internet was held by six powerful companies. These companies fought to prevent governments from obtaining access to their methods. They worked harder, mainly with millions of dollars spent lobbying politicians, to prevent regulations designed to hamper those methods. The spin they put out claimed they were protecting the privacy of their clients. They did not give a damn about personal rights. These companies designed and implemented ways, from tracking activity to actually spying on users, to create psycho-demographic profiles on billions of people worldwide."

"They maintained profiles on billions of people?" Amanda asked. "Why?"

"They cataloged everything from purchasing habits to travel and leisure pursuits," Tab answered. "By constantly improving their algorithms they were eventually able to predict a person's next purchase, next vacation destination, or when they were likely to cheat on a spouse and with whom."

"Funny," Amanda said.

"He isn't being funny," Veronica said. "I've seen the period files. They were sophisticated enough to predict potential criminal behavior. That was scary, but scarier was when they discovered a construct to predict government actions based on the profiles of people involved with making final decisions."

"The governments of the world allowed this?" Black asked.

"They didn't know how evolved the profiles became," Adekola answered. "This was why they fought to prevent oversight or government access to any part of their systems. No one wanted people to know how little privacy they actually had, and none of the corporations wanted others to get access to their methods and steal their advertisers."

"Something changed," Amanda guessed.

"A Romanian hacked one of the most powerful internet social platform providers. He sold the entry key to the Iranians. They leased it to the Russians, and the Chinese stole it from them. Once those countries learned how to defeat the security for the first platform, their cyber-ops used it to create similar breaches in the others."

"The whole world of virtual reality and social insecurity was about to come to a screaming halt. Connectivity was going to end globally, sending the world back to telephones," Veronica said.

"Telephones?" Amanda asked.

"Different history lesson," Tab told her. "The point they are trying to make is private businesses came under attack by mega-governments. A losing battle."

"A losing battle for everyone," the unit commander said. "The Super Six ran to the US government. Actually, they went directly to the President. The information-age world faced armageddon."

"What could the President do?" Amanda asked. "He didn't run those other governments."

"Not directly," Adekola said. "He did command the cyber-ops units located at the Pentagon, the NSA, the CIA, and two-dozen other locations. In return for help, the six had to pledge allegiance to the United States of America. They signed documents giving the US complete access to anything they wanted anytime they wanted it, and the platforms would assist in future operations when requested."

"A blank check," Tab said.

"They had no choice," Veronica responded.

"I still don't know what the President could do to stop those other nations from releasing the information they stole, or use it themselves," Amanda said.

"Sure you do," Adekola said. "The great solar flare blackout."

"Twenty-first century solar flare wiped out communications worldwide for a day," Amanda said. "It wasn't a solar flare?"

"The scientists called it a coronal mass ejection. A CME is similar to a flare, but a whole lot more powerful. Effects on Earth begin within eight-minutes of the ejection. Besides magnetic storms in space, a CME affects communications, power grids, and electronics," Veronica answered. "Only it wasn't a CME. World War Three began and ended without ninety-nine-point-nine-percent of the population ever knowing."

"USA military and intelligence agencies' cyber-ops organized and launched a unified response to aggression by foreign powers," the Nigerian answered. "They shut down every computer and telecommunications system on the planet. Over two-hundred nations went dark. Ten-billion people clueless. All to cover wiping out operating systems for Iran, Russia, and China. They erased the information stolen from the Super Six. They sold the national infrastructure operating codes back to the thieves."

"At what price?" Amanda asked.

"The nuclear agreement to eliminate everything bigger than a tactical-nuke occurred within months of the flare," Tab said. "Funding for terrorism dried up around the same time. Several terrorist leaders were apprehended or killed within a year of the flare. I'm guessing those where partial payments."

"Good guess," Adekola said.

"Miranda Muse?" Amanda asked.

"Marine Cyber Intelligence and Media Research Division created the original pod-cast and her multi-platform personality in the mid-twenty-first century. With the assistance of the major companies, she became the highest followed personality in history. She continued as number one through wars, the pandemic, unification, and today."

"Why am I here?" the Major asked. "Exactly."

Tab answered.

"I didn't know the details, but being around for thirty-plus years, you hear rumors," he said. "I knew we had a relationship with Miranda Muse. She is considered an independent voice who reaches over one-billion followers. That's post-pandemic numbers. The kind of numbers media platforms would pay incredible amounts to own."

"Offers received daily and turned down," the other Colonel interjected.

"Until now," Tab said. "We know at least three of the Camarilla Dissolvere conspirators control huge multi-media businesses. No way those businesses and subsidiaries have not made offers for the rights to Miranda Muse. You, Major Amanda Black, will become the latest incarnation of Miranda. Feelers will be discretely sent out you may be interested in a sponsor."

"I don't look anything like Veronica," she protested.

"No image of any Miranda has ever been released," Veronica said. "Thousands of concept caricatures have been created over the decades, and no two alike. Miranda Muse could be anyone."

"I'm a good talker, but I can't compete with the sophistication, the power displayed by Miranda Muse."

"I appreciate the compliment," the current Muse said. "I'm sure I speak for my predecessors as well. I'll continue to create the streams. You need to be familiar with a few of my pet phrases, and my current take on events. No one in the media will expect you to be 'on' when you meet them personally. A President once called the press 'fake news'. The actual truth was 'fake professionals' massaging the news for profits. Anyone in the management side of the business will expect no less from you."

"Miranda Muse is open to listening to an offer," Major Black, Marine Intelligence officer and long-time undercover agent said the concept aloud. She wanted it in the light to see if it held up. "An invitation comes from someone associated with a Camarilla member. Miranda isn't going to listen to an agent, but will need assurance from the top. She gets near them, they get her near the others. Marines sweep in and the Dissolvere is dust."

"Could work," Veronica said.

"Sounds doable," Adekola said.

"Might be our best chance," Tab added.

"Me as the Voice of Sanity. My ass is fried," Amanda countered.

"Part one of your scheme is in play," Amanda said to Tab. They rode in his antique hover-landcrawler on the journey from northern Virginia back to Washington, DC. "What's the next part?"

Tab engaged the hover-thrusters to lift the vehicle over a crumbling section of highway. He floated down and resumed all-wheel-drive once the pavement seemed more intact. The shock absorbers and special coils reduced the otherwise bone-jarring ride to simply jarring.

"While you decide on a disguise and study the material Veronica provided, I'll fly up to Toronto and speak with Admiral Patterson. We need her support for part two. We may be Marine's, but The Board of Governors placed Space Fleet in charge of military actions involving the Camarilla. She'll need to give the final go on the mission."

"I thought Prime Minister Arcand had final approval?"

"He does, but he's going to accept what Pam tells him. With the future of the UEC at stake, he isn't going to play politics. This will be a military option."

"Military?" Black questioned. "You can't use regular assets because the Camarilla may have eyes and ears embedded we haven't found yet. They had someone as high as second-in-line to command Space Fleet, two Space Rangers, and no one knows how many others scattered throughout the other branches."

"Which is part two of the plan," Tab replied. "Operators not actually associated with any of the branches."

"Mercenaries? You want to risk our lives, excuse me, MY life by trusting people who are only loyal to money?"

"Not mercenaries," he responded. He activated hovers once more and added, "Not even close."

Chapter 5

Earth

"Taking out key members of the Camarilla Dissolvere has given us more time, but the UEC remains vulnerable."

Guy Arcand, head of the United Earth Council's Board of Governors, made the statement from his seat at the table.

Admiral Pamela Patterson noted, "Stephen Hawks is dead. Herman Reinhardt, Hamed Attaran, and Benny Claflin are in custody. Saleh Abd al-Rashin is on the run. Without those people they can't launch their campaign to dissolve the Council and return the planet to regional rule."

"We are in danger as long as Al-Rashid is loose. He, and his father before him, spent decades to build a network of people who will benefit from the failure of a centralized government," Paris Cassel interjected; the third person at the table. He was Director of the United Earth Security Establishment (UESE), responsible for espionage, counterespionage, and threats against the UEC. "The media are primed to report only the failings of a centralized government overseeing world-wide laws, trade, and military forces. They continue to blow up any stumble as cataclysmic. Not being able to publicize the actions of the Camarilla does not help."

"We should be able to shine a light on these bastards," Patterson said. "Can-Am reestablished a free press shortly after the Pandemic. The current UEC bylaws support a free and open press."

"There is no free press, Pam," Cassel said. "The media has been purchased and those who control salaries and decide who receives air-time control the message. If an owner or ownership group has an agenda, it will be supported by the news. Ideas to the contrary will be suppressed."

"I cannot buy reporters bowing to such heavy-handed pressure," she countered.

"The on-air personalities no longer report facts or worry about truth. They see their job as providing an interpretation of events," the security expert responded. "An interpretation enhanced by slick sets, mesmerizing graphics, and a panel of experts prepared to validate the narrative or deride opinions of others. Others they treat as less informed or worse, corrupt."

"People are not stupid," the Admiral replied. "They will recognize the truth if we present them with facts."

"It isn't that simple," Cassel replied. "It's who gets to interpret the facts. The modern media exert the type of influence the Pope and Cardinals of the Catholic Church once held over all Christians. People could read the bible, but they had to agree with the interpretations sent out from Rome or be branded as heretics."

"A news report can be slanted in the same way religious extremists persuade their followers a natural disaster is actually God taking action against those with a different ideology. The fact of the disaster is obvious. Reporters who disagree with our style of government will ask 'Could the UEC have done more to prevent loss of lives and property? Is the government reacting properly? Do government agents show preferential treatment to certain segments of the population and ignore the suffering of others?'" Arcand asked the possible rhetorical questions.

"Of course we do not show preferences during a major disaster," Patterson argued.

"We do not," Arcand agreed. "Honest answers to those questions would prove that, only those answers do not get reported. Questions are presented and left to simmer. Facts are unimportant. A former President of the United States was despised by the media during his time in office. Every move he or the government agencies of his cabinet made were reported as failures. When a so-called failure began to show success, the major reporting platforms simply walked away from the story. When they could not attack a decision, they created doubt regarding motivation."

"That was a time when people sought affirmation of their opinions, not unbiased news," Patterson countered. "Journalists were caught creating stories and citing sources who did not exist. Worse, sources used reporters to broadcast false information. The courts found entire media corporations in contempt. They opened them up for lawsuits. Once they screwed themselves out of their First Amendment rights, things changed."

"Pam, the lessons of the past are valuable only to people who study history. Too many people prefer ignoring inconvenient facts when they get in the way of personal agendas. The Camarilla continues to take jabs at the UEC through the media," Cassel added. "Space Fleet's defeat of the Prophet makes the entire galaxy a safer place. World-wide streams asked why Earth squandered assets and humans lost their lives in a war between aliens. Why did people die trillions of miles from home?"

"You already said it, Paris," Patterson replied. "The galaxy is safer. Earth is safer."

"Is Earth safer? How do we prove it?" Cassel asked.

Patterson sat back, silenced by his question. She knew the truth, but recognized how truth could become a fluid substance.

"We cannot publicly recognize the conspiracy," Arcand replied. "It would only draw more fanatics to their cause. The Council realizes people fear losing their cultural identities. The movement to erase borders following the pandemic required force and speed to maintain the rule of law. The first Council's decision to slow progress toward completely centralizing all government functions was an attempt to prevent a fever of nationalism from sweeping the good being accomplished into the gutter."

Arcand, the dapper representative for Can-Am, controlled the power behind the political scene. The United Earth Council of elected representatives presented the world with an example of cross-cultural unity. For the example to develop into a truly united world, Can-Am provided the military forces to shepherd the planet in the preferred direction.

"The glitter from providing a cure for the Pandemic and providing stability and law following the chaos is fading quickly," he told the other two. "We need people from every corner of the planet to recognize the benefits of centralizing control of militaries, trade, and laws. At the same time, we must honor cultural heritages. A strong breeze can blow us off this high-wire."

"We have seen a collective pride in our accomplishments in the Aster System," Patterson countered. "The fact aliens are receiving better treatment is proof humans are accepting our new position among other civilized worlds."

"The Prophet and the Mischene expansionists also demonstrated aliens possess the desire and the ability to force their way into our lives," Cassel said. "We bested them this time, but what if there are more powerful aliens out there? What if they decide to attack?"

"Precisely why we need allies," Patterson countered. "The technology provided by Fell and Rys have improved our capabilities far beyond anything we could have accomplished alone. The races in the Aster System are using their ship-building expertise to construct a new carrier to replace the Fairchild. The Mischene who never believed in their government's actions, and those who now know they were deceived, do what they can to repair relationships with the other races and species harmed during Soren's rule."

"Social scientists once surmised the only ways our planet could unite would be as a result of a world-wide disaster or the intervention of extraterrestrials," Arcand said. "We have experienced the one-two punches of both events. If ever a centralized government would succeed, now is the time."

"There are important actions which must be concluded before we can call our system a central government," Cassel responded. "We must rebuild the Institute of International Law and the International Criminal Court. We have a legislative body, and a military. We need an executive branch and a constitution."

"The military is stretched far too thin," Patterson interjected. "I'm proud many exceptional people joined Space Fleet, but they left the other service branches to join us. The added ships and the losses in the Astor Farum system have me pulling cadets from the Academy sooner than I would prefer."

"The aliens?" Arcand asked.

"When the Star Gazer returned to Osperantue, ninety-percent of the refugees went home," she replied. "Some of those who stayed have become Fleet personnel, but most are employed in civilian jobs. Our population growth has been more controlled than prior to the pandemic and the loss of five-billion souls. We do not have the number of volunteers needed to fully staff the UEC Army, Navy, Air Force, or Marines. The Navy, Marines, and Coast Guard are sharing personnel, facilities, equipment, and other assets. The Army and Air Force have dedicated personnel, but are sharing several facilities and work closely to maintain control over the more militant factions trying to challenge the UEC."

"Space Fleet must continue to build alliances beyond our solar system," Arcand said. "We cannot maintain peace on Earth if we are faced with another Prophet. You are our goodwill ambassador, as well as our military force for defense above the surface and throughout the galaxy. Operations like the repatriation of Phisor are costly but crucial if extraterrestrials are to take us seriously."

The Governor turned to his Chief of Security and said, "Paris, you must protect the UEC from enemies within. I expect you to communicate and work with Pam and every other military command when necessary to accomplish your goal."

Cassel and Patterson first worked together thirty-years previously when he was a spy working for her mother and she a freshly minted Naval Intelligence officer. He nodded to his life-long friend, and she returned the gesture.

"The remaining Camarilla?" Cassel asked.

"We are on the verge of announcing a global financial system," Arcand revealed. "With it will come the first draft of a Constitution. That will precede the establishment of a functional judiciary and the formation of an Administrative Branch. If the Camarilla continues to influence public opinion, these initiatives will be viewed as despotic. We must break their influence."

Hours after the meeting with Arcand and Patterson ended, Paris Cassel sat in his office in downtown Toronto. His butt in his comfortable leather chair. His eyes on a wall of holographic bio-pics. His top asset stood in front of the images, arms folded, memorizing the faces and information.

"These are the leaders of the Camarilla Dissolvere," he said. "Saleh Abd al-Rashin, former Saudi representative to the UEC is the chief strategist. He and his father recruited the others. His goal is to return regional rule. His family can then reclaim its heritage as rulers of the Middle East. He has the backing of radical Islamic groups, is well financed, and is currently in hiding."

The back-lit photo dimmed, and another brightened. A woman in her mid-fifties with hawk-nose, high cheekbones, and the eyes of a predator.

"Alexandra Vasluianu," Cassel said. "Russian ancestry, but Can-Am resident. Owns or has control over one-fourth of the social media platforms used by the world's population for news and sports coverage. Descendant of oligarchs and claims to be related to the original Russian Czars."

As the Russian's image dimmed, the face of an older, attractive, though fierce-looking woman glowed. Her dark skin and scowl gave her the appearance of an African Tribal Queen. Not someone to be questioned or toyed with.

"Katherine Chinda of Nigeria," the Security Chief gave a name to the bio-pic. "Leader of the largest anti-unity militia on the planet. Based in Nigeria, but with alliances spread across the globe. Former Nigerian military officer. Nationalist and cultural purity proponent."

The holographic image alongside the African militant was an opposite in all appearances.

"Sir Daniel Miller. United Kingdom representative to the UEC. You can find his highness at the best bars and clubs in Toronto on any given night. He's into gin, boys or girls, expensive suits, and hopes to one day become Chairman of the Board of Governors. Since he has no qualifications other than heritage, his only way to the top is by providing intel to the Camarilla."

"Arnold Montack," Cassel said as the following holo-photograph backlit. "Financial genius. If the global economy becomes a single unit, trade becomes less profitable. He represents profit-seekers and rich clients fearful of losing their positions if equality becomes reality. His friends include people with controlling interests over one-third of the mass media outlets on the planet. With Vasluianu, they have nearly sixty-percent of the mass media platforms under their thumbs. He's a Cam-Am citizen and lives in a fortified compound in Utah."

Cassel swiveled enough to watch his agent. "Lorena Aragon," he said.

Light brown skin, dark hair pulled back into a bun. Brilliant blue eyes. A beautiful woman with a sly smile. The scar along her right cheek added to her exotic appearance.

"Head of the illicit drug cartels. Mexican heritage, but lives anywhere and everywhere from Tijuana to Buenos Ares. If the UEC reestablishes the International Criminal Court, she becomes number one on their hit list. I believe you have a history with her."

The agent did not answer. Did not move. Did not react to the holo-pic or the Director of Security.

Cassel turned away, lit the final bio-pic.

"Daughter-in-law of the current Japanese Emperor. Half-Japanese and Half-Chinese. I would be gracious to call her a conniving bitch who wants the Far East to become what the Chinese wanted before the pandemic they released on the world. A society onto itself. A closed, self-contained segment of the planet where she rules. Wei Zhou Nanke. She is called 'The Power.'"

"My job is find them," he said. "You job is eliminate them. Questions?"

None.

Hours after the meeting with Cassel and Arcand ended, Admiral Pamela Patterson sat in her office at the Space Fleet complex north of Toronto. Col. Barnwell sat facing her.

"Tab, I appreciate your being cautious regarding the use of military units to back you and Amanda. I get it we may have spies and traitors inside the ranks. But what you are asking is a bit much," Patterson said.

Chapter 6

Earth - Toronto

"Stacey, do you think I will ever fly anything more important than a shuttle?" Chaspi asked. The Bosine sat within a virtual display of a cockpit from a space-station transport. Her side of the dorm room converted into an interactive training model.

Stacey, her blue-skinned roommate from Fell, sat cross-legged on the bed across the narrow space. She looked up to see Chaspi's spiky brown hair above slumped shoulders. The Bosine's chin dropped to her chest as she concentrated on flying the make-believe shuttle through a computer-generated ion storm. From this short distance, the display wavered as if reacting to the ionic currents. Or Chaspi's repeated sighs.

"You've already flown a Wraith," the Fellen reminded her. "How many people in the galaxy can say that?"

She resumed flipping pages on her flexisheet data reader. The flight manual for a Spirit-class three-operator fighter holding her attention. She scanned and memorized the operating limitations, performance data, and loading information for the carrier-based craft. With her eidetic memory, once she completed reading, it would remain available in her mind forever.

"That was kind of cool," Chaspi said, followed by another sigh. "The nav-computer did most of the flying. I sat in the pilot's seat and pointed her in the right direction. It feels like forever ago. Do you think we'll ever know what happened to Coop and Cassandra?"

With her back to Stacey, Chaspi could not see the other girl's cat-like eyes shift from gold to orange rimmed in red. Her skin darkened a shade as her blood pressure rose. Normally physical signs of anger, or the fight aspect of fight-or-flight response to an attack. In this case, the bio-changes indicated the level of frustration the alien felt regarding the disappearance of Daniel Cooper, his ship, Cassandra, and the avatar Cassie. For months she communicated with family members on Earth, on Fell, and in space

actively searching for the missing man. No clues emerged. No
trails. Nothing to indicate he vanished by choice or force.

Space Fleet supposedly maintained a search, but no one considered it an active response any longer. Besides the time lapse,
Coop was no longer a member of Space Fleet. Sky (ASkiilamentrae), Storm (AStermalanlan), and her brother, Sparks (ASparquila) spent hours daily for weeks chasing ghosts and monitoring
communications from around the known galaxy.

Sky eventually returned to Fell to help establish the new military force created to assure no one successfully invaded their
planet again. Storm rejoined the John F. Kennedy, PT-109 as the
Communications Officer. The ship, originally under the command
of Cooper, now operated with Elena Casalobos as Captain. Sparks,
co-creator of the STORM-HATCH tachyon-based communications
system remained on Earth to continue his work with Manny Her-
nadez, Trent Industry's lead engineer, and the H in HATCH. AS-
parquila was the A. It did not not require brainpower to realize
Storm created STORM, the solid-state operating hardware used to
imprint and decode messages embedded on tachyon particles.

"You ask that about twice a week," she said. Stacey took a
deep, cleansing breath to reduce her level of anxiety. Getting
worked up again would not help. A year older, the intake of air
raised her bosom, reminding her how she was beginning to look
like the other women in the AS tribe. She retained her narrow
hips, similar to her sisters ASkiilamentrae and AStarratrae. Her
chest, firm before, now more rounded and full like her cousin
AStermalanlan.

"I know," Chaspi answered. The pink-skinned alien from Osperantue swiped off the virtual display. The manifestation rod lay-
ing atop her bed blinked off. The device a prototype and gift from
Billy Elkman. He designed and constructed it as an engineering
project. Stacey assisted by programming the system and import-
ing the images. Billy and Stacey were on a fast track to complete
their certifications and join Space Fleet. They hoped the virtual
display would help speed up Chaspi's path toward her pilot's certification.

Stacey watched her friend stand, turn, and straddle the chair. Her roommate wore boxers and a tight tank. She noted the girl's recent dedication to physical fitness. Slender and muscled from exercise and combat training with Sensei Kai. Her body a contrast to her Bosine appearance. Big brown eyes set further apart than Stacey's. Wide nose and flared nostrils. Small mouth with tight lips. Her ears, covered by the light-brown hair, had tipped upper lobes. Bosine represented prey, not predators. Except Chaspi fought the stereotype. If she did not make it as a pilot, she could always become a Fleet Marine.

"At least I'm not asking every day anymore," she said, turned to face her friend.

Two species living together on the world of a third. The two aliens shared a desire to make a difference in the expanding galaxy. They shared something else. Friendship.

"Have you memorized the entire manual yet?" Chaspi asked. Only a few trusted souls knew of Stacey's eidetic memory. Always fearful she would be transferred to some research and development program if people learned she could recall anything she saw quicker than a computer could search and recover data.

"Memorizing the flight manual is easy," the Fellen answered, shutting down the thin sheet made from organic film. "It's understanding how and when to implement procedures when normal turns to abnormal or an emergency occurs. It's also the difference in flying for Earth and piloting a ship for any of the other Trade Alliance worlds."

"Don't I know it," Chaspi said. She moved from the chair to her bed, replicating Stacey's cross-legged position. "Computers do the flying, navigating, and respond to all conditions. Pilots are trained as babysitters, or take the yoke only if a catastrophic meltdown of the operating system occurs. There's no . . . " Chaspi hesitated trying to find the proper word in Osperantue, which would then be translated automatically to Fellen by the translation and communications chip embedded in Stacey's neck.

"Initiative," Stacey said, using the English word.

"Exactly," Chaspi agreed.

"Speaking of initiative, did you and Billy have sex yet?"

The Bosine's light pink skin dropped several shades darker. Her pupils, already big, grew larger. The black pupils obscured the brown irises.

"Billy is my friend," Chaspi stammered. The attempt to infuse horror, or disdain, or some level of shock into her reply failed. The response came out flat. "Not one with benefits," she added. More emphasis and less embarrassment in her tone. "Why would you even ask?"

"Because he's in love with you, has the hots for you, and you always spend extra time trying to look nicer when you know he's going to be around," Stacey answered.

"I'm trying to look older, not nicer. More mature, so people will take me seriously," she explained. "You honestly believe he has the hots for me?"

"You remember the workout with Kai yesterday?"

"Of course. He made us practice contact drills until we were drenched."

"Billy could not keep his eyes off your tits," Stacey said. "Wet tank top stuck like glue. I nearly killed him with a backhand because he kept peeking at you."

"He's a boy. Boy's get stupid around boobs, regardless of the size, shape, or dampness of the shirt," Chaspi responded. "Of all people you should know that."

"Billy doesn't drool over my chest. He notices, but when he looks at you it's with full-on lust. I had the impression you liked him."

"I do," Chaspi admitted. "But I don't want to get involved. Becoming a pilot, a real Space Fleet pilot is hard. I'm not a natural, like you. I can't afford to get distracted."

"I didn't ask if you were going to marry him. I asked about sex."

"That would be more distracting than marriage," Chaspi countered. "And if it's such a no-big-thing, I haven't noticed you with anyone."

"Nice maneuver, pilot. Change course and distract the enemy," Stacey answered without answering.

Billy Elkman ducked his head and drove both palms up to contact the pistol. The pew sound of laser fire shockingly close to his ears. The beam, redirected by his action, passed harmlessly over his lowered head. He drove a right knee into the groin of his opponent. As his foot landed back down, his hands, fingers wrapped around the barrel, pressed down while keeping the barrel pointed away. He jammed the weapon into his attacker's mid-section. He then stepped in with his left foot, adding momentum to his move. Both hands now twisted, pressing the pistol sideways, against the shooter's wrist until it came free. With the pistol his, he stepped away, putting distance between them. The weapon now turned on its owner.

"Perfect," Aya Ishihara complimented the younger human. Head of the UEC's Exo-Legal Affairs, she also acted as an assistant instructor for her father, Kaito. The semi-private training taking place in her father's dojo located in a shopping strip-mall north of Bathurst College in northern Toronto. She bowed.

Billy returned the bow.

Her hands now covered the barrel of the pistol, and three fingers of her right hand also gripped his palm. She twisted left, quickly reversed right and continued, dropping down. Her weight, and the pain from the grip caused Billy to follow, losing his balance. He looped into an awkward fall, felt the pistol ripped from his numb fingers, and lay still.

"Took my bow too low," he said.

"Never take your eyes off an opponent, Billy," Aya said. "The fight might not be over."

He pushed himself up, stood, and faced his instructor. He bowed once more, this time making sure his eyes remained focused on the Japanese woman.

"You've improved a lot in a short time," she said. She tossed the practice-pistol to him. It looked and worked like a laser pistol, down to the unique sound. It only produced sound and flash, no deadly light beams or bursts. "Secure the pistol."

As he returned the prop to its place in a locked cabinet along the back wall of the dojo, she asked, "Why such hard work on martial arts, Billy? I understand you are doing exceptionally well at the Academy. Engineering and technology certifications do not require proficiency in combat skills."

"I asked Sensei Kai, your father, for more help because I want to join the Space Fleet Marines," he answered, returning to the mat. "I think I could help a lot on missions. Things often go wrong, and the average Marine is damn good at making do, but what if problems could be fixed immediately? How many lives could be saved if equipment was repaired under combat conditions, and not abandoned? I looked into military history texts and in the twentieth and twenty-first centuries engineers normally accompanied troops into battle zones."

"The Space Marines are difficult to join," Aya remarked. "Tough standards and a long waiting list of special operators from military and para-military branches around the world. Made more difficult with aliens now accepted for combat positions. Applications have arrived from several planets."

"I don't have a special operator background," he said. "I'm not coming from a military branch. I do have specialized skills I hope the command-level officers will recognize as valuable. Especially for Marines deployed in hot zones far away from normal support systems. If I can match engineering know-how with the ability to handle myself in a fight, I might stand a chance."

"You also have some important people who would endorse your application," the attractive attorney said. She untied the hair ribbon, allowing her long, straight black hair to fall. It framed her oval face, accentuating the black eyes full of intelligence. "People who know you and realize you are capable of handling yourself in a fight."

"Except I got knocked on my butt during Col. Barnwell's rescue," he replied. "Stacey did the real fighting. Chaspi carried me back to the Wraith."

"Stacey is Fellen," Aya said. "She has trained to fight since she was a child. The report I read said you delayed several bad actors long enough for the others to arrive and save Barnwell. I did not see anything mentioned about you being carried."

"She didn't actually carry me," he admitted. "Maybe Captain Cooper would vouch for me, but he isn't here. He might never be here again."

"Daniel Cooper is not someone you count out, Billy. He would certainly support your application to the Marines, but there are others equally as important."

"Your father might, and Admiral Patterson, maybe. She might not want to. It could look like she used her position to force me on the Marines," he responded. "Same for you, Aya. You're the Head of Exo-Legal Affairs. As a civilian, it might appear you are using your position to request a military unit take me on."

Aya untied her black belt. The gi top opened enough to display sand-colored skin beaded with perspiration and ripples of abdominal muscles. She folded the belt and placed it over her shoulder, indicating the session was done. Billy would remain and clean the dojo; the price for his lessons. Her father's residence, located behind the dojo, was a second home to her. She would shower, change, and return to the UEC complex.

As she walked away, she said, "We would all back your decision, but the person I was speaking of is your grandfather."

She disappeared, the door closing behind her. He stood, mouth agape. If she knew who his grandfather was, how many others did too?

"He works very hard," Ishihara Kaito remarked as his daughter entered the compact kitchen.

"He has purpose, tōchan," she replied, using the Japanese casual term for father. "You know what that can do."

"Our family is an example of ikigai," he replied from the table where he nursed a porcelain cup with hot tea. "A life with purpose is a happy life. Are you happy, Aya?"

The daughter of the sensei removed a bottled water from the fridge; sipped before answering.

"I enjoy my new position as the Head of Exo-legal Affairs for the UEC," she said. "It is demanding, and there is much to learn about alien legal matters."

Kaito waited. Her response was not an answer.

"Practice and being with you make me happy," she added. "But I admit, I sense something is missing."

"Children?"

Aya laughed. "You are always eager for grandchildren, tōchan. I think to make you happy, not me."

"Children can bring much reward," he said. "They can also be a pain in the ass."

"Yes, well this pain in your ass needs to shower and return to her real work." She bent to kiss the top of his head before leaving the kitchen.

Rosz watched the cyanobacteria react with the discharge from the black diamond shard from Rys. He hit the shard with a low-energy laser to create a reaction. The dead soil surrounding the colony of cyanobacteria began to change color. It turned from a light brown to a richer auburn red.

The entire process occurred within a simulator, but the parameters used to create the experiment were real enough. The chrono-gauge indicated an elapsed time of thirty-six-hours-twelve-minutes-ten-seconds before the dead soil began the color change.

"That was quite a success," the lab monitor, a professor at the University's eco-engineering department of the Environmental Engineering School, complimented the Bosine. "I see why the planet-recovery program on Rys accepted your application to study with them. This idea of yours could speed up the warming of a planet's surface by decades."

"Rys has the longest and most successful history of reviving planets and restoring them for life," he said. "Warmth, atmosphere, and water are the three keys. It traditionally requires a century or more to get the three elements in place, and decades before they have evolved to support plant growth. If the surface can be warmed more quickly, everything else speeds up."

"You said your theory came to you while working in the Saudi desert," the professor remarked.

"I was part of the University field study. The Saudis manage the largest cyanobacteria farms on Earth, as well as algae tanks and other components used to revitalize over-cultivated land. Their work was reproduced on Mars by the original robots sent to establish a permanent encampment," the young Bosine male responded. "Elliott Fairchild's wife, Dr. Katharina Ikonen, an exo-botanist, designed new bacterial hybrids capable of thriving on Mars. The pine forest there is named for her."

"The field trip was to introduce Dr. Ikonen's Martian bacteria back to Earth," the monitor said. "I remember reading the synopsis requesting the funds. I also remember it did not produce results."

"Nothing worth creating a paper or requesting additional funding," Rosz admitted. "But I spent my free time trying some of my own experiments. I broke the bacteria into separate bacterium. I also explored the desert, trying to find places with more rocks and ground water, and less sand. One of the bacterium did appear to have a minor effect on rocky soil at the edge of the desert. I dropped my headset by accident and the crystal chip popped out and onto a square where I poured the algae-based bacterium liquid. The minor charge caused the liquid to gel. The soil became a little darker."

"You didn't report your experiment to the supervising professor?" the woman asked.

"By the time I returned to the base camp with the sample, the soil was the same as before," he said. "The change of color could have been hopeful imagination."

"Hopeful enough to try a more dedicated charge from a more powerful source," the lab professor said.

"A simulated attempt," he corrected. "The twenty-third to be honest," he added. "The first using specs for a black diamond crystal."

"It appears you have a starting point, Rosz. The scientists on Rys may become the students instead of you."

[Rewind To Admiral Patterson & Col. Barnwell]

"Tab, I appreciate your being cautious regarding the use of military units to back you and Amanda. I get it we may have spies and traitors inside the ranks. But what you are asking is a bit much," Patterson said.

Her surface office in the Space Fleet Administration building within the United Earth Council complex north of Toronto, Canada did not offer the view her office on the Earth-Moon Space Station (EMS2) provided. From the forty-third floor, the windowed corner office looked out across an impressive landscape. From here she could see a mix of modern buildings, courtyards, and, in the distance, Toronto's skyline.

The Marine Colonel placed a data chip on the Admiral's desktop.

"Ishihara Kaito," he said. "Former Japanese military special operator. Became a member of the Tokyo police department when he left the military. Joined the Royal Guard and retired as their commander. Father of the UEC's head of exo-legal affairs, Aya Ishihara. Recently hired by you as the lead instructor for hand-to-hand combat training at the Space Fleet Academy."

He placed another chip on top.

"AStasaei of Fell," he said, releasing the chip. "Currently enrolled in the Pilot Certification track at Space Fleet Academy. Demonstrated ability to fly and advanced combat skills when she helped rescue one Titus Andronicus Barnwell, Jr. from the Camarilla Dissolvere. During the unsanctioned mission she took on and took out multiple targets without firing a shot. Communications expert and considered a computer systems genius by her host on Earth, one Admiral Pamela Patterson. Eyes-Only after action report by ex-Captain Daniel Cooper referred to her as 'bad ass.'"

The third personnel background chip joined the first two.

"Chaspi. A Bosine and native to the planet Osperantue. Refugee from the spaceship Star Gazer. She assisted on the same rescue with AStasaei. Currently a cadet in the Pilot Certification program at Space Fleet Academy. An early entry to the Cadet Corps based on the recommendations of several current and former Space Fleet personnel."

"Including me," Patterson said.

Tab nodded and set down a fourth chip.

"Rosz, another Bosine from Osperantue. Enrolled at Bathurst College in the Environmental Technology school. Within a few credits of completing his undergraduate degree in less than two years. Accepted to the Planet Reclamation Research Foundation on Rys, the leading group in the known galaxy for establishing viable habitats on barren planets and moons."

"Because?" she asked.

"He's studied the environment in the deserts of Saudi Arabia. He knows the topography better than some of the locals," Tab answered.

Producing another chip he said, "William 'Billy' Elkman. Besides experience with the others in my rescue, he's trained with Ishihara. He transferred from Environmental Studies at Bathurst to Engineering and Technology at Space Fleet Academy. He appears to have discovered his niche. Instructors consider him a whiz, especially at analytical analysis and repairs on mechanical systems. He is expected to test for certification and receive a commission and assignment to a Space Fleet ship within three months. He's advanced through the ranks faster than any former cadet, human or alien."

"Kai because of his skills," Patterson said. "Stacey because she can do it all. Pilot, computers, fighter, communications. Chaspi is your pilot back-up and support person. Rosz knows the terrain and might give you insight into getting in and out of the complex. Billy is there to fix equipment when they go wrong, and things always go wrong on missions. None are currently military, and no one would expect a bunch of cadets to attack a fortified location in the Saudi desert."

"I don't expect them to either," Tab said. "I trust them to back Amanda and me when we go for al-Rashid. I also know the mission will not get leaked by using operators from outside the normal pool."

"What if you discover al-Rashid is somewhere else?" Patterson asked.

"Everyone but Rosz would still be applicable," the Marine answered. "I'll either find someone with local knowledge or rely on virtual mapping and topography."

"You have another chip in your hand," Pam noted.

"This one is special," he said. "Someone you know, and do not know. This one is on faith alone. Truth is, I will need someone else's permission to recruit this agent. Thought you should be aware since the mission will be a joint operation."

"Sounds intriguing," the Admiral replied. "Before I agree or kick you out, tell me about your last team member. Then I need to tell you a secret about one of the others so you know exactly what you are requesting."

"Sounds intriguing," Barnwell mimicked.

Chapter 7

Earth - Virginia

While Tab travelled to Toronto to request the personnel transfers from Fleet Admiral Patterson, Amanda Black returned to rural Virginia. Her assignment was to confirm a lead concerning Saleh Abd al-Rashin.

The lead concerned the new construction in the middle of Saudi Arabia discovered by the Geospatial-Intelligence Agency. Barnwell believed it to be the work of al-Rashid. He dispatched Major Black to confirm his suspicion.

The UEC Reconnaissance Office, located in Chantilly, Virginia, south of Washington, DC was home to the Imagery Intelligence (ROII) division of the Geospatial-Intelligence Agency. The location, a short drive from Fort Belvoir and GEOINT, was kept separate to provide greater security. Far fewer people could access the ROII than wandered the sprawling campus at Fort Belvoir.

Black, dressed in civilian clothing, sat beside a young woman of African heritage who smelled like a tropical breeze. They lounged comfortably in leather ergonomic chairs with back supports. They were inside a dark studio within a high-security bunker located several levels beneath the surface. Low light emitted from floor-level sconces kept the room from being totally blacked out. The woman tapped an imaginary keypad, and the interior brightened. The planet Earth appeared in the air before them.

"Based on the parameters you requested before arriving, I coordinated the collection and began analysis of information from airplane and satellite reconnaissance of the Saudi region of interest." Her voice soft, but carried. No accent the experienced spy could discern. "I collated and merged images by military services and the UEC Central Security Agency."

The planet expanded as they zoomed down, virtual-soaring to the Middle East. The display continued to track down, finally leveling off and skimming the surface.

"The largest city remaining north of Riyadh is Hail." The surface became a four-lane highway with sand drifting across the cracked asphalt in several places.

"I'll speed this up," the analyst said. The surface blurred, and the angle pulled back and up. The outskirts of a community zoomed into view. Abandoned petrol stations, homes made of common and exotic materials, and a mosque whizzed by. The image stopped; frozen on a cityscape. They saw a mixture of shuttered industrial sites, abandoned parks with monuments, and once palatial, now dilapidated hotels. One forsaken hotel appeared forlorn. Dried fountains and scrub palms created a feeling of sadness and anger. A once beautiful Arabian metropolis destroyed by the Pandemic, which took two-thirds of the population, and then ransacked by survivors. Vehicles, left to the desert sun decades earlier, littered side streets.

"Hail," Tamra Jones, the ROII analyst and Middle Eastern expert said. "Before the Pandemic this was Saudi Arabia's wheat and grain hub. The city evolved in the center of agriculture. Located in a valley with two major mountains hemming it in. Once half-a-million people lived here. About one-hundred-thousand live in and around the urban area today. Most are farmers, or merchants who have reclaimed the center of the city."

The virtual tour continued over and beyond the city. The view once more travelled a pock-marked highway.

"Old Highway-Seventy," she said. "Twenty miles northeast of Hail it runs through the ancient village of Baqa'a. A mosque, a grocery store, and a school for children too young to work the fields is pretty much the extent of Baqa'a now. A road leads south toward another small town called Ash Shaalaniyah. Between the two is what you are interested in."

The image ascended, providing a view from above, but without the three-dimensional aspects of the tour to this point.

"This area is in the northern center of Saudi Arabia," Tamra said. "We don't have any overflights or surface video during active construction."

"How is that possible?" Black asked. "The construction must have required months."

"Someone knew when aerial assets would be in range," the tech answered. "Crews worked whenever we were blind. They covered the area in sand-colored tarps to disguise the work and hide the encampment's interior layout."

"No one got curious?"

"Eventually, but not until the location became active and the people no longer cared who saw movement," the reply. "I've stitched together imagery from satellites orbiting the region since we began to understand it was an unusual development. I also have closer aerial recon from drones. I can't give you more than the exterior images and the layout from a high angle."

"The placement of buildings, access roads, and barrier fences make it look like a military base," Black said. "Except the one building in the center."

"A mosque," Jones explained. "Official records and permits for construction were finally made available. After everything you see was completed. The mosque is the central hub for a community service project. South of the mosque is a medical aid building."

"Servicing two insignificant villages in the middle of nowhere? Who paid for the construction, and who runs the operation?" Black asked.

"International charity foundation did and does," the reply. "Planet Peace Initiative is the corporate name. No one on our watch lists directly associated with the group, but if you drill down deep enough and follow enough loose threads you can find possible connections to businesses owned or associated with Camarilla members."

"The multi-story structure on the eastern edge?"

"Plans call it staff housing and support. Analysts call it barracks."

"I count five bunker entrances, four smaller buildings, security huts, and a helo-shuttle landing pad," Black said, pointing at holographic images as she spoke aloud.

"Storage, camouflaged batteries, garage, offices, and a communications center capable of receiving signals as far away as space, and able to broadcast around the world."

"The entrance is a u-turn security trap, and the whole compound is surrounded by double fences. Old-fashioned, but photo-electric or laser grid barriers wouldn't last long under the desert sun. Roadway inside and outside the fence for vehicle or foot patrols," the Major noted.

"Open land around the four sides," Jones enjoined. "Single entry-exit road from the highway. Houses at the abandoned town have been renovated. Anyone not staying in the barracks is living in those homes. The renovations were also used to distract attention and provide an excuse for vehicles delivering materials."

"A base of operations?" Black asked.

"Base of operations," Jones confirmed. "Too much secrecy in the permitting and construction, and too many military aspects for a civilian or religious compound. Add the uber-powerful communications and the landing zone and you have a command center."

"Located in the ancestral home of the al-Rashid family," Black added. "I believe we just confirmed Col. Barnwell's gut."

Chapter 8

Devisator

Devisator is a planet of extremes.

The Devisator system is a trinary. The planet orbits a late giant carbon star that trapped a white dwarf star. The dying dwarf had negligible effect on the larger star. From the planet the smaller star creates the effect of a dark pupil within an iris of burnt orange. The name of the double-star (translated) is Cyclops.

The planet remains in a stable orbit around Cyclops, but the elliptical pattern creates extremes in weather. Outrageously hot summers and freezing winters with only short, temperate times between.

The system contains another dozen planets and planetoids varying in size and atmospheric conditions. None are hospitable for life, but several produce minerals and gases with valuable applications.

The Devee, forced to adapt to extremes beneath the ever watchful eye, evolved into a society adept at creating useful products from everything available. Following their expansion into local space, the resources mined from other planets in the system rapidly improved their civilization. The discovery of wormhole travel opened the galaxy to the resourceful species.

The third star in the Devisator system is a hot blue emission star called Aquae for its watery appearance in the night sky. It sits six-times further away than Cyclops at Devisator's longest orbital arch. The distance insured no affect on the planet's orbit. The distance between the two major stars mitigated the instability found in the majority of multi-star systems.

The trinary did affect the system's two wormhole gates. Wormhole gates tended to appear at the edges of star systems. Planets moved nearer or further from a portal according to their orbits. The gravitational effect of three stars created an anomaly. One gate constantly remained proximal to Devisator. The wormhole tunnel elongated or contracted behind the portal as the gate moved with the planet.

The second gate opened onto a massive planet located midway between Cyclops and Aquae. The planet revolved, but did not orbit. The gate remained locked above the frozen world and within the dense-core orb's strong gravitational pull. Ships entering the system via this gate were yanked to the surface with catastrophic results.

Ginae[10] Tabilis massaged her temples with the middle-fingers of both hands. The pressure from the tiny concentric circles provided little relief from her headache. She needed a VigaTea, but the painkiller played hell with her cognitive facilities. The weekly updates from the Videolios[11], the Councils in charge of the major departments within her government, required she be sharp. The low-grade migraine improved her focus on each report as she concentrated on the information to push the discomfort aside.

"What the fuck was Atticus Soren thinking?" she demanded from Sypha Chai. The migraine did not improve her mood.

"I do not believe the Mischene Prophet put much faith in thinking," the Devee charged with oversight of the Mischene as they advanced their manifest destiny doctrine replied. "Without the guidance of his father, Governor Soren, he acted precipitously."

"Hundreds-of-years of manipulating those bastards wasted," the Ginae said. "Gently pushing Soren into attacking the other Trade Alliance worlds, providing him and his closest associates with Longgevi-tea to extend their worthless lives, lost because his power-mad son decided to attack the Aster System and goad the humans into a confrontation. At least he's dead."

"We did increase our trade profits by filling voids created when the Mischene disrupted routes and eliminated competition," Chai said. "We also discovered the planet Phisor and the remark-

---

[10] Ginae: Leader. Combination queen and president.

[11] Videolios: Council of Supervisors overseeing the work of the caste dedicated to a profit center or study crucial to the civilization's continued success. The Supervisors report to the Ginae.

able fur the creatures there have. Synthesizing the fur's qualities will provide a new income stream."

"Chimia Elotho, do you still believe Chimia Scalah will have completed her experiments when our ship arrives to collect her?" the leader asked the stout brunette seated beside Sypha Chai.

"Scalah is my best chemist," the Chimia Videolio representative replied. She rested clasped hands atop her round belly. "She will discover the answers by the deadline."

"She'd better," Tabilis responded, not amused by the smug attitude of the alchemist. "The Devee spent a great deal of resources keeping the Mischene rebels and their pet lizards supplied. I would like to see a return on our investment. The trade created by others who will want the products we manufacture from Phisoran fur will be essential for recouping our expenses."

"The sexual experience enhancement from the pheromones will be desired by dozens of our trade partners," Elotho replied. "A synthesized spray will create a healthy return on our investment. I'm more concerned about the Earth forces on Phisor. They may try to stop Scalah from leaving."

"Fuck those humans," the Ginae spat. "The Devee abducted creatures from Earth before humans walked on two legs. Their jump up the evolutionary ladder occurred quicker than any of our Tuito[12] predicted. Right Tuito Bailis?"

The willowy blonde sat with her arms crossed beneath melon-sized breasts.

"We have studied alien behavior for centuries. Our research has been used to manipulate others, predict their actions, and increase the Devee influence across several alliances and confederations. Humans are confusing," she answered.

"That's your professional opinion, Tuito Bailis?" Tabilis' anger dispatched her migraine. "Humans are unpredictable. You placed a spy on their planet decades ago. All you have learned from her is humans are confusing?"

---

[12] Tuito: Psychologists and Exo-Political Pundits

Bailis remained calm in the face of her leader's ire. The tiny squint of her hazel eyes the only indication she did not appreciate the Ginae's tone.

"Our spy has introduced major disruptions into their society," she replied. "The humans adapted quickly. Their response to disaster is resolve, not despair. When we learned they discovered a Nakki ship with a space-fold array, our agent was dispatched immediately. Every attempt to gain the secrets of space-fold have been failures, while the humans, against the odds, have deciphered the technology and implemented it without destroying their social fabric in the process. They are unique, Ginae. Our experience shows civilizations given such powerful assets follow a pattern of ever increasing corruption until they fall or are defeated by a more powerful enemy."

"Not Earthers?" Ginae Tabilis asked, her anger receding as her curiosity grew.

"Not entirely," the vague reply by the expert in political maneuvering. "Humans are not actually a civilization. They are a single species, yet they are broken into hundreds of societies. They coexist and cooperate despite major ideological differences. A few, mostly individuals, but some of the more radical social groups, could be manipulated for our benefit."

"Why aren't we manipulating them?" Sypha Chai asked. "I have manipulated the Mischene for centuries."

"With the end result a failure," Bailis countered. "My agent on Earth identified the most powerful of the individuals, groups, and former nations most likely to exchange power and prestige for the technology secrets we desire. She is developing relationships."

She directed her comments to the leader, allowing Chai to fume silently and ignored.

"You predict a success?" Tabilis asked. "Will humans fall into line?"

"I believe we can use the weak-minded and greedy among the humans to create sufficient havoc to disrupt the planet's security services. Then we use simple bribery to gain access to the tech we want. We will attain Nakki secrets they deciphered and human technology to advance our own," Tabilis replied. "My experts do not believe humans, as a whole, will ever fall in line, nor continue to be manipulated for an appreciable term. Resources spent controlling them would be wasted after we extract their sciences."

"Recommendation?" the leader queried.

"Annihilation. Wipe them out before they become a greater threat to our interests."

"Which we cannot do while they hold the advantage of space-fold, as well as their advanced weaponry," Echnee[13] Hor chimed in to the discussion.

"We can if we take advantage of their major weakness," Bailis countered. "They are trusting fools. They also believe in second chances. If we cannot defeat their tech, we defeat them through their sensitivity."

"There is your answer, Chimia Elotoh," Ginae Tabilis said. "When our ship arrives in the Phisor System to collect Chimia Scalah, we will implement Tuito Bailis' suggestion. Consider it an experiment. Trick the humans into allowing us near by appealing to their overly trusting natures. Then annihilate them."

"The Mishene and Zenge on Phisor?" Elotoh asked.

"Fuck them," Tabilis responded. "We'll have everything we wanted from both sides. Let the Mischene and Phisorans fight it out. Whichever side wins can have the planet. Echnee Hor, has your caste constructed the weapon from the plans the Galvari general, Saytuss, provided. We traded two dozen sex slaves for those plans?"

"Built, tested, and being prepared for our more powerful ships," the Engineering Representative responded. "It requires a massive energy source, but produces the results as promised by Saytuss. I would call the trade a bargain."

"Pidita[14] Xeneau, you have been quiet," Tabilis noted. "As the principal administrator for trade, your caste has an interest in everything being discussed. Comments?"

---

[13] Echnee: Technology Specialist. Includes spacecraft and weapons.

[14] Pidita: Trade / Merchant

Xeneau, an older woman with grey streaks in mousy brown hair which hung straight to the center of her back, sat with perfect posture, her hands folded in her lap; an image of composure.

"Trade has made our world rich," she said. "Our decision to remain in the shadows while others go to war allowed us to take advantage of the chaos. We follow behind to sweep up valuables left in the wake of conflict. Because our Tuito caste is masterful at manipulating weak minds, we know when best to act and when it is prudent to leave an area and avoid losses."

Tuito Bailis nodded her blonde head to Pidita Xeneau in recognition of the compliment.

"My trade delegations are able to open routes closed to others because of the diversity of our products. The Sypha and Chimia create incredible brews and merchandise. The Echnee reproduce bartered technology cheaper than the original, and often with added features. The Devee slavers and reavers deliver prized species and valuable objects easily exchanged on the black markets for other difficult to obtain merchandise."

"A wonderful synopsis of our superior abilities," the Ginae said. "Is there a point?"

"We may or may not have reached a tipping point, Ginae Tabilis. The time may be near when Devisator is no longer content to merely influence galactic politics."

"You believe the Devee should begin to consolidate our resources and connections. You suggest we become the empress and not the king-maker," Bailis said.

"I believe a test of our strength is nigh," Xeneau responded. "The arrival of humans created a power shift in the galaxy. A shift similar to the one we hoped to control through the Mischene. This one likely to wash over the Devee if allowed to continue. It was a wise move on Ginae Tabilis' part to send a spy to Earth when we learned of their discovery of a Nakki installation. With foresight she ordered our spy to intercede in the human's path to unlocking the secrets of the Ancients. Our lack of understanding human perseverance and persistence may actually have strengthened their resolve. We may have, unwittingly, advanced their arrival by attempting to thwart it."

"We had only abducted humans to study," Bailis countered. "Usually infants raised to become slaves or trade bait."

"I meant no aspersion, Tuito Bailis," Xeneau said. "In fact, I agree with your earlier recommendation. Humans are unique in our experience. With anything unique you must consider its trade value. It could be priceless, or best trashed rather than suffer the maintenance costs."

"They will not be easily defeated," Hor interjected.

"Annihilating the human race, as Bailis counsels, would be the victory needed to announce our decision to rule rather than simply profit," Elotoh chimed in.

"The Devee would no longer be the most profitable of the Trade Worlds, we would control the markets for this entire quadrant of the galaxy," Ginae Tabilis pronounced.

""We may not be in a position to defeat them," Xeneau cautioned. "We may possess the technology to defeat the humans. We may not possess the battle experience or the military ability to win."

"Why is it the Pidita sect can never stand behind a single choice?" Echnee Hor asked aloud. "If we attack the humans, we may win. If we attack the humans, we may lose. This is true of every barter, regardless of the stakes; we win or we lose. The question is do we try?"

"Chimia Scalah expects a ship in ten days," Tabilis interrupted. "Hor, will the ship to Phisor have the new weapon?"

"No," the short answer.

"Bailis, you must send a message to the commander of that ship. Instruct her how best to persuade humans she represents no danger. She must get near enough to their ship for our conventional weapons to destroy it," Tabilis ordered.

The blonde nodded.

"Echnee Hor, I want our finest ship outfitted with the Galvari weapon. Our plans included a visit to Earth within the month. We will change our plan from a covert mission to a trade delegation. It is time the Devee introduced ourselves to Earth as a fellow member of the Trade Alliance Worlds. It will be our first and final introduction."

Ginae Tabilis had made her decision. It was time to test their ability to lead.

Hor nodded. "Everything is prepared. My guild can install and test the new weapon within forty-eight hours," she assured her leader.

"I want every guild to reset mission clocks. The ship to Phisor will exit the wormhole gate in two days and take another eight days to reach the planet. The Carrier designated for the Earthers' system will require two days to install the Galvani weapon. It can reach Earth's system in five days using the advanced wormhole drive. Four or five days more from the gate to the planet Mars in the Earth system. Within two-weeks we test the humans. Hor will provide updates as events require."

Nods of agreement and acceptance passed through the council chamber.

"It is such a wonderful word," the Ginae said. The others looked to their leader. "Annihilation."

Chapter 9

Phisor

Captain Onour Cadee walked well behind the line of Zenge as they searched the ruins. He kept his laser pistol in one hand and the Zenge-zapper in his other. The jittery white-haired Mischene never received officer training. He survived long enough to receive promotions based on attrition. He became a sergeant by simply joining the Prophet's army by choice and not coercion. They made him a lieutenant when the RMM arrived on Phisor. After a year of ducking assignments where others were killed or disabled, his cowardice was rewarded with Captain's rank. No longer able to hide when dangerous work needed to be done, he found himself in charge of a squad dispatched to locate, capture, or eliminate the crew from a downed enemy fighter. An enemy crew who already eliminated the first squad sent to find them.

In the dark, surrounded by the ruins of a ghost town, in command of aliens he feared as much as he feared the enemy, he maintained a low profile. He placed his thirty troopers in a line and ordered them forward. The vicious lizard-like killers moved without stealth. They tossed debris aside and charged into any place a person might hide. They acted without fear of an ambush. There was no doubt they would ravage anyone they discovered. No prisoners would be returned to the General.

Cadee heard stories of Zenge blood-rage. His damp fingers squeezed the transmitter developed to administer shocks through a collar worn around the neck of every Zenge soldier. If they found the flyers and went mad, he intended to keep his distance. He would shock the shit out of any lizard attempting to get near him.

Because he cared more for his own safety, and because he was woefully unprepared to lead a squad, he did not notice his line bunch to the center. It was a natural action, and experienced battlefield leaders would periodically remind their team members to maintain spacing.

He stopped behind a battered transport vehicle. A bus or rail-car left to rust in the street. The Zenge cleared the interior and moved forward. As his squad began working their way up a rise in the landscape, he sat down for a drink. A little water mixed with a little something extra discovered in an abandoned bar.

Cadee wanted to order the Zenge back. He wanted to call off the search and return to report no success to his superior. He wanted his radio to work to confirm the enemy Marines on the far side of the city were being kept busy, but the jammers used to interfere with the enemy screwed communications for everyone. He began to play a game in his head of all the things he wanted. He made it to an image of a girl he attended army training school with when the first laser fired.

Storm lay in a depression across from the building where Elie and Jon-Jon waited. Water pooled in the bottom of the rut, but the METS kept her dry. Her head rested on her forearm, allowing her eyes to see above the rim. The integrated helmet's optics and heads-up display on maximum field observation.

The crater probably resulted from a blast because the area around it was clear. Whatever once stood atop the low hill became a target. Now it provided her with a great view and a foxhole.

"Elie, a line of Zenge are starting up the street," she said, certain the closed trans-comm signal would not be overheard.

"Storm [static-crack] . . . mers . . . your sig . . . [ack-static-ack] . . . king up."

The jammers used by the Mischene proved powerful enough to interfere with the chips, though separated by less than a city block.

The METS software kept a running account of each enemy signature. By assigning a number, the computer kept the Marauders pinpointed and provided an on-going count as bodies appeared via one of the optic-programs. Her display reached twenty-three, the last one popped up from her lower right side, when Number One stopped to appraise the nearly complete structure across the street.

Not waiting on fellow Zenge, the soldier advanced.

Storm lifted her chin to free her arm. The laser rifle's barrel now sat atop the rim. She did not fire on the one entering the hideout, maintaining her focus on the half-dozen bunched and behind it by fifty-feet.

Her heat-sensitive scanner showed a form flow out of the doorway and remain low to the ground. It moved quickly and disappeared behind rubble located on the edge of the avenue, a dozen yards north of the building. The speed meant it was Elie moving to a new location. It also meant the Zenge entering the old store did not receive a hospitable welcome. She wiped the Number One. Numbers twenty-four and twenty-five replaced it.

"Elie, . . . art . . . reet," was the garbled message she received. She replied, "Storm, jammers are affecting signals. You're breaking up."

Realizing her message probably made no more sense than Storm's, she quit talking and began watching. She placed her laser rifle at the bottom of the doorway, the sight facing the street. She then used her METS helmet optics to access images from the sight. She could see without taking the chance of being seen. It was necessary to rely on optical enhancements because of the Zenge's lower-than-normal body temperatures.

As the first attacker moved toward the building, she pulled the combat knife from her boot sheath. Knowing Jon-Jon could see her with his system, she held the knife up to warn him of her decision.

The wide, flat feet of the alien soldier stepped on the laser rifle. When the elongated snout dropped to see what he stepped on, Elie used her enhanced strength to grab his rifle and pull. She fell backward, bringing the three-hundred pound alien with her. His stomach landed on her knees, and he continued to roll over the living shadow, coming to a jarring landing on his back.

Jon-Jon used his rifle as a bar across the creature's neck, placing his entire weight on either end to stop him from calling out a warning.

With two hands, Elie buried the point of the blade in the Zenge's chest, penetrating light body armor, the thick scales of its hide, and breaking a bone before entering the heart. Only a Space Ranger could have delivered the force necessary to drive a knife that deeply.

She left the blade, finding it too difficult to remove, and started out the door. She collected the rifle and sprinted for a mound of debris. The location would give them triangulated fire coverage.

Jon-Jon stopped at the open door and dropped to a knee. Rifle up. Optics on. Breathing steady. All of the training necessary for being a fighter pilot coming to fore a long way from the sky overhead.

When the half-dozen Marauders following decided to join their buddy, Storm opened up, taking down three before they realized they were in an ambush.

Elie caught two, and Jon-Jon blasted the only one able to get near the doorway, sending the big body backward with a hole through its mid-section and a portion of spine disintegrated.

Cadee dropped to his stomach, his fortification spilling onto the ground. When he realized no bursts came in his direction, he scampered to the front corner of the vehicle. His squad was caught on the slope of the hill. It looked like his entire team had gathered for a leisurely walk up the avenue.

The distinctive ack-thack sound a laser rifle produced sounded as one, two, three beams from three locations atop the hill tore into the reptilians.

Palmer halted and lifted her fist.

"Laser fire," she said. The three waited, verified the direction, and sprinted toward the sound.

Galetti's team had already run in the same direction.

MSgt Palmer attempted to contact Galetti to coordinate their approach. Proximity to the Mischene's forcefield and sophisticated jammers produced static and chirps. The two three-member teams would be cut off from each other, as well as unable to warn the downed crew of their proximity.

When she rounded the corner of a suburban home, the flash of lasers atop the hill pinpointed the action. Peter, sure-footed and fast in the rubble, already knelt in the building's cover. Khaled joined them ten-seconds later.

The Phisoran pointed out, over, and slightly up. Galetti's team were leap-frogging up the far side of the rise. Two holding their ground to provide covering fire if needed while the third moved forward. When the team member on the move stopped, the last person in line began their sprint to the front.

Palmer raised her rifle and tapped Peter on the shoulder, pointing the path up the hill on their side of the narrow street. As soon as he found a secure spot and stopped, she sent the Egyptian out. The corporal raced to Peter's location, hesitated for a split second, and then continued forward. When he came to a halt, Palmer began her ascent.

In this manner, both teams advanced toward the top of the rise and the action.

The targeted fire from the three Space Fleet flyers ripped into the Zenge, killing several. Those wounded, saved by their protective armor and thick skin, ignored the pain and the danger. Adding war cries to the ack-thack of laser fire, they charged forward with those uninjured. They overran Storm's position first.

The Fellen fired point-blank into an elongated snout filled with razor-sharp teeth before two others tackled her. The extended talons of the Zenge ripped at the METS. Rows of jagged teeth snapped at the woman as they attempted to bite down on her arms or legs.

Storm fought with the strength and skill of the residents of Fell. Her right hand smashing into the scaly enemy while her right slashed with her combat knife. It was quicker to retrieve the knife than draw her sidearm.

The blade gashed the throat of one. The other got his mouth around her wrist and bit down. The suit prevented the teeth from penetrating, but the immense pressure trapped her arm. The mortally wounded Zenge continued to rip at her as blood loss from the mortal wound weakened it. Claw tips caught a minuscule seam where the helmet integrated with the bodysuit, ripping it open and scratching the blue skin beneath.

She drove the knife beneath the chin of the bleeding Zenge, finishing it. When she attempted to recover the blade and hammer it into the one biting her wrist, another joined the fray in time to snare her free arm.

The Zenge with his teeth latched to Storm's wrist dug the claws of his free hand into the opening below her neck. He threw a muscled leg across her lower body to control her. The other Zenge continued to hold her other arm. The enemy trooper dropped to its knees, landing atop and pinning Storm's left leg.

Talons capable of ripping sheet steel began to peel the METS away, tearing skin and spraying blood as the claws raked down and over her chest. The blood-lust washed over the two in anticipation of feeding on the woman while she still lived.

Elie laid down withering fire but could not prevent three of the Marauders reaching Storm's position. Incoming laser fire laced the pile of debris she used for cover. Refusing to hide while Storm and Jon-Jon were under immediate threat, her METS saved her four times when hits landed. The latest version of the tactical suit deflected the lasers, but could not stop the force of the impacts. Each hit landed like a blow from a sledgehammer. The fourth glanced off her helmet, rattling her already tender brain.

She brushed aside the cobwebs. She had to help Jon-Jon by taking out the Marauders advancing on his position. Then she needed to hot-foot it to Storm. As she raised her rifle, a thick muscled arm of green scale snaked around her throat and lifted her off the ground. One of the Marauders, the only one to not make the mistake of bunching with the others, had made her way around the conflict. She moved in from behind Elie. Foggy from the laser impacting her head, and not fully recovered from the crash, the Ranger did not notice the proximity alert on her heads-up display.

Jon-Jon stood in the doorway. Feet braced and rifle up with sights linked to his helmet optics. Twenty of the Marauders were down. Killed by Storm, Elie, and his weapons. Three reached Storm. Elie quit firing, but the Zenge had not advanced on her position. She must have taken a hit. Six of the twenty dead lay on the ground in front of his position. Another half-dozen remained active, following behind those dead or dying, using the initial wave as fodder. He took out two more with clean head shots before another barreled through the opening. Three others followed. The structure, once used to protect him from enemy fire, now prevented Storm or Elie, if either still lived, from targeting the Zenge inside with him.

Storm's tears were not the result of pain. They were anger-driven. Angry she would not be able to help Elie and Jon-Jon. Furious she would never know what became of Daniel Cooper.

The Zenge biting her wrist unclamped in order to bury its teeth into her exposed chest. A fur-covered body hit the crazed creature's upper torso with the force of a runaway car. Peter, unable to fire into the tangle of bodies, simply ran as hard and fast as he could. His arms wrapped around the Zenge's head and the momentum from his assault pulled its head around. The body followed, releasing the hold on the Fellen to fend off the attack by the Phisoran.

The second Zenge roared in anger. The roar cut short by two laser pistols at a distance where a mistake could not happen. Abbie and Khaled fired together, blasting the beast's head to green, grey, and red splatter. The heat of the laser instantly cauterized the massive wound. The headless Marauder collapsed.

The Egyptian pulled medical spray from a utility pocket to close Storm's ragged wounds. The Brit jumped forward to get a better aim and assist Peter. She did not need to fire.

In the roll, Peter pulled his Space Fleet issued laser pistol from the Sherpa thigh holster. The redesigned pistol slid easily from the quick-release. When the two bodies came to a stop, the muzzle fire was hidden by the Zenge's body. The spray of body parts and armor from the Zenge's back were visible in the dark night. The Phisoran struggled to push the heavy body, all dead weight, off. MSgt Palmer helped, grunting as she lifted and Peter pushed.

"Elie. Jon-Jon," Storm said loudly. She stood. Khaled stood with her, keeping the med-spray aimed at her bloody upper chest.

Elie had enhanced speed and strength. The Zenge had the advantage of surprise and leverage. The METS helped, but the strength of the alien female Marauder would be sufficient to snap the human's spinal column.

A knife cut the Zenge's forearm to the bone. Severed muscle and tendon lost control, and the pressure around Elie's torso eased. The follow-up slash cut the length of the Zenge's other forearm, from wrist to elbow. The pain lost in blood-lust, but the destroyed nerves unable to respond to orders from the enraged brain.

Elie dropped to her feet as soon as the arm around her throat fell away. A firm hand pushed her aside, and a person in a METS continued to attack the Marauder, landing multiple blade-strikes to the much larger opponent's stomach and chest. The attack would have persisted, the knife-wielder eventually killing the enemy with dozens of punctures, except Elie delivered the coup de grâce with her laser pistol. The beam drilled a hole between the female's eyes.

"Thanks, Ash," she said, recognizing Daniel Cooper's favorite combat knife before the young woman disconnected her helmet.

The black hair and red skin of the Hana Kay race from Aster Farum 1 stood revealed. Ashauk Livist Tolnikiton had been a sex-slave for the Prophet. She and her sister rescued by Coop and Hiro when they assassinated the Mischene rebel leader aboard his space ship in the Aster System's deadly vortex. Coop gave the Hana Kay his knife so she felt capable of protecting herself and her sister.

"Reconnect your helmet," Elie ordered. "We have to help Storm and Jon-Jon."

"Yes, Captain," Ash replied, the helmet hood flipped on and the convex faceplate made of organic film back in place in seconds.

C.C. and Haz reached them as the two women raced away. They hurried to catch up. Elie easily pulled away. She noted Storm and three others in Space Fleet METS moving toward the hideout. Elie juked left, happy to know Storm remained alive and mobile; worried about her co-pilot and friend inside the abandoned store.

Elie entered first. Two Zenge lay dead, and two others screamed and hammered closed fists against Jon-Jon's curled body. She fired, aiming high to target the bigger Marauders and not accidentally hit Jon-Jon. Storm added her fire, followed a second later by Ash. The three women decimated the remaining enemy.

C.C. and Haz took positions outside the doorway, scanning and protecting the perimeter. Abbie and Khaled held spots on either side of the avenue to make sure no one surprised them from up or down the street. Peter remained where he was, watching for anyone trying to sneak in from the east. The five watched and waited.

Ash exited first, her rifle up as she swept the area. Storm walked out next, her left arm hanging, her head exposed since she removed the damaged helmet and visor. In the dark, no one could see her expression.

Elie came last, Jon-Jon in her arms. She lay the young man on the ground, taking a seat beside him. Her helmet disengaged. The others, except Khaled and Peter, who remained on sentinel, took the cue from Captain Casalobos. They removed their helmets and joined the group around the downed pilot.

"He's dead," Elie told them. "The suit kept them from getting to him, but they beat him too hard and too much." She stopped talking. It was obvious Jon-Jon's METS could not prevent the repetitive concussive blows from damaging his internal organs.

"Top," Khaled Hafez called Palmer. "I have a heat signature at the bottom of the hill. It appears to be moving away, back toward the shield."

"Probably the Mischene officer in command of the Zenge," Abbie Palmer surmised. "Do we let them go, Captain?"

"Storm, did the forcefield drop before the first Marauders found Angel 7?" Casalobos asked.

"No," the short simple answer.

"Did anyone notice if the forcefield dropped long enough for this size team to exit the city?" she asked aloud.

"The forcefield hasn't lowered since the last time they took a shot at the 109," Palmer answered. "That was days ago."

"They have a tunnel in and out," Ash surmised. She joined the Marines on Phisor as an underground mining and tunnel expert. The Hana Kay mined precious minerals on AF1. They were also explosives experts. Ash volunteered to survey underground openings in an attempt to find ways into Marauder fortifications.

"Who's in command of your team?" Elie demanded.

"Master Sergeant Palmer," Abbie came to attention and saluted Captain Casalobos.

"Top, assign your medic to transport Lt. Johnson's body to your vehicle. There's a grav-sled in the store you can use. Storm will go with them."

"No fucking way," the Fellen responded. "I will not leave you out here."

Elena Casalobos, Space Ranger, former Spanish Legionnaire, fighter pilot, current Captain of the PT-109, and second in command in the entire system to General Gregory Anton, turned on her friend with the controlled fury of an officer on the battlefield.

"You will take your useless arm and escort Jon-Jon back to the team's vehicle. If you do not hear from me, you will take yourselves and Jon-Jon back to h.q.. You will do this, AStermalanlan, or I will shackle your blue ass and assign two more soldiers to carry you back. Which will it be?"

Storm, true to her name, fumed. She broke before blowing, realizing her injury would cause more difficulty than her presence would be an asset.

"Yes, ma'am, Captain," she replied. "But you better be careful and you better come back in one piece."

"Palmer," Elie called.

Palmer responded by ordering Cpl. Hafez to recover the sled, load Lt. Johnson's corpse, and escort him and Storm back to the hidden SVT.

"Your team?" Captain Casalobos asked.

"Peter is a Phisoran resistance fighter. If we get inside the forcefield, we have to get the Phisoran hostages out of harms way for the 109 to fire on the city. They will listen to him."

Elie nodded, appreciating the reason for the presence of a native.

"Ash knows tunnels and explosives," Palmer continued. "If they did use an underground passage to exit and reenter the city, she's our best bet to locate and clear it. If we need to blow something up, like a forcefield generator or cannon, she has the experience."

Another nod.

"Sgt. Tankian is my most experienced fighter. Staff Sergeant Galetti is my right hand," Palmer said. "Both good as any Space Fleet Marine I have served with."

Elie turned to the female Marine in the METS and said, "C.C.?"

The young woman turned to face her and replied, "Nice to see you, too, Elie. I'm sorry about Jon-Jon, Captain."

The others waited for an explanation, but neither the Staff Sergeant nor the Captain explained how they knew each other.

"We're ready," Khaled called. He stood beside the grav-sled carrying Jon-Jon's body.

Storm hugged Elie with her one good arm. "Come back," she whispered.

She then surprised the others by giving the same hug to Sgt. Galetti. "And, you," she said. "Come back and bring Elie with you."

"Top, do you still have the heat signature?" Elie asked Abbie.

"Six-by-six," the reply. "Bougie headed north and in a hurry."

"Lead," the Captain ordered. She waited until the other four newly formed team members followed Palmer single file before taking rear guard. She did not look back.

"She doesn't seem bothered by her co-pilots death," Hafiz said as he watched Casalobos fade into the shadows.

He failed to notice the Fellen's good hand ball into a fist.

Storm turned slowly to face the corporal.

"She is concentrating on the mission, and on keeping her team safe," Storm said. "She will mourn for Jon-Jon when there is time. Do not mistake strength for a lack of feeling, Corporal. And do not make the mistake of saying anything similar in the future when I am near enough to hear."

She began the long trip to the SVT, running fingertips across the body of her friend as she walked beside the sled.

Hafez guided the grav-sled from the front, saying to himself, "You are one dumb shit."

Chapter 10

Aboard the John F. Kennedy, frustration described the emotional state of the day.

"Comms, surface report," General Gregory requested.

"Colonel Duval reports a massing of Marauder assets inside the shield near the Marine's main base of operations," Ensign Timothy Rutledge replied. "Our communications systems are strong enough to keep the base and Kennedy in touch as long as we beam to a distant repeater first. The Mischene jammers are disrupting the ground units. Mobile forces can't carry generators with the power needed to break through the static or send and receive via the repeater."

The holo-display of the Phisoran city provided an overhead grid-view of the metro area.

"Marines are massed at the Northeast quadrant, one-mile outside the shielded area. Marauders are assembling inside the barrier. We do not have a location on the mobile pulse cannon," Rutledge reported. "A dozen scout-intel teams are deployed across the face of the shield from five miles east of the main camp to five miles west. With surface comms unreliable, teams are using Phisoran volunteers as runners to convey messages."

"Runners?" the General asked.

"Runners, bikers, and using vehicles when surface conditions allow," the Comms operator replied. "Low-tech, but the most effective way to maintain links between command and field assets."

"The other quadrants?"

"The destruction around the city limits made other locations impassable or too open for covert activity. The places where the outskirts are leveled are being monitored by the 109. The southwestern quadrant is a mix of structures, cleared spaces, craters, debris, and untouched areas. The quadrant is cut off by two rivers and a major ravine. With bridges destroyed, it has been considered an unlikely location for Marauder activity."

"Until Angel 7 crashed there," Anton said. "Duval report anything from the team he dispatched to find the crew?"

"No, sir. Because it required crossing a river to get into the area, no messenger will be used. We may not know anything until the team returns."

"Kennedy, scans from the area show anything?" the surface operations commander asked the ship's AI.

"No communications. Visual scanners may have detected small arms' laser fire," the AI replied. "The forcefield creates disturbances in the atmosphere. Enhancing the feed produces imperfections in the view. I cannot be certain, but considering the location, a firefight occurred."

"Occurred?"

"There are no more indications of laser fire at this time," Kennedy replied. "You could dispatch the shuttle LBJ," Kennedy added. "They could perform a flyover, return, and provide a more detailed report."

"And we could lose another ship," Gregory countered. "The jammers play hell with flight electronics. We know they have a pulse cannon, but we do not know where it is located. They could drop shields long enough to use their plasma cannon. The LBJ does not have the maneuverability to avoid a blast coming in at plasma speed. Until we hear from Duval we take no action. Continue to monitor the area of the crash for signals."

Kennedy did not reply to the directive, leaving General Gregory to wonder who the AI considered in command. A question he heard voiced by Daniel Cooper on more than one occasion.

"I want eyes and ears on the Marine encampment," he ordered the command personnel. "If the Mischene are placing assets into the quadrant, something is about to happen. We need to be prepared to warn the ground troops, and provide support where, when, and how needed."

"Heat signature is gone," Palmer said. "Anyone else have it?"

C.C. and Ash both reported losing the signature at the same time as Palmer. Peter did not wear a METS with optical enhancements and Elie concentrated on the area behind them while Tank split time watching the flanks.

"Move up and keep an eye out for anywhere he might have hidden. Someplace able to shield his body temperature," Elie ordered.

The avenue continued toward the mid-city area, but the Mischene running from the fight veered right before his signal disappeared. Peter figured out what happened.

"There's a utility maintenance shed on this side street," he told the others, pointing at a hut-like building set twenty-feet back from the street. "Workers monitor gauges and access underground energy and communications conduits."

"Underground?" Ash asked. "You can get down into utility tunnels from this shed?"

"Not from every location, but some," the Phisoran answered.

"This might be the access methods the Marauders use to send out squads without needing to drop the forcefield," Elie said. "Ash, you're the tunnel expert. See if you can find an access to the underground. If you do, let Sgt. Palmer lead to make sure no one is below on guard."

The Hanna Kay and the Marine entered the building. No loud pops or sounds of an ambush. The others set a perimeter and waited.

Palmer reappeared at the doorway and waved the others closer.

"We found an access panel in the floor. Ladder to a maintenance tunnel below. Signs of a lot of use, but no guards. No sign of any trips or alerts. Ash is scouting ahead, but promised to stop and retreat if she runs into the enemy," the Top Sergeant told them.

"Let's go," Elia said. "C.C. you lead. Top, then Peter. Sgt. Tankian, follow me."

Low voltage lighting strips did not furnish a lot of illumination. The systems within the METS' optical package used the soft light and enhanced it to provide the Marine's with near perfect vision. Peter seemed to have no difficulty operating in the dim tunnel. Ten minutes after Elie and Tank landed on the underground corridor, the team caught up with Ash. She sat with her back against a wall.

"The access turns in two directions here," Elia said. "Any guess which tunnel we take?" she asked Ash.

"Up," the Hana Kay answered, standing. She pointed at rungs embedded in the cement wall to her left. "The tunnels in both direction show sign of disturbance, but not the kind of disturbances you would expect from squads of Marauders. More like small teams exploring. I think they entered and exited from above us. I did not look, in case there is a guard."

"Scans?" Elie asked.

"Nothing on visuals, obviously. Body-heat scans are not reliable because the Zenge have lower core temperatures and it is night. I have not heard anything on audio enhancement, but the access panel may be thick enough to dampen sounds," Ash answered.

"Looks like we have to hit the door and take on whatever we find," C.C. said.

"Which means I lead," Elie said.

"Ma'am, that's against team protocol," MSgt Palmer interrupted. "Team leader does not take the forward position into an unsecured space. You're highest rank. That makes you team leader."

"I appreciate your concern for rules, Top, but those protocols did not take into consideration Space Rangers," Elie replied. "I'm the only one here strong enough the throw the lid up, and fast enough to get on top before anyone waiting can react."

"Can't argue with facts," Palmer replied.

"C.C. follows me," Elie said. "Top, since you're the actual team leader and protocols are important, you follow C.C."

Palmer gave the Captain a snide look hidden behind her METS faceplate.

"Peter, Ash, and then Tankian. No one sticks a head above the surface if I make contact with the enemy," she warned. "C.C., you wait until I give you the 'all-clear'."

"Yes, ma'am," the staff sergeant answered.

"Ash, you're my tunnel expert. When you exit, find a way to make sure the lid stays closed unless you want it open. Can do?" Elie asked.

"Yes, ma'am."

Elena Casalobos began her military career as an officer in the elite Spanish Legionnaires. She was a member of the 19th Special Operations Group, known as the Maderal Oleaga, when she volunteered for the Space Rangers Project. A long time in the past, but her instincts as a special operator never deserted her. She slung her laser rifle across her back and loosened the Velcro on her pistol's holster. She let her right hand drop to make sure the combat knife attached around her right calf was within easy reach, only to find it missing. She remembered leaving it in the chest of a Zenge.

She went up the ladder. She did not hesitate at the top, hitting the square panel above her head with both hands, shoving it upward. The simple latch holding it snapped with the pressure applied by muscles six-times stronger than the average human. As the hatch flipped back on hinges, she launched herself from the rung her feet rested on. The plyometric leap propelled her slender form through the hole. When her feet landed on either side of the opening, her laser pistol, already in hand, swept 360-degrees.

Elie stepped away from the opening, crouched, and accessed every scan her METS unit offered. While she ticked off optical, audio, heat, sound, and movement reports, C.C. exited and took a position behind her, facing the opposite direction. She instituted her own METS scanners.

Abbie Palmer exited with Peter a step behind. They took positions so the four could cover the cardinal points of a compass.

Ash egressed, ignored the others, and began examining the tunnel hatch before Tank emerged. As the other five closed scans, coming to the shared conclusion they were alone and unobserved, Ash pulled items from her satchel, closed the lid, and worked quickly. Once finished, she called the others in.

"The lock is shattered," she said. "I've hooked up an explosive charge to the hinges. Anyone pulls up on this lid and a blast radius of ten-yards will leave nothing but dust. Any of us can disarm the detonator. I set it on channel one. Get within twenty-five-yards and say 'disarm.'"

"Seriously, Ash?" C.C. asked. "Disarm?"

"Thought it would be easy to remember," the younger woman replied. "One more thing. At ninety-seconds the bomb rearms.

You have ten-seconds afterward to say 'disarm' again. In case you need more time."

"I thought you attached it to the hinges," Peter said. "What if the lid is open when it rearms?"

"Ten-seconds and boom," Ash answered.

"I'm glad you made the disarm code easy to remember," C.C. said.

"It's damn stupid to leave an access point unguarded," Palmer noted. "I'm not showing signs of non-intelligent alerts. Nothing."

"Best guess is they are low on personnel," Elie replied. "They probably did have sentries, but they may not have planned for the number of losses. It could also indicate they are massing personnel somewhere else. Either for defensive or offensive purposes."

"Don't look a gift horse in the mouth," C.C. said. "What's the plan, Captain?"

"The Mischene command center is located in a medical center three miles to our east. We know they have a plasma cannon located within the complex, and they have Phisoran hostages housed in close proximity to the emplacement. The forcefield generator is believed to be in the same complex, most likely hooked into emergency generators for the medical facilities. Sgt. Palmer, Peter, and I will head there, recon, and decide what happens next based on what we discover."

"Which leaves Tank, Ash, and me," C.C. said.

"Two miles east and two blocks north is a high-rise building. Tallest one in the city, so you can't miss it. Top floor has been converted into a prison. Phisorans are held there. Next floor down holds quarters for Mischene and Zenge guards. Below them the floor has been cleared, walls removed, and windows taken out. It's the location of their communications jammers. Ash is our explosives expert. I need to know if we can blow the jammers without killing the Phisoran prisoners," Elie said.

"We need to get near enough to make a decision and then find you with the answer?" C.C. asked.

"Problem, Sergeant?"

"Seems like if we get that close, and we decide it can be done, makes more sense to do it than waste time finding you for the okay," the young woman answered. "By the time we returned, the situation could change and we would be back at the square one."

Elie stood silent. In her METS outfit she looked like a curvaceous reconstruction of the robot from the ancient movie The Day The Earth Stood Still. A day Earth made first contact and discovered aliens did not appreciate the lack of care humans gave their planet.

"I agree," she finally replied. "If you can accomplish destroying the jammers without collateral damage, go for it. I trust you to make the best decision."

As Casalobos opened her map-app to confirm locations and distances, Ash turned to the other non-human on the team and said, "I know what a gift is," she told Peter. "What's a horse?"

The Phisoran shrugged.

Chapter 11

Earth / Saudi Arabia

"I trust you to make the best decision," Wei Zhou Nanke said. "My concern is the opportunity seems too convenient."

"The contact request came through a third-party with a connection to my largest media supplier," Arnold Montack said. The narrow face and sunken eyes of the planet's most connected multimedia mogul displayed via archaic means. His image broadcast onto a pixilated screen in the communications center of the new Camarilla stronghold in Saudi Arabia. "Similar feelers were received by others within my organization. Considering producers and media managers from every platform on Earth have tried to connect with Miranda Muse for decades, it was only a matter of time until one of the Muses decided to cash in on her fame."

"Exactly," the Japanese princess said. Her image did not appear in the secure studio beneath the mosque. Only her voice represented the powerful woman. "A matter of time. At a time when we prepare to push the UEC into a corner. A time following the loss of several important members of our organization. A time when the UEC, the security agencies, and the military are desperate to discover our plans."

"Two of my top people also received word Miranda Muse might be open to the idea of associating with a single production company with multi-media access," Alexandra Vasluianu chimed in from her private comms-center in Omaha, Nebraska. The transplanted Russian media giant's ruddy complexion and redshot eyes beneath heavy lids, appeared on a second video screen. "One brushed it off as rumor, but the other knew the person willing to facilitate the connection. Not someone he trusts, but someone of great self-importance. The price to set up a meeting was substantial. With no guarantees beyond a face-to-face audience."

"To force the United Earth Council to disband, we must persuade the majority of the world's population they are better served by local governments. We must paint the UEC as greedy and uncaring about cultural history or family pride. The loss of borders is the same as the loss of individuality. We have laid the foundations, and many are concerned the centralization of government is the first step toward centralizing thought, religion, and social justice. A neutral voice of reason, such as Miranda Muse, adding her opinion with ours could tip the scales," Saleh Abd al-Rashin said.

He sat in an uncomfortable chair in the cramped communications center. To make the room unassailable by eavesdropping methods required thick walls of exotic materials with anti-detection embedded within the walls, ceiling, and floor. The center contained the latest developments in broadcast technology. The dichotomy of using antiquated communications channels and hardware forgotten by most of the world as an added layer of security not lost on him.

"It is worth pursuing," Nanke said. "I understand the value. I counsel care."

"I told my social-media manager to send a message indicating our interest," Montack said. "I did not want to miss this opportunity by allowing another agency, one not controlled by myself or Alexandra, to act before we could make a full appraisal. I also contacted Lorena Aragon."

"Why would you contact a drug dealer?" al-Rashid asked. Aragon was a member of the Camarilla Dissolvere. Her resources and contacts invaluable to the success of their operations, but the strict-Islamic fervor which still coursed within him detested the woman.

"Drug dealer?" Montack asked. "Aragon controls every illegal cartel in the western hemisphere," the thin man said. "She did not become the most powerful person south of Can-Am without knowing how to watch her ass. I asked her to assign her best people to oversee the communications between my manager and Muse's people. They will make sure no unwanted government agencies are behind the scenes."

"A wise decision," Nanke said. "It appears you have made several decisions without waiting for a quorum."

"I've placed pieces on the board," Montack replied. "Whether we play the game is for the Camarilla to decide."

"Chandra and Miller are unavailable," al-Rashin said. "I assume Lorena Aragon is in favor of our next move since she is supplying pieces for Arnold's board. With Arnold's vote, we need two more in favor of contacting Miranda Muse and giving Arnold control of negotiating a deal. If we are assured it is not a trap."

"I say yes," Vasluianu said. "I wish it were my people and my syndicate, but better Montack's group gets her than someone we do not control."

"As I said before, I trust Arnold to make the best decision," Nanke said. "I believe Aragon will make sure we are not compromised. I'm equally sure she will make anyone trying to harm us pay a heavy debt. Yes."

"My vote is moot, but I also say yes," the Arab said. "Arnold, you have the blessing and the resources of the Camarilla. Buy us a revolution."

With the communications channels closed, al-Rashid turned to the stunning African woman seated beside him.

"A revolution you will ignite," he told her.

Katherine Chandra, former Nigerian military officer and leader of the largest terrorist militia operating on the dark continent, squeezed the therapy ball she habitually carried. Dressed in a loose dress with long sleeves and high neckline in deference to the location beneath an Islamic compound, she also wore an ankle holster with an automatic pistol. Old tech, but effective and easy to conceal.

"I have no problem attacking UEC or local government offices, schools, or religious sites," she said. "With the information on military units you have provided, we easily hit and disappear. Igniting a revolution places my people in the middle of much larger population centers, and with less opportunity to escape. I must be sure it is not a suicide mission."

"We are within reach of success," al-Rashin assured her. "More than fifty-percent of the world's information is controlled by people loyal to our mission. We have enough agents within the military to provide crucial intelligence on operations. Those same agents will create havoc when we incite protestors to riot. Once the UEC forces take lethal action, and those mass killings are blasted across every mass-media platform, more people will rise up. The fire we light in Africa will burn across the Middle East, into the rest of Asia, and throughout Europe."

"The UEC is headquartered in the Western Hemisphere," Chandra reminded him.

"Lorena Aragon controls gangs and cartels from Mexico to Argentina," he countered. "They may not be the disciplined military units you command, but they will unleash a storm of death and destruction. UEC military units will be forced to respond, leaving all branches spread thin. The UEC will be back where it began. Can-Am alone."

"They were strong enough to unite the planet after the Pandemic."

"They were seen as heroes delivering a cure," he replied. "This time they will look like bullies. Their own news media will crucify their actions. The UEC will fall."

"You think Miranda Muse will help us speed the destruction of the UEC?"

"She is the bastion of reason. With her voice added to our chorus, those on the fence will turn against a centralized government. But we must begin soon."

"My army is always prepared," Chandra assured him.

"Good. Miller sent word the Board of Directors is close to revealing the plans for a single monetary unit, as well as the final draft for a United Earth Constitution. Arcand has been secretly working to place judges around the world and reopen the World Court. If these items are accomplished, creating a popular uprising will be much more complicated. Muse questioning the validity of such actions, and demanding more details be made to the public, can delay the government implementing the reforms."

"What about Space Fleet?"

"They will be kept busy with other problems," he answered. "There are others who also prefer Earth return to concerning itself with Earth-issues and leave the galaxy alone."

Japan

"I trust your decision, but do you think it wise al-Rashin knows you are Devee?" Keiko Takei asked.

"Perhaps not, but it is expedient," Wei Zhou Nanke answered. "I need the Camarilla to succeed at disrupting the attempts to unify this planet. I also need al-Rashid to coordinate his attacks on the UEC with the arrival of our spacecraft. I could think of no other way than to reveal my true self."

Keiko, the daughter of a Japanese family with ties to royalty for hundreds of years, acted as Nanke's personal aide. The Devee agent found her as a toddler in Tokyo, both parents dead. She raised the girl to be her aide, confidant, and protector. At thirty-five-years-of-age, Keiko Takei was brilliant, beautiful, and deadly.

"Does he know you created the virus which caused the Pandemic?"

"No one knows but you, Keiko," the Devee chemist and secret agent replied. "I was a different person then. Chinese. Now I am Chinese-Japanese, wife of the Emperor's son, and a respected business woman."

"I still find it difficult to understand the vision of your Ginae to send you to Earth more than three decades ago."

"You are too intelligent to see simplicity," Nanke replied. "The Devee knew of this planet for over three-thousand years. Our reavers collected humans, plants, and animals for experimentation several times in the past. When humans discovered the Nakki outpost on Mars, the Ginae sent me to observe. When I saw the advantages humans harvested from the ancient technology, I decided to slow them down."

"The virus wiped out half the population of the planet," Keiko said.

"It delayed research, but Fairchild and his people were still able to decipher the Nakki language. Nakki technology and ancient sites have been discovered across the galaxy, but no one could break their codes or successfully reengineer their technology. Until humans. It was, it is, totally unacceptable."

"You have worked to steal the secrets of Mars since I was a child," Keiko said. "With little success."

"Unintended consequences," Nanke whispered. "The Pandemic led to the unification of the planet. The strength of the Can-Am alliance created Space Fleet. The secrets found in the Martian hangar helped develop the methods used to safeguard those secrets. I left China because the virus destroyed much of the country, and because Chinese were blamed for the outbreak. I had surgery to alter my appearance to pass as part-Chinese and part-Japanese. I did not wish to wear out my glamour shield. My skills as a Chimia helped me seduce the son of the Japanese Emperor."

"And place us in a position to discover a way to take the Martian files," Keiko concluded.

"Which is why I joined the Camarilla Dissolvere," Nanke added. "The chaos from a revolution will provide the opportunity to break into the vaults on EMS2 and take the Nakki data. If that does not work . . . "

"The Devisator Warships will invade Mars and take the secrets directly from the source," Keiko said.

"We must coordinate the Camarilla actions on Earth to coincide with the arrival of the Carrier," Nanke said. "Which is why I made my identity known to al-Rashin. He is enraptured by the hope of recovering his family's rule over Saudi territory. He does not care about Earth's position among the galactic worlds. If he had his way, all aliens would be imprisoned or ejected off the planet."

"The UEC security forces are searching for al-Rashin. They know of the other Camarilla directors, including you, Nanke-sama. Communications must be secure," the woman raised to provide the Devee's safety warned.

"The Arab has installed the best communications systems and jammers available on this world," Nanke assured her aide. "The Quantum Key Distributors used by the Devee are more secure than anything known throughout the galaxy. Even the Fell do not use QKD communicators. They may not operate faster-than-light, as the tachyon-based systems Space Fleet now use, but our photon-laser optical channels are impossible to hack."

"The photon qubit cannot be copied, and the qubit collapses as soon as our receiver measures it," Keiko said. She trained on the photo-laser communicators from a young age.

A Devee ship would transmit a signal through a wormhole. The diluted laser would pass through a wormhole gate without the portal opening. A Devee ship within the system would capture the signal. The operator would see the message, memorize it, and pass it along. No system could copy the optical data. Because the qubit collapsed, data could not be stored. A rebounder placed in systems, usually on asteroids, moons, or uninhabited planets, could redirect the signal to a surface receiver.

Such a rebounder existed on one of Uranus' moons. Nanke stayed in contact with Devisator, though messages often required weeks to reach their final destination.

"We know a ship will arrive within two weeks," Nanke said. "I must do everything I can to push the Camarilla to action. Once the ship arrives, communications will be much quicker. We will attack Earth from within and from space."

"In the confusion, we steal the Martian files," Keiko said.

"Afterward, Earth and Space Fleet will not exist to interfere with Devee business interests," Nanke added, summarizing the most important aspect of the venture. That, and Nanke's long-awaited return home.

Chapter 12

Phisor

C.C., Ash, and Tank moved through the city streets, each taking lead while the others covered. The tall building with the electronic jammers always in view. Two miles required forty-minutes of leap-frog through the eerie cityscape. With electricity cut off, the ghost-city appeared green and grey in their night-vision. C.C. pushed on a door to a store two blocks from the target. When it opened, she signaled the others to join her inside.

Sure the grime-covered windows would block the illumination, Galetti placed a blue-light emitter on the floor. She removed the cowl of her armor-suit and stored the soft faceplate in a pocket lined with material designed to protect the shield. She reached behind her head to pull on an elastic band. Dark curls fell across her shoulders.

"I had to shake it out," she told her companions. "I feel like I've crawled in dust for a decade."

The Hana Kay removed her helmet and stored her faceplate. Short raven-black hair sweat-plastered to her carmine skin.

"It is not as bad as working in mines," she said, "but it is close. You have beautiful hair. Hana Kay have straight hair. Yours reminds me of an ocean."

"A muddy, filthy ocean of sweat and tears," C.C. quipped. "I usually like my hair. Reminds me of my mother and the Jewish side of my family. At the moment, I could go for short and straight like yours."

"What is Jewish?"

"A religion on Earth. One of several, and not something we have time to discuss."

"The jammers?" Tank asked. He did not remove his helmet, remaining at the doorway with his scan systems active.

"We need to cross two more blocks and find a way inside first," the top sergeant said. "I'm shocked, happy, but shocked we did not run into patrols getting this close."

"I noticed the lack of activity also," Ash replied. "Like not having guards posted at the tunnel. Captain Casalobos said they may be short of personnel or repositioned."

"Shortage I can go for. Assigned somewhere else scares me. The only place more important than their h.q. and these jammers would be Colonel Duval's location," C.C. replied.

"They may be planning an attack. Or they decided to try to escape the city," Tank said. "When we liberated Fell we had over forty-thousand personnel," the Lebanese NCO remarked. "We have a brigade here."

"Force required without having to mount another volunteer army," Galetti replied. "Whether the Marauders plan to sit, attack, or escape, our people need the ability to communicate."

She turned her attention to the Hana Kay and said, "I know you and your sister were hostages on board the Prophet's ship. We may need to blow up the Mischene jammer arrays. Phisorans could be caught in the blast."

"You mean killed, not caught," Ash corrected. "My sister and I were not hostages, Sergeant Galetti. The Prophet used us for sex . . . and other things. We would have traded our lives for his death. The Phisorans inside the building will feel the same."

"C.C.," the Marine told her. "Sergeant Galetti sounds too official, and I cannot stand the sound of Sarge."

"Humans are an interesting species," the Hana Kay said. She pulled her head covering back over her skull. "Tough and resourceful. Willing to die for others you do not know. Possessors of advanced technology and military skill. Dedicated to being informal. Daniel Cooper told me to call him Coop, because his friends did. Dr. Kimura insisted I call him Hiro. Captain Casalobos taught me to address her as Captain, unless we were alone or among friends, and then it was to be Elie."

"It helps us remember to be human," C.C. said. "Embracing informality is our way of interacting with others as equals."

"Other humans?"

"Once, before we knew we weren't alone in the universe. Now, I hope, it means treat all others as equals."

"Even your enemies?"

"Yep. I'm always willing to treat my enemies to equal ass-kick-ings," C.C. answered, returning her hair to confinement before pulling on her helmet.

"Do we have a plan?" Tank asked.

"My father has a sign on the wall of his office. It says DON'T TALK. DO. Of course my mother, who is a linguist, has her own that says DON'T TALK. LISTEN. Our plan is to decide what we do one step at a time. And keep our ears and eyes open."

"Good. I prefer simple plans," the Lebanese Space Marine said.

They worked their way to the street where the skyscraper sat. Short by Earth standards at twenty-stories, it was the tallest build-ing in the city. Phisorans did not flock to metropolitan areas. Most of the population preferred rural homes and villages. Phisor, be-fore the invasion, looked a lot like Earth in the early to mid-nine-teen-hundreds.

A single Zenge with a laser rifle stood sentry at the front en-trance.

Using hand signals, C.C. ordered Tank to remain on watch while she and Ash reconned the building.

An alley loading dock on one side appeared closed and barri-caded. The rear entrance to the building had metal panels bolted across the doors and first floor windows. The other side faced an-other building across a narrow walkway. Both facades with noth-ing but windowless walls and no entrances.

Returning to the front, they joined Tank behind a concrete planter to concoct a plan.

C.C. scurried away, disappearing into the shadows. Ash lay low to the ground, peering around the corner of the planter to watch the watcher. Tankian did the same on the opposite side. They saw the Zenge react to a noise from the far corner of the building. An area bathed in darkness. A second sound resulted in a raised laser rifle. A third and the sentry moved toward the shadows.

Ash was on her feet, Falkniven combat knife in hand before the guard traveled two lizard-legged strides. Light on her feet and fast as a snake, the petite female covered the distance and launched herself. With two hands on the knife, she slammed the tip into the sentry's nape, plunging the wicked blade into the creature's spinal column.

The Zenge folded, his body no longer following orders from his brain. By the time C.C. and Tank reached them, Ash had slit his throat. Following the tedious walk to the building, and the time-consuming recon around it, the furious action seemed to occur faster than actuality. And it happened damn fast.

The two women pulled the three-hundred-pound corpse into the deeper shadows and tossed the laser rifle into dying ornamental bushes.

Silence remained an operational imperative. C.C. took lead and Ash followed. Tank covered the six. At the entry. C.C. pulled the glass door open. Ash rushed inside, laser rifle swinging left-right-up-across while her optical scanners searched every corner of the foyer. C.C. followed, her rifle up to cover the second-floor railed walkway overlooking the atrium. Tank entered, but remained at the door, seeking any movement.

The team again relieved, surprised, and concerned with the lack of additional security.

They could not chance the confinement of an elevator. They located the stairwell and raced upward. The METS suits provided cooling and extra oxygen. The superb physical condition of the warriors allowed them to cover fifteen flights in a few minutes.

C.C. stopped them on the fifteenth landing. Deciding a whispered conversation was more important than attempting to decipher hand signals, she removed her faceplate. Ash and Tank mimicked their team leader.

"Three floors up should be the jammers. There will have to be guards and technicians there, no matter what else is going on," C.C. said.

Nods of agreement.

"Next is the floor for Mischene and Zenge personnel, and then the floor with the hostages. I say we bypass the jammers, see if we can clear the nineteenth floor, and recon the twentieth. Then we decide on how to destroy the tech."

Ash remained quiet, but gave her human teammate a rather searching stare.

"I know," the young human said. "You could set your explosives beneath them on the seventeenth floor and we could be long gone when you detonated them. I can't help thinking about the prisoners. I'd hate myself forever if I didn't try to get them out first. You can set your blasters while I move up. Tank can stand guard. If I don't get back in thirty-minutes, get out and blow the building."

Ash remained quiet, but delivered a sinister stare. She gave C.C. a single shake of the head before replacing her face-plate. Then she started up the stairwell. Tank gave a muffled snort of amusement at the Hana Kay's action. He waited for C.C. to tag behind the short alien before following.

Ash continued higher, past the floor with the jammers and up to the next exit. The Hana Kay stopped and faced the door connecting the stairwell to the corridor beyond. She slowly turned her head left to right and back again. The faceplate came off to allow her to whisper to C.C. without fear of electronic detection.

"I don't register any heat signatures," she said.

C.C., her own faceplate off, replied, "Zenge don't normally show on thermal scans."

"I've turned up audio, and I've scanned for motion," the red-skinned woman replied. "I think the entire floor is empty."

C.C. motioned Tank forward. He was the most experienced urban fighter on their team. She pushed down on the handle mechanism. The bolt disengaged. Tankian, rifle ready, stepped passed C.C. and into the dark corridor. He moved forward as Ash and C.C. followed. It required only ten-minutes of searching to reach the far end of the hallway.

"Doors open and rooms abandoned," Tank said. "Junk tossed around, but nothing personal, and no weapons I could see. The troops housed here left, and left in a hurry."

"Let's move up to the next floor," C.C. said.

They followed the same protocol on the twentieth floor. They did not find the same conditions.

Elie, Peter, and Palmer sat in a booth in a dark corner of an abandoned restaurant. The building used as the command center for the RMM was located one-block-west and one-block-north of the diner. The front window blinds kept light from entering. Palmer placed a compact blue-light emitter atop the booth's table, allowing the two humans to remove their helmets and still see.

"Medical complex," Peter said. "We knew that already."

"But now we know the important stuff is in the hospital section, not the administration or support buildings," Elie said. "Three entry points with two exterior guards and at least two interior guards. One Mischene and three Zenge at each location. Two sets of roving pairs circling the building. Zenge. Lights showed on all six floors. No obvious guards on the other buildings, and only a couple of windows with lights on."

"I'm surprised we haven't seen more troops," Palmer said. "Only two pairs of walking sentries on the way in. No electronic detection systems. A lot fewer guards for a command center, even for this time of night. They have a lot of confidence in the shield."

"Maybe," Elie replied. "Maybe they have fewer personnel than we estimated. Maybe they don't fully staff at night. Maybe they are repositioning troops. None of it matters. That hospital houses the shield generator. We know the cannon is located on the ground between the buildings, but the generator could be anywhere. Ideas?"

"Do you know if this city is prone to flooding?" Peter asked.

"Nothing in the reports I read mention it as a problem," Elie replied.

"The generator and back-ups are likely in the basement or sub-basement," he said. "The hospitals near my home place them there. Those closer to rivers or oceans with a potential for flooding place them on the roof."

"Makes sense," Elie responded to Peter's logic. "It makes our mission less difficult. The plasma cannon is on the ground because it creates too much vibration for them to install it on a building. The force shield generator will have a dispersal dish on the roof. Assume the power comes from the hospital's basement."

"That makes three potential targets," Palmer said. "How does it make our mission less difficult?"

"All we need to do is take out the generator and back-ups," Elie replied. "The dish emitting the shield will fail. Once the shield is down, the 109 will take care of the plasma cannon. If Peter is correct about the power plant's location at the basement or sub-basement level, we only have to get inside and down a floor or two. If we had to go up we would need to clear a lot more obstacles."

"Did you believe anything Cadee said?" the Mischene Officer-of-the-Day (OD) asked the sergeant monitoring systems normally covered by five technicians.

"I believe he ran and left the Zenge sent to locate the crew of the downed space fighter behind," the sergeant answered. "I don't believe he fought until the last moment. I don't believe he encountered fierce opposition. He's a coward."

"I'd send a team to check out his story, but every extra trooper has been ordered to the forward shield encampment," Lt. Asper said. She was average in most aspects. Dark skin and white hair. Average height and average weight. Middle of the graduating class from the academy. She joined to fight with the Prophet because he made her feel more than average. She got OD duty at h.q. for the worst time slot because she remained average.

"What did you do with Cadee?"

"What could I do? He outranks me, and I was not going to wake the General with his story. He left to find someplace to crash. Someone higher than me can order him to report after the sun comes up. Anything interesting on the monitors?"

"Nothing. Same as always," Sergeant Turnor answered. "Exterior cameras show it's dark outside. Interior cameras are Phisoran and grainy as a beach in a wind storm. Comms automatically scan for enemy and friendly talk. Readiness display for the plasma cannon is always green. Also a bunch of gauges I'm not sure what they should read, or what they are reading. I'm not a tech-head."

"Non-combat personnel were assigned weapons and bussed to the front," Asper reminded the NCO. "There is a support ship arriving to take out the Earther battleship in orbit. When that occurs the General intends to send everyone at the enemy camp. Once the humans are eliminated, ships will land to take us off this planet."

"So he says," Turnor said. He played with a focus on an exterior camera feed, giving up when the dark picture became darker. "Until then a skeleton crew provides security and monitors electronics here. If things go bad we don't have enough firepower to hold off the enemy."

"With the fighters from the support ship providing air-support, nothing will go wrong, Sergeant," Asper assured the NCO. "One more day and we'll be off Phisor and on our way to a secret RMM location. The Prophet's dream will come true. Mischene will one day rule the galaxy."

Turnor did not bother responding. He was career military. When he chose to follow the Prophet he locked his fate to Soren. Now it was locked to the RMM.

Chapter 13

Galetti sat on her heels with her lower back pressed against the stairwell wall and her head tucked between raised knees. Corporal Tankian stood on the landing, one hand on a rail to prop his weight. He stared down the steps, but his eyes, hidden by the METS faceplate, looked far beyond the stairs descending to the lower level.

The door to the building's top floor slowly opened inward. Ash stepped through, pulling the self-closing door shut, not waiting on the mechanism to do the job. She removed the suit's helmet. Her normal carmine complexion turned to a deeper, currant hue.

"I made one more sweep," she said. "No one alive."

"I cannot believe they murdered every single hostage," Tank said.

"Don't use the comm," C.C. whispered. She did not lift her head. Her own helmet faceplate lay between her feet.

The big Lebanese NCO released his faceplate. "I can't believe it," he repeated. "Adults and children. All dead. Why?"

"They no longer needed them," Ash surmised. "They did not want to transport them, and they did not want to guard them. They poisoned their food."

"Still doesn't explain why," Tank replied.

"They're leaving," C.C. answered, rising by pressing her back against the wall as she uncoiled her legs. "A single guard out front. The floor used as a barracks deserted. The lack of roving patrols. They are prepping for an escape."

"To where?" Tank asked. "How? We have ground forces ready to attack if the shield drops. The 109 is overhead. Where would they escape to?"

"The hospital ship from Devisator," Ash murmured. Louder, she added, "It is the only way they could get off the planet. The Devee are not honorable traders. If the Mischene offered them a profit, they would take it. That ship with supplies and medicine for the Phisorans is a fake."

"It's the only thing that makes sense," C.C. agreed. "We need to take the comms center and get word to Captain Casalobos. She needs to warn Kennedy."

The three hurried down the stairs, METS suits intact and rifles up. Tank on lead did not bother with subtleties, firing a laser blast into the lock and slamming the door open with his muscled shoulder.

C.C. followed, taking his right flank, with Ash taking left. The floor's interior walls had been demolished to hold banks of tech, a massive crystal-powered magno-generator, and a section set up as a break area with cots. Six dish-arrays and two spherical antennas with monopoles stood at eight windows creating a sweep of communications disruptions.

The three turned their attention on two moving bodies. One rising from a bunk, and the other jumping from a chair in front of a control console.

Ash was nearest the cot. She rushed the Mischene trying to untangle herself from a sheet and blanket.

The Mischene at the console pulled a laser pistol as he turned to face the intruders. Tank raised his laser rifle, but C.C. took the shot first. The blast removed his head and singed the wall above the electronics.

The two Marines worked in a well-rehearsed protocol to clear the rest of the floor, including a makeshift bathroom with showers. Satisfied no other threats were present, they hurried to join Ash.

The Hana Kay pinned the Mischene to the bunk with one knee planted atop her stomach. Her combat knife's tip pressed against the woman's throat. A tap on her left shoulder signaled the Hana Kay to back off.

C.C. replaced the knife point with her pistol barrel. With her helmet-cowl down, the human made sure the black-skinned RMM saw the determination in her eyes.

"First, how do I shut down the jammers, and second, where are the other Mischene and Zenge?"

"The jammers are monitored and serviced from this location," Asper answered. "Only someone with code-clearance can shut them down, and that is done remotely from the Command Center."

"Where are the others who work here?" C.C. demanded, placing more pressure from the pistol against the woman's neck.

"Sent to the front," Asper answered. There was no reason to lie or stall. There was nothing the human could accomplish with or without the truth.

"Why?"

"I am only a tech," the officer lied. Some falsehoods made sense. "I take orders, but no one bothers to explain them. I and Sgt. Turnor were ordered to stay and monitor the jammers. A rotating Zenge guard is sent for security. Everyone else was ordered to report to the forward encampment near the Earthers."

"What about the Devee ship? What's their plan?"

"I don't know anything about a Devee ship," Asper answered. "The jammers are on continuous operation. There can be no communications, including with ships in orbit."

"Ash?"

"I can blow the generator," the ex-miner answered. "When it goes the jammers will cease functioning. The Mischene command will know immediately."

"It will put the Captain and her team at risk, too," Tank added. "When this location blows, they'll go on alert expecting something else."

"The Captain will adjust," C.C. responded. "we will warn the 109 the Devee ship may be a Trojan Horse," C.C. replied. "Ash, set the charges and program a remote. We'll try to get to the others, but we need to be ready to shut down these jammers if it takes too long to find them."

"You can't blow the generators," Asper said. C.C. used the laser pistol to prevent her from sitting up. "There are civilian hostages on the top floor. Evacuate them before you set off an explosion."

C.C. pulled the pistol away, her eyes appraising the enemy.

"You don't know, do you?"

"Know what?" Asper queried.

The team leader turned to her explosives expert and said, "Set it up, Ash. We don't have long. Tank, secure our prisoner. Unfortunately, we have to take her with us."

Without the barrel to stop her, Asper sat up and said, "Did you not listen, or don't humans care about others. There are hostages upstairs. Including children."

C.C. backhanded the Mischene hard enough to draw blood from a split lip.

"Tie her up, Tank. If she keeps talking, gag her. If she gives you any trouble, shoot her."

"So much for easy," Palmer said. She, Peter, and Elie huddled in an alleyway across from the medical complex. A dilapidated trash dumpster and rubble provided cover from the entry. With the buildings on three sides dark and abandoned, Elie decided they could risk discussing the situation.

"They don't have many guards, but they have them deployed perfectly," Elie agreed. "The roving pairs are timed to keep two entrances covered. If we take out the exterior sentries, the interior ones will be alerted, and the rovers will hit us from the backside."

"Is there a solution?" Peter asked.

Before Elie could reply, all three heard the double clicks. A slight hesitation, followed by two more clicks. C.C.'s team asking for a location.

Elie replied with a single click. She would give another every ten-seconds. The tracking program integrated in the METS would follow the trail of clicks to the alley.

Peter and Palmer took up positions on either side of the narrow entry. When Tank arrived pushing a half-dressed bond Mischene, they waved him in. The two watched Ash and C.C. enter, remained long enough to assure no one followed, then backed into the alley.

C.C. quickly explained the Mischene, what they learned at the location of the jammers, and their fear the Devee ship closing was not friendly.

Asper's head snapped up when she overheard the one who slapped her tell her superior officer about the murdered Phisorans. Peter turned on the Mischene with hate-filled eyes the gloom could not hide.

Asper raised her tied hands, palms out, and said, "I did not know. I swear. I did not know."

"Would you have tried to stop it if you had known?" the resistance fighter asked.

"I don't know," she replied. Her hands lowered as her chin dropped. "I honestly don't know," she repeated. Her body language accepted her guilt. The collective guilt of association. If the Phisoran executed her in this alley, she accepted his right to do so.

"Back off, Peter," Elie ordered. "I need her."

The two Zenge sentries at the back entrance to the hospital went on alert. Laser rifles raised and talons on the triggers. Walking toward them was a Phisoran, herded by a female Mischene wearing a uniform shirt, no pants, and a pair of boots. She held a laser pistol at the back of the furry alien's head.

"I am Lieutenant Asper and I have a prisoner," she called, making sure the light spilling from the building caught her charcoal skin and white hair. "Where is your team leader?"

"Stop there," one Zenge ordered. The other stepped back to the glass doors that once acted as the hospital's emergency entrance. He waved to someone inside before returning his attention to the intruders standing in the middle of the driveway.

A Mischene sergeant came through the doors, laser pistol in hand.

"What is this?" he demanded.

As he came forward, two Zenge sentries rounded the corner. Having heard voices, they came prepared for trouble.

Elie, one of the best shots in all the armed forces, fired two laser bursts from cover. The Zenge on guard duty at the Emergency Room exit dropped, cauterized holes through their chests, evaporating their hearts.

Palmer and Tankian emerged from shadows. Their METS allowed them to blend into the pre-dawn darkness. They sliced the throats of the two roving sentries. The thinner scales covering their squat necks no match for the hardened alloy of the Marine-issued combat blades.

Peter pulled the concealed laser pistol from behind his back and blasted the sergeant from less than twenty-feet. The super-hot beam of light aimed center-mass destroyed the man's uniform, chest, and exited, melting his spine along its path. He pivoted to face Asper, who already extended the disabled pistol with one hand while she held the other open and away from her body. The Phisoran took the offered weapon. Neither adversary sure how near he came to finishing Asper's life, with or without provocation.

Elie, with supernormal speed, was at the glass doors before the Mischene sergeant's body hit the concrete. The sliding door's sensor seemed to take a lifetime to recognize a body standing at the entrance and automatically begin opening. The last Zenge on guard at the rear entrance rushed away from the doorway and toward a box centered on the far wall. A box with a prominent red button. An alert, possibly a fire alarm that would warn the entire complex of a breach.

Casalobos did not wait for the panel to slide completely open. When she had space for the hand-held laser, she thrust it around the edge of the glass and fired. Not relying on aim alone, she triggered multiple bursts.

Four of six hit the running Marauder. That he was massive and slow helped. His huge body came to a halt as a heap of singed green flesh spread across the floor tiles three-feet from the wall with the alarm.

C.C. and Ash rushed past Elie, located the stairwell, and were through the door and on their way down before Peter followed with Asper. None-too-gently he forced her to her knees, shackled her wrists with glue-cord, and turned his attention on the entrance.

Elie replaced the pistol with her rifle and took a position which allowed her to watch the corridor portal connecting the lobby of the former Emergency Room with the rest of the building. Sgt. Palmer and Cpl. Tankian would remain outside, hidden in the shadows. If the short firefight was loud enough for other guards to investigate, they would deal with them. If they maintained the same pace used earlier, the second pair of roving sentries would round the corner of the building in fourteen-minutes.

C.C. led the way into the basement. She had rank, but in this instance, Ash was the most important member of the team. She had the explosives.

The human hurried down the dark hallway, her METS scan systems extending in every direction for sound, movement, or a thermal signature. The Hana Kay followed two steps behind, her systems equally revved up to provide a warning in case anything alive presented a threat.

The integrated system delivered a heads-up signal to C.C. to inform her the third door on the left side led to a substantial void with a power-signature most likely the main generator. Not having the luxury of time, she set aside personal safety and kicked the door inward. Her rifle sites scanned one-hundred-eighty-degrees at the same time the METS systems cleared the area of lifeforms. Since nothing exploded, and no alarms sounded, the room was not wired.

Ash entered and walked around the massive power generator placed in the center of the room. She ducked twice, avoiding conduits and power leads in her appraisal march. Once the circuit was completed, she dropped to a knee and pulled her backpack off. While C.C. watched the door, Ash activated remote detonator switches on a dozen packages. The charges were of various sizes and different compositions. Each designed for a specific purpose. Ash planned on using all of them for one purpose -- blow the generator to hell.

Charges activated, she made one more three-sixty-circuit, placing the magnetized packets at positions she felt would cause the highest degree of damage.

Leaving the empty backpack, she hurried through the door and down the hallway with C.C. covering their six. When the two exited into the Emergency Room lobby, Ash gave Elie a thumbs-up on her way outside. C.C. stopped to lift Asper to her feet, and she and Peter half-carried and half-pushed the Mischene out the doorway and into the night. Elie backed out, clicked three-times with her trans-comm to let Palmer and Tank know the job was done, turned and followed the others. Her heads-up read twelve-minutes-thirty-six-seconds. A minute-and-a-half before the exterior sentries would see bodies lying outside the hospital's rear entrance.

They rendezvoused at the alley entrance, and with more than thirty-seconds before an alarm would be sounded by the guards, Captain Elena Casalobos of Space Fleet activated the detonator to blow the power generator supplying the forcefield and the explosives Ash set to destroy the jammers.

She sent the signal.

Chapter 14

Earth - The Arabian Peninsula

The decommissioned Space Fleet shuttle Picard crossed the Indian Ocean fifty-feet above the surface of the water. The identification transponders, locators, and most of the electronics removed from the ship following removal from active service. Because several museums and private groups were negotiating to preserve the shuttle with the historic name, in-atmosphere flight capability remained. The Aerospace Maintenance and Regeneration Group felt the ship would be easier to deliver by flying it to its final destination. This was the second time it had been "borrowed" for an off-the-books mission requiring stealth.

"Twelve-degrees port," Stacey said from the right seat. Without electronics, she handled the navigation duties while Chaspi flew the shuttle. "That will take us up the Red Sea until we turn for the coast of Saudi Arabia."

"I can't believe we're doing this," the Bosine said. "Again."

"Not exactly the same as before," the Fellen replied. "This time Col. Barnwell is with us. Last time we had to find and rescue him."

"You know what I mean. You and me, with Sensei Kai, Rosz, and Billy on a secret mission. A couple of days ago I was practicing flying on a virtual system in our dorm room, and today I'm flying a Space Fleet shuttle across an ocean."

Stacey did not respond, busy with her data pad and making calculations as they flew from the Gulf of Aden into the Red Sea. The darkness prevented ships and shore locations from spotting the compact craft. The low altitude kept it off scanner screens. It also made the flight dangerous. Chaspi needed to follow Stacey's directions on faith. If the altimeter Billy hastily affixed to the hull and connected to a personal comm-screen taped to the console in front of the pilot's seat failed, she could plow them into open water. The young Bosine never felt as alive as in these past hours.

"The lights to our starboard are Jeddah," the blue-skinned alien said. "Two-hundred-miles more and ninety-degrees to starboard. We'll cross over the coastline north of Yanbu, turn fifteen-degrees north-east, and you will need to come up to one-hundred-yards above the surface."

"Drop below Mach 1 to prevent a sonic boom," the pink-skinned pilot said aloud. She remembered the mission points presented to the team by Col. Barnwell before they entered the stolen shuttle. "Three-hundred-eighty-miles to the landing zone Rosz suggested."

At seventy-five-percent of Mach 1, the craft covered the desert terrain in less than thirty-minutes. A full moon lit the ground below, transforming the landscape into something alien.

"Rosz," Chaspi called aloud to her fellow Bosine seated on the floor behind the cockpit. The seats removed along with electronics.

"Yes?" he asked, his head between the two pilot seats, the ever-present earbuds playing music only he could hear. Chaspi and Rosz grew up as neighbors and friends on Osperantue, their families escaping the Zenge invasion of their home-world aboard the Star Gazer. In the years since Rosz received his first headset as a child, she had rarely seen him without the latest version. How he could listen to music and carry on a conversation was beyond her, yet he always knew what was going on around him.

"What are those circles on the surface. They are everywhere," she said.

Without bothering to look out the cockpit window, he answered, "Farmers' crop circles. Not nearly as many as before the pandemic. They use a central pivot point to spray water for irrigation. It sprays in a circle so the crops grow in a circle. It's the most efficient method of using water in the desert for plants. The location of the Camarilla mosque is on the southern edge of what used to be wheat fields. I picked a landing site atop a yardang three-miles west of their location."

"Yardang?" Stacey asked. "I have no translation." The comm-trans units used by the majority of Space Fleet personnel were developed by engineers on Fell. They translated alien languages or translated spoken words into alien languages.

"It's a unique word for sure," Rosz answered. "Turkish, actually. Wind erodes the surface into the shape of a long bowl, or yardang. We'll park on the ridge, which was built up by the same winds."

"Slow down and fifty-three-point-zero-four-degrees west of north," Stacey said. "The entry into Rosz's dang yard is one-half-mile.

"Yardang," Rosz said, turning and returning to his space on the floor beside Billy.

Billy gathered the equipment he had worked with since they departed. He placed everything inside two cases to protect them from a rough landing. He noted Sensei Kai remained eyes-closed. Asleep or meditating. In the rear of the shuttle, Tab Barnwell held a hushed conversation with the added team member.

The young woman was attractive, but not overtly pretty, nor feminine. Her short white-blonde hair shone against deeply tanned skin. Brown eyes appraised everything the way predatory animals surveyed their territory. She wore military-style combat top and bottom, moved like a cat, and spoke softly.

She felt the stare and glanced in his direction. Rosz dropped his eyes to the floor. Bosine were prey. It was their nature to be non-aggressive. Chaspi one of the few exceptions. Himself? Verdict still out, but under the woman's glance, he felt defenseless.

Chaspi rose the ship sideways along the curved wall of the yardang, slipped the shuttle over the edge and onto the ridge with as little dust and sand blown up as possible. Three-miles in the desert, with a full moon, was near enough for any disturbance to be seen. Luckily, dust devils and wind-blown sand were not unnatural.

"Perfect," Stacey told her friend.

"Good job to both of you," Tab said, joining them at the front. "Cam and I will scout the area. Take a rest."

The side door opened wide enough and long enough for the two to exit.

"Does anyone know her whole story?" Billy asked.

"I am certain Colonel Barnwell will tell us what we need to know when the time is right," Kai said. The Japanese martial artist and close combat instructor's history included work as a police officer and royal guard for the Emperor's family. Clandestine operations were not new to him.

"A team requires trust and a complete understanding of the capabilities and potential liabilities of every component by every member of the team if it is to function effectively," Stacey said, quoting from the Space Fleet Marines' field manual.

"This is not a military operation, Stacey-chan," Kai corrected. "This is a spy mission, and for those, everything is need-to-know. You are told only what you need know to complete your portion of the mission."

"It still requires trust," Stacey countered.

"Do you trust Col. Barnwell?"

"Yes."

"Then you have the trust you need. Trust Ms. Valverde because Col. Barnwell obviously trusts her," the Japanese warrior said.

"And because she looks like she can kick ass," Billy added.

"Impressed much?" Chaspi asked.

"In this case, yes," Billy replied. One of the few times he ever spoke with conviction to Chaspi when it applied to a personal point of view. Up to now he stammered if he thought he might say something to upset the Bosine.

"Billy grew up," Rosz whispered to Kai, who gave a tight nod in reply.

"I suppose we also have to trust Captain Black will be inside the compound," Stacey interjected.

"That was the plan," Billy said, sitting down again, pulling his bags beside him.

South Carolina / Three Days Previously

"Captain Black returned from Salt Lake City and her meeting with Arnold Montack and Sir Daniel Miller," Tab informed his newly formed team.

After each potential member contacted agreed to the invitation to join Barnwell's team, he and Admiral Patterson came up with plausible reasons for them to be absent Space Fleet Academy or university for a short period. Patterson provided a public transportation ticket that eventually brought them to Walterboro County, South Carolina. Barnwell met each one at the local airfield at different arrival times.

They were driven into swampy forests and across dirt roads to a private hunting lodge.

"I cannot believe this world has so many striking landscapes," Chaspi observed aloud from the second floor balcony of the three-story centuries-old manor.

"A planet of extremes," Tab replied. "Earth is covered with incredible scenery. Is Osperantue different?"

"We have mountains and forests. There are wide plains, and vast oceans, but not the seasons and variations in temperature as Earth," she answered. "My world is much calmer."

"Fell has fewer topographies than Earth," Stacey said. "Because our atmosphere is always moist, the majority of the planet remains at the same temperature. Plant and animal life are similar across the continents. Only the northern and southern polar regions are harsh. I always thought my world was exciting and diverse until I came to Earth. I know of no other world as beautiful, and dangerous, and exciting, and colorful as this one."

"It is also peaceful," Kai added. "It is calming to be here amid the tall pines and ancient oaks covered with moss. Ponds and streams around every turn. A great habitat for animals and birds."

"And insects," Billy said, slapping at his arm. "Biting insects. But otherwise it is peaceful. Kind of strange for a place people visit to hunt wild animals."

"Hunting game only occurs twice a year," Tab explained. "There are some animals which no longer have predators to control their numbers. We place limits and stipulate the age and sex of animals which can be hunted for kill. The meat is prepared and distributed to local families. The ponds are used for fishing. There are a couple of species of wild birds we must cull occasionally."

"We?" Rosz asked.

"My family owns this land," he answered. "I have family members living around here, all the way to the coast."

"If any strangers were in the area . . ." the Japanese began.

"I would be told," the African-American finished.

"You were saying Captain Black has returned," Rosz said from the rocker he claimed the moment he stepped onto the balcony.

"She's sure they bought her story," he said, turning his back on the view to concentrate on the mission. "The legend Cassel's people built obviously stood up against a background check, or they would never have taken her to Utah. She convinced them she already felt sympathetic to the idea of regional rule over a central government. She hinted at her desire to profit from her inherited role as Amanda Muse and let Montack present her with an offer."

"Money?" Stacey asked.

"Money, property, continued fame, and power," Tab answered. "They all but offered her a place on the board of the Camarilla Dissolvere. She hedged, requesting more assurances than she felt Montack and Miller could provide. She told them she needed proof they could pull off breaking up the United Earth Council and not end up in prison. Then she left."

"Do you mind telling us how you stay in contact with the Captain, Colonel?" Kai asked. "I would think the members of the Camarilla would be most severe in their security arrangements."

"Old school, Sensei," Tab said. "I don't know if Coop ever told you guys, but I'm a history buff. Military mostly, but I love all of it. Spy-craft goes back thousands of years, and passing messages and information without getting caught was key to the success of every major espionage story."

He pulled a rectangular devise from his pocket and tossed it to Kai.

"That's a mini-recorder from the twentieth century," he said.

Stacey took the devise from Kai and examined it.

"Mini?" she queried. "It's huge. Pulleys and bulky wiring. You actually have to push down on metal buttons for it to operate."

"Small for that time in our history," Tab explained. "Outdated and only found in museums and private collections these days. Mostly forgotten. I have two pristine models. Amanda Black has the other one. We have pre-arranged locations where she can drop it and pick up the twin. When she needs to make a switch she logs-on to a world-news research agency and uses operational code words within search requests. The system alerts me when a search with two or more code words occurs. It's how we stay in touch."

"She isn't overheard?" Rosz asked. Doubt from an alien who listened to music non-stop and overheard everything said in the room.

"Once more, old methods still work," the Marine intelligence officer answered. "She only uses the recorder after she has scanned a room for bugs, and she makes sure there is running water nearby."

"Surely the Camarilla searched her belongings," Chaspi said.

"And found a vintage voice recorder," he answered. "The kind of quirky item someone who makes a living as a communicator might feel attached to. Did I mention I had a mech-tech genius rework the tape?"

"Tape?" Stacey asked.

"The film inside on the rollers is voice-recording tape. You press the START-TALK buttons at the same time and it records what you say into the mic. Hit REWIND and PLAY to listen to what was recorded. But if you press START-TALK-FASTFOR-WARD at the same time, your voice is recorded on the lower half of the tape. Anyone who listens will hear only what was recorded on the top half. Unless you know which buttons to use to hear the hidden message."

"I guess it's better than writing with lemon juice," Kai said, bringing a smile and chuckle from the Colonel.

"I'm not the only history buff," he said to the martial artist. "When you write with lemon juice it is invisible. When you heat the paper, the words magically appear."

"Older people are weird," Billy whispered to Chaspi.

"And now?" Rosz asked.

"We wait and prepare. If they take the bait, Amanda will be taken to the operation center. The location we suspect is in Saudi Arabia. She will require total access, including meeting with al-Rashid, and details on the final plan."

"Then?" From Rosz.

"Extract Captain Black and the info is our mission. Along the way if things get destroyed, or bad guys get killed, shit happens."

"Killed not captured?" Kai asked.

Barnwell did not answer, which was the answer.

"How do we get into the compound?" Chaspi asked.

"Quietly," he answered. "Two to three crews for insertion, recovery, defensive action, and back-up in case those going in don't come out. "

"Which leaves the question as to how we get to Saudi Arabia, and how we get out," Stacey said.

"You provided the answer, Stacey. I believe I hear it now," Barnwell turned to look out at the dense forest.

A grey Space Fleet shuttle skimmed the tops of the tallest pines.

"It's the Picard," Stacey said. "You stole it again?"

"Borrowed," Barnwell corrected. "She took it the same way you did when you used it to find Coop in Canada. Flew it out of the maintenance yard without an official requisition. No one will report it missing for a few days."

"She?" Stacey asked.

The group trotted down the back steps to the open courtyard behind the lodge. The shuttle landed neatly between hedges, missing the decorative fountain, but crushing a row of roses.

The side panel slid open and a lithe figure stepped down. Shaggy cut white-blonde hair and sun-kissed skin. Eyes hidden by over-sized aviator shades, and her shape disguised by a baggy military shirt with multiple pockets tucked into black combat pants, tucked into black jungle-style boots. The only thing for certain was a tiny waist and a bright smile. She flashed it as she hugged the taller (by six-inches) Barnwell.

"This is Morena Campo Valverde of the United Earth Security Establishment (UESE). She works directly for Director Cassel. Cam, this is our support team."

The smile disappeared as the agent surveyed the people standing before her.

Without offering an opinion, she turned to the Colonel and said, "An alien space craft has entered the solar system. A delegation from the planet Devisator with an ambassador requesting to join our defense alliance. They say they are members of the Trade Alliance Worlds."

"Members not particularly cared for by the others in the Alliance," Stacey said.

"Dangerous?" Tab asked.

"There is no history of open warfare by the Devee," the Fellen replied. "It's a world of females-only and they live for the trade. Fair or unfair, they will always get the best deal for their Ginae."

"Ginae?" Kai asked.

"Their leader," Stacey answered. "They barter for anything, and they are known to trade in less than ethical goods. That includes slaves, bio-chemicals, and weapons."

"A world of women only?" Billy asked.

Chaspi elbowed Billy.

"Centuries ago they decided procreation could be accomplished in other ways. Males were culled during the genetic process and soon disappeared."

"We're opening communications with a lot of new planets," Tab said. "I guess we should have expected visitors to start coming to us. Doesn't sound like they are the type to cause us any trouble."

"I do not care for the timing," Valverde said.

"The wormhole's current location means between two to three-weeks to travel from the gate to MSD for standard alien vessels," Tab said. "Another two or three days to get around the sun to Earth. We'll be done, good or bad, before they get near the planet. The Devee ship is Patterson's problem. Our job is to make sure the UEC is around to greet the Devee representatives. It's time for dinner, people. I say we move this to the kitchen."

During the following two days the team members studied their primary assignments, practiced, and cross-practiced for the mission. Chaspi and Stacey flew the Picard at night. Stacey memorized coordinates and salient landmarks for the flight to the middle of Saudi Arabia.

Billy created an altimeter for the space ship. The young engineer occupied most of his time reconfiguring explosive discs from military stock. The new grenades could be locked magnetically to metal, or flung like a frisbee. For practice, he introduced the off-worlders to frisbee discs. The front yard of the hunting lodge soon looked like a green space on a college campus with flying discs sailing between the four friends.

Rosz studied notes from his trip to Saudi Arabia, and compared his information to the data Barnwell provided on the recently constructed Camarilla compound. He was to locate a secure landing zone and map out the most efficient, least dangerous paths to-and-from that site and the compound.

Kai worked with everyone on close-quarter combat drills. Each person practiced with the weapon they were most comfortable with, as well as becoming more comfortable with something they might be forced to use.

He spent two hours away from the lodge with Valverde, returning and refusing to say anything other than she was "more than capable."

Barnwell and Valverde spent most of their time huddled together over the information they believed impacted the mission.

On the afternoon of the second day Barnwell called everyone together, issued orders as to what they could and could not take with them, and informed them they would take off in one hour.

"Did Captain Black contact you?" Stacey asked.

"No. She was taken from the apartment Cassel arranged in Bethesda. No one made a prior contact. The watchers said it took less than four-minutes from the time the Camarilla agents knocked until she left with them. Satellite followed them to a local airstrip. Hover-shuttle took off a few minutes later. It stopped transmitting locator signals after it crossed the coastline."

"We don't know if they are headed for Africa, somewhere else, or decided to drop Captain Black in the Atlantic," Billy said.

"We're going to Saudi Arabia," Tab told them. "If I'm wrong about the location, we'll make adjustments from there. But I'm not wrong," he assured them.

Tab asked Kai to walk with him to the manor's study. Cam joined them.

"If I had a choice other than these kids, I would have taken it," he told the older man. "I need you to make sure they don't do anything stupid. I don't intend to console any parents when we return."

"I can assure you, Colonel, these are no longer children," Kai said. "They have the spirit of youth, but they also have wisdom beyond experience. I have trained hundreds of young men and women over the years. These four are special. Not since my own daughter, Aya, have I seen such determination."

"Determination will not keep them alive," Cam said. She stood in front of a wall with photographs from past hunts. Pictures of men and women long dead. It seemed an appropriate backdrop for the mysterious young woman.

"They have skills, Onna-bugeisha." Sensei Kaito called her by the ancient Japanese title for a female warrior. Warriors who fought alongside samurai. Women of royalty trained for battle. "They are not as skilled as you, but I have met few with your ability."

"I do not need approval or praise, Sensei," Cam replied. No rancor in her tone. "I need to know they will watch our backs without getting killed or in the way."

"They would die for you, Señorita Valverde, but they will not get killed carelessly," he assured her.

"I still need to know you will watch over them, Sensei," Tab interjected.

"I know my role on your team, Colonel-san. You and she are a team. I and the cadets are the other team. You are the sword, and we are the arrows."

"They are the arrows, Kai," Tab corrected. "You are the archer. And the back-up sword if needed."

The older gentleman bowed in understanding, leaving the two to prepare for the journey.

"We could have done this alone," the Brazilian said.

"I know how you prefer to operate, Cam, but we need help on this one. Daniel Cooper trusted them enough to fight beside them. They're better now than they were then," Tab told her.

"Daniel Cooper fought beside my grandmother and she died," Cam reminded him.

"Ali Campo died saving Coop," he reminded her. "I know the man, and I know not one day goes by he does not wish he had died and she lived. That is a long time for someone to carry grief."

"My mother carried the same grief, and she never blamed Coop. He made sure she was always cared for. She went to school and became a great teacher. He was there when I was born. He has never judged me for my choices. I turned my mother's grief, my loss, into passion. Daniel Cooper does the same. Every pain he endures is turned into action. It will not wipe away the grief, but it makes a payment."

"A payment?" the Space Ranger asked.

"We will meet those we have lost one day," she replied. "Space Rangers like you and Coop may have extended lifespans, but everyone dies, Tab. Those who went before us will greet us then, and those we wronged will expect payment. The more good we do now lessens the cost we must pay then."

"And those we kill in the name of good? Will they expect a payment?"

"No. They will be too busy suffering in hell."

PART 2

con·tra·dict

käntrə'dikt

deny the truth of (a statement), especially by asserting the opposite.

be in conflict with.

Chapter 15

The Void Between Star Systems

The Wraith was positioned to exit Clyde, the Nakki transport ship. **I Can See Clearly Now** by Johnny Nash played over the ship's speakers. The song selected from Key Largo's[15] reggae collection.

"Almost home," Coop said from the pilot's seat.

"There will be things I will miss," Cassie responded from his right. She sat in the co-pilot's seat with her eyes closed.

"I'm pretty sure I can talk Manny into installing a shower with real water," Coop replied.

The avatar smiled and opened her eyes. "Hangar doors opening," she said. "Clyde says we are in the void between the Aster Farum and Fell systems. He also says 'Good luck.'"

"Not good-bye," Coop murmured as he pushed the fighter across the deck and into space.

Cassandra sped into the starry expanse. Clyde disappeared.

"What?" Coop asked, noticing Cassie's pinched expression while she stared into space.

"We're in the right place," she said, "but my chronometer is rebooting."

"So?"

"The alignment of stars is making my operating systems recalculate and reset time functions."

"And?"

"The ten days we were gone just became eight-months-thirteen-days and six-hours."

Jimmy Cliff replaced Johnny Nash, singing **Many Rivers To Cross**.

"Eight months?"

---

[15] Key Largo: Book 4 / CONNEXIONS. A human alien abductee rescued by the Nakki agent Verace D'Sey. Discovered his heritage and embraced all things Jamaican.

"Thirteen-days-six-hours," the avatar added.

"The trans-dimensional travel variations Doc mentioned," Coop said. "The fact we needed to travel around a black hole to get to the other side of the galaxy probably added to the time distortion."

"I am able to receive communications and data from various sources now we are back in our own space," Cassie reported. "It will take a few minutes for me to process everything, but I should be able to discover what has been happening with Earth, Space Fleet, and any non-terrestrials communicating with our people."

"Coop noted the term 'our people' by the holo-avatar. The trip to aid the Hellacene Alliance against the Kasch Empire added layers to the personality of the woman created by computer programmers and a modified 3-d organ-tissue printer.

"There is a general notice for anyone who sees you or Cassandra to report the sighting to Space Fleet command," Cassie told him. "The active search for us ended two-months-three-days ago. We are officially Missing In Action."

"Maybe we should take advantage of being MIA," he said. "We could find some unexplored part of the galaxy and start over. OWWW!"

Cassie pinched him on the forearm. Hard.

"Do not think for one moment I will allow you to go back to being the dark, brooding, loner you were becoming before D'Sey pulled us out of space-fold," she warned. "You joined a crew of pirates, saved two princesses, rescued an alliance of peaceful planets from doom, and enjoyed the entire experience. Remember the keep it simple rule."

"I remember," he replied, rubbing the spot on his forearm. The Space Ranger project activated his Methuselah gene to extend his lifespan. The alien soup his body was emerged in reengineered his genetics. His cells regenerated daily, allowing his physical body to age slowly. The improvements prevented ninety-nine-percent of pathogens from infecting him, gave him six-time-normal-human strength, and tripled his speed. Anything but an immediate killing blow would heel. But it did not stop the pinched skin from aching.

"Stop overthinking every little detail, and no more feeling responsible for every tragedy in my life," he recited. "Keep it simple, shit-head. Take what comes and do what feels right."

"And be happy about it," she added. "I like you better with a sense of humor."

"Since you come with the ship, and I plan on keeping the ship for a long while, I suppose it is important I keep you happy."

"Damn, skippy," she answered, her artificial eyes on the data streaming across the heads-up display on her side of the cockpit window.

"You're certainly becoming more human. Pinching me. Using phrases like *damn, skippy*. That or you've morphed into my conscience."

"If you're giving me compliments so I'll fuck you, don't bother. All you need do is ask," she said.

"Because you're programmed to be my sex-slave?"

"Because I enjoy fucking you," she answered. "I'm part of the artificial intelligence operating Cassandra. That means I evolve with experience. I no longer require a system code to make decisions. If I have sex, it's because I want to, not because I have to."

"You are definitely becoming more human," he said. The smile indicated he approved of the evolution. "Speaking of Cassandra, how is my ship?"

"The Wraith is structurally sound. The dog-fights with the Kasch Shroud ships scorched her paint, and there are dents and scratches, but no breeches. The food-replicator we got from Clyde means your food and fluid supplies are sufficient. You will need to find another origin-source when you run out of the replicant-food-cubes D'Sey provided. We are out of projectiles for the rail-guns. The tachyon cannon is available and charged. All four wing-fixed laser cannons are functional. Anti-detection systems are positive, and the optic-camouflage enhancements Clyde added to the hull are available."

"Power systems?"

"Ionic-fusion one-hundred-percent. Space-fold array reads in the green. No damage or movement of the power crystal. The Rys black-diamond forcefield emitter shows no problems. We have power, weapons, and defensive capabilities," she concluded.

"The STORM-HATCH communication system is obviously working," he noted. "Had enough time to find out what's happened since we left?"

"A lot," she answered, "but the latest reports from Space Fleet are the most important. The 109 is located above the planet Phisor. Mischene and Zenge elements loyal to the Prophet were using the planet to reunify their forces. Admiral Patterson mounted an operation to take them off the world. They have the invaders backed into one city. They named themselves the Revolutionary Mischene Military or RMM following the death of the Prophet."

"Sounds like the Fleet is doing a good job," Coop said.

Cassie swiveled her seat to look directly at her companion and captain.

"Angel 7 was shot down by the RMM. Elie, Storm, and Jon-Jon were aboard. A Marine S&R team has been sent to find them, but communications are jammed on the surface. No word of survivors," she told him.

"How long before we can make the Phisor System?" he asked.

"Less than one-day," she answered. "Coop, a Devee cargo ship carrying medical aid and supplies arrived in the system. It will be at Phisor before we can get there. You remember what D'Sey said about the Devee?"

"He felt they were a bigger threat to this quadrant of the galaxy than the Mischene," Coop answered.

"All communications from the Phisor System have been cut off," she added. "The communications experts on Fell say it could be a natural phenomenon. An anomaly may be disrupting ion fields."

"Or someone," Coop said. "Are nav-coordinates in for Phisor?"

She nodded.

"Let's go." He activated space-fold and sent the fighter toward friends-in-need.

"Do you want me to inform Admiral Patterson?" Cassie asked.

"Not yet. The Devee may be able to intercept communications. We have eighteen-hours-forty-one-minutes until we reach the planet. The Rys force-field will activate at the system's edge. We can travel to the planet without dropping out of space-fold to readjust. Pull up the intel D'Sey provided on the Devee. Let's learn about this potential new threat before we engage."

The holographic image of Nakki agent, Verace D'Sey, stood atop the table in the galley. The projection came from the data-pad lying on the table.

"I'll make this short," the image said. "The Devee must never, ever, under any circumstance be trusted. The species is driven by an obsessive need to win. They count their winnings in the fortunes amassed through trade. As such, they will trade anything for something of greater value.

"The Devee are a completely female society. Originally a ma-triarchal culture, over time the females in charge decided men were unnecessary to maintain the species. They do not appear to hate males in general. They made a practical decision. They justify every decision made to benefit the Devee as practical.

"As you know, I have been away from your quadrant for nearly one-hundred-years. Nakki listening posts, and ships like Clyde, keep watch on the Devee. Actually, they keep watch on everyone and everything. I have a personal dislike for them so I keep up with events with Devee involvement."

The hologram hesitated, apparently D'Sey arranging his thoughts before continuing to record the information promised Cooper.

"I have attached files with a breakdown of Devee social struc-ture. They are segmented and assigned to castes. Each caste is tasked with improving profit centers for their world. The Devee trade with several alliances, federations, and are suspected of dealing with closed systems. They are excellent at persuading oth-ers to barter. Their spy network and psy-ops professionals discov-er what another race covets, and they dangle the bait. In the be-ginning of a relationship, the Devee are willing to trade at a loss to establish a connection. Soon they find ways of changing the odds, and eventually the Devee come out on top.

"The Devee will manipulate any situation to improve their position. Conflicts and wars have been fanned by these assholes so they could profit from the results. I do not have proof, but I know the Devee have been in contact with the Mischene. Both sides, Coop. They worked with Soren and with his son, the Prophet. I believe they are attempting to create a galaxy-sized conflict to extend their reach into the pockets of every system caught up in a war. This includes societies without the ability to travel between star systems."

The image hesitated once more before continuing the monologue.

"They're incredibly sophisticated, Coop. If not for being sociopathic, they could be a benefit to the entire galaxy. They have the capability of taking any drug, tech, weapon, or theory and improving it. I know for a fact they use personal glamour shields. These shields allow a Devee to appear to another species as anything they program into the projector. Most often they appear in a form a trade-partner will find unappealing, and therefore dismiss, or extremely appealing and unable to resist. They possess advancements in communications, weapons of destruction and disruption, and have ships capable of far more than they allow others to witness.

"Again, everything I know and everything the Nakki have discovered, along with educated guesses are included in the files downloaded to Cassandra. This little monologue is so you understand, captain to captain, man to man, if you have to face off with the Devee, one single moment of hesitation, or sympathy, or doubt will be all they need to win."

D'Sey stood a moment longer before the hologram projector closed down.

"That was ominous," Cassie said.

"Have you looked at the additional files?"

"They are equally ominous," she replied. "One of the educated guesses D'Sey alluded to is a prediction the Devee will eventually start a war against other planets instead of instigating from the background. Phisor might be their first step."

"If it is, the 109 and a lot of our friends are in their path," Coop responded.

"I have new information which may affect more of our friends," Cassie told him. "A Devee ship carrying a delegation to negotiate an alliance with Earth is already in the solar system. PT-89, the John A Macdonald is the only Space Fleet battle ship in the system. Most of the fleet remained in the Aster System."

"UEC and Space Fleet installed defensive cannon on both space platforms, and on the surfaces of Earth, Mars, and the moons. There are two non-orbital satellites with weapons," he said. "It would require a lot of firepower to get through. More than one ship could possibly carry, regardless of how dangerous D'Sey believes the Devee."

"He said the Devee are devious, Coop. I realize I still have much to learn, but I know humans are gullible. You always look first for good in others, which is a fine quality, but it leaves you open to a sucker punch."

Coop stood quietly contemplating everything D'Sey said, and Cassie's observations. D'Sey was not human, despite his appearance. No one ever said, or possibly knew exactly what kind of being D'Sey was. Cassie was not human, regardless of her programming to make her appear and act human. Both questioned whether humans would survive an encounter with the Devee. The pirate by inference and the avatar straight out.

"The Devee have a history of winning," he said. "They destroyed their own natural order because they saw it as a weakness. If they have decided to attack Earth they will discover a new lesson. We prefer winning, too, only we do not believe you must become a total dick to come out on top. I'll take humans, with all of their flaws, against the Devee in a fight to the death. When humans see the possibility of defeat, we redouble our efforts and keep charging ahead. When it becomes clear they are losing, the Devee will cut their losses and retreat. That single distinction in character will make the difference."

Cassie stood facing Coop, one hand over her mouth and holographic tears gleaming at the edge of hazel-colored eyes. She was not moved by Coop's observation. She was trying to control laughter.

"What?" he demanded.

"You're talking about an entire species of females, and you use phrases like *becoming a total dick* and *coming out on top*," she replied. "You are really, really bad at making a speech."

Recognizing the bombastic nature of the soliloquy, he could not help but laugh at himself.

"You're right. I'll stick to flying and fighting."

"You're forgetting one other f-word," the stunning woman said as the clothes she wore dissolved.

Chapter 16

Phisor

"Izzy, updates," Lt. Lesego Ndaba requested. She sat in the command chair for the shift. Genna, who required separation time from the AI, slept in her quarters, leaving Ndaba the ranking officer on the bridge.

"Nothing new from the surface," Dominczyk answered from the Systems station. Her voice reflected the weariness the entire crew felt. Concern for their Captain and Angel 7 crew frayed nerves and cost many much needed rest. "The Devee ship remains on course and speed. They should set orbit over Phisor in fourteen-hours-twelve-minutes. Same old same old."

Sitting in the Pilot's chair, the final member of the skeleton bridge crew, Fallenitsch, a Bosine from the planet Osperantue, said, "I'm glad to be back aboard the 109, but there is no same old same old anymore."

Nicknamed Folly, she had been a member of the Star Gazer's flight crew, the cruise ship carrying refugees making first contact with humans. Now she served with Space Fleet and watched the forward SHD screen with big brown doe-eyes. The planet revolved on the screen. The serenity of the moment a contrast to the truth playing out in and around the Marauder-held city directly below their orbital position.

"Captain Casalobos, Storm, and Lt. Johnson missing. Captain Cooper missing. Too many friends injured or dead from the battles with the Mischene and Zenge. My own people returned to Osperantue. I would give anything to hear from any of them," Folly said.

"Explosions on the surface," Izzy yelled, unnecessary with the others within a few feet, but a reaction to the sudden actions below. "The building we designated as housing the communications jammers and the hospital building in the medical complex where the plasma cannon is located."

"Kennedy, the Devee ship is a fake. Shields and all-stations to alert," the commanding voice of Captain Casalobos issued from every bridge-connected comms unit, including the trans-comms the crew wore, the embedded speakers, and across all channels. She was reaching out to the ship's AI, but she fully intended for those on the command bridge to hear the warning.

"Sub-light power plant revving to full rpm," Izzy reported. "Sonic shields are up. The Rys force field array is now active, adding a second layer of shielding. Kennedy is moving the ship out of orbit."

"Kennedy, confirm that was Captain Casalobos," Ndaba called aloud.

"Confirmed," the AI answered. "Communications on the surface and to-and-from the surface are available," the ship's master operating computer added. "Forcefield shielding the city is offline. The surface plasma cannon is cycling. Anticipate it firing on us within four-seconds."

The ship tilted and despite the gravitational dampeners, the three on the bridge needed to grab their seats to stay off the floor.

"Harnesses," Ndaba ordered as a beam of super-heated plasma swept past the port side of the PT-109.

"The Devee ship has launched torpedoes. One dozen smaller spacecraft have departed the ship and are headed for our position," Kennedy said.

"Confirmed," Izzy added. "The ship no longer scans as a cargo vessel converted for medical aid. I'm getting data indicating multiple cannons, missile launchers, flight bays, advanced shielding, and, well, shit . . . it's a fucking battle carrier. How the hell did they disguise it?"

"Who is in the chair?" Casalobos called.

"Lt. Ndaba, Captain," the South African answered. "The Devee ship has launched torpedoes at the 109. A dozen fighter-class ships have departed the main craft. I don't know how, Captain, but they disguised a battle carrier as a refitted cargo ship. They tricked our scans."

"Lieutenant, keep my ship in one piece," Elie said. "Send a message to Space Fleet. Warn them of the Devee sneak attack.

When you can, target the plasma cannon here and take it off the map."

"Captain, this is Kennedy," the AI interrupted. "The Devee ship has spread an ion-disruption field throughout the region. It will prevent the use of tachyon particles for communications. We cannot contact Space Fleet, or anyone else with the STORM-HATCH system. They are also emitting white noise into the gas clouds."

"They have cut the system off and using the white noise limits your shield protection to the Rys array," Casalobos responded. "Hold, 109."

As the bridge team awaited the return of Captain Casalobos, First Officer, and temporary Captain, Genna Bouvier and General Gregory, both informed of the situation by the AI, arrived on deck.

"Captain on the bridge," Ndaba called, unstrapping quickly to stand and step away from the command chair.

Under normal circumstances, those stationed would stand until released by the arriving ship commander, but harnessed in for battle, such polite actions were ignored.

"Captain Casalobos, this is Genna. General Gregory and I are on the bridge," the avatar said aloud, knowing the AI would transmit the message. Using standard communications meant a slight delay would exist between contacts.

"Genna, Anton you have to keep the 109 safe," Casalobos said, repeating her earlier order. "Space Fleet does not have enough ships to lose another. The Marauders have mounted an offensive against Col. Duval and the Marines. We're going to help down here. You have the stars. Loba, out."

"She used her callsign," Gregory said. "She's going to war."

"So are we," Genna replied. "Lt. Ndaba take tactical. Lt. Dominczyk, move to communications. Fallenitsch, remain as pilot. Kennedy, have Dr. Cosoi report to Systems Control, and Ens. Diego Pablo to Navigation."

"Four torpedoes incoming," Ndaba reported. "Thermal-explosive warheads."

"Shoot them down, Lesego," Genna told Ndaba. The use of the Tac-Officer's first name meant the ship was going to battle. Rank, titles, and positions were secondary to quick and decisive action. Team work. Brothers and sisters.

"Izzy, tell the Captain to clear any personnel from the medical complex area. First chance we get, we're taking out the plasma cannon," she informed her Comms Officer. "Anton, you have a team on board as a fast-response group."

"Tier One, the Battle Bots," he confirmed.

"Get them to the LBJ," Genna said, telling him to have his people board the ship's shuttle. "If I get an opening, I'll launch the shuttle. Duval may need additional help."

"Since he hasn't called for reinforcements, I suspect he has his hands full," Gregory replied. "I'll be on the shuttle if you need me," the general said as he departed the bridge. The Space Ranger would no longer remain on the sideline directing operations.

"Torpedoes destroyed," Ndaba reported.

The computer expert, Dr. Nadia Cosoi walked onto the bridge, a cup of coffee in one hand and a bag of chips in the other.

"What's happening?" she asked.

Standing in front of the portal nearly cost the Romanian her breakfast when Ens. Pablo rushed through, made a titanic effort to avoid the diminutive woman, spun and landed on the arm of the command chair.

"This is not your station, ensign," Genna said, sending the young officer off the chair as if shot from a laser pistol.

"No ma'am," he replied, reaching the navigator's chair beside the pilot. "What's up," he asked Lesego.

"To the crew of the John F. Kennedy," Genna opened the ship-wide communications system, "this is acting Captain Genna Bouvier. First, Captain Casalobos is safe. She has managed to disable the Marauders' communications jammers and their forcefield."

The cheer could be felt more than heard coming through the hulls, floor, and ceiling of the command bridge, strategically located amidships.

"I do not have a report on Storm or Lt. Johnson. The enemy has launched an offensive against our Marines on the ground. It appears this is in cooperation with the Devee ship we thought was delivering charity medical aid and supplies. It is actually a battle carrier and they have attacked this ship. We are at war, and I expect everyone to battle stations and to perform your duties. We have a Captain to recover, Marines in need of assistance, and a planet to protect. They have the finest ship and crew in Space Fleet to do it. Bouvier, out."

Cosoi did lose her coffee when the grav-dampers did not compensate for the sudden descent of the warship. The craft dropped in space as a lift would fall from the highest floors of a skyscraper if its cable snapped and the brakes failed.

"The Devee ship and the surface emplacement fired plasma beams at us simultaneously," Kennedy explained. "I pulled a Cooper."

Discomposed by the abrupt action of the AI, everyone still managed a smile at the phrase *pulled a Cooper*. Daniel Cooper, the ship's original Captain, was known for making up maneuvers on the go when in battle. He was an expert at warfare in the multi-dimensional battlefields of space.

"Lesego, prep every weapon and load tubes. Diego, navigation line from here to one-hundred-miles over the surface cannon. Folly, put her on the spot Diego gives you. Now, people," the avatar-ship commander ordered.

"Damn girl looks twenty-four and acts like Attila the Hun," Cosoi said to herself. "Not a bad act to follow."

"We need to clear this area before the 109 takes out the plasma cannon," Casalobos told the others. "If I know Genna, she'll use the tachyon cannon and make damn sure it gets toasted with one hit. If we're within a mile, we may get crispy as well. C.C., take point and head for Duval and the Marines. Peter, then Ash and Tank, with the prisoner between you. I'm behind Tank, and Sergeant Palmer will cover the rear. GO, people."

"Captain!" Peter shouted. "The hostages?"

"Damn," Elie cursed herself for failing to remember the Mischene placed civilians to thwart the exact attack she just ordered.

"Kennedy, it's Elie. With the forcefield down and the jammers offline, can you locate the civilian hostages being used as shields in the hospital complex?"

"Forty-three Phisoran-signatures on the top floor of the hospital, and sixty-one on the top floor of the building two-hundred-sixty-five-degrees from the cannon emplacement," Kennedy reported across the private trans-comm.

"Inform Genna," Casalobos ordered. "Hold fire on the cannon until we can clear the hostages. Elie, out."

"Palmer, Peter, and Tank. Take the hospital. Go in through the Emergency Room. Kill anyone not Phisoran who gets in your way. Do not hesitate."

The three sprinted back toward the hospital.

Elie turned to the Mischene prisoner, her fingers tightening on the laser pistol.

"I won't give you any problems," Asper promised. "Let me go first. If guards see a Mischene, they'll hesitate. I don't want to see the civilians killed any more than you."

Elie pushed the Mischene toward the administration building west of the cannon emplacement. She, C.C., and Ash followed.

"We must get clear of this building," General Vinier told the two Devee chemists.

Emergency lighting provided illumination. Dust, shaken free by the explosions in the basement below, spread from the ceilings, defusing the yellow glow.

"Who caused that explosion?" Scalah demanded.

"I don't know," Vinier snapped. "I do know we are under attack and the generators have been destroyed. That means no forcefield. The Earth ship in orbit can destroy this place."

"Our ship will destroy the humans first," Scalah replied. The lack of conviction in her tone indicated a higher level of concern than the Devee wished to exhibit in front of the Mischene. "Portence and I will collect our research and samples. Where is the best location for a transport to pick us up?"

"There is a park one-mile west," the general answered. "How many will the transport carry?"

"A drone can seat two," she answered. "Take only what you must and we will meet in the lobby. My personal communicator will act as a homing signal."

Aboard the Devee battle carrier the communications officer reported to the ship's captain, "Chimia Scalah requests extraction from a park one-mile west of her current location."

"Send four of the drone-fighters," the captain replied. "One to collect Scalah and Portence and three to attack the human troops."

"The Mischene-Zenge forces are already engaged with the humans," the comms officer reminded her superior. "The drones may not be able to differentiate."

"It doesn't matter," the captain answered.

"Four fighter-sized enemy ships headed for the surface," Cosoi reported. "Eight headed for us," she added a heartbeat later.

"We're in position to launch the LBJ," Folly called. "Hangar doors are open."

"Launch the shuttle," Genna ordered. "Lasers spread pattern to intercept the incoming fighters. Lesego, fire the tachyon at the Devee carrier. Let's see if they can stand up to that big of a blast."

"Lasers firing. Tachyon burst on the Devee ship," NDaba answered.

"The plasma cannon on the surface is cycling," Cosoi yelled.

Cycling meant it would fire a superheated beam at them in less than three-seconds. With the tachyon cannon firing and the hangar doors in the process of closing, they may not be able to move quickly enough to avoid the impact. Within a few-hundred-miles of the weapon, the ship's shields might deflect most of the beam, but they were going to get kicked in the teeth.

The world inside the bridge shifted. It lasted only five-seconds, but everyone needed to catch their breath.

"Current location is 66,137.56527 miles from last position," Ens. Pablo informed everyone from the nav station.

"I took the liberty of engaging space-fold," Kennedy said through the embedded speakers around the bridge.

"The plasma beam missed," Cosoi said. "Obviously."

"Kennedy, put us back where we came from."

Five-seconds later the 109 emerged from space-fold into natural space.

"Engage the enemy carrier, and use the rail-gun on the fighters," Genna ordered. "We need to hold position until we get the signal from the Captain. What was the effect of our tachyon on the enemy ship?"

"It missed," the angry retort from Ndaba. "They are faster and more nimble than anything displayed earlier. The smaller craft from the carrier appear to be drones. No life-signs present inside the shells. They are varying laser wavelengths. The white noise renders our sonic forcefield useless, but the Rys shield is holding. They are attempting to find a laser frequency able to seep through."

"Kennedy, possibilities?" Genna asked aloud. She could have gotten the reply via her electronic interface with the ship's AI, but wanted everyone to know the situation.

"I have not studied the Rys field-generation system sufficiently to provide an answer, but the probability would be high. An application created by power from a crystal-based array, even a black diamond, would require a tight construct of particles. Particles would bind through vibration. Something operating at the same frequency would, theoretically, join or pass through the bond," Kennedy replied.

"What's powering the drones?" the acting Captain asked.

"Ion-fusion, similar to our sub-space-fold power plant," Cosoi reported. "Smaller, with minimal thermal signatures. They either use a more efficient power plant, or they mask the thermal output with insulation. The only way I can identify the source is because the ships vent ionic waste."

"Can we lock torpedoes on their thermals?" Genna asked.

"I doubt it," Ndaba replied, her eyes scanning a dozen lines of code as she interpreted the information to give her commander an answer. "The heat-signature is minimal and deep inside the ship. The torpedo would need to be near the drone to scan the thermal output. The drones are faster and more maneuverable than our torpedoes. A dozen plasma loads headed our way form the carrier," she added. Her alert delivered in the same tone as her report on the drones. It took a second for the warning to make sense.

"Evade," Genna ordered Folly, or Kennedy; whichever could act faster.

"Six-point location spread," Lesego NDaba called. "You have to fly between two of them to evade the rest."

Unfortunately, neither Folly nor the AI could swing the patrol boat around quickly enough to slip between the paths of incoming super-heated plasma. Kennedy did not try space-fold again so soon after the last time. The stress of activating the drive a second time proximal the gravity well created by the planet could damage hull integrity. It could potentially make members of the crew fold-sick.

Fallenitsch did manage to move the 109 fast enough to avoid five of the loads, taking the sixth along the stern. The force field stopped the hot-shot from penetrating, but the impact shook the ship stem-to-stern.

"The LBJ?" Genna asked before the hull ceased vibrating.

"Nearing the surface," Lesego answered. "Three drones are strafing the Marines on the ground. One has made a landing in-side a green-space one-mile west of the Marauder's h.q.."

"Izzy," Genna called out to her Comms officer. "I haven't heard anything from you."

The petite blonde lieutenant most often described as cute, but a proven battle-tested warrior turned from her console, tears be-hind the glasses she wore to make her appear more mature.

"Jon-Jon is dead," she said.

In the quiet that followed, Genna Bouvier felt the over-power-ing emotions she usually avoided by hiding behind her guise as an engineered being with implants and wiring instead of a heart and soul. Those close to her knew her emotions ran as deep as any young woman. Those not close to the engineered being saw an aloof, dispassionate machine made to look like a twenty-something human female.

As the face of Jonathan Johnson, always smiling and often red from embarrassment, flashed through her memory, her senses came to life. She saw each tear fall along Izzy's cheek. She could smell the stench of fear and adrenaline in the perspiration of the bridge crew. She heard the soft whirr of data being reported by hundreds of sensors to dozens of consoles. She felt the soft fabric covering the metal arms of her command chair compress as her fingers squeezed it to near tearing.

"Storm?" she asked.

"Injured," the reply, releasing some of the tension and saving the Captain's chair from damage.

"The Marauders are advancing on Duval's camp. They have a mobile pulse cannon. Probably the same one used to bring down Angel 7," Izzy reported. She was throwing herself into work-mode, pushing aside the thought of never seeing Jon-Jon again. "The Devee drones have the Marine's and Phisoran fighters penned. General Anton and his team are separated from the others by over a mile. The drones are working back-and-forth between the two groups. The LBJ has taken several laser hits and is not expected to fly again. It is currently offering cover and the crew is using the laser cannon to engage the drones."

"Captain, do we try for atmosphere to help the surface teams?" Lesego asked.

Genna sneezed, clearing the smell of sweat from her nostrils. She scanned the room, seeing every face looking to her for an answer. This was why she never wanted the ship's captain to leave on away-missions. This was the hidden fear that dogged her dreams. Alone, in charge, and without a clue. A child hidden inside the body of a woman.

"Take control," Kennedy's voice sounded inside her head. "Remember what Captain Cooper told you when he ordered us to leave him at the edge of the solar system with the Star Gazer? When you said you could not captain the ship?"

"This is about keeping Earth safe," the avatar said aloud.

"I'm sorry, Captain. What?" Lesego asked.

"Our first responsibility is keeping this ship operational," she said to her crew. "Gregory, Duval, and Captain Casalobos will figure out a way to handle the surface. The PT-109 is a space ship. We take down the fucking Devee ship, otherwise they might believe they can attack Earth ships whenever they want. Folly, take us toward the carrier."

"Yes, ma'am," the Bosine replied.

"Lesego, start planning your attack sequence. Some combination will work. Kennedy can supply the previous battle schemes the 109 and other Space Fleet ships have used successfully. Steal something or create something unique."

"Yes, ma'am," the Tac officer called.

"Lizzy, inform surface teams we will engage the Devee carrier and remaining drones to keep them away from the planet. Until we complete our mission, they are on their own."

"On the horn, Captain," the Comms officer replied.

"Diego, we need attack and evade routes. We may also need a couple of escape plans. Start working on angles and mapping obstacles in the system. Use Kennedy's help and work in short space-fold hops if needed by determining the length of time necessary between them to mitigate illness."

"Working," the ensign answered.

"Nadia, allow Kennedy to monitor the scans. She can decide what data I need to form decisions."

"And me?" the Rumanian asked.

"Find a way to hack into the enemy carrier, or the operating systems for the drones. If we can't figure out a way to shoot them down, I want to kill them from inside."

The savant hacker returned a smile mixed equally of evil and child-like mischief. She extracted her personal operating platform from beneath the console, linked it into the 109's mainframe, and began to play.

UEC Space Fleet PT-109, the John F. Kennedy headed for battle. Captain in command.

Chapter 17

Palmer and Tankian fired laser rifles from the darkness, taking out two Zenge standing over the body of the Mischene sergeant. Peter rushed forward. The Emergency Room lobby lit by low-wattage back-up lamps appeared empty, but he never hesitated to make sure.

The Phisoran resistance fighter ran up the stairs in the dimly lit well. His eyesight equal to the enhanced visuals the humans received in their battle suits. He could hear the footfalls of his teammates following, at least a level behind. He could also detect the sounds of hurried activity as he passed the third and fourth floors on his way to the fifth and final floor. So far, no one ventured onto these stairs to exit the building. What he did not know, could not know, was these stairs were restricted to the Devee and the highest Mischene officers. Everyone else used the stairwell on the opposite side of the building.

Luck ran out as he rounded the last turn. A Zenge sentry was posted at the entrance to the top level. The guard heard the running feet coming up the stairs, but because access was limited to high-ranking individuals, she did not have her rifle in a position to challenge. She also did not have the benefit of night-sight.

Peter fired as he raced upward. The ack-thack of shot after shot echoed in the contained space. The bright flashes of deadly light strobed across the walls.

When Abbie and Tank arrived, Peter was assuring the hostages they were safe. The explosion already had everyone out of bed and worried. The arrival of the humans in METS nearly created a panic as these people had no idea Earth had sent troops to recover their planet.

While Peter and the two Space Fleet Marines calmed the civilians, General Vinier and the two Devee, unaware of how close they were to the enemy, used the same stairs to exit the building. The body in the foyer and those outside the entrance made Vinier wish he had taken his guards with him instead of sending them down the non-VIP stairwell.

With Peter in the lead and the two Fleet Marines covering the rear, they herded the weak civilians down the five flights. They held everyone in the dim lobby while the three reconnoitered the area outside the entrance.

Ash warned them via her comm before she emerged from the darker shadows.

"We have the hostages out and the Captain is taking them south," she said. "There are still soldiers in the main courtyard with the plasma cannon. I had a group of seven-to-ten pass me in the dark. They were headed west."

"Any trouble reaching the hostages?" Abbie asked.

"Nothing we couldn't handle," Ash replied. "Biggest problem was keeping the Phisoran from killing our prisoner. Funny, since she actually helped by distracting a couple of guards along the way. Gave us the chance to take them down before they could fire."

"Peter, go get your people," Palmer ordered. "Warn them to be quiet. Anyone sick or too weak needs to be helped by the others. As soon as you get them here, we'll head south and catch up to the others."

Vinier deployed six Zenge fighters and two Mischene troopers around the perimeter of the park. Portence rushed ahead pushing a grav-sled loaded with tech-repositories of various size. Chimia Scalah followed with two over-sized satchels. These were filled with data drives detailing every experiment, failures and successes achieved while on Phisor. The value of the research guaranteed her a comfortable life on Devisator.

Scalah used her personal comm-unit to inform the drone of their position.

"You're stronger and faster than you look," the Mischene general said to the chemist. She still appeared in the glamour of a thin, older hag. Portence maintained a similar disguise. As far as Vinier knew, two aging scientists pushing a sled and carrying bags of data outran him from the hospital complex to the park. All he carried was a laser pistol.

The 109's laser cannons hit the plasma cannon emplacement. In the early morning light, the prism affect created by the impact fanned across the sky in green shimmering light streaked with veins of red. The ground trembled and leaves fell from trees.

"Your ship has not stopped the Earther vessel," Vinier said to Scalah. "We may come under fire when we attempt to fly away."

"Have faith, General," the Devee answered. "By the time we reach space we will have a clear path to our carrier. Portence and I will take the first drone. There is not enough room for the containers, satchels, and three of us. I have ordered a second drone to pick you up and follow us to our ship."

Vinier watched Portence load the grav-sled into storage beneath the drone. She stored Scalah's satchels behind two seats placed forward inside the craft's fuselage. When she turned back, the Mischene held his laser pistol in Scalah's face.

"Come join the other crone," he ordered. "I will take this one and the two of you can follow. With your valuable research with me, I think my chances of making it to the carrier will be greatly improved."

"Not very gallant, General," the chemist said.

"I do not trust you, hag," he replied.

"You are mistaken about us, Vinier," the Devee said as she pressed the hidden switch on her glamour shield buckle. The hag disappeared, replaced by an attractive woman. "We hide our true selves for protection." The black and red wraps parted to reveal a feminine body.

Vinier's eyes dropped to drink in the soft skin and round curves. The distraction allowed Portence to move closer and spray a chemical into Vinier's face. The intense pain from the fatal mixture overpowered Vinier's mind. He made no sound as his body crumpled.

The two Devee rushed to board the drone. The guards, seeing their commander slumped on the ground, rushed forward. Their lasers bounced off the shielded skin of the fighter, leaving them to watch the ascent and departure of the drone.

C.C. tried to keep a quick pace, but needed to balance getting clear of the potential blast radius when the 109 fired on the plasma cannon with not running into an ambush. The short Phisor night ending and the sun beginning to rise made their journey more difficult. The advantages provided by the METS, especially the camouflage and night-fighting enhancements would be diminished in daylight.

"Go," Peter told the sergeant. He added a tap to her left shoulder sending her ahead to the next adequate cover. In this case, an over-turned metrobus. Ash and Tank joined Peter behind a planter separating the sidewalk from the narrow avenue. Lt. Asper sandwiched between them.

The avenue provided the most direct route to the Marauder forward camp and the Marines five-hundred-yards further. The squad could hear the pitched battle. The air reeked of ozone from lasers. An underlying odor of burnt chemicals meant one or both sides were lobbing explosives.

After Palmer's group joined the others, Elie told the civilians to head westward and go at least three miles before they looked for a place to hold up. She provided a Phisoran female, who innately took charge of the two groups, with a locator.

"As soon as possible Marines will locate you and bring medicine, food, and supplies," she promised the woman. "We have to go help our people."

Light flashed across the pale night sky, followed by the roar of thunder. The ground shook, and the rubble around them wobbled. The prism effect of the cannon being destroyed by laser bursts dissipated in the pale blue sky.

"Genna got my all clear signal," Casalobos said. "It won't be long before the entire planet is free of invaders."

The Phisoran did not say anything, but the hug she gave the Spaniard spoke for all of the hostages.

"Go," Elie said, arriving to witness C.C. take a position behind the corner of the bus.

Sergeant Palmer backed in as Peter ran ahead.

"**Everyone stop and drop**," Palmer called over the team comm. "Vehicle approaching from our six, and coming in fast."

Peter and C.C. pivoted and raised rifles. Behind the planter, Ash placed a hand on Asper's back and flattened the Mischene officer against the rough sidewalk. Tank, Elie, and Abbie set a line with rifles up.

"It's an STV," Tank said.

"It's our STV," Abbie added, lowering her weapon.

The big transport slid to a stop, the side-panel opening before the wheels ceased rotating. Storm stepped onto the street.

"I would have called to warn you we were coming," she said, "but I didn't want to chance being overheard."

The team loaded after C.C. and Peter hurried back. Elie the last to enter, falling onto the bench seat behind the driver.

"Can you get us to the Marines without running into the enemy line?" she asked Cpl. Hafez.

"Could, but not going to," Khaled answered.

"Duval is pinned down, and Anton can't get past the drones to help," Storm said, taking the seat beside Elie. "The Marauders' pulse cannon is set up on a high point. It's preventing the Marines and Phisoran fighters from advancing or retreating. The Marauders are moving toward them."

"We're behind everyone," Elie said. "We take out the cannon and put the enemy in a crossfire."

"My thoughts exactly," the Fellen replied, her fangs displayed.

"Jon-Jon?" Elie asked.

"Secured to a bench. No one left behind."

"Huddle up," Elie called. "We have a plan. Cpl. Hafez, we'll talk while you drive. Move out."

The Marine STV with five humans, one Hana Kay, One Phisoran, One Fellen, and one Mischene prisoner sped down the avenue.

"You were supposed to take the STV back to the Marine encampment," Elie said to Storm. She kept her voice low.

"That was never actually discussed," Storm answered in a similar low voice.

"You brought it back to where we followed the Mischene into the tunnel and waited," Elie surmised.

"Yep."

"When the shields fell and the jammers were destroyed, you heard everything."

"Yep."

"You decided to come get us and take on the Marauders."

"Yep."

"Thanks."

Storm did not answer, but closed her fingers around Elie's.

"All clear from Captain Casalobos," Izzy announced.

The tachyon cannon needed to recycle before being able to fire again. Not wanting to wait, Lesego used the laser cannon attached to the ship's upper deck. Folly tilted the 109 on request by Tac, and the South African triggered repeated bursts, sending a half-dozen laser bursts on a line to the hospital complex below them.

"Plasma emplacement destroyed," Cosoi reported. "Actually, using the laser instead of the tachyon did the job with a lot less collateral destruction. If Captain Casalobos and the others put a half-mile between themselves and the cannon, they should be safe. Devee fighters are back."

Chapter 18

"The drones continue to probe our forcefield with laser fire," Lesego Ndaba updated Genna. "Nothing I've tried has been effective against the Devee ship's shields."

"One of the drones from the surface is on a course to return to the carrier," Kennedy reported. "The ship will need to lower its forcefield for docking."

"Lesego, prep every weapon capable of covering the distance between us and the Devee ship within the time estimated for the drone to pass the barrier. You will have that much time to cause as much damage as possible," Genna told her Tac officer.

"Ready," the coffee-hued woman from the southern tip of Africa assured her commander.

"The drone continued past the carrier," Kennedy informed them. "It is taking a position further out. The carrier is moving to intercept our current course. Twelve additional drones have launched. It appears their fighters, like weapons, can pass through the shield when leaving the ship. The Rys forcefield we use has the same capability."

"I attempted the EMT-Laser combination against them," Ndaba said. "The EMT had no effect. The shield must not be created by an electro-magnetic generator."

"They must use an array similar to the Rys forcefield emitter," Genna replied. "Kennedy, did the engineers on Rys provide insights on possible methods of defeating the forcefield?"

"No. The gyroscope and emitter were not originally designed to create a shield. The first one given to Captain Cooper for the Wraith would not allow weapons or communications to exit. The second generation was adapted to allow for operational functionality. Tests to determine weaknesses or means of overcoming the system have not been successful," the AI answered.

"Folly, you need to fly this ship and keep enemy hits to a minimum," Genna told the pilot. "Nadia, anything?"

The hacker gave a thumbs down, continuing to work on a solution.

"Kennedy, run virtual scenarios against the forcefield array. Find a way to get through it. Ndaba, the rail-guns may be our best option against the drones."

"Agreed, Captain, but the dozen launched are headed for the surface. I think they intend to wipe out our ground forces."

"Izzy, warn Duval and Gregory. Let Captain Casalobos know what's about to arrive. Tell her we are currently in a stand-off with the Devee ship. The drones are a wildcard."

"The 109 reports twelve more drone fighters inbound," Casalobos told the others. "Anyone experienced with a cannon like this?"

The blended team now held the mobile pulse cannon. Four Zenge and three Mischene lay dead around the weapon and the hauler it was bolted onto. The flatbed also held a crystal-drive power generator. The trailer with the weapon system attached to an equally large truck with all-terrain tires and an engine powerful enough to move quickly.

The squad operating the cannon and vehicle concentrated on the Marines in the distance. It cost them their lives when Casalobos' team rushed in from behind. Ash was setting charges when the Captain received Izzy's warning.

"It's a pulse cannon," Cpl. Tankian said. "The dials are in some language I can't read, but it should operate on the same principal as our military cannons. Build a charge, aim the gun, release the charge, and a pulse of compressed atmosphere slams into the target. The ones in space ships are bigger and require the atmosphere be channelled into the chamber from within the ship. Ones like this suck air directly into the compression chamber. The crystal generator is unique, but operates like any other crystal-fed power source."

"Can you operate the targeting computer?" she asked.

"Not if I can't understand it," he answered.

"I can read Mischene," Ash interrupted. "Tell me what to look for and I will translate."

"Tank and Ash will operate the pulse cannon," Elie said. "Storm and Khaled will stand guard. Abbie, C.C., and Peter with me."

"When we fire the cannon at the first drone, they will target this location," Storm said.

"Which is why you will wait long enough for my team to get in behind the Marauders," Elie responded. "When Tank begins firing and the drones redirect, we'll lay down suppressive fire on the enemy. With the drones pulled from overhead, it should provide the Marines time to uncover and fire on the Marauders. Tank, any guess how long it takes the cannon to recycle?"

"Don't have to guess," he answered. "They fired on our troops every thirty-seconds."

"Take as many shots as you can, but the four of you abandon this location before the drones arrive. Storm is team leader. Follow us and join up as quickly as you can. Khaled, the prisoner?"

"Doped and tied in the transport like you ordered," he answered. "She'll be out for hours."

"Elie, the drones are shielded," Storm reminded her friend and commanding officer.

"You know the one major flaw with crystal-laser systems?" Elie asked. When no one offered an answer, she said, "Stability. The lasers hitting the crystal's facets need to be on target. Precisely on target. If the crystal moves inside the faraday cage, it becomes just another rock."

"The pulse from the cannon might be able to dislodge the crystals," Storm said.

"Same way it knocked Angel 7 so hard it almost killed me," Elie replied. "Let's go to work people."

C.C. led down the slope with Peter, Elie, and Abbie following. Storm and Haz took positions at either end of the rig, while Tank sat in the gunner's seat with Ash on his left side. The Hana Kay read the screen, changed the target acquisition, and the barrel of the gun swept upward and the entire weapon moved on a swivel.

"When the two red lights merge and turn green, fire," she told the big Lebanese soldier.

The first pulse slammed into a drone as it slowed to change course to fire bursts into the area the Marine's held. The protective tarps and METS suits had prevented any deaths, but hits still hurt. The ground pounders could not move out from beneath the fiber shields. METS were not constructed to stop direct body shots from ship-mounted laser cannons.

Elie wanted to let out a whoop when the Devee ship spun out of control, cartwheeling through the air to crash and burst apart.

As the two remaining fighters peeled away and their on-board computer systems determined a new course of action, Elie made contact with Duval and Gregory. Aware they had a short window to act, Colonel Duval ordered his Marines to prepare to attack. General Gregory split his team into two squads, sending them in different directions to move up and flank the Marauders.

Elie's team, hunkered in depressions or covered by debris, began firing targeted shots from behind the enemy. They aimed at Zenge and Mischene elements in the forward positions, hoping the unexpected cross-fire would make the others seek cover.

A second drone went spinning as Tank connected with a pulse. A beam, most likely from the LBJ, cut into the gyrating fighter, destroying the ship in mid-air. While this pulse did not disable and destroy the target, it obviously did what Elie hoped. The array was shaken enough to disable the shields and allow a laser to finish the job before the autonomic system could realign the crystal.

Her left hand ached from steadying the rifle as she found enemy soldiers in her sights and single-tapped them. The METS maintained a comfortable temperature, but it could not stop sweat caused by the tension of battle. It stung her eyes, and she could not remove the faceplate to wipe it away. She blinked hard until her vision cleared enough to set the next target.

"Kennedy, it's Elie," she whispered to activate the trans-comm chip beneath her parotid gland.

"Elie, this is Kennedy," the AI replied. "The ion-diffusion and white noise discharged by the Devee carrier is interfering with communications. This channel is unstable."

The reply came through with static, and Casalobos needed to assume certain words, but it sufficed for a short message she did not want the Devee to hear.

"The drones, possibly the carrier, use force field generators similar to the Rys array. If the crystal is shifted or any of the lasers knocked out of line, the shields fails until the crystal can be repositioned. Tell Genna, and be careful. Without sonic shields, the 109 is vulnerable in the same manner. Elie, out."

C.C. and Abbie were almost as accurate with their rifles as Elie. The newer design used black diamonds and weighed less than older models. This resulted in less operator muscle strain. They also provided more repeats before the crystal waned. Peter did not have their experience with the rifles. He took more time between shots, and looked for enemy soldiers closer to his position.

They realized the last remaining drone had destroyed the pulse cannon when the blast echoed down the hillside. No one turned to confirm the loss of the cannon, or verify the rest of their teammates abandoned the rig in time.

The final Devee automated fighter zoomed across the battlefield. It did not fire. Duval's Marines used the distraction and destruction caused by the pulse cannon to cover the ground between them and the Marauders. The battle changed. It was now close-quarter combat.

The regiment of Space Fleet Marines under Col. Duval numbered two-thousand-fifty. Another one-hundred-forty-five Phisoran resistance fighters worked with them. Anton's two-dozen special operators were closing in from east and west. From her vantage Elie estimated the Zenge forces approximately equal with a scattering of Mischene attempting to direct the ferocious lizard-like aliens.

"Hi," Storm said as she dropped down beside Elie. "Everyone got away before the drone destroyed the cannon. I sent them to pair-up with the others. Sit-rep?"

Elena Casalobos, a life-long military specialist, could not stop the smile. Storm, a communications and computer genius from a planet where the inhabitants preferred living in tribal villages, first met a human less than three-years earlier. Now she lay beside her asking for a situation report like a seasoned UEC Marine.

"The fight is turning hand-to-hand," she told her friend. "The Zenge are beginning to show signs of blood lust, which will make them harder to stop. They already out-size our troopers, and their thick hides are as tough as METS. We aren't going to be able to target individuals much longer from distance. It's going to come down to hand-held lasers and blades."

"Those twelve drones are on the horizon," Storm said, directing Elie's attention to the West. "The one left is hovering. With the two groups mingled, they can't fire without potentially hitting Mischene or Zenge soldiers. At least that helps."

It would have if the incoming fighters cared about not injuring their allies. With the chemists and their research off the planet, the Devee only cared about annihilation of the forces from Earth. If the attack killed Mischene and Zenge, it was an acceptable cost.

The hovering drone received updated instructions from the carrier, joined the incoming fighters, and laser fire rained down on the bodies below.

Chapter 19

"What are we facing, Lesego?"

"The Devee ship has six plasma and twelve laser cannons. It can launch drone fighters with laser cannons, but I cannot estimate the number available. Currently twenty-four have been dispatched. Sixteen to the surface, and eight engaged with the 109."

The Tac officer did not read off the data. She had it memorized.

"The carrier uses forward torpedo-missile tubes port and starboard. We know they can disperse ion-particle disruption to disable communications. They know enough about Space Fleet defenses to incorporate white noise emissions with the diffusers. The forcefield protecting the ship appears similar to the Rys system we currently use. Since it is not electro-magnetic generated, it is not affected by EMT attacks."

The woman with short dread-locks and active dark eyes turned to face the strawberry-blonde in the command chair.

"There isn't anything exotic in terms of weaponry or defense," she said. "The methods used to camouflage the ship and fool our scans are unique. The way they can prevent communications and disable our sonic forcefield are innovative. The ship is five-times our size and carries drone fighters. We have space-fold speed, better maneuvering capabilities, and a wider selection of weapons."

"Captain Casalobos suggests attempting to dislodge the power source for their forcefield emitter," Kennedy chimed in from everywhere. "She also recommends caution, as the same tactic could cause our own shields to fail."

"Nadia?"

"I'm getting fat trying to find a way into their systems," the computer hacker answered. She unwrapped and popped a piece of chocolate into her mouth. When she stressed she craved the caffeine and bitter-sweet taste of the dark candy.

"Captain, the drones sent to the surface are firing on our people," Lizzy announced. "They are in close-quarter-contact with the Marauders, but the drones don't appear to care. They are firing on everyone. They need support, Captain. Quickly."

"Folly, turn us back," Genna ordered. She explained; "There's no point in maintaining a stand-off with the carrier. We need to place weapon-systems where we can try taking out those surface air elements."

"The Devee ship has increased speed and released a dozen torpedoes," Ndaba called. "The drones have doubled their laser-fire-rate and are concentrating on the stern. They know where our Rys array is located. They're attempting to shake us enough to disrupt the shield."

"Rail-guns on the incoming torpedoes," the avatar ordered. "Folly, continue toward Phisor. Tachyon cannon, fire on the Devee ship. Slow it down and rattle it. Kennedy, increase power to gravitonics, and increase the levels in the area around the Rys forcefield emitter. Place the cabin housing the forcefield emitter inside a blanket. Laser cannon; return fire on the drones. Do not allow them to hit this ship uncontested."

Chemia Scalah and Portence watched the action from a safe distance. The carrier kept them informed of events between the Devee ship and the Earth ship, as well as action on the surface.

"How long will this continue?" Portence asked.

"According to the Captain of the carrier, the Genai sent a ship to the Earth system with advanced weaponry and technology. Her mission in this system is to collect us and keep the attention of Earth's Space Fleet on this location. By disrupting communications during a time of stress, our political psychologists believe humans will be more concerned with the lack of information and potential peril their forces face on Phisor than the arrival of a diplomatic mission from Devisator," Scalah answered.

"This is just a distraction?"

"It is also a means of collecting valuable data on the capabilities of Earth's warships, as well as learning more about their battle tactics. The longer we prevent the space ship from leaving the system and contacting their command, the closer our ship gets to Earth. If it can slip inside their forward defenses before attacking, the more likely it will succeed in its mission."

"Their mission is to attack Earth?"

"To prove we can attack Earth," Scalah replied. "The actual purpose is to steal the secrets of the Ancient Seeders discovered by humans. If we can learn how to decipher the Ancients' language, we can begin to harvest those abandoned sites our explorers have charted over the centuries. We will also gain access to space-fold travel. That one piece of information is more valuable than all other trade goods combined."

"Stories of the first civilization and the miracles of their technology have passed around the galaxy for millennia," the chemist's assistant said. "Ancient sites discovered. Some with ships left to sit for hundreds-of-thousands of years. No species has ever decoded the secrets of the Seeders. How is it humans did what more advanced civilizations could not?"

"How they did it does not improve the value," the pragmatic Devee replied. "When the Devee gain control of the information, we reap more than profits for everything the Ancients created. We will no longer be the power behind others."

"We will be the power," Portence concluded, calculating the return on investment.

"Captain, the Devee carrier continues to fire on us. Our lasers are disrupting the drones attacking the 109, but we're only pushing them around. They continue to fire on the section housing the shield array," Ndaba reported. "We can fire on the surface, but the air-fighters attacking the battlefield are flying random patterns. I cannot anticipate a shot. If the weapon misses it will impact the surface and kill more of our Marines than the drones."

"If we head for the surface to engage the drones, what are the chances the Devee carrier follows and begins targeting our troops?" Genna asked.

"High," Kennedy answered.

"FUCK!" the avatar said aloud. The inability to find a solution caused the emotional display. The frustration of their situation weighed on everyone aboard the ship. No one thought less of the woman with the responsibility for thousands of lives to express herself. No one except the woman herself.

Engineered in a lab on an orbital space platform and created to integrate with an artificial intelligence designed to operate in outer space. Genetically altered to be smarter, faster, stronger, and less emotional than the human building blocks within her normally evolved. From concept to sitting in the Captain's Chair of the John F. Kennedy required less than ten years. More experience with aliens and combat in the previous three years than any other being from the planet Earth. It was a hell of a time to discover the depth of her emotions. The pain of frustration. The fear of failing. The realization she would be responsible for the deaths of comrades and friends.

The heartache of being alone. Proof the avatar was human.

Chapter 20

"Cassie?"

"Exited into natural space one-hundred-thirty-nine-point-four-thousand-miles to the star-side of Phisor," the avatar reported. Coop sat alone in the cockpit of the Wraith. Cassie dissolved her solid form prior to entering the system and now acted as the interface with Cassandra; the ship and AI.

"PT-109 engaged with Devee carrier and eight non-AI operated fighter drones. No damage apparent to the 109. Space Fleet Marines hand-to-hand with Zenge and Mischene forces south-by-southwest of the city. Thirteen drones are firing onto the battlefield. The drones are not attempting to select targets. Both sides are receiving casualties. General Gregory is with a force of twelve Marines on the western edge of the fight. Another twelve operators are engaging from the eastern rim. Captain Casalobos, Storm and a group of six fighters are behind the enemy lines. They are firing at the drones, but laser rifles are ineffective against the ships' shields. The LBJ is on the surface, also firing at the drones with the shuttle's laser cannon. I have made contact with Kennedy."

"Kennedy, it's Coop. Short and to the point."

"We cannot fire weapons on the surface drones without a high probability of hitting our own people," the AI answered. One thing about artificial intelligence - it never acted surprised. "We are attempting to disrupt shields for the Devee ship and fighter drones attacking us by causing vibrations strong enough to misalign the power source for their shield emitter. They are doing the same to us. Our situation is stable. The forces on the surface need immediate assistance."

"Coop, out."

He spun the ship toward the city on the surface and hit the haul-ass.

"Shuttle LBJ this is Daniel Cooper aboard the Wraith ship Cassandra. Do you copy?"

"Ensign Wallace, Captain Cooper," the shaky reply. "Thought you were dead, sir."

"Ensign I intend to hit the drones over your position. Target your cannon on any enemy fighters to lose shields. Be ready, be fast, and be accurate."

"Sir, yes, Sir!"

"Cassie, when we clear the upper atmosphere of the planet, close off the galley and maximize gravitonic control inside the cockpit. After I level, deploy the rear horizontal and vertical stabilizers," he ordered. "The rail-guns are empty and I can't deploy the tachyon cannon because it would cause major aerodynamic problems in atmosphere. Prep the wing cannons and set limits on the bursts. I don't want any misses by the lasers hitting the surface."

"Limits will require not firing the cannons unless we are within one-hundred-feet of the target," the avatar-AI informed her captain.

"The plan is to get a lot closer than that, Cassie," he warned her. "I plan on shaking those drones so hard anything slightly loose will fall apart. I'll concentrating on the flying. You control laser fire. Knock anything with a shield away from our troops. Kill anything without a shield. Copy?"

"Knock 'em up or knock 'em down," she answered.

"Elie, Storm, Anton, and Kennedy, this is Coop. Don't talk. Listen. I'm coming in hot to the surface. Plan is to disrupt the drones and try to bring down their shields. Cassandra and the LBJ will shoot down anything with a broken shield. Order our personnel to the edges of the battlefield and find cover. Kennedy, keep the Devee in space busy. When they realize a new player is in the game, they may try to fire on the Wraith. I'm not worried about hits. The misses from weapons that powerful could wipe out everyone in the area. Keep them occupied. Coop, out."

"That was rude," Cassie said. "Your friends haven't heard from you in over eight months. You're listed as MIA and probably dead."

"I do not have the time for conversations and explanations at the moment," he replied. "With them or with you. Exiting the stratosphere and entering troposphere. Begin converting the Wraith from space ship to in-atmosphere fighter."

Storm and Elie were engaged acting like teenage girls, hugging and laughing. The arrival of the Wraith at Mach 6 occurred before they could stop to locate the little ship in the silky blue sky. The results of Coop's sudden return from oblivion were easier to see. He drove the fighter into the swarm of drones, actually connecting hull-to-hull in two cases. The combination of surprise and the wind-pressures generated by the pass blew the drones in several directions. By the time the sonic boom blasted the landscape, the LBJ's laser took out one of the drones hit by the Wraith. Rear laser fire from Cassandra took down the other.

"Elie, Storm, this is Anton," Gregory's voice sounded inside their heads. "He's alive, he's here, and he's on time. I've ordered our personnel to head for the outskirts of the battle zone. I need you protecting them. Party later. Anton, out."

"How did he know we were partying?" Storm asked.

"'Cause he did the same thing, only he stopped sooner," Elie answered. The soreness in her arms disappeared as she lifted the rifle, rested the front barrel atop a piece of block from a demolished building, and began scanning for targets.

Gregory's special operators did the same, and as Marines made their way to the outside of the kill zones, they turned and added their own fire to help protect the ones following.

Unable to handle the confines of the METS helmet any longer, Elie pulled the faceplate, slipped it into a special pocket, and yanked the hood-helmet off. The stench of old sweat, new blood, and ozone assailed her. It also energized the warrior within. She located a Zenge Marauder and removed its head with a tap of the trigger.

Storm, operating with only one good arm, used her hand-held laser. It did not have the range or accuracy of a rifle, but she could make Mischene and Zenge hesitate by firing at them. Busy ducking, it allowed Marines more time to bug out. Noticing Elie's decision to go topless, she also removed her headgear. It took longer with one hand, but the breeze pushing across her head and the release of her dark auburn tresses felt orgasmic.

"It's against rules to remove any part of the METS during battle conditions," C.C. Galetti said as she plopped belly-down beside Elie. Ash duplicated the dive, landing alongside Storm.

"Bite us," Storm said.

Ash pulled her helmet off. "It stinks as badly out here as inside my suit," she said.

"I doubt that," C.C. said, removing her headgear. "You have a better line-of-sight from here than our position," she said. "Mind the company?"

"Never," Elie answered.

"I believe the ship I saw blowing through those drones was a Trent Industry design," C.C. added. She turned her look on her commander. Eyes filled with mirth, hope, and tears that did not reflect the horror of the battle in front of them.

"I believe you are correct, and here it comes again," Elie answered, confirming C.C.'s hope.

"Cassie, can the Rys forcefield be directed to cover one exterior hull section with a thicker shielding?" Coop asked.

"The gyroscope spins consistently to produce the effect of an external shield," she answered. "Because of the consistency scientists were able to discover a way to send weapons' fire and communications from inside to outside the shield wall."

"Which actually increased the effective range of the lasers as an unexpected result," he replied. "I know the history of the system, Cassie. It conducts the energy created by the crystal-laser into the faraday housing to prevent a charge from inside the cage blowing up the array. The external charge is directed to the Wraith's hull. If we disconnect the leads connected to the rear of the cage, will the extra power be funneled forward?"

"In theory."

"No better time than the middle of a dogfight to experiment," he quipped. "Disconnect the rear leads," he ordered.

With the delta wings of the ship tilted backward and the rear multiple stabilizers active, the ability of the Wraith to maneuver in the heavier atmosphere of the planet far exceeded the capabilities of the one-size-fits-all drones. Craft designed to operate effectively in the voids of space, but only able to make do within the troposphere.

Daniel Cooper began his military career as a grunt. Became a sniper, team, leader, and received a field commission. Following the Space Ranger Project, offered the opportunity to serve in any position with any military force on the planet, he opted for Navy pilot. Between then and resigning (sort of) as a Captain in Space Fleet, he spent the majority of his life as a test pilot.

The skills required to operate experimental craft came roaring back as Cassandra performed an impossible bank at Mach 5 and returned to the battle zone. Picking up speed.

In comparison, the Devee fighters looked like heavy balls tied to a string. They appeared to hang in midair for someone to take a swipe at.

Coop did not swipe. He walloped. The Wraith slammed the first drone, actually turned to hit and second and third, and left a trail of bouncing ships caught in its wash. The first ship slammed into the ground, exploding. The second pulled up in time to not hit, and the third was destroyed by the LBJ. Cassandra's lasers sliced the one drone which avoided the ground in half as it attempted to gain altitude.

"EARS!" Elie shouted. Without the METS helmets, the sonic boom following the Wraith could destroy their hearing.

The four dropped weapons, clasped palms over ears, and dropped to the ground. The sonic wave vibrated the surface, bouncing smaller pieces of debris into the air while shifting larger pieces. Even with their ears covered, the four experienced ringing.

"What did you say?" Elie asked C.C. She watched the younger woman's mouth move, but did not catch the words.

"Ash has the firmest ass I have ever seen on a humanoid," the Marine sergeant repeated. "The boom was loud enough to make her butt jiggle."

Casalobos looked at the Marine sergeant with curly brown hair plastered to her skull, and a smile of perfect white teeth. Shaking her head, she added her own smile, then told her foxhole companion, "Your parents named you perfectly."

Storm and Ash overheard the exchange, with Storm making an effort to look at the Hana Kay's rear.

"It is pretty damn firm," she said.

The red-skinned alien shook her own head, smiled, and went back to killing Zenge.

"Captain, we have a problem." The call came through the suit's comm, the speaker now around Elie's neck.

"What have you got, Palmer?"

"The Marauders have decided we're covering the weak side of the box," Sergeant Palmer replied. "Mischene officers are marshaling soldiers and looking this way. I think they are about to mount a charge to escape the kill zone."

Elie set her own rifle aside to take in the bigger picture. Sometime, when you concentrate on individual target long enough, the world shrinks.

"I think you're right, Abbey. Anton, this is Elie. We're about to get overrun. Any chance for help?"

"Elie, Anton," he replied. "Get your people out of the way, Elie. You're too far for anyone to provide support in time to matter. No way you can stand up to a couple hundred Zenge. Let them through. We'll find them later. Anton, out."

"Listen up team," Elie began to order her people to retreat. A laser blast missing by less than a foot stopped the order. She dropped, spun completely over, and fired up the hill behind their location toward the shooter.

Behind cover, and with the advantage of higher elevation, Captain Decadee, the cowardly officer who abandoned his squad when they engaged Elie and Storm the first time, returned fire.

He had commandeered a room on the second floor of the building with the jammers. The explosions, more than a dozen floors above him, did little but shake him awake on the dusty sofa he passed out on.

He made his way to h.q., lucky enough to be slow enough to be far enough away not to be injured when the plasma cannon was destroyed by the 109.

His luck growing, he found the guards who allowed the Devee to murder General Vinier. The two Mischene and four Zenge remained with the officer's body, unsure of their next move. Decadee took command, leading his new team toward the sounds of battle. He was no braver than before, but saw few other options. With the jammers destroyed and the force field down, he opted for joining up with more Marauders over running into angry Phisorans or a squad of Earthers.

From the hill where the rig carrying the mobile pulse cannon smoldered, they watched the Wraith's initial run through the drones. They also noted the location of the eight enemy soldiers firing from above the battle field, but below Decadee. Realizing the advantage of location and surprise, he ordered his crew to cover and to open fire on the enemy.

"Sgt. Palmer's hit," Khaled called. "Took a laser in the back. METS saved her, but I think she has broken ribs."

"Peter, Tank," Elie called back.

"We're fine," Tankian responded. "Singed, but those turds can't shoot worth a fuck."

"They don't have to," C.C. said. "If they keep us pinned, the Marauders will overrun our positions."

"Coop, this is Elie. I know you're busy, but my team is located on the northern side of the battle zone, half way up the hillside. We have four-to-eight shooters above us, and the enemy below is headed our way. Elie, out."

Elie turned to C.C. and said, "You have command. Storm and Palmer are both injured. Try to bring the other four here and fortify this position best you can."

Mouth open to question the order, Galetti closed it when Elena Casalobos set her rifle down, pulled her combat knife, and exited so fast, so fluidly, the Marine questioned her senses.

"She's going hunting," Storm said. "Catherea protecting her cubs."

"Catherea?" Ash asked.

"Jungle cat on Fell," Storm explained. "My tribe nicknamed Elie The Catherea because she eliminated a squad of Zenge chasing us after Demon went down."

"Galetti, it's Tank. Palmer is too bad to transport to your location. Peter and I will stay here with her and Khaled."

"We'll come to you," C.C. responded.

"Don't," the terse reply from the Lebanese. "Look over your shoulder. The enemy is headed our way, and there is a whole lot of them."

The thick hide resisted, but Elie's strength forced the sharp knife through the scales. The blade penetrated into the brain, and the Zenge died. She kept a knee on the creature's back as the body shuddered. Working from her right to left, this was her second kill. The helmet and faceplate back in place, the METS suit did not blend in as well with the rising sun spreading light, but moving through shadows kept her invisible.

A glance down the hill placed an anvil on her chest. The Marauders, at least three-hundred, were starting up the slope. Her team - her friends - fired from two locations. Their cover little more than depressions. On her right, at least four enemy soldiers fired sporadically at the two groups below. Despite her speed and skills, the mob escaping the kill zone would overrun the two positions before she could clear the hill.

The Wraith was coming in less than fifty-yards off the surface. The eight remaining drones placed themselves in a picket. Coop would have to get through them before he could lay down suppressive fire on the attackers.

She moved into the shadow of the smoldering big rig, then slipped beneath an opening between the cab and the trailer.

Coop had to come in fast to evade fire and hit the drones with enough force to knock their forcefields off-line. That fast, with the drones operating near the battle below, it would be impossible to target and fire lasers accurately on the Marauders.

"Fuck this!" she said aloud. She rose from the far side of the damaged transport, aimed at the backs of two black uniforms with snow white hair above the collars. One Mischene stood five feet in front of her, and the other twenty-yards right and down range.

The first shot burned through the uniform and exited, taking burned flesh and organs with it. Her second shot entered the second Mischene beneath his left scapula, cooked his heart, exited his far side, and blew debris up as the force of the laser burst slammed into the ground.

Three lasers answered her, two missing, but one catching her in the abs, tossing her backward, into the grill of the transport. She collapsed onto the street.

The drones opened fire on the incoming delta-wing fighter. Coop counted the distance in miles, then yards, and finally feet. Trusting the advanced gravitonic controls Nathan Trent incorporated in the ship's design specifically for high-speed dangerous maneuvers within the confines of an atmosphere, he spun the ship.

No one would engineer anti-G-Force tech for a craft traveling over Mach 6 to purposefully scrub speed by twirling like a ballerina. Especially a ballerina plowing into a line of drones protected by forcefields and firing lasers.

His eyes had fuzzy brown webbing at the edges, and his nose bled from both nostrils. His hands on the yoke nearly crushed the grips, but he and Cassie fought to bring the ship around. The bouncing into and off drones hurt and helped. The jarring impacts bruised his hips and shoulders, despite the ergonomic wrap of the pilot's seat. He felt his jaw disconnect and reconnect, and the pain stabbed up through his cheek. The pin-ball effect did drop his speed from four-thousand-six-hundred-miles-per-hour to coasting in less time than for him to press his left foot against an imaginary break pedal.

The ship ended facing away from the hillside, and, unlike in space, he could not simply flip the craft. He pressed the throttle, swung an arc, and came back from the opposite direction. Coop, the fighter pilot, test pilot, and trained sniper placed Cassandra feet above the surface.

The four swivel-mounted cannon under the wings laced white-hot solid light into the bodies advancing up the slope. Dozens died or were terminally wounded within seconds. Those who panicked and tried to rush up the hill were washed over by the ship's lasers or cut down from the two positions held by Elie's team.

The Marauders retreating, rushing back to the battle field and to the hundreds of soldiers lost and leaderless in the open kill zone, were allowed to leave.

"Cassie, drones?"

"Four destroyed by our impact or by impacting with each other," she reported. "LBJ destroyed two, and the other two have apparently been recalled to their ship. The Devee must have decided to limit their losses. I believe you said we would call this the bowling-ball maneuver."

"Set 'em up and knock 'em down," he said.

With the threat to the teams on the hill retreating, Coop turned his ship to face the kill zone. Hovering and without the need for aerodynamics he lowered the bomb-bay doors on the stern and deployed the tachyon cannon.

The remaining Zenge and few Mischene dropped weapons, and raised hands.

"Coop, it's Anton," Gregory called on the private channel. "We'll take over. The 109 needs your help, and where the hell have you been?"

"Elie, Coop. Status?"

A special METS, one redesigned by a team at Trent Industry following the near fatal laser shot to Daniel Cooper while preparing for Operation Crossroads, was built for Space Rangers. It was heavier and came with more dispersement than those worn by normal people. While the wind was knocked from her, and the colors on her flat stomach would be bright and varied for weeks, the suit did not allow penetration.

"Fuck," she said again, with much less fervor.

Thinking her dead, and marveling at the actions of the Wraith, Decadee and the two remaining Zenge stood watching their forces beaten by one small ship.

Elie lifted her pistol, decided her line of fire, and snapped off three blasts. Three hits. Three targets down. Mission complete.

"Elie, Coop. Status?"

"Coop, the hill is cleared. Looks like the fight is over." She did not mention her stomach felt like a mule kicked it.

"Coop, Elie, it's Storm," the Fellen joined the conversation. "Palmer is awake, in pain, but Khaled swears she will be fine. Broken ribs only. Everyone is okay. That was incredible flying, Coop. C.C. and Ash say thanks. Where the fuck have you been?"

"Ash as in the little girl with the big knife, and C.C. as in our C.C.?"

"Didn't mention them before because I thought you had enough pressure to deal with," Elie answered. "Since Storm asked, I'd like to know where you've been, too."

"I promise answers soon, but the 109 is still in danger, and a Devee ship is in our solar system. Coop, out."

"Fuck that man!" Storm said.

"First chance I get," Elie quipped.

"You can have seconds. Storm, out."

Ash and C.C. could not hear all sides of the private channel communications, but she heard enough to ask the Marine sergeant, "Who are you? Everyone seems to know you, but me."

"I would love to hear that answer," Tank said, dropping into the depression with Sgt. Palmer in his muscled arms. He gently set the Top Sergeant down. Her midsection wrapped in compression shielding to help prevent further injury.

"Me, too," she said. "I'd like to know why every commander on the planet knows you well enough to give you hugs instead of expecting a salute."

Cpt. Hafez and Peter slipped over the low rim and plopped down. Both beings beaten down by the battle. Both glad to find a quiet moment and a deep breath.

"Constance Cooper Galetti," Storm said. "Galetti is her mother's name. Mara Galetti."

"The woman who decoded the Martian files?" Palmer asked, sitting up and rudely reminded of her injury by the pain the movement caused. She lay back down. "That Galetti?" she asked from a prone position.

"Yes," C.C. confirmed.

"She's married to Nathan Trent," Khaled said. "Your father is the Head of Sciences for Space Fleet and owns Trent Industries?"

"Yes," C.C. replied. With her faceplate off and helmet cowl around her shoulders, it was impossible to not see her skin coloring moving closer to Ash's red shading. "I was named for Admiral Patterson's mother, Constance, and Daniel Cooper's father."

"Holy shit," Palmer said, holding an arm against her body. "If I had let you get killed I would have every big shot from the Admiral down to answer to. Thank you for staying alive C.C. But if you think I'm going to give you easier assignments, forget about it. I'm impressed, but I still got rank."

C.C. smiled. Always fearful the identity of her parents would cause friction with other Marines, glad to discover she had earned the respect of her team leader and parentage would not be an issue.

"Why did they name you for the Admiral's mother and Daniel Cooper's father?" Tank asked.

"That is a long story, and can wait until we make it back to Earth," the young woman answered.

"If there is an Earth to go back to," Elie said, joining them after hiking down the slope. "Coop said a Devee ship is in our solar system. It explains why disrupting communications was important to the Devee. That and keeping the 109 too busy to space-fold to a place where we could contact Space Fleet."

"They didn't want Earth warned," C.C. surmised. "What do we do?"

"We lick our wounds, make sure the prisoners are under control, and give the planet back to Peter and his people," Elie said. "Coop's obviously back from wherever, and he will warn Admiral Patterson."

"The Devee ship in this system?" Peter asked.

"Coop's first stop," Elie assured him.

Chapter 21

"There are two drones exiting the planet's atmosphere," Kennedy announced. "The Devee carrier has launched sixty-torpedoes."

"Sixty?" Genna asked.

"Four tubes releasing torpedoes every twenty-three-seconds. Fifteen total rounds."

"I wasn't questioning your math," Genna told the AI. "It seems like a large number. We could avoid all of them using standard space drive."

"Scans indicate the warheads are explosive and thermal-nuclear with proximity detonators," Kennedy added. "They may be intended to shake us with sufficient force to disrupt our shield emitter. The drones probing our shield defenses have backed off."

"Folly, pull back and give Lesego time to target the incoming torpedoes," Genna ordered.

"It may be more efficient to launch our own torpedoes," The Tac officer said. "I can set proximity detonation and with the incoming fish fairly bunched, I should be able to take out three or four of theirs with one of ours."

"Make it so," the avatar agreed. "The rail-gun is deployed. Use it to take out anything getting through."

"Aye, Captain," the South African answered. "Torpedoes armed, sequence set, and forward tubes are launching now."

Cosoi, oblivious to the battle action going on around her, left her station and walked across the bridge to stand beside the command chair. She offered Genna a wrapped candy.

"Go ahead," she said. "I know you steal them when I'm not around."

Genna popped the unwrapped bitter in her mouth and gave the Rumanian a questioning eyebrow raise.

"I can't hack the Devee," the person widely considered the best computer hacker on Earth informed her commander. "Not the carrier, and not the drones. I can't find a way to get a signal inside their ship. Unless they open a channel for communication directly between us, everything is closed tight."

"Forty-six incoming torpedoes have self-destructed," Lesego announced. "Their proximity settings triggered when ours detonated within range. Rail-gun is targeting the remaining fourteen. I have the laser cannon tracking in case I need to supplement."

"Have you ever come against closed environments before?" Genna asked. As someone permanently linked to a computer, she had a curiosity regarding potential threats relative to her own self-preservation.

"Sure. Everyone who gives a shit about security attempts to close their systems from outside influence, but unless the system is a self-contained operation without any external communications, and I mean none at all, there is always a vulnerable spot. Time is needed to locate it, and the real trick is deciding how to take advantage without setting off alarms. The Devee system may be the only one I have seen or heard of which maintains external communications and has no vulnerability. I mean, the whole time I've been searching for a back door, the ship has been communicating with the drones," Nadia said.

Genna realized she could not taste the chocolate melting under her tongue. The constant low hum, a sound like a faraway fan running on the lowest setting, which always reminded her she was in contact with Kennedy, did not provide the comfort it normally did. Never had she felt disconnected and distracted to this level. It was interesting and frightening.

"Genna? You okay?"

"I'm fine, Nadia," she assured the woman. "I'm trying to figure out how they can be invulnerable. They possess the ability to mask not only their exterior appearance, but create interiors capable of fooling our scans. How do you know they communicate with the drones? Have you monitored their transmissions? Can't you piggyback into their systems through the messaging?"

"All torpedoes are neutralized," Lesego announced. "Captain, while we were engaged the two drones from Phisor and the one standing off docked."

"They dropped shields?" Genna pushed the thoughts of closed computer systems aside and returned to the more dangerous issue at hand. "Did we take a shot?"

"No," the brown-skinned, dark-haired lieutenant answered. The simple answer given in a tone mixed with self-recrimination and shame. "No excuse, ma'am. I let the torpedoes occupy me and did not notice the change in their forcefield in time."

"Well, I have an excuse," Folly said from the pilot's chair. "Exhaustion. We've been going non-stop for hours. The torpedoes were fired to force us to retreat. The number fired guaranteed we would concentrate on preventing them from impacting the 109. The eight drones harassing us did not return to their ship. They played us to give them time to bring their other drones home."

"Kennedy, what's the carrier doing now?"

"Moving away," came the answer. "They have abandoned those left on the planet, collected whatever assets they could, and disengaged with us. The drones remaining in space have taken positions between us and the carrier's retreat."

"Nadia, how did you know they were communicating if you could not intercept the messages?" Genna asked again.

"Action and reaction," the older woman answered. "Drones are drones, and you can only preprogram x-number of variables. War creates way too many factors to design a logic train in advance capable of providing every response. When unexpected crap happened, the drones acted or reacted to the new circumstances after a short delay. The delay indicates they were accepting new directives. Anything preprogrammed would have kicked in seamlessly. No delay."

"Do you want me to follow the carrier?" Folly asked.

"John F. Kennedy, this is Daniel Cooper. Captain Bouvier, do you acknowledge?"

His voice came over the bridge communication speakers, which means through Kennedy. She already knew who was calling, verified authenticity, and piped him through. Why did he not use their private channel?

"Acknowledged, Captain," she answered. Silently she asked Kennedy, "How long have you known?"

The internal reply, AI to avatar, "He contacted me for a situation report before entering the Phisoran atmosphere to provide air-support for the Marines. We were busy and you needed to concentrate on the Devee ship."

"We will talk later," she promised the AI. Aloud she said, "Happy to know you're alive, Captain. I understand you've been busy on Phisor."

The others on the bridge turned to watch the commander. All were thunderstruck by the appearance - in voice at least - of the missing former Space Fleet officer. Now they were discovering he had engaged the Marauders on Phisor while they dealt with the Devee overhead.

"Communications in the system will remain spotty until the ion-fields clear," he said. "I thought I should inform you Captain Casalobos and Storm are secure. The planet is completely under the control of General Gregory and Space Fleet."

A howl erupted on the closed bridge. Pent up fear, anger, and frustration released on the word of good news. Much needed news. Genna glanced at her control displays embedded in the chair's left arm. Coop's news was being broadcast across all ship channels. Everyone heard. Now she knew why he opted for open communications. He intended to boost morale.

"The Devee carrier is making for the wormhole," Genna said. "Any opinion on the 109 following and re-engaging?"

"I'm not your commander, Genna, but if all you want is an opinion, I'd let them go. Kennedy and Cassandra have been exchanging information, and you appear to be too evenly matched to accomplish anything of value at this point. Whatever they wanted to collect from Phisor, they have. Their other mission was to keep you from contacting Earth and warning them about the potential of a Devee sneak attack. They blocked tachyon particle communication, and they know you will not abandon your position with the drones they left behind."

"If we go after them, or if we space-fold to the rim of the system, the drones will attack the surface," Genna said.

"Whoever the Devee truly are, they are experts at manipulating others," he said. "What they did not expect was Cassandra."

"You're leaving to warn the Admiral," Genna surmised.

"I'll send a message as soon as I clear the system, and will be there in less than a day," he confirmed. "The drones are nimble, but you should be able to bracket them with your remaining torpedoes. Shake them, then take them out when their forcefields drop. Your other option is blanket an entire region near them with a tachyon spread from your cannon. The sympathetic waves from the explosion will hit them with close to the same force as the tachyon blast. Between the two, I think they will lose shield integrity."

"Coop, it's Izzy. I hate to interrupt, but I may have something you can use when you return home."

"Then you should interrupt, Izzy. What do you have?"

"Nadia Cosoi has been attempting to hack into the Devee systems."

"Without any luck," Cosoi added aloud.

"I heard her bitching about closed systems impossible to hack," the communications officer continued. "It got me curious, so I went back to reexamine every scan. I extended the parameters for sound, data, visual, or other means of messaging. I began searching for any signs of particle wave disruption, ultrasound, or high and low frequency emissions. I found evidence of photon impaction."

"Quantum Key Distribution!" Cosoi yelled the three words. "QKD optical channels used with a diluted laser. Scientists on Earth gave up on them over a century ago. The links were too sensitive. They collapsed if a butterfly sneezed around them."

"Obviously the Devee made them butterfly-proof," Coop replied. "Thanks, Izzy, and you, too, Nadia. Genna, keep up the great work. Nice to see the 109 is still in capable hands with the best crew ever assembled in this part of the galaxy. Cooper, out."

"Wait," Diego called out. "He didn't say where he's been."

"Right now, it's more important where he's going," Genna said. "Lesego, detonate the rest of our torpedoes on top of those drones, and then finish them. Afterward, I want everyone replaced. You have performed exceedingly well under duress. Rest. As soon as we make sure Phisor is secure and our people are back on board, I believe Captain Casalobos will be taking this ship back to our own solar system.

Silently she asked Kennedy, "Did you learn anything from Cassandra?"

"Quite a lot," the AI replied. "Do you like stories about pirates and princesses?"

PART 3

contranym

ˈkäntrəˌnim

a word with two opposite meanings,
     e.g., sanction (which can mean both 'a penalty for disobeying a law'
and 'official permission or approval for an action').

Chapter 22

Earth

"I realize you are hesitant to bring the woman here," Sir Daniel said to al-Rahsid, "but Arcand is pushing his agenda through the Council. Should he accomplish half of his goals to solidify the government, tearing it apart will be twice as difficult."

"Which is why we need to concentrate on completing our own goals," the Arab countered. "Wasting our time convincing Miranda Muse to support regional rule is foolish."

"One of the cornerstones for success is convincing the public they will be better served by local governments. Equally important is turning public opinion against the UEC. We cannot target individual countries or regions. Civil unrest in a few locations will be quashed by the armed forces. To create a worldwide call to action, we must have voices people will follow. Voices the average person, regardless of where they live, will believe. The persona of Miranda Muse is the most influential social agent on Earth."

"She is not real," al-Rashid responded.

"The person behind the scenes is real, and for billions of people, Miranda Muse is real. They know the actor changes, but they do not care. I know I sound a bore, but let me repeat: billions around the world follow Miranda Muse."

"Fine. You and Montack met with the woman. Why is she ready to accept a sponsor?"

The Brit eased back into his chair. The argument was won. Now it was simply providing the man driving the Camarilla Dissolvere justifications he could understand and accept.

"I believe she is driven by two powerful motivations. She has her own doubts regarding a centralized government. She understands the purpose of the original creators to help safeguard the population and take control of resources from profit-mongers and warlords. She also sees the potential for massive corruption by an organization with limitless power."

"She sounds intelligent," the Arab conceded.

"Exceedingly bright," Sir Daniel added. "But I sensed another factor, and Arnold agrees. This current version of The Muse, Miss Amanda Peppers, is driven by more than providing well-thought-out commentary on current issues. She would like to profit from her position."

"Why do you and Arnold believe this?"

"Arnold's media interests are far-flung, and he has access to skilled researchers. Once we knew her real identity, a thorough background check was done. She is from a poor family in the mountains of Kentucky in the former United States. Had grades more than sufficient for college, but needed to work full-time as a waitress to afford school. Even so she excelled, especially in political science and philosophy."

"Sounds industrious, not mercenary."

"I never said she was a mercenary," Miller replied. "She is another post-Pandemic child with hopes and dreams, but living in a world where essential skills, not artistic abilities are valued. The loss of billions of people included the loss of labor. She has worked hard, moved ahead, and continued to write on social-political issues. Her op-ed pieces placed in minor publications and local platforms were recirculated on larger media sites. Her pieces resulted in the former Miranda Muse contacting her as a potential replacement."

"You sound as if you admire this woman."

"I will admit to it," Sir Daniel nodded as he answered. "She lives a simple life, in an inexpensive apartment, and sends funds and supplies to family she has left in Kentucky. She is not a stupid person. She sees an opportunity to change her life, become the person she dreamed of, and help her family. I would not call her a mercenary, but she is an opportunist."

"Your arguments are impressive, and I trust you and Arnold. Why must I meet with her?" al-Rashid asked. "Why here?"

"She knows who you are," the Brit answered. "Your public outing, and the constant notices across news platforms seeking your location make you the most important member of the opposition. However, I had the impression she did not care if you granted a personal interview. She wants proof we can accomplish our goal.

If she is to place her reputation, the reputation of Miranda Muse on the line to support the movement to dissolve the UEC, she wants to see the infrastructure. As she said to us, 'A movement does not move far on hot air.'"

"If we bring her here, and prove we have resources more substantial than hot air, she will work for us?"

"No. She will work for Montack Media Groups, and she will be paid a great deal of money, including a lifetime trust. Montack will relocate Ms. Peppers to an island in the Bahamas with a fully-supported studio she can work from. She will be given the deed to a substantial home located on the same island and a thirty-five-foot boat as a bonus."

"Honestly?"

"As I said, the young woman has dreams."

"From the sound of it calling her a mercenary would be polite." From his tone and body language, Saleh Abd al-Rashid felt better knowing Miranda Muse came at a steep cost.

"I'll arrange for security to transport her tomorrow," the British representative to the UEC said. "We made it clear she alone would be allowed to come. If you agree. I will have her picked up without notice. Once our people are with her, she will have no access to any communications. She will not be told the final destination, nor allowed to look out of any windows."

"She will know she is in a desert when she tours the facilities," al-Rashid said.

"But not which desert, my friend. Until Ms. Peppers is broadcasting with our people watching, we shall all be vigilant."

"More than that, my friend. When she agrees to our sponsorship, I will expect her first opinion to be broadcast from here. In fact, until her island home is prepared, which will not happen until the UEC is in ruins, I expect her to broadcast all of her future material from here.

"She may object."

"She may, but she will either do things my way or she will never leave this desert."

Amanda was excellent at getting people to relax. Attractive, but not beautiful, slender, and able to carry on a conversation about anything, or simply chatter. She once pretended to be a Space Fleet officer able to command a ship. The operation came close to ending in a catastrophe. She could be a seductress, which required her to set aside personal morality and replace it with duty. She was first-class at spying because she was adept at reading people.

"This ship can really move," she said.

Two security agents, a male and female, the same two who collected her from the Bethesda apartment sat at the rear of the cabin. Arnold Montack and his assistant, a pretty young man with a flair for Italian clothes, including soft leather shoes, sat on recliners facing her.

"I understand the reason the blinds are closed, but you can just feel the speed, can't you?" she directed at the assistant.

"Mach 3 top end," he said. The two bonded earlier over his choice of designer footwear. His smile growing as she gushed over the shoes.

"Don't know what that means, but it sounds fast," she replied. She knew exactly what it meant. Two-thousand-three-hundred-miles-per-hour. They may or may not be flying at top speed, but she now had a reference. They allowed her to keep her vintage wristwatch (after a detailed electronic scan proved it to be a vintage wristwatch). She would be able to estimate distance from Maryland. Unless they were flying in circles.

"Fastest non-military speed allowed by in-atmosphere shuttles," he responded. "Allows us to get anywhere on the planet quickly. And in luxury. Would you like more wine?"

"Myron, stop showing off," Montack said. "It's gauche."

Myron wrinkled his nose and gave a little pout at being corrected in front of his audience. Amanda thought he was too pretty to only be an assistant, and now knew he was Montack's boy-toy.

"What does the Camarilla think about Arcand's announcement of the new UEC constitution being brought up for a vote?" she asked the mogul.

"We think it's a waste of time, Ms. Peppers. The Governor is trying to solidify his hold on the world by legitimizing a central government. It's proof he's afraid people are ready to reject unification."

"And the release of the timetable for converting currencies to a single standard?"

"An attempt to change worldwide conversation from disillusionment to debate over financial stability," the older man answered.

"The reopening of the International Criminal Court?"

"A feeble warning to those like ourselves. If we continue to work for the overthrow of Arcand and the UEC, we face prison."

"I would not do well in prison," Myron said.

"Actually, you would do rather well," Montack replied. The snide comment indicated the relationship between the two might be waning.

"What do you think of those items, Amanda?" Myron asked, ignoring the slight and working his way into the discussion.

"I agree with Mr. Montack," she said. "He appears to have an understanding of Governor Arcand's motives."

Montack nodded and presented her with a smile of appreciation - or recognition of her fine judgement. His eyes slid down to where her short skirt and crossed legs provided a show of creamy skin. Montack was a switch-hitter, and Myron's time on the playing field was coming to an end.

She flicked a glance at the gay aide. He noticed and noted his Sugar Daddy's interest in Amanda.

She twisted her head as if relieving tension in her neck to take a glimpse of the two agents behind her.

Ex-military or similar training. She decided so when they first appeared at her door and began giving orders. From that moment she took little opportunities to act flustered, or stumble over impediments. Once she pretended to be startled by someone anyone with a little training would have seen coming from a long distance. She wanted them to mark her down in the column headed: civilian / low risk.

Arriving at the private hangar with the shuttle, she handed over her watch, necklace, and travel bag. These were taken to be thoroughly scanned, and anything a tiny bit suspicious would be left behind.

The female agent escorted her to a restroom where Amanda stripped and received a professional body search. At the appropriate times she giggled.

Since boarding the ship, the guards took their seats and began talking. Their disregard for her presence proved she had succeeded in lowering their estimation of her threat level. Zero was a pretty good number.

"We have another two-hours, Amanda," Montack informed her after checking his personal comm-data mini-pad. "Myron, pour the wine. And find us something to snack on. I don't know about Ms. Peppers, but I hear my appetite calling."

Myron just received his demotion from assistant to gopher. Amanda ran the numbers silently, and the time at top speed would place them in North Africa and Saudi Arabia. It could also place them in Japan.

Chapter 23

Tab and Cam lay atop a dune one mile east of the compound.

"The shuttle belongs to one of Montack's corporations," the black man said. The optics gun aimed at the craft not only captured an object and presented a detailed image on a screen attached to the barrel, it interfaced with a Marine Intelligence Division search engine. The specs on the craft, from dimensions to registration, were available for the asking.

"There is a reason special operations are not done under a full moon," Cam complained. "I feel exposed."

"One; we did not have a choice. Two; could be the skin-tight suit you're wearing."

"The suit was designed to allow me to blend into shadows. It is not meant to be worn in sunlight or beneath bright moonlight. I'm sorry if it distracts you."

"Doesn't distract me, but you left two young men with their jaws dragging the ground when you came out of the shuttle in it," Tab said. "Wasn't enough that it hugged you like a second skin, but with two slim-set Model .22 pistols holstered and a knife sheathed on both calves, I'm pretty sure you walked out of a graphic multi-player game."

"You think they would like to play with me?"

"I think they know better."

"Is Captain Black in there?" Cam asked, returning their attention to the issue.

"Probably. Two shuttles parked inside. The number of roving patrols have increased from the previous observations. Armed track-vehicles are in the open. The tracks have been spotted by overflights, but not the actual transports. Lights on in more buildings than normal for this time. Either they know we're here, or they have a VIP on site."

"Or both. The compound has sophisticated tech. They could have seen, heard, or been warned of a ship in the area."

"Maybe," he said. "If so, I would expect more activity outside the perimeters. Until we know otherwise, assume Amanda is inside. When she has the info or access to their plans, she'll send a sign. Until then, we do what we do."

"We wait," the Brazilian said.

"What are we waiting for?" Arcand demanded from Cassel. "If your analysts, the Marine analysts, and Col. Barnwell believe the Camarilla's new headquarters are in that compound in the middle of Saudi Arabia, why don't we send in operators?"

"Because al-Rashid is not stupid," Cassel answered. Called to a meeting with the head of the Board of Governors before breakfast meant the leader of the UEC was impatient. The Director of Security arrived knowing he must remain cool and calm to offset his fellow French-Canadian's desire for action.

"He built a mosque and a hospital for local children in the middle of his cloister. There are communications facilities capable of broadcasting over multiple media platforms, including bouncing signals off satellites. If UEC forces attack, the world will see us attacking a religious and humanitarian site."

"Send them in covert. That's what you do. Covert."

"Wouldn't matter," Cassel replied. "The Camarilla controls three-fifths of the news media. The experts they hire will make sure people think the UEC is behind any attack. We need to let Barnwell handle infiltration and elimination his way."

"What is his way? I haven't seen a single report on his mission plan. If it wasn't for you and Patterson telling me he's out there, I wouldn't know," the Governor complained.

"You haven't seen a report because we aren't creating any," the Director answered. "The Camarilla has shown they have spies inside the UEC, as well as the ability to hack secure communications. This operation is completely off the books. Tad Barnwell is a Space Ranger, a life-long Marine Intelligence officer, and a special operator. Captain Amanda Black is the best undercover agent on the planet. She has worked for the Marines, Space Fleet, and my agency since she graduated from the academy. Agent Valverde is my number one asset. Those three alone are more valuable, and more capable, than a platoon of soldiers."

"Make my day better, Paris," Arcand said. He took a deep breath and relaxed behind his desk. "Give me an idea of why you're backing Barnwell's plan. Convince me so I can move onto normal business."

"The compound is a hard site. We don't have a complete picture of how much firepower they have, but we know how al-Rashid works. It will be more than sufficient. A few special operators are more likely to get through security than a company of soldiers."

Cassel reminded Arcand, "We need their plans, not just two or three scalps. For that we need a spy on the inside. If we take down any of the leaders, we can't afford for them to come across as martyrs. There has to be proof the people in control of the operation are working for personal profit, and not motivated by philosophical differences. al-Rashid understands the importance of appearances, which is why he built the mosque and hospital."

With the cool that kept him alive as a spy for decades, Cassel continued his methodical explanation.

"We have a public relations war to win as important as preventing an armed revolution. If Barnwell fails, it's a blip. If we send in troops, or order Patterson to blow the damn place off the map from outer space, it pushes aside everything positive you are rolling out. The UEC becomes the devil."

Cassel stood still, allowing his arguments to settle.

"Do we have a back-up plan?"

"No. It would require planning and preparing assets, and we can't take the chance of warning the Camarilla."

"Do YOU have a back-up plan?"

"Of course," the Director and life-long top spy answered, adding a smile.

"You can turn it on," Stacey called.

Standing atop a formation of rocks, Billy activated the Fellen camouflage projectors. Four poles had been erected around the Space Fleet shuttle. Together they projected an image of the surrounding landscape Billy added to the program installed on the thin tablet given to him by Stacey with short instructions on how to take a picture, add it, and activate the pole-projectors.

"How's it look?" the girl from Fell asked.

"Perfect. From the top, it looks like the rest of the surface. You'd have to be standing on the ground looking directly at the shuttle to see it," he answered.

"When the sun comes up we're going to cook," Rosz said, wiping the dirt from his hands after helping install the poles.

"The shuttle is insulated for space flight," Chaspi said. "The maintenance staff removed most of the electronics, including the environmental controls, but it should keep us at least twenty-degrees cooler."

"I stand corrected," Rosz replied. "With an outside temp over one-hundred, we won't cook. We'll baste."

"We will be fine, Rosz-san," Kai said. "Perhaps a little uncomfortable, but nothing we cannot survive."

Billy joined Rosz as the Sensei left to explore the bowl behind the ship. The depression carved into the sand by years of winds.

"Speaking of uncomfortable, I thought you were going to melt when Valverde caught you staring at her," the human poked his alien friend.

"Caught us both," Rosz replied. "I recall your eyes dropping to your boots when she looked back."

"I'm beginning to believe my entire male life will be spent around women out of my league," Billy said. "Think about it. Stacey is gorgeous, brilliant, and kick-ass. Chaspi drives me crazy, and I know she's like your sister, but you can't tell me you don't see how hot she is."

"I see it," Rosz admitted. "Kai's daughter, Aya is an older Japanese version of Stacey. I feel like a child when I'm around her. At least I think she sees a child."

Billy nodded his head in understanding and sympathy, adding, "Now Valverde. Did you notice the outfit?"

"I saw what was inside the outfit," Rosz replied. "And the pistols. And the knives. She could kill us both."

"Easily," Billy agreed.

"What's easy?" Chaspi asked.

The two young men both started, unaware the girls had moved away from the shuttle and closer to where they stood talking.

"Nothing," Rosz answered quickly.

"True that," Billy added. "Nothing's easy."

"Sensei suggested we sleep while the shuttle is cool," Stacey said. "I reminded him we have METS aboard. If it does get too hot, we can use their environmental system to avoid heat stroke. Come on, Chaspi. The pilot and co-pilot seats are the softest things left on the ship."

"And they recline," Chaspi added with a smirk, heading back to the borrowed ship.

"If I have to watch Valverde walk around in a skintight suit, and see Stacey and Chaspi wearing those METS again, I'm going to need a cold shower," Billy said.

"If we are forced to wear METS suits we may need towels, but not for a shower," Rosz replied. "We'll have to tie them around our waists."

Billy needed a moment to follow. He looked down at his crotch, thought about the effect the women would have on his physiology, and said, "Shit."

Chapter 24

"After sunrise I will show you the communications center and the hospital," al-Rashid told Black. "You will be able to see the women's section of the Mosque, but no more."

"I understand," the undercover agent replied, making sure respect exuded from her tone. al-Rashid exhibited the ages-old attitude about professional women still held by the more radical elements of Islamic societies. Her best course of action was to control her natural tendencies toward such misogynists.

Of course he never came straight out to question her choice of profession as a woman, but he made all the little check points along the way. In less than two-hours of her arrival and initial meeting, he asked if she needed to recover from the trip; gave her advice on how to act around his soldiers, male or female; spoke on times changing and women becoming more independent (and not in a tone of appreciation).

"Four of our most important members are women," al-Rashid told her for the second time. "During and following the Pandemic, many males died. Post-pandemic, women were more abundant. The loss of skilled male workers opened many positions for women. It is important the world realize the centralization of government functions, especially laws and courts, will steal many advances women made over the past century."

Amanda wanted badly to scream that a centralized government meant less opportunity for men like al-Rashid to put their boot on a woman's neck. She choked it back, smiled, and allowed the Arab his moment.

"You have our operational outline for the coming months," he said, indicating the data-sheet in her hand. "When you select any item on the agenda, you will see a synopsis of activity. I'm afraid I cannot provide a more detailed guide until we have concluded our business and you have become an official member of the Camarilla Dissolvere."

"I understand," she said. "It makes solid operational sense."

The leader of the opposition stopped for a moment to look at the slender young woman with him.

Amanda provided a vacant smile in return, kicking herself for using a phrase like 'solid operational sense.'

al-Rashid smiled and nodded, and moved forward, expecting her to keep pace.

"These bunkers are where we work and sleep. The barracks would prove impractical, and it would not be secure for you to use one of the refurbished homes near the road. If you have special needs, should it be that time of month for instance, someone on staff will be able to find items for you."

Prick, she thought, but said, "Thank you. I have everything I need in my overnight bag."

"It has been a pleasure to actually meet the famous Miranda Muse," the olive-skinned man in the traditional garments of an Arab prince assured the out-of-place woman. "It will be a short night. I hope you rest well. Mr. Sweetwell has visited before. I am sure he would be happy to escort you to your quarters."

Mr. Sweetwell was Myron, who nodded politely.

"Ms. Muse will be staying in Room Fourteen. Her bags have already been delivered," al-Rashid told them both.

After being thoroughly examined, Amanda knew.

"Arnold and I have a few more details to discuss, and then we will be off to bed ourselves."

Black nearly choked, considering Arnold Montack's current relationship with Myron, and al-Rashid's unintended phrasing.

Montack and al-Rashid continued down the corridor, while Myron directed Amanda to the left, along an intersecting hallway.

The two security agents from the shuttle followed the pair.

"He's an equal-opportunity prick," Myron said to Amanda. He made sure his voice did not carry back to their guards.

Amanda nearly giggled.

"He dislikes modern women and gays equally. He dislikes the UEC more, so if working with women and gays helps overthrow the current condition, he'll live with it."

"After the overthrow?" she asked.

"He'll be another prick in the Middle East. We'll have our own places in the world. If I understood correctly, Arnold is looking for a suitable island in the Bahamas for you. Dreamy."

"Montack is considering replacing you," Amanda said. She liked this flip young man, regardless of his affiliation with the wrong side.

"Won't be the first time," he confided. "He has to sample from time to time, but he always calls, apologizes, and brings me back."

"You come every time?"

This time Myron was the one unable to stifle giggles.

"I cannot believe you asked that?" he said between little hiccups.

Amanda, realizing her own malapropism, began laughing. The two stoic watchdogs remained at a distance. Neither seemed pleased with babysitting children.

"You would think someone who makes a living using words would be better at conversation," Amanda said.

"Yes, you would," Myron agreed. "Here is your room, Amanda. The door will be locked, but you will find everything you need inside. Unless, of course, I need to run to the apothecary for feminine products," he quipped.

"I'm fine," she assured him.

"Good. I will knock at seven and escort you to breakfast. Tomorrow will be a busy day. Amanda."

"Yes, Myron?"

"I'm glad you're here," he said in earnest. "It's a pleasure having someone real to talk with. Goodnight."

Amanda Black closed the door and leaned her weight against the metal. Tomorrow would be a busy day.

Tab woke Cam.

"Stay low," he warned. "The sun is coming up behind us. Our silhouettes can be seen from the compound."

"Did you stay awake all night?"

"Benefit of the Space Ranger Project," he said. "My metabolism can maintain a higher level of activity longer, and I require less recovery time."

"Do you think they will ever revisit the program?" the granddaughter of another Space Ranger asked.

"Would you volunteer?"

"In a second."

"If they ever find out why twelve survived and nearly two-hundred died, they might," he replied. "I would vote against it."

"Only ten Space Rangers are alive. Do you want to keep it a private club?"

"It's no club," the African-American said. "For the most part, we're friends, but we've all experienced pain as a direct result of the project."

"I thought you regenerated. Injuries healed miraculously."

"There's no miracle about being a Space Ranger, Cam. Our physical wounds heal because of genetic reengineering, not because of divine intervention. The pains we cannot beat are emotional. Like watching family and friends grow old and pass on."

"You can make new friends," she said. "We're friends."

"And the pain will cycle through again and again," he answered, voice weary as he fell to a moment of introspection. "The increase in our lifespan guarantees we will experience the loss of people we love over and over."

"You could stop caring," she replied.

"Then we would live without a soul," he answered. "What would be the point?"

"Tab, you always speak of your new self . . . your abilities and your liabilities as we and our. You rarely say what you experience."

"Compensation," he answered. "One way of making myself feel connected, and not freaky. Don't want to be the cat in a yard filled with dogs."

"It's not so bad as long as you're a panther," she countered.

"Cam, I understand you want to be the wildcat in the jungle," he told the much younger woman. "You are a copy of Ali in many ways, but you need to learn something she did not."

The Brazilian rolled to her side. Her odd glacier blue eyes turned on the American, waiting.

"Use your brain. If you let your emotions rule your actions, you'll place yourself in a position you won't walk away from."

"My emotions are under control," she assured the mission commander. "Until they are not," she added, looking back toward the compound. "Then it will be others who do not walk away."

Changing the topic, the Brazilian said, "I believe Captain Black is on a field trip."

Barnwell placed the optic-rifle-display atop the dune and focused on a group walking from the office building toward the communications center.

He gave a low whistle. "This is what we came for."

Myron knocked at precisely seven-o'clock.

Black, conscious of her potential errors the previous day, purposefully answered in a tone indicating she was awakened by the sound. The fact she slept soundly, and late should indicate a lack of military training.

"Sorry, Myron," she called. "I forgot to set my alarm. If you have a key, come on in."

The dapper man entered, dressed in smart desert attire one would expect from a modern Lawrence.

Amanda sat up on the bed, rubbing her eyes. She wore a thin tank-top.

"Give me five," she said. "I need a quick shower. What should I wear?"

"Light colors, and cover your skin," he called to her back as she lurched to the attached bathroom. Dressed in only a tank and a pair of pink panties indicated she was too sleepy to care about his seeing her nearly nude. Perhaps because he was gay, she didn't care. Perhaps she did not care regardless.

"Cover myself to show proper respect to the men?" she asked, leaving the door to the bathroom open.

"Because the sun will give you skin cancer and wrinkles," he answered.

"Skin cancer I can deal with, but not the wrinkles," she quipped before stepping into the spray from the shower.

Continuing her fieldcraft, and because Amanda Black was not someone known for modesty, she soon returned wearing a towel.

Once she collected underwear, a long-sleeve beige shirt, khaki slacks, and socks from her bag, the towel came off.

"You look like an athlete," Myron complimented her.

"Good genes," she answered as she dressed. "I couldn't run a block without having a heart attack. Working on the research, preparing and putting out the Miranda Muse commentary doesn't leave much time for exercise."

When they arrived at the mess, she found the kitchen provided a variety of food options, and a distinguished, if evil, group of people to share breakfast.

al-Rashid and a beautiful woman with Asian features sat at the head of a group of tables pushed together. She placed her tray on the table and took the open seat beside al-Rashid. Myron was relegated to a place at the far end of the tables.

"Good morning, Ms. Muse," the Arab said. "You know Arnold, and I am sure you know most of the others here by reputation. Beside you is Alexandra Vasluianu. Your commentaries are broadcast on many of her social media platforms."

The Russian said, "All of them." The woman could be fifty or seventy. Plastic surgery lifted worn skin, and smoothed it across prominent facial bones. Expensive work, but done a few times too many not to show. She had rich red (dyed) hair and watery grey eyes.

"Sir Daniel Miller sits on Alexa's other side."

The British lord and UEC member leaned forward to nod before returning to his food.

"The gentleman next in line is Imam Fahad Dardir. Imam Dardir is a well-known Islamic scholar. He is in charge of the mosque and leads us in prayer."

The hawk-nosed man wore a white turban and matching thawb. He made no effort to make eye contact.

"Across from you is Princess Wei Zhou Nanke of the Japanese Royal Family."

"Wei Zhou hime," Amanda said, addressing her as a Royal; adding a compact, respectful bow.

The Princess returned a smaller nod, but said nothing in return.

"Keiko Takei is Princess Wei's personal assistant."

The two young women nodded across the table.

"Next to Ms. Takei is Ali Khadr, my Chief of Security."

Another Arab, male and muscled, did not make eye contact, continuing to down his cereal. He wore desert cammo.

Myron, seated beside the Security Chief, appeared inconsequential.

"When we complete our meal, I will take those interested on a tour of the facilities. I have been assured by Sir Daniel we do not need to concern ourselves with satellites, drones, or high-altitude overflights, so we can travel above ground. It is not as cool as using the tunnels, but provides a more impressive view."

Tunnels. No one mentioned a tunnel network in any of the analytical reports on the compound. Amanda wondered if Tab knew, and decided he did not. He would have mentioned tunnels.

Chapter 25

The display provided names and biographies for the people with Amanda. It supplied truncated resumes for the half-dozen security guards attending the VIPs.

"The security jumped when they came out of the office building," Cam said. She watched the whole picture while Tab concentrated on individual targets. He returned his focus on Amanda, looking for any signs of apprehension.

"Good," he said. "It means it will drop lower when the field trip is over." He named each person. Some he knew by sight, and the others identified by the optic-search link.

"You were right," she said. "al-Rashid and most of the major players in the conspiracy are here. Using Miranda Muse for bait was genius. When do we move in?"

"Once Amanda gives me a signal she has their plans," he said. "You have to promise me this isn't a kill-only job for you, Cam. Otherwise, I go in alone."

"The brains behind destroying thirty-years of work, thirty-years of developing the foundation for a unified planet are one-mile away, and days from turning Earth into a fractured world again," she said. The normal calm control tamped down by the anger in her voice. "al-Rashid's father started this conspiracy, and he built the movement on my grandmother's murder. I was sent to eliminate the threat."

Tab lowered the optic-gun to watch and listen to Cam.

"I have no problem eliminating the threat," he said. "If we kill Miller or Nanke the threat will escalate. There isn't enough proof we could give the Brits or the Japanese to justify assassinating them. Montack's and Vasluianu's people will go nuts flashing their deaths across every single news-platform around the world, and they will push the narrative the UEC attacked free speech. al-Rashid will become a martyr. A devout Muslim slain on the doorstep of a mosque."

"I'm an assassin," she said, the cold returned to her tone. "You knew that when you asked Paris for my help."

"You're an operator," he countered. "You have the ability to get in, get close, take out your target, and escape. I need those skills, except only take out targets which pose an immediate threat to the success of the mission."

"Someone trying to kill you or me?" she asked.

"Fine. Or Amanda," he added.

"We could end the Camarilla now," she argued.

"We could do it by firing a tachyon cannon at them from EMS2," he replied. "That would not stop the movement."

"What have you decided will stop the movement?"

"Light," he answered. "Bad critters come out at night. Things that will rip you to shreds, but shine a light on them, and they run. We are going to get the information Amanda collects, and we are going to use it with the other evidence agencies have collecting for the last thirty years to put these bastards on trial."

Cam rolled to her back and placed a hand over her mouth to stifle laughter from crossing the still desert landscape.

"Our mission is to collect evidence for a trial," she said. "A trial could take a decade with the resources these people control. Do you think they will not continue their plans?"

"Not from prison cells," he said. "The UEC will announce the return of the International Criminal Court in a day or two. The court will not allow the Camarilla to post bail. The warrants for their arrest will include warrants for search and seizure. Government and military agents will be raiding businesses, including media offices, around the globe. The detailed search of records, including breaking through encryptions of anyone who fails to comply, will also take years."

"Your light includes placing the leaders of the Camarilla into dark cells," she said. "The grand plan is to strangle the conspiracy."

"All the time showing the world what they are, what they were attempting, and the personal profits they intended to gain."

"News leaks?"

"News Releases," he countered. "As evidence is brought forward for judges to consider, the UEC PR division will allow some made public to prove the government is acting honorably, giving the conspirators an open and public trial," he replied. "And news leaks, too," he added.

"You have all of this planned out. But you do not control the media or the social platforms the way Montack, Vasluianu, and their circle of friends do."

"Greed," he said. "The same motivation behind the Camarilla Dissolvere will be the driving force behind their failure. With the heads of the conglomerates locked away and their assets tied up legally, two events will occur."

"Their circle of friends will move in to snatch away pieces of their empires," Cam surmised quickly.

"With a little assistance from UEC agencies in charge of business and financial operations," Tab confirmed. "The government cannot allow the free press to fail, nor allow the men and women of information superhighways to lose their jobs because their owner is mired in criminal charges."

"Stewardships will be offered to competitors, with the promise they will receive full rights if the criminals are found guilty," Cam added. "Brilliant."

"The UEC Communications and Civilian Information Freedom Agency within the UEC Trade Department will be vetting the top officers and administrators working for Montack and Vasluianu. Some will be asked to take more administrative control."

"Kill them from within," she said. "Small bosses become big bosses, and to make sure they stay on top, provide shit on their former bosses. Greed."

"We get Amanda, get out, and the wheels of justice begin to turn," Tab said.

"If that's the plan, why not let Amanda get the info and bring it out when she leaves?"

"Time. We've been watching, listening, and analyzing. Every intelligence agency working on any part of the Camarilla conspiracy agree something explosive is about to happen. Adding Miranda Muse is the capper. Because we believe time is crucial, they may not allow her out until their plans go operational. Finally, the evidence. No way they will let her take out anything damaging. It would be her word against theirs."

"We're not going in alone, are we?"

"Kai and I will locate and extract Amanda, including any physical evidence she has or can get her hands on. Stacey and you will hit the communications center. She will hack the mainframe while you set explosives. Billy will be placing explosives around the outer perimeters. When we contact him with our quickest exit route, he'll open the path."

"Chaspi and Rosz fly in for pick-up, and off we go," Cam concluded. "Only the compound has four batteries, one massive mobile strike vehicle, three smaller patrol vehicles, and four guard towers I can see from here, and probably more dangerous secrets I cannot see. The shuttle will be toast."

"Have faith, Cam," he said. "Have faith."

"From this location we can access the world," al-Rashid said.

"We should be able to access the galaxy," Wei interrupted. "The funds spent on this one facility are greater than all other expenses combined."

"Worth the investment," al-Rashid assured the Japanese member of the Camarilla.

"Dr. Sonam Sharma is my Director of Communications," the Saudi introduced a thirty-something woman of Indian heritage. "She will give you an overview of what we are capable of accomplishing and how."

Her dark hair pulled back made her dark eyes appear larger. The light olive complexion of her skin indicated she did not often venture into the harsh sunlight of the desert kingdom. Wearing a vibrant tunic and cream slacks indicated she did not cow-tow to the local Muslim sensibilities. The doctor knew her value.

"You stand before augmented reality," she said, sweeping her hand in an arch to introduce her tech-heavy studio. She slipped an open electronic glove over her right hand, the fingers and thumbs covered with wires connecting them at a banded wrist cuff.

A virtual globe of the Earth appeared in the center of the crowded room. It startled a couple of the people when they found themselves surrounded by the planet.

Sharma shrank the display and raised it above their collected heads. "You are viewing the world through a technological overlay. I can request real-time digital information from anyplace we can access via a communication link," she informed them.

"If I access any video system and a person's face appears, the overlay will display the person's name. With a finger-click I can recover all data on that person stored within multiple storage banks operating on Earth."

"Do you have access to government and military communications?" Amanda asked.

"The lower level communications," Sharma answered. "The Camarilla is working on accessing the more secure systems from another location."

al-Rashid coughed. Sharma received the warning to limit her discussion to this location.

"We have overcome language barriers with real-time translation," she said to bring attention back to her operation. "With everyone sharing their lives through community platforms, there is a wealth of information available. Similar to how the first great social media giants used this wealth to produce content to change how people perceived the world. We are mining this data to create messages to lead people away from the concept of a united planet."

"When the governments discovered the depth of manipulation available to those giants, laws were enacted to curtail their access," Amanda reminded the doctor. "Our personal communications devices now come with filters to prevent collection."

"Direct collection, yes. But no public domain platform is secure from being overheard or viewed," the tech expert said. She walked to a console and a beam shot from the desktop into the virtual Earth hovering overhead. "We have artificial intelligence controlled eavesdropping programmed to search for specific targets of interest and recreate their conversations or image sharing. These are stored, cataloged, and used however best benefits the Camarilla."

"You don't have the ability to recreate everyone's communications," Amanda said.

"It would be too much data, and ninety-nine-percent trivial and worthless," Sharma responded.

"Dr. Sharma supplied our media platforms with information and insights which allow us to create messages more likely to resonate with people who watch or listen," Montack interjected. "She has been able to help us define our messaging in ways that impact specific regions, as well as develop catch-phrases and concepts which resonate globally."

"A major goal of our center is to change how people think," al-Rashid said. "That alone is worth the cost of research and development. But we can also broadcast."

"There are two major broadcast capabilities," Sharma said. "We can directly communicate with our operatives on a highly secure network. Using the satellites owned by the Montack and Vasluianu corporation, and securing our private communications by using encryption through a Japanese satellite, we can speak openly among ourselves without fear of being hacked."

"For example," al-Rashid tapped a bud worn in his right ear. "Commander Chanda, are your assets in place?"

The globe overhead changed as it zoomed into northern Africa, and then Egypt. The image of the Nigerian rebel, Katherine Chanda appeared beside the virtual map.

"I have units in Cairo, Jerusalem, Tripoli, and Algiers," she answered. "When we announce a wave of unrest, my people will make sure the unrest is violent. I have others dressed in military uniforms of the UEC forces. They will make sure a large number of civilian casualties are blamed on the new government."

"Lorena," al-Rashid said aloud.

The virtual globe, whirled around and displayed Central America. The image of the Latina Lorena Aragon appeared above the Caribbean Sea.

"The UEC administration sites in Mexico City, Nicaragua, Panama, Bogota, and Caracas are covered by my cartels," she said without prompting. "When they are attacked, the UEC will send forces. When they arrive, we will attack and the locations assure many people will be caught in the crossfire."

"The media, ours and all others, will rush to show the carnage and the despotic nature of the UEC," al-Rashid said.

The images of the two women disappeared.

"You intend to call for world-wide demonstrations to object to the centralization of world government," Amanda said. "When the people move into the streets you plan to ignite violence in certain locations. You will then broadcast UEC forces reacting with greater violence. A lot of innocent people will die."

"You can help us reduce the number of innocent deaths, Ms. Muse," the mastermind of the conspiracy responded. "With your voice added to what we already control, you can bring more people out to show their support for regional rule. The more people, the less likely the UEC will act forcefully."

"But it will not change your plan to instigate violence in North Africa and Central and South America," she countered.

"No," he admitted. "To fan the flames where the public will turn against the UEC, they must see blood. People will be sacrificed, but fewer than if we have to continue the process across more continents."

"What if the UEC shuts down communications and prevents your outlets from distributing the images?"

"That requires controlling hundreds of orbital satellites," Wei answered for al-Rashid. "Space Fleet is tasked with maintaining satellite surveillance, and they will be otherwise occupied."

The Japanese Princess continued, "Their own communications will be disrupted, leaving only this center capable of worldwide distribution of voice and image data for at least a few days."

"Crucial days," al-Rashid added.

"I see you have made your plans, but I don't see how you can disrupt government and military communications without interfering with your own. Unless I understand how you get around the problem, I can't see putting my brand on the line."

"Modern communications rely heavily on ionized atoms," Sharma decided to answer the question. "Communications pass through the atmosphere, or through space, riding atoms which have been made electrically positive or negative. Even the incredible STORM-HATCH system relies on tachyon particles. If the ability to ionize atoms is suspended, communications are suspended. Except for antiquated hard-lines, which no one has used for several decades."

"I understand basic communications tech," Amanda replied. "You pick stuff up when you rely on the systems. If you could suspend ionization, which is doubtful, you take down your own systems."

"Unless we do not completely rely on atmospheric sound waves," Sharma answered. She could not hide the smug satisfaction in the less-than-specific reply.

"Quantum-based communications use photons which are particles of light," Wei interjected, stealing the spotlight from the Indian. "Communications between photon particles require low-frequency lasers. We have installed reflectors on the satellites we control. This way we can communicate with our resources around the globe. We will also be able to transmit images over the commercial networks. Sound will be a problem because those networks are not adaptable for voice. You, Ms. Peppers, in your role as Miranda Muse, will be our voice."

"I'm getting a bit overwhelmed," Amanda admitted. "I'm your voice, how?"

"Your show is transmitted in several formats, including a blog-style. We can transmit your words across the images," the Japanese Princess explained.

"You sit here and write," Sharma said, indicating a simple chair and desk. "The words are scanned into a photo-imager, then reproduced and translated for wherever we broadcast using the quantum key-net Princess Wei provided."

"Tonight you will deliver your first message predicting the failure of the UEC to act as a humane organization. You will join the voices on other platforms encouraging people to peacefully demonstrate their opposition to a central government," Sir Daniel entered the conversation.

"Our most respected on-air personalities have already begun to disseminate this message," Montack added.

"In two days you will be the only voice the entire world hears," al-Rashid said. His tone added gravity to the proceedings.

"Reads, not hears," Sharma corrected.

"Whatever," the Saudi Arabian responded to his pronouncement being stepped upon with a blistering stare at his communication expert.

"I get my island, and I keep my show?" Amanda asked, ready to set the hook on the people who thought they were the anglers.

"I have three possible sites for you to choose from," Montack answered.

"Two days?" she asked.

"Three at most," al-Rashid said. "We must act before Arcand can complete his legitimization of the UEC. We hope to disrupt the communications grids within this time, but we are prepared to move forward regardless. If this is the case, you will be one of many commenting on the vile acts of the military against civilians."

"I'm in," Amanda said. "Now what?"

"We complete our tour of the compound, though everything else will seem dull. Then you can begin preparing your shows," the Arab said.

"Will you provide enough information for me to make edits on the go?"

"You will have access to many more details. The outline sheet I gave you will be linked to Dr. Sharma's system. However, from this point forward you will have no access to anyone outside of this compound. Do you understand, Ms. Muse?"

"Completely," she answered.

Exiting the Communications Center, the group walked past a platform. No one explained it housed a laser cannon. A few steps beyond the battery emplacement, on the path toward the front entrance to the Mosque, Amanda became agitated.

She began slapping at her chest and shoulders, and whirled. Without warning she stripped her shirt over her head and waved it.

Myron quickly wrapped arms around her, more to cover her exposed skin than stop her gyrations.

"You can't take your clothes off in front of a bunch of Islamic extremist at a mosque," he whispered urgently into her ear.

"Something was inside my shirt," she complained. "I think it stung me."

"Put your shirt on, Amanda, or you'll get worse than stung," he told her.

She pulled the top on, explained for the others what occurred, and lived with the looks of humor by infidels and anger by believers.

"What was that?" Cam asked.

"A think that was our signal," Tab replied, pushing backward to skinny down the dune without being seen.

"You think?" she asked, belly down to slither along side.

"We couldn't be sure how she would be able to make contact," he answered. "She said to expect something dramatic."

"That act was pretty dramatic," Cam agreed. "Or something with a bite got inside her clothes."

Chapter 26

"Cam, Kai, Stacey, and I will enter through the front gate," Tab told the team gathered inside the shell of the Picard. "The bus used to bring and return kids to the local villages and farms leaves at eighteen-hundred-hours. The sun sets at eighteen-zero-six, and it will be in the guards' eyes. We'll have long shadows and a grey sky to enhance the METS optical camouflage ability."

"How do you expect us to get close?" Kai asked. "Even with the METS, trying to cross an open area with motion detectors, sensors, and eyes watching will be impossible."

"I doubt they have sensors on the road itself," Tab said, "and I asked Admiral Patterson for a favor."

"You risked communications this near their compound?" Chaspi asked.

He tapped his neck and replied, "Private channel. It's possible to detect, but doubtful. Besides, I had no other choice. The Admiral and I discussed the possibility before the mission began. A prearranged two-word signal to call for the distraction. The team will reach the entry gate while everyone looks the other way."

"What could make everyone look away long enough for you to get into the compound?" Chaspi asked.

"An abandoned satellite is going to drop out of orbit. The resulting fireball will be to the east as it plummets for the Red Sea. The Space Force division which monitors objects around the planet already began issuing alerts about the expected failure. It's a huge platform replaced a long time ago, and large enough to come down like a comet."

"If you get inside, how do you locate Captain Black?" Billy asked.

"From what we observed, they must be using underground bunkers. The office building beside the mosque is the obvious entry point. Once we get underground, I have a low-yield radium-226 detector integrated within my METS."

"Radium-226?" Billy again.

"Antique watches sometimes used radium-226 to make their faces glow at night. It allowed the wearer to see the face without an external light. Amanda is wearing vintage pieces of jewelry, including a watch. It makes it appear to be a style-fetish for her."

"Stacey and I will head directly for the communications center," Cam said.

"How do you get out?" Chaspi asked.

"We have to assume we're going to trip alarms or come up against opposition," the Marine Colonel said. "Billy goes with us to the front gate, but he breaks off. He will place charges at four-to-six locations around the perimeter."

"The fences will be tagged, but I doubt they will have sensors too near them. The two systems would constantly be tripping each other," the young engineered said. "I won't be able to set up anything capable of taking out both barriers."

"They use vehicles to inspect the outside," Chaspi added. "Billy will be exposed."

"It will be getting dark," Tab replied. "The exterior sentries aren't on a schedule, and they may not take a ride with the VIPs inside the compound. If they do he should have time to hunker down and rely on the METS."

"If they still see him?" she asked, her concern obvious.

"How do I know when and which section to blow?" Billy asked, changing the subject.

Tab pulled a satchel out of a storage net and placed it at his feet with a mischievous smile. "Glad you asked," he said.

He extracted hand-held devices with knobs and metal antenna, handing one to each team member. Next came earbuds with wires attached.

"These are called walkie-talkies," he announced. "A couple-of-hundred-years ago, these were how field operators stayed in touch."

Stacey pulled on the metal tip of the antenna and it extended. She said, "You're kidding."

"Nope. The headsets are plugged into the unit. The first knob selects the channel, and the second one controls volume. Push down the button on the side to talk, and let go to listen."

"There's only two channels," Chaspi noted.

"Everyone set your walkie-talkie on channel One," Tab ordered. "Put your earbuds in so someone calling you won't be overheard, and make sure you keep the volume turned up because we will need to speak softly."

"We'll be detected," Rosz said.

"Not likely," the Marine with an affection with old things answered. "They broadcast over the electromagnetic spectrum at 460mhz. No one uses the lower frequencies anymore. These units are only effective up to three-miles."

"Your plan is to use the latest military technology integrated within the METS to locate Captain Black by tracking an antique watch, and we stay in touch with wacky-talkies?" Cam asked.

"WALKIE-talkies," he replied. "Each step in the mission plan will be designated by a two-word phrase. After we're inside the gate, I'll say Mango Stamp. Billy, Chaspi, and Rosz will know we've begun the next step."

"Mango Stamp?" Rosz asked.

"Random generated words so if something is overheard it will make no sense," Barnwell answered. He turned on a holo-board display and expanded it to list the salient mission objectives and the two words that would indicate object accomplished.

"At least you are successful at making no sense," Rosz remarked as he read the phrases.

"If we make it to the point of exfiltration without raising an alarm, we'll use the lasers to cut through the inner fence. Billy, will blast a hole in the outer fence and join us," Barnwell continued. "Memorize the mission objective terms."

"Rosz and I?" Chaspi asked.

"When the explosives take down the barrier, that's your cue to get airborne. You have sensors installed to locate us. Land, pick us up, and off we go," Barnwell said.

"Bullshit," Chaspi replied. The doe-eyed alien with the soft pink skin was red-faced and angry. "It is because we are Bosine," she added. "We are the docile aliens. We cannot be trusted to fight at the front, or take the kill shot, so we get left behind to be bus drivers."

She stomped from the shuttle.

Stacey, Billy, and Rosz started to follow when Sensei Kai ordered, "Stop! I will talk with her. You continue your planning."

The Japanese instructor caught up to the young woman as she stopped at the edge of the yardang.

"Chaspi, I am ashamed at your stupidity," he said. His tone gruff, in the manner used when he displayed annoyance at a poorly executed punch or kick.

"Stupidity?" she fired back. "Bigotry. I am not a coward. Rosz is not a coward."

"You are a Space Fleet Cadet," Kai countered. "What is Rosz?"

"An alien?" she answered with a snide questioning tone.

"A civilian," the older man responded. "What is your responsibility regarding civilians?"

"To protect and secure their safety," she murmured.

"What is your position on this team?" he demanded.

"Back-up pilot," she answered.

"Chaspi, that is only one reason Col. Barnwell recruited you. You are a pilot, a communications expert, and a soldier. If anything happens to any of us, you are the one person capable of taking their position and completing the mission. Col. Barnwell is not leaving you behind because you are an alien or untrustworthy. He is counting on you to protect Rosz and to do whatever is necessary to protect his team. The Colonel trusts you the most, Chaspi. Please do not act like a child."

The tone was harsh, but the words moving.

The Bosine from Osperantue hugged the man from Japan, wiped her eyes dry, and replaced a tiny smile with a stern face.

"Thank you, Sensei," she said, giving a short, formal bow. "I will never act like a child again."

She returned to the shuttle with purpose, her friend and teacher proud to walk beside her.

"I need the room," Wei told the two techs monitoring the communications center.

Aware of her status, they made no comment, and certainly no objection, leaving The Power and her aide the privacy she demanded.

Wei sat down and booted the laser-optical channel designed to operate when the other systems failed.

"Giving al-Rashid and his lackeys the secrets to quantum key distribution was necessary for the success of the mission," she told Keiko. "But it also makes it easier to communicate with the Ambassador. The QKD system I brought with me from Devisator is not easy to transport."

"His communications professionals have made significant improvements," the young Japanese woman replied. "This station is much more powerful than the one we use in Tokyo, and they miniaturized transceivers for their field units."

"Those smaller units can only communicate with the central command located here," Wei said as she aimed the laser situated above the roof toward the region in outer space the Devee Battle-Naut occupied. "It is a pain in the ass for orders between units to be bounced here first."

"With time, they will find a solution," Keiko said.

"Ambassador, this is Tuito Wei."

"Tuito Wei, this is the Ambassador. Pidita Jax is available."

"Jax, the pieces are in place on Earth. I need to know when you will arrive."

"I am twenty-hours from beginning the mission," the ship's commander replied. "Depending on the level of resistance, I suspect another few hours to eliminate any threats and recover the Nakki data. I will proceed to Earth thereafter. I estimate forty-nine-hours."

"Which is more than three-Earth-days, Pidita Jax," Wei complained. "The operation to create chaos and interfere with the response by the Earthers must begin sooner. Too many pieces of my plan are in place."

"Then your plan will begin and we will arrive when we arrive, Wei," Jax replied. Unlike the people she bullied on Earth, the captain of the Ambassador, and a member of the Traders' caste did not fear Wei. "However, I see no reason I cannot move our timetable forward a few hours. I can use additional speed. The Ambassador could possibly arrive in forty-hours."

Wei wanted badly to scream at the Pidita pisser on the far side of the sun, but recognized she needed the Devee ship and its firepower. It was her ride home. Antagonizing the captain would accomplish nothing.

"Thank you, Jax. I wish you the best bargain in completing your mission and free sky reaching Earth."

"Good bargain and large profits, Wei, on your grand plan. I will contact you when we begin the turn for Earth."

Wei sat back. The bitch had told her *don't call me, I'll call you* in Devee.

A knock at the door interrupted her hateful thoughts. One of the techs looked in and said, "You might want to come above ground. The sky is on fire."

Wei looked to her aide, who explained, "The satellite reentering the atmosphere today," she reminded her boss. "I believe that is what he means."

"We might as well go watch the sky burn," the disguised Devee said. "I have nothing to do now but waste time."

Chapter 27

Barnwell, Valverde, Stacey, Ishihara, and Elkman walked along the right side of the paved roadway connecting the compound to the highway. From the shuttle, they crossed open country and connected to the road half-way between the two points. It required hours of difficult travel across rocky land, sandy dunes, and weird circular patches of farmland. The METS kept them comfortable, but the trek was tiring.

They took a break at reaching the paved path wide enough for trucks and buses to pass in different directions.

The team came prepared with technology spanning centuries of tactical warfare.

They carried compact weapons which could be concealed inside the highly-evolved METS, making strange bulges and leaving bruises. Bladed weapons, the choice of special operators for thousands of years, were strapped to thighs, calves, or across backs. The Twenty-First-Century walkie-talkies attached to their upper arms with a hard-wire snaked through a pin-hole in the suit's fabric for an earbud. If any vehicles came, they planned to drop into the shallow ditch created when the road was built.

Their optic enhancements picked up the incoming satellite long before the naked eye would see the burst of light and the fiery tail.

"If we pick up the pace we should be at the gate when the main section of the platform is the most visible," Barnwell said. "But don't run," he warned. "The faster you move, the less refracted light, and the more visible you become."

One-hundred-yards from the entry point, they stopped. The 10x magnification provided by their helmets showed four sentries transfixed by the light show in the cloudless Arabian sky.

"Billy, go," Barnwell ordered.

The young man, his suit the strangest looking (when visible) because of the number of explosive discs he carried, ghosted toward the outer fence. Because of the discs, he did not carry a firearm.

Luck was with the other four. The bus carrying children home from the medical facility or lessons at the mosque stopped inside the u-curve designed to slow vehicles and prevent a high-speed surface attack on the compound. The driver and a group of children stood watching the fireball. Because they were on the way out, the barrier gate stood open.

The team skirted the fence and the bus. Attention remained on the guards in case anyone turned around at the wrong time.

They continued down the first line of the U, hugged the corner, and back toward the bus and gate before entering the compound grounds. A High Mobility Multi-Purpose Vehicle (HMMV) with hover capability and a mounted laser mini-cannon sat atop a circular pivot beneath a sand-colored canopy. It caused a moment of concern until it became obvious it was unoccupied.

To the right of the pivot, which allowed the HMMV to drive in and then be swung around for deployment without using reverse gears, sat the entrance to an underground supply or maintenance bunker. Above and behind rose a guard tower. With no alarms sounded, anyone in the tower was likely staring at the sky.

Barnwell brought them to a halt between the HMMV and the bunker entrance. They removed faceplates to talk in whispers.

"Lime Ballast," he said over the radio. Then addressed those with him; "On the other side of this bunker is a battery and then the barracks. I saw a bunch of people standing on the grounds in front of it watching the show. There's a tower behind the barracks, but it isn't tall enough to look over the building onto the interior.

"The one-story white building directly in front of us is the main office. It will have the most direct way down to the spaces below and where Amanda will be. Kai and I will go through it."

"The communication center is across the compound," Cam said. "It was in front of us when we rounded the bend at the entrance. There are a lot of people standing outside of it, as well as in front of the mosque. I don't like our chances of getting from here to there unseen."

"When the satellite crashes, the sun will have gone down," Tab replied. "People will still be excited by the fireworks, but they will also have an adrenaline drop. When they leave the grounds, use the darkness to make your way over. Stay close to the gateway fence for extra cover. Everyone ready?"

Three nods and faceplates reattached.

The African-American Marine and the former Japanese Royal Guard moved away from the shadows and quickly covered the few yards to the office building. Cam and Stacey knew they were there, and knew where they were going. They had difficulty keeping an eye on the two men, even with the enhanced optics the METS provided. It was a strong indication the enemy would not see them at all.

The two women stood at the fender of the big vehicle and waited. They watched the death of the once important space platform. It went to a watery grave in a blaze of glory. Hopefully not an omen.

The stealthy entry into the office, then locating the passage to the underground complex proved easier than Barnwell anticipated. The show arranged by Space Fleet's Space Force Group not only pulled people outside, they left doors open behind them.

CCVScanners were visible on walls and at portals. The METS units continued to function brilliantly. At least no alarms were sounded. Fortune does, sometimes, favor the brave.

Tab activated the radium-235 detector, and a blip appeared instantly. He requested a sonar scan of the corridors and rooms below the surface. Within a few seconds an overlay of outlines representing walls appeared in front of his left eye. The blip came from a room three corridors ahead, right, and three rooms down on the right. He airdropped the representation to Kai's suit, waited on a thumb-up, and moved forward.

He remained near the wall on his right expecting the grey paint to be easier for the camouflage element to reflect than open air. Kai followed his lead.

Twice they needed to freeze in place when someone entered the corridor. Once the person moved away. The second time a man in a slim-cut European style suit passed them with less than two-feet of clearance. Head down and engrossed with his data pad, he did not look up and continued away from the two inter-lopers.

At the door to the room containing the radium signal, a plate with eye-scan recognition provided security.

Prepared, Tab requested biometric data on al-Rashid and Daniel Miller. As members of the UEC, both provided biological data from retina mapping to palm prints for security access. While al-Rashid's access was now denied, his data remained on file.

Expecting the top ranking members of the Camarilla to have the highest security clearances, Barnwell came ready.

al-Rashid's iris appeared on the Marine's faceplate. He placed it in front of the auto-scan and the mathematical pattern-recognition software responded with a click of the lock releasing.

Had the doors above not been left open, he would have used the same trick to gain access to the bunkers.

Tab entered, laser pistol in hand and Kai's hand on his left shoulder. He quickly cleared the space. Amanda Black seated at a desk, turned to see who unlocked her door. From her coy smile, Tab knew she understood who the nearly invisible intruders were.

Kai pulled the door closed after confirming a similar security scanner existed on the inside wall of the studio apartment.

"The new METS are incredible," Amanda said. "I'm watching and know you're there, but still see only ripples. If you weren't moving, you would be totally invisible."

Tab and Kai disengaged the cammo-modes and removed their faceplates, leaving the soft-helmet hoodies up.

"I assumed the strip-tease in the courtyard was for my benefit," he said to his partner. "Do you have what we need?"

She held up a data sheet.

"They gave me practically complete access to plans and loca-tions," she answered. "I don't have names for all the specific indi-viduals associated with the Camarilla, but most of the more im-portant contacts necessary to move their agenda forward. It in-cludes military contacts at international sites, as well as who has access to classified communications."

Tab took the soft plastic-like sheet and placed his faceplate, made of similar material, over the top. A scan provided the answer he needed.

"There is a lot of data. It's linked to this sheet, and not embedded into a storage trap," he said. "If we leave with only this piece, it can be wiped remotely. Give me a second."

He activated a tap-trap on his faceplate and placed the cover directly onto the data sheet. A green flicker occurred two-seconds later.

"Everything has been transferred to my data storage," he told her. "They can wipe this and it won't matter. As soon as we clear the jammers, I'll transfer everything to Marine Intelligence. Are you ready?"

"I am, but I don't suppose you came with a METS for me?"

"No. You'll have to walk out like you own the place. Kai and I will silence anyone who tries to stop you," he replied.

"And when all hell break loose?" she asked.

"We run," he answered. "Fast," he added.

"Where to first?"

"Meet Cam and Stacey at the communication center. Can you get us there from here?"

"Could, but the bunker complex is lousy with Camarilla VIPs, security, support personnel, and others. If the show you arranged upstairs is over, it might be best to go up and across the surface," she answered.

"I was afraid you might say that," he replied. "Lemon Bridge," he said to his upper arm, gaining a quizzical stare from Black.

With the show over and night falling rapidly, the throngs of curious people returned inside.

On hearing Lemon Bridge Cam and Stacey moved quickly across the open spaces, hugged walls or fence-lines when available, and reached the communication center without a challenge.

The external lock was a simple palm-print. Cam reproduced al-Rashid's on her right glove. The palm would be visible as the image overlaid the refraction elements, but worth the risk.

The door slid aside and the two women entered. As it closed behind them Cam calmly shot the two techs seated at consoles.

"Was that necessary?" Stacey asked with her faceplate off and the cowling of her helmet pushed down.

"It was," Cam answered. "Can you operate these systems?"

The Fellen inspected the console while Cam pulled the two bodies off to the side.

"Banana Silk." Cam announced their success at reaching the comm center, and Stacey answered her question.

"They were monitoring communications. Systems are open, so I don't have to hack into them."

"Communication storage?" Cam asked, her own helmet off.

"Found it. I can send the record of past communications directly to Space Fleet."

"Wait," Cam warned. "Have any and all information prepped for transfer before you send anything. As soon as you uplink, people will know we're here.."

Stacey nodded in understanding and returned to the console interface.

Five tense minutes passed and a strange knocking came from the entrance.

"What was that?" Stacey asked.

"Shave-and-a-haircut," Cam answered. "More of Tab's fascination with the past. It's his secret signal."

The door slid open and Amanda Black came through, followed by two ghostly shadows.

Tab and Kai soon appeared, removing their own helmets.

"Wanted to warn you before we opened the door," the Colonel said. "I remembered you being rather quick with a laser."

"She still is," Stacey said, eyes cutting to the bodies pushed against the far wall.

Before Tab could comment the communications systems shut down.

"You?" he asked Stacey.

"No," she answered.

"Ms. Muse, I am disappointed," al-Rashid's voice issued from speakers inside the studio. "Security warned me as soon as I entered your apartment. We watched you and two nearly invisible people make your way to the communications center. Now you have a choice. Surrender or die. I assure you the METS will not be sufficient to stop the number of weapons currently trained on the center."

"Fuck," Cam said.

Tab turned a circle, keeping his eyes on the inside of the face-plate in his hand.

"Thermal and sonar readings indicate we are surrounded, and by a lot of bodies," he reported.

"Our personal comms are jammed," Stacey reported. "We can't call Billy or the shuttle."

"We have two laser pistols, a sword, and knives," Kai said.

"If we can keep the door to the grounds and the one leading into the subterranean corridors blocked, we can hold out until someone notices," Amanda said. "al-Rashid isn't going to destroy his communication center. He needs it to complete his plans."

"What's the timetable?" Barnwell asked.

"Basically, tomorrow," Black answered.

"So we can't warn the UEC, but then he can't communicate with his assets either," Barnwell said.

"Actually, he can," Stacey said. "I memorized as much information as I could while preparing the units for a data drop, in case something happened."

"You memorized information?" Cam asked, her expression between shock and disbelief. "There was a mountain of data being zipped for transfer."

Stacey ignored the comment, not wanting to waste time explaining her eidetic memory.

"The shuttle Captain Black came here on, and the one Princess Wei used have the capability of communicating with most of the Camarilla outposts. They don't have a quantum capability, but they have the necessary range for standard methods."

"A major part of their plan is to broadcast multi-media with the specific content they want disseminated," Black said.

"They can record and edit and broadcast from either shuttle," Stacey replied. "If anyone tries to interfere, they can take off and fly above jamming."

"But they won't be able to jam UEC and Space Fleet signals like they could have using their connections to satellites in orbit," Black said . . . hopefully.

Stacey did not answer. She sat back and her eyes glazed. The Fellen needed a moment to mentally replay data which flashed by earlier in seconds.

After three eerie minutes clicked by, Tab gently shook the young woman, concerned for her silence and the pale-blue color her skin turned.

She blinked, looked around to reposition herself mentally, and trembled.

"Sorry. It happens sometimes when I try to remember something instead of allowing the memory to occur," she said. "They may be able to run a hardline from Wei's shuttle to the compounds satellite dish," she said. "They will have to enhance the power couplings, but it would be possible to jam communications if they know specific channels."

"They cannot hear our conversation, can they?" Kai asked.

Stacey shook her head. The effects of being caught in a mental-loop left her shaken.

She pointed at a simple toggle switch and said, "I cut off internal signals," she said. "It's an emergency switch used to make the center completely blacked out. Simple, antiquated, and effective."

"Stacey, Admiral Patterson told me you were probably the most qualified communications and computer operator on Earth. She said you had skills only your brother and cousin came close to replicating. Can you get this center operational?"

"The center is operational," the alien replied. "What it does not have is power. Without a power supply, there isn't anything I can do."

"If I contact Billy, can they trace the signal?" Barnwell asked.

"They will need to triangulate, which will take at least a minute, but the short answer is *yes*," she replied.

"Then we have to keep it short," he said, pulling out the ancient walkie-talkie. "Billy, it's Tab, come in."

"It's Billy. The detonators are set."

"Quick as possible, we're in the comm center and they cut power. I need to transfer data to the shuttle, how can I do it?"

"Pull the feed from the main supply to the console, open the power box on one of the laser pistols, connect a couple of transformers to prevent an explosion, and fire the pistol. It should deliver a sustained power source for five-to-ten-seconds. Zip-tight your data and burst it. You'll have one shot, no pun," the engineering genius answered.

"Where do I get transformers?" Barnwell asked.

"The METS use circuit relays and transfers located in the armpits of the suits," he answered. "The ones under the left armpit should snap into the laser pistol converter. Wrap the exposed leads from the console around the barrel."

"Got it," Barnwell replied. "Move, Billy. They may be locating you now. Tab, out."

"You may have gotten him killed," Stacey told the mission leader.

"I need you and Cam out of the suits," Barnwell replied, ignoring her comment. "Cut out the circuit boxes under the left armpits while I prep the power cord to the console. Kai, use your blade and pry open the power-converter box of the laser pistol."

While the four of them got busy, Amanda removed the clothing from the two dead techs for Cam and Stacey. Cutting into the fabric designed to resist blades proved the most difficult task. In five minutes they had everything laid out atop a console. Barnwell and Stacey worked silently to put the parts together.

"Stacey, when I pull the trigger, key the data."

"I have Chaspi's comm-ident preset," she replied. "She will be able to rebound the message to Space Fleet."

"When Stacey keys the communications, those outside will know," Kai said aloud. "They already know we have someone nearby. They will attack us and try to locate the others."

Once again Col. Barnwell ignored a comment, saying to the Fellen dressed in over-sized fatigues, "Ten-seconds."

He held one hand up, fingers splayed. The other hand gripped the laser pistol. One at a time, a finger retracted. When his thumb closed to form a fist, he pulled the trigger.

The surge of power restricted by the multiple-converters caused the pistol to shake. The comms console lit up and Stacey sent the data burst. With the message sent, she backed away from the board.

Tab released the trigger, but the power already built up continued to feed the transformer, pass into converters, travel through the hardline and into the console. He released the weapon a moment before it glowed a brilliant yellow-red. Everyone feared an explosion. People dropped, covered, and braced.

The pistol simply melted. A flare of sparks issued from the rear of the console, and smoke trailed upward as the lights and dials on the front of the board died.

They looked up, relieved no shattering detonation occurred.

The building shook. Explosions and laser fire erupted outside.

"Here they come," Tab said.

Chapter 28

Stacey watched the Brazilian agent tie the loose shirt into a tight knot at her waist. She pulled the military-style web belt tight around her waist, locked the friction buckle and cut off the extra length.

The Fellen pulled her shirt tails together to tie. Cam pushed the knife across the floor toward her. She smiled at the young blue-skinned teammate, and went back to tightly rolling the cuffs of the borrowed pants above her ankles.

Finished with her own belt and cuffs, Stacey handed Cam back the knife. She used it to cut the laces from the boot of a corpse. Without asking, Cam moved behind Stacey and used the lace to tie her long auburn hair into a ponytail, then bobbed it and tied it again.

"This way no one can grab your hair in a fight," she said.

"Some of those explosions were Billy setting off his bombs," Tab announced. He pointed at his walkie-talkie, indicating he was in contact once more with their engineer-teammate. "He has the HMMV backed to the front door. Says there is a floorboard entry underneath the chassis. Get ready, people. When I open the door we go quick. Under the wheels and up the chute."

The others had and held a number of questions. At the moment, action was more crucial than answers.

Barnwell popped the door and stepped through with the only laser pistol left operational. He used the open door as a shield for his back and opened fire at anything his optics considered a threat.

The weapons aboard the HMMV laid down continuous fire and provided more firepower than anything the compound forces could use in response. The four major batteries were designed to repel air-threats and could not depress to an angle necessary to target the ground vehicle.

Black went through first, bending to scurry beneath the tall vehicle, protected by the alloy construction and the oversized all-terrain tires. She reached the open hatch, jumped up to grab a hand-bar to hoist herself into the belly of the beast.

Stacey followed, helped into the HMMV by Black. As soon as the Fellen landed inside, Black left to join Billy in the forward cabin.

Kai came next, followed by Cam. As soon as her unshod feet disappeared, Barnwell ceased his cover fire to join the others. Once inside, he hurried to the front.

The special plasti-metal windshield was cracked and scorched, but held. Testament to the design and how much enemy fire the vehicle received in a short amount of time.

"I left the comm center door open," he told the engineer in the driver's seat. "Can you turn us around and send a round through?"

"No need to turn," Billy answered. The heads-up display rotated. A red-pinpoint lit at the rear of the ghosted image of the HMMV. The entire truck vibrated as a miniature missile lifted from a rear-mounted tube.

The missile's explosive head detonated against the far interior wall of the building, reducing everything inside to ash and metal flake. The building itself remained whole. Had a similar missile hit against the exterior, the result would have been negligible. The Camarilla constructed a site to withstand a massive assault.

"Uh-oh," he said. "The supply hangar on the far side," he said, indicating a second heads-up display with an outline of the compound and structures. "They are bringing out a mobile launcher. If they have penetrating rounds, the skin on this baby may not be strong enough."

"Get us out," Barnwell ordered.

"The compound jammers are off-line. I have three messages," Black said from the shotgun seat. "The Admiralty acknowledges receipt of our data. Army units are being dispatched with warrants."

"Warrants?" Billy asked. He swung the controls to slide the big vehicle into a one-eighty arc, slinging unharnessed passengers at the same time. "Sorry," he called. "You may want to find seats and straps. I hope they plan on bringing more than warrants."

"Chaspi is off the ground and east. She's stayed low to avoid the surface-to-air battery cannons," Black continued.

"Smart girl," Billy said. "Detonating discs," he announced.

The exterior fence beyond the compound's landing pad and the communication center blew apart. A second detonation took out two of the four pillars supporting the guard tower overlooking the eastern perimeter.

"One of the shuttles on the LZ is powering up," Black announced. "It's the Japanese transport."

"Billy?"

"Too late," he said. From the cracked shield, the three watched as the shuttle made an emergency liftoff and darted upward into the night sky. "But we can seriously fuck up the other one."

A laser cannon on a swivel fired a continuous beam at the second shuttle, slicing a major gap along the starboard side.

The rear of the big vehicle rose violently, driving the forward bumper down into the hard desert soil.

"Missile impact from the mobile launcher," Billy called. His eyes scanned the various displays while his fingers danced over an invisible control board. "Rear plates held, but buckled. Rear missile tube compromised."

The HMMV's reinforced hood slammed into the inner fence, plowing the electrified metal and carbon fiber barrier down, allowing the reinforced tires to roll across and through the damaged section.

"If they hit the same part of the bus again, it may not hold," he warned. "Make sure everyone is located as far forward as possible and in straps. That includes you, Colonel," he cadet told Barnwell. "I know you're strong enough to hold on, but there may not be a lot available to grab."

"The third communication," Captain Black said. "We're about to get rain."

Billy turned to the woman seated on his right, noticed the smile on Barnwell's face as he took the seat directly behind the Captain. He asked, "Really? The third communication was a weather report?"

"Not that kind of rain," Barnwell answered.

Chapter 29

"What's the current position of the Devee ship?" Admiral Patterson asked Lt. Sanchez.

Following short, restless naps, showers, and dressing in fresh uniforms, the two met in Space Fleet's newest Command Operations War Room. Sarcastically referred to as the COW.

A spatial-model of the solar system hovered in the air. Lasers used to excite nitrogen and oxygen molecules created a projection that could be disconcerting. The realistic images of planets, moons, asteroids, and even artificial satellites looked as if they could hurt if the hit. In fact, anything solid would pass through empty air.

Sanchez wore a finger-thumb interface. By swiping, pinching, or wiggling her index finger and, or thumb she could control the projection. She wore a mic to interface her comments to the AI operating the display.

She wiped away the satellites, artificial and natural, leaving the sun, planets, and the asteroid belt between Jupiter and Mars. She created a bright green dot beyond Jupiter, and then wiped off the planets beyond.

"The Devee ship is called the Ambassador," she said. "Twenty-million-miles from Jupiter. Jupiter and Mars are currently on the far left quadrant of the sun. Venus is located on the far right quadrant, with Mercury and Earth lined up on the side."

"Contacts?"

"Aya Ishihara, and her exo-legal team are making arrangements for the Devee delegation. They will reach the Mars Shipyard and Docks in approximately seventy-three-hours."

"Has Trent determined how the Devee are capable of traveling over one-million-miles-per-hour inside the solar system?"

"No. We reached out to Fell. Sky replied and said they have no records of a Devee ship with such extreme speed capability. They do have reports of Devee raiders able to run for short distances at one-third the speed, but nothing else. The Rys representative told us the same. As did Admiral Senait's contacts in the Aster System.

The Devee are demonstrating a technological evolution not witnessed before this visit."

"To intimidate or to demonstrate?"

"Director Ishihara's reports indicate the Devee representative has been cooperative and friendly. When asked about the ship's power source, she would not reveal Devee secrets, but did admit the ship was the first of its type. The representative made it clear the advances were on the table for possible future trades," the Latina said.

"Weapons?"

"Scans are inconclusive. Ishihara asked the same question and was assured the Ambassador was built for diplomatic and trade missions, not battle purposes. The ship does use forcefields for defense and to protect against damage to the hull by space debris. Their communications system is not FTL. It does use accelerated particle enhancements for faster messaging than normal speed-of-sound networks."

"How do we communicate if we aren't on the same network?"

"Their system adapts to ours. We can pick up their signals with conventional listening devises, and they can accelerate our signals. And, yes, it is available for potential barter."

"Sounds like everything we have heard about the Devee is correct," the Admiral said. "The deal is the goal. No history of overt militaristic tendencies."

"The reports I read show a race without a strong moral compass. They tread water between legal and criminal behavior, including slavery, abductions, and trading in unsavory markets," Lt. Sanchez said.

"Morals based on human traditions and customs," Patterson reminded her aide and friend. "We cannot continue to appraise the actions of non-terrestrials by our codes of ethics. Our own ethical and moral rules change over time. Who are we to judge?"

"Which is why I sent a personal request to Judge Korr on Aster Farum 3," Sanchez admitted. "She said, and I quote, 'Keep eyes on them at all times. Know where your children are and keep a weapon nearby. Just in case.'"

"Pass the warning along to Aya," Patterson said. "Contact Captain Jobert on the 89 and have her place the Macdonald between Mars and the Ambassador. We may request a security boarding before we allow the Devee onto MSD."

"Yes, Ma'am," the Aide replied. She stood, but Patterson kept her another moment.

"Contact the Mars Colony," she ordered her Aide. "Tell them to lock down the hangar and secure every file. Close down any open communications between the hangar, science labs, and the colony base. Keep comms open to listen to MSD and to Space Fleet only. Broadcast only if they have an emergency."

"You want them to go dark so the Devee cannot crack any of their systems?"

"The Devee may be here to establish an alliance, but it does not change the fact they seek items for trade value. Nothing in our solar system is more valuable than the secrets on Mars."

"Do you think it wise to display the ship's speed?" Echnee Kailah asked. A member of the Technology Videolio, Kailah was in charge of the technical specialists aboard the Devee ship.

"Does not matter what any of us think, Kailah," Pidita Jax, the ship's commander, answered. "We have a timeline and the only way to reach the humans' space station orbiting the planet they call Mars is by maximizing the fission reactors. When will we need to begin deceleration?"

"Before we enter the asteroid belt. To scrub sufficient speed we will shut down the reactors in two hours. We must be in the G-Chambers by then. The ship will drop to a constant speed of two-hundred-thousand-miles-per-hour. The automatons and automated operating systems will handle the ship until it is safe to exit the chambers," Kailah answered.

"I find it amazing our bodies are capable of handling traveling at millions-of-miles-per-hour as long as the speed is constant, but we must hide in chambers required to dampen gravitational effects when the ship accelerates or decelerates," Jax mused aloud.

"I am a technician, not a biologist," Kailah rejoined, "I have seen what happens to organic life not protected by the chambers. I have no wish to become a jelly blob."

"The Earthers have plasma cannons deployed on asteroids," Jax said. "The tachyon cannon emplacements on four of the moons around their Jupiter will be too far away to concern us. We will target the asteroid sites with conventional weapons. The newly installed Galvani weapon will handle the tachyon cannons on the space station and on the planet's surface. It will also remove their space craft as a threat. If it works as described."

"The science is correct, and the tests we ran before installing it aboard the Ambassador met all specs," the tech specialist replied. "I find it difficult to believe these people allowed us this near their inhabited sites."

"The Tuito predicted their actions based on how we presented ourselves," Jax replied. "It would appear humans are more predictable than the Ginae feared. I find it more impressive the jump in evolution they made in fewer than two-hundred-years. It was not long ago Devee Reavers culled humans, plants, and animals from a backward world. Now they represent a danger."

"Speaking of the Tuito, are we still in contact with Tuito Wei on Earth?"

"She is busy starting a revolution," Jax answered. "Between her work on the surface, and our surprise, humans will regret their sudden rise to significance. When we learn how Earthers deciphered the Nakki codes, control of the ancient secrets will make Devisator the most powerful planet in the galaxy."

"We have only seven Devee and fifteen-slaves aboard. It should not take long, but I must prepare the G-Chambers."

"I will contact the human representative, Ishihara, and tell her I will be unavailable for a few hours. It does speak to human intelligence a female is in charge of liaisons. Be sure the asteroids are targeted and the Galvani weapon is prepared," Jax reminded Kailah. "When we exit the asteroid belt I intend to begin our true mission in this system."

"As ordered," the Echnee nodded and departed the constricted command bridge.

"Captain Jobert, the Devee ship is decelerating," Tactical Officer, Lt.JG Markku (Mark) Tilkanen informed the PT-89's commander.

"Approaching the asteroid belt," Jobert surmised. "Most dangerous objects are hundreds-of-thousands-of-miles apart, but it makes sense to slow down if you have not run the belt before."

The 89's central command bridge consisted of the Captain and six consoles for Sciences, Systems, Communications, Tactical, the Pilot and the Navigator. Unlike the previous PT-designated warships, the 89 did not use an AI-Avatar master operating system. The newer design included more technology, fewer crew members, and more weapons. Design changes made after conflicts with the Zenge and Mischene.

"The scans of the Devee ship are amending , Captain," Specialist Renny Murphy said. The Irishman manned the Systems Console, port-forward on the ship's bridge.

"Amending how?" Jobert asked

"I believe the scan enhancements are due to ferromagnetic asteroids. The belt is sixty-percent metallic. The Devee ship uses a magnesium diboride superconductor to generate radiation shields to protect the crew. The magnetic attraction created by the asteroids is reducing the ship's shield integrity. The Devee apparently use scanning intercepters and deflectors powered by the same superconductor."

"As they near iron-rich asteroids, they deflect less of our scans," the Captain concluded. "What do your new readings show?"

"They use nuclear fission reactors to power the ship," Murphy informed her. "That's how they create a high rate of speed without using space-fold. Theoretically, they could add another five-million-miles-per-hour."

"Reactors release radiation, Mr. Murphy."

"Yes, Captain, and they do not appear concerned," the Systems Operator answered. "The reactors are shielded to the ship. Radiation and heat are vented directly into space. Not the most environmentally sound concept, but not dangerous unless they use the reactors close to an atmosphere, or a trailing cloud of radiated dust is blown onto a living planet."

"What else have you learned?"

"Because the magnetic fields are fluctuating, I cannot confirm, but the ship appears to be twice the size we thought. I count twenty-two lifeforms."

"Lt. Tikanen, it would be prudent you check our weapons and prepare a possible scenario for confronting the Devee ship," Jobert informed her Tac officer.

"Communications, send the Admiral an update. Make sure it's A-Coded and directed to the Admiral's private comm."

The Captain sat watching the representation of the asteroid belt play across the SHD screen dominating the forward interior hull.

"Devee may be short for devious," she said aloud. "The Macdonald is on yellow alert. Inform MSD and Mars of our status and my suggestion they raise their threat awareness level."

"Aye," the Comms officer replied. A bead of sweat trickled from the young man's hairline and down his spine. The environmentally controlled atmosphere did not control nerves.

"Pam, it's Coop, do you copy?"

"Coop, Pam. Where the fuck have you been? Are you alright? Where are you?"

"I'm fine. Can you talk openly?"

"I'm home with Sam, who would also like to know where you have been?"

"Too long a story for now, but I'll catch you up when I return. I'm twenty-three-hours from the solar system. Pam, I left Phisor where a Devee ship attacked the 109. Is there a Devee ship still in the solar system?"

"Entering the asteroid belt on their way to MSD," she answered. "They claim to be a delegation sent to open alliance discussions, but Captain Jobert has her doubts. She placed the 89 on

Yellow Alert and suggested MSD and Mars do the same. I agreed with her assessment."

"Smart Captain," Coop replied. "The Devee can masque their ships, inside and out. They have been supplying the Mischene and Zenge elements since before we engaged the Prophet. It seems like they are tired of making money by working all sides and have moved on to creating conflicts."

"Are they an imminent threat?" the Admiral asked.

"Yes. I believe they intend a sneak attack. They are greed-driven, Pam. They're after the Nakki secrets."

"Say again, Coop. Whose secrets?"

"Sorry, Pam. The Martian hangar and saucer, with the advanced tech, were left by a race called the Nakki. One of many things I learned while away."

"You think the Devee will attack Mars?"

"They have access to advanced weapons, automaton fighter drones, and other advanced tech, Pam. The 89 will be overmatched. They know how to use white noise to disable our sonic shields. They also know if they shake our ships hard enough, they can disrupt the Rys shield generators."

"I'll warn Captain Jobert. Why are you contacting me, Coop. What happened to my people in the Phisor system?" The concern in the Admiral's voice unmistakable.

"You have casualties, but Space Fleet performed above and beyond expectations, Admiral. Phisor is completely in the hands of Anton, and the 109 has the Devee on the run. They used a particle diffuser to disabled tachyon-based communications. They will be out of touch until the field dissipates. It's why I needed to leave the system to contact you."

"I'll warn our communications people," she answered. "If they do the same here, the time-lapse will be a problem with Mars on the far side of the sun."

"Cassandra is sending the data collected on the Devee, as well as information provided by a reliable source on their history and tactics. The Comms Center in Toronto is getting it now."

"Coop, send it directly to the 89, in case the Devee screw with communications before we reroute."

"Copy, Admiral. One more thing. The Devee use a version of QKD for secure communications. You can program your scanners to listen for low-frequency quantum distortions. They will be short and directed, but you should be able to fix signal generation and reception."

"Did you know Devee ships can travel at over one-million-mph inside a system?" she asked.

The hesitation would have been answer enough, but he replied, "The ship in the Phisor system did nothing similar. The data from D'Sey did not mention extreme in-system speed capability."

"What's a deesay?"

"A who," he answered. "A pirate who owed me for some work. I'll stay in touch via STORM-HATCH. Cassandra is fast, but if the Devee can travel at those speeds, the 89 will face them alone. Coop, out."

"Did he say where he's been for nine months?" her husband, Sam Patterson, asked. He stood wide-eyed listening to only her side of the conversation. Coop's voice coming through the Fellen trans-comm chip embedded in her neck.

"No, but I think he was working for a pirate," she said, hurrying past her dumbfounded spouse. The quiet evening at home another casualty of responsibility.

Chapter 30

Jobert discerned the important points from the data dumped on her from Space Fleet Central Headquarters on Earth and the civilian space craft Cassandra, piloted by former Space Fleet Captain Daniel Cooper.

"Systems, increase atmospheric density inside the cabin holding the Rys force field emitter. Increase gravitonic control fourtimes. Bar access to anyone as long as those standards are maintained."

She noted the 'Aye' and moved on.

"Communications, we may need to operate without STORM-HATCH. Make sure standard messaging is available between us, MSD, and Mars colony. Check time-lapse. Do the same with SFHQ on EMS2 and Earth."

The ship's Tactical Officer and second in command, Lt. Tikanen had also scanned the incoming reports on Devee capabilities and possibilities. Weapons and power systems checks were being performed before an order arrived. Jobert noted the activity displayed by her embedded data analysis screen in the arm of the Command Chair. She smiled in appreciation for a second with initiative.

"Navigator, plot a dozen jump-points for in-system space-fold with durations of fifteen-seconds to one-minute. Make sure we don't hop into an asteroid or planetoid gravity well if we need to make a sudden change of location."

"Aye," the reply. Tension on the bridge began to mount as the Captain issued orders. The crew knew something changed, but were not yet aware of the significance of the communications coming in from various locations.

"Pilot, disconnect safety protocols."

At this order, heads turned, including Lt.JG Jasmine Park, less than three-months from graduating the pilot cert program at Space Fleet Academy.

"We may need to maneuver more radically than the computer-safety-protocols allow," she said. "The potential lag between your making a move and the system checking your sanity could leave us vulnerable. Disconnect those protocols, LT."

"Open all channels. This is Captain Jobert to the crew of SFPT-89."

The bridge crew did not need to look at their commander to hear her over the speakers, but they all did. They witnessed a person become a frontline officer. A calm spread over her features as she sat back in the oversized command chair, crossed one leg, and turned her eyes to the view of space projected across the forward wall.

"The Devee ship is not here on a peaceful mission," she told them. "We do not know its exact purpose, but Space Fleet Command believes it to be hostile. This ship is currently the only battle-worthy asset in the solar system. Our job is to prevent the Devee from nearing MSD or Mars. If we are lucky, analysis may be incorrect and the Devee will respect our space. More likely we are about to engage in the second major conflict with non-terrestrials within our solar system.

"The last time we drove the enemy off, but that battle took place at the far edges of the system. This time the fight will occur in our own backyard. Mars, MSD, asteroids and satellites now have defensive capabilities we did not have before. But make no mistake, the John A. Macdonald is the barrier between this potential new enemy and our homes.

"We are now at Red Alert. Report to battle stations and prepare to meet the enemy. Captain Jobert, out."

Chapter 31

"We have exited the more dangerous section of the asteroid belt," the pilot informed her commander.

"The Captain of the Earth ship requests your attention, Pidita Jax," the communications tech said.

"This is Pidita Jax," the woman said from her seat. "You wish to speak with me, Captain Jobert?"

"Pidita Jax, cease forward movement. Bring your ship to a complete stop," Jobert demanded.

"I do not understand, Captain. We are visitors seeking an alliance. Is there some problem?"

"We have monitored quantum key communications coming from your ship," Jobert replied. "We detected your superconductors venting radiation into our system also enhances a scanning refraction system you use to hide the true size of your vessel. Reports from the Phisor system worry out leaders. The Devee have used advanced weapons in support of Mischene rebels against Trade Alliance military units. You will bring your ship to a complete stop, or I will stop it for you."

The other Devee on the bridge watched their stations. The Earth ship's commander had much more information on the Devee than anyone realized. If they knew so much, they might also possess capabilities the Devee Council was unaware existed.

"Captain Jobert, our systems are for defense only," Jax responded. "We have never been in your system before. Contact with your species has been limited."

"We can discuss your position after you come to a complete stop," Jobert stepped on the Devee commander's communication. "Do it now, Captain."

"We cannot decelerate from our current speed to all stop without harming the crew," Jax replied. "We will begin a controlled deceleration that will allow us to remain active. Do you understand, Captain?"

"Just do it, Captain," Jobert's curt response.

The ship's engines began to reduce power to the huge thrusters. The vessel continued forward through the vacuum, dropping speed as it went. Pidita Jax sat in silence, deciding what her next move would be.

"Captain Jobert," she called, "We are reducing power. I am terribly troubled by the report of a Devee and Trading Alliance dispute in the Phisor system. There must be a misunderstanding. I wish to send a message to my home world for clarification. I do not wish for it to appear offensive."

"How long before you receive a reply?"

"Approximately twelve-hours," Jax answered.

"Do not direct any communications toward Earth," Jobert warned. "Do not engage any systems other than your communication arrays," she added. "We are in contact with our people on Earth, Mars, and those currently located in other systems. I hope you are correct, Captain, and a misunderstanding has occurred. However, please be aware a substantial number of weapons are trained on the Ambassador. I would hate for any further misunderstandings to end violently."

"As would I, Captain Jobert. We will remain here until we hear from Devisator. Ours is a mission of peace, Captain."

With the communications closed between ships, Jax ordered her bridge crew, "Ready offensive systems, including the new Galvani weapon. Do not make any overt acts which might warn the Earthers. Have everything prepared up to the point of bringing them on line."

The communications hub located at Space Fleet Headquarters north of Toronto crackled with energy. Normally a busy place, at this moment it was a zoo. Not only were the communication operators operating, the spacious suite held supervisors and line officers. No one bothered saluting, and the visiting high ranking officers learned to stay out of the way or get plowed over.

Systems analysts dissected information and flipped it to the next level most likely concerned with the data or messages contained.

Supervisors watched over shoulders and listened on earbuds. The most watched console currently monitored the SFPT-89. A close second was the conversations between Mars and MSD.

"QKD signal detected," a tech called. She stood at a panel with a single icon floating above a holo-board. "Direction is toward the wormhole."

"Can we hack it?"

The question came from a visiting Admiral of the Navy. The unveiled looks of disdain set the older man back on his heels.

"What?" he asked.

A Naval Captain assigned to the UEC explained, "QKD signals cannot be hacked, Admiral. They are point-to-point and exist only in those two locations."

The Admiral gave the young woman a look of disbelief, decided against asking more questions that would date himself, and ended up leaving the hubbub. He would read the details later.

"That was mean," a nearby tech said to the Captain, sliding an open palm out for a quick low-five.

The Captain silently slapped the palm, smiled, and said, "We needed the extra space."

"Rebound burst coming in from an unidentified source," a comm-tech Ensign called from the far end of the suite. "Holy shit," he added. "Super!"

A young Lieutenant JG linked in with her earbud and synced her hand-held data reader to the console. Her eyes widened and she ordered the Ensign "One, Two, Three and Four, NOW!"

The tech dispatched the burst directly to four receivers without bothering to send anything through analysis.

The signal from an unknown transponder located in the middle of Saudi Arabia was relayed in whole to the Office of the Chairman of the Board of Governors, the Fleet Admiral of Space Fleet, the Chairman of the Joint Chiefs of Staff, and the Director of UEC Security.

"Anyone not assigned to space, dedicate your systems to the Middle East, Red Sea area, and Saudi Arabia specifically," the LTJG ordered.

Supervisors and visiting officers attempted to link to the new communications priority, but the data received had been sealed.

When an Army Colonel ordered the LTJG to tell him what the communication contained, the woman leaned in to whisper, "Fuck off, and if you bother me again I will have you tossed out of the building."

"Do we want Director Ishihara to contact the Devee ship?" Governor Arcand asked.

"Not yet," Admiral Patterson replied. "Captain Jobert has convinced the captain of the Ambassador to cease any forward movement. The ship sent a quantum-based communication to their world for instructions. Until they receive an answer, which will take approximately twelve-hours, let them wait."

The video conference between Arcand, Patterson, Paris Cassel, and Nathan Trent was arranged to discuss the situation developing between the asteroid belt and Mars.

"It gives us time to analyze the reports Coop sent regarding the Devee confrontation over Phisor," Trent, Director of Sciences for the UEC, added. "We're unsure of the Devee's capabilities. As of now, Captain Jobert is running a bluff, pretending we know more than we do. I agree with the Admiral. Let them stew and wonder if we're prepared for anything they might have."

Three alarms sounded in unison. Alerts of highly classified and extremely important communications being sent to their private receivers.

"It's the mission plans for the Camarilla Dissolvere," Cassel said. "Barnwell and Black were successful."

"And in trouble," Patterson added. "Reports of explosions and laser fire at the compound in Saudi Arabia."

"There's enough here for me to get warrants from a Criminal Court judge," Arcand interjected. "The nearest military units are at Camp As Sayliyah on the Persian Gulf northeast of the compound. I will forward the warrants to the Army to deliver."

"The compound is heavily fortified and has a mosque and a hospital," Patterson reminded the Governor. "Sending Army units guarantees a fight."

"A fight we have a legal right to wage now we have proof of the conspiracy," Arcand countered. "I will instruct the Army commander to take precautions regarding the mosque and medical facilities, but we have to act. The Camarilla has gone beyond a war of social unrest using their media contacts. This indicates a plan to incite riots and turn them into bloodbaths."

"If the members of the Camarilla move into the mosque and request sanctuary, you cannot force your way inside," Trent said. "Even if the mosque was built to protect against a UEC attack, or as a possible escape."

"If they want to live the remainder of their lives inside a mosque, so be it," Arcand answered. "It will make as effective a prison as any other."

"We have people under imminent threat," Cassel interrupted. "The forward base at As Sayliyah is close, but not near enough to save Barnwell's team. Admiral, the Colonel requested a special back-up."

"I'll send the order. She should be there in less than ten-minutes," Patterson replied.

"Who?" Arcand asked.

The Eskan Air Force Base south of Riyadh, the former capital of Saudi Arabia, closed down a century earlier. The village was originally built to provide housing for Bedouin tribes, but the nomadic people preferred their freedom and living in the desert. The US Air Force housed personnel in the complex until it became too dangerous for non-Muslims to remain in Saudi Arabia. When things returned to normal, the base was not reopened.

One building added to the complex following the transition to military housing had been a special transport hangar. Designed for new vertical-hover shuttles used to move personnel from the village to the military sites around the region.

The top of the hangar rolled back and a ship rose from the darkness into the starry sky. Ion-fusion thrusters engaged and the craft accelerated to Plus-Mach 5 in seconds. Direction. North.

"Captain Jobert, you have a communication request from Fell," the current Comms Officer interrupted the Captain's meal. Lea, pushed aside her plate, but left her personal chair in the recline position.

"Send it through," she instructed.

"Captain Jobert, my name is ASillamentrae. I am the mother of the Fellens you know as Sky and Sparks."

"I'm aware of who you are ASillamentrae," the Captain answered, "The members of the AS tribe of Fell have been important allies of Earth during the past few years. Your own family has done a great deal to improve our technology. You have fought beside us as friends. How can I help you?"

"I received a call from Daniel Cooper," the matriarch said. "I have a reputation among my people as a tough negotiator. In my years acting as a trader there have been occasions when I dealt with the Devee. He thought it may be of service if I were to provide you with insight into their methods and practices, considering the current situation."

Lea brought the chair to an upright position.

"Captain Cooper was correct. I would appreciate anything you can share to help guide me through the next few hours, ASillamentrae."

"I am pleased to help, Captain Jobert, but you must call me Silla."

"And you must call me Lea, Silla. Where do we begin?"

"Pidita Jax, we have received a message from Devisator. It is from Ginae Tabilis," the communication operator informed the captain.

Alone in her cabin, Jax opened the end-point communique with her personal QK trans-receiver. This would prevent the comms operator access to the message, insuring Jax would be the only one aboard to hear the Ginae's reply.

Quantum messages could come in any number of formats, and because they were dispatched by low-intensity lasers, images were as simple to send as texts. The image of Tabilis appeared above the repro-disc atop her transceiver.

"Pidita Jax, the Videolio is split. Some believe you should continue your original mission and do whatever necessary to secure the Nakki technology and how the humans decoded the Nakki language. Others are concerned the humans are too well prepared. No one expected the Devee carrier to fail in its mission to the Phisor system. The fact the Earthers have been alerted to our actions there puts a different light on your chances of success. We all desire the advantages the Nakki secrets offer, but it would be a bad trade to lose the Ambassador, our position among the Trade Alliance Worlds, and not come away with those secrets."

Jax wanted to yell at the insufferable woman's image. Thus far she wasted valuable time with useless prattle.

"You have command of our most powerful vessel," the Ginae continued. "The Galvani weapons, along with the extensive improvements made by the Echnee Videolio make it possible for you to face and defeat the military forces of any known world. Tuito Bailis believes the humans are trying to bluff us into backing down from a confrontation. The Echnee analyst, despite the years of data provided by Tuito Wei, are unsure of the level of sophistication Earth has attained. They have Nakki technology, the technology bartered from the Fellen and Rys worlds, as well as military and state secrets they may have taken from the Aster system."

If Jax could stop the message and no longer hear the ruler talk, make a comment, make a counter comment, and talk more without saying anything useful, she would. Unfortunately, once a quantum signal was opened it needed to run its course. Closing the channel would delete the remainder of the message.

"You are our representative on sight," Tabilis said.

"Here it comes," Jax said aloud.

"You must decide what is in the best interest of the Devee. If you think you can destroy the Earth ship and render their defenses useless, and take the secrets from the planet they call Mars, then act. But those secrets must be returned to Devisator. A move so bold as to attack this new system will tell the other worlds of our decision to take control of this quadrant of the galaxy.

"I am assured Space Fleet vessels from the Aster system and the Phisor systems are being recalled to Earth's defense. If they arrive before the Ambassador can reach the wormhole, you may or may not be capable of destroying them.

"However, if you decide to continue, if you believe your ship can defeat the humans, you must follow two orders. First, you will abandon the second phase. Once you have acquired the Nakki secrets, make haste for the wormhole. We will deal with Earth and recover Tuito Wei later. Second, send a message. As soon as we know your intention to attack, several Devee battleships will be dispatched to the system. Once they emerge from the wormhole gate, they will provide more than enough firepower to insure your safe retreat."

"I knew it was going to fall back on me," Jax whispered aloud. "Fucking bureaucrats."

"You have our complete trust, Pidita Jax," the image assure her before it disappeared.

"Echnee Kailah, meet me on the bridge," Jax ordered.

Chapter 32

"Will the Galvani weapon work against the Space Fleet vessel?"

"They use ion-fusion propulsion," Kailah answered. "It will work."

"The plasma cannons on the asteroids?"

"Two are within range to fire effectively on the Ambassador," the tech specialist replied. "Both will be in the same zone as the Earth ship. The weapons require ion conversion. When we remove the Earth ship, the plasma cannons will also become useless."

"Communications?"

"The disruptors worked before. We will not need to add white noise emitters since their sonic shields result from their engines creating sympathetic vibrations. No engines. No shields."

"They have back-up shields."

"Crystal-laser-based arrays according to our trade-spies," the tech explained. "On a ship that size, there will be thin areas. The drones will find them. Our pulse cannons alone might disrupt the flow and eliminate the force field. Their offensive weapons can be neutralized by our own. If we cannot destroy the ship, we can make it worthless."

"Their docking platform and the military defenses on the red planet?" Jax asked.

"Both too far away for the initial ionic disruption to reach them," Kailah admitted. "We may have to endure some hits until we are near enough to silence their systems. The Ambassador has multiple shield generators and unlimited power. It might be a bumpy ride, but nothing more."

"Then?"

"We use the AI Intrusion we traded for and improved to attack their computer systems. Once we have received every file, the platform can be eliminated. Drones can land on Mars and dispatch land-bots. While we use the Intrusion to steal their files, the land-bots can collect items, people, or anything else we decide we want. Once the drones return, we target the habitat and the mountain."

"Retreat to the wormhole and hope the Space Fleet ships on their way back do not arrive in time to stop us from gating out, or Ginae Tabilis actually has Devee warships here to cover us," Jax added.

"You're going to call the patrol ship captain's bluff?" Kailah asked.

"If we return to Devisator with the ultimate prize, the secret to unlocking the Nakki language, we will never work a day again in our lives, Kailah. The Ambassador will earn a place in Devee history unequalled by anything before. The beginning of the Devee conquest begins today."

"I thought the first step began in the Phisor system," the technician reminded her commanding officer. "It doesn't sound like it went well."

"Then we don't stumble," Jax said. Her next order would bring the systems waiting for more than twelve hours on line.

Before she could make the order, comms informed her, "A call from Captain Jobert of the United Earth Space Ship Macdonald."

"Yes, Captain Jobert?"

"The message from Ginae Tabilis was quite interesting, Pidita Jax," Jobert said.

On board the Devee vessel, an epidemic of wide eyes and held breathes raced among the bridge crew hearing the human's pronouncement. Intercepting quantum-based communications was impossible. It defied the laws of physics. It simply could not be done.

"Before you make a rash decision that places us at war, let me educate you, Jax," the eerily calm voice of the woman commanding the ship one-fifth the size of the Ambassador washed across the open bridge. "Your title is Pidita, so you know the value of receiving free information, don't you Jax?"

Jax made no reply.

"Of course you do," Jobert continued. "You must always weigh the potential return on your investment against the cost of doing business. In this case, you must decide if you are going to force the issue, take your booty and escape home, or if you will continue to act like a ship on a peaceful mission.

"You would not be here, alone, if you did not believe you had the upper hand. Maybe you are trying to see exactly what Earth is capable of. If true, the Ginae is sacrificing a significant investment hoping to use the information gained to improve the Devee position later."

Jobert allowed her words to settle.

"Might be a decent investment if you could send back the facts before you and your ship were obliterated. Destroyed. Smashed into Devee crap and tossed into the asteroid field. Which you might be able to do with QKD, except we know how to intercept those messages. You probably didn't know that before, did you Jax?"

"We are here on a peaceful mission to make contact with Earth as a fellow member of the Trade Alliance Worlds," Jax said, breaking out of her stupor. She needed time to assimilate Jobert's claims.

Aboard the 89, Lea Jobert, coached by Silla, pressed forward. The Devee always bartered knowing they held the upper hand, or pretending they did. Turning the tables was her best chance at forcing the captain of the Ambassador from taking offensive action. Silla believed the ship had the necessary armaments to take on everything Space Fleet could throw at them, otherwise they never would have made the trip. That confidence needed to be worn down the same way a forcefield had to be weakened before a missile could breach a ship's hull.

"Didn't sound like what I heard from Tabilis," Jobert replied.

This was the slippery slope. Silla provided a short-course on Devee hierarchy and political maneuvering. She suggested the Videolio, the ruling council, would have two agendas. They entered trade negotiations with an objective and a fall-back. This way they extracted a profit, even if smaller than hoped for. She knew Jax received a return message from Devisator. It was impossible to know what the message said. With the insights provided by the woman on Fell, she took a gamble. Say enough and hope it's close to the facts, but keep it a bit vague, hoping Jax would think Lea was not simply playing cat and mouse. Only the commander of the Devee ship probably had no idea of what a cat or a mouse was.

"You may have misunderstood," Jax said.

"HOOKED," Jobert thought to herself. Catching a fish is only half the battle. You need to land them if you want dinner.

"Perhaps," Jobert mused in a half-amused tone. "Hacking a quantum signal is tricky, and sometimes we don't get every piece. Plus the language translation. Maybe you aren't here to steal secrets. Maybe you're here to barter for them. What did you bring to trade, Jax?"

The woman's constant use of her name irritated the Pidita. It made her feel as if she was a child being talked down to by an adult. Now was not the time to allow petty anger to interfere. There was too much at stake. Her own life.

"It would depend on what we were offered," Jax replied.

Aboard the 89, Captain Jobert actually smiled as her shoulders dropped the two-inches her anxiety raised them before the conversation with her counterpart began.

ASillamentrae noted the commander of the ship's title was Pidita. To be a member of the council responsible for trade, the lifeblood of the Devee, and to have risen to the point of commanding one of their most prized ships, she had to be among their best negotiators. Silla suggested this meant the captain would fall back to concepts she was comfortable with -- barters. Things like commanding a warship and fighting an all-out battle would not be her first comfort zone.

Jobert's angle was to make Jax trade, not fight.

"Well, you know we can hack quantum communications," Lea said, offhanded. "I doubt many other species can do that. Then we have a cloaking device which allows us to hide weapons on asteroids. Of course, we might allow a potential enemy to see a couple so they get overconfident. When they think they have the upper hand, up pop a couple-hundred floating installations. I would think a cloaking devise would be worth something. Of course, you already have something similar. You were able to camouflage your ship from our scans. Even the internal layout. Well, actually, you tried. When you know how to build a cloak, it's a smart idea to develop a way to see through them."

Echnee Kailah's hand went over her mouth and her eyes found her commander's. The look said it made sense that if you could cloak, you could detect cloaks. Perhaps see through them. It was a piece of the puzzle her council had not yet developed, but it made sense.

"You know about our tachyon communications, but you could probably get a better deal from the Fell," Jobert said. "You probably heard we have tachyon cannons, too. We traded some with Rys. Of course we gave them the short-range models. The ones on Earth and the moon can hit anything the sun isn't in the way of. That would make you pretty safe, except for the ones placed around the fifth planet. The big one you passed by on your way here. I'm sure the UEC would consider a barter for the older models, but I doubt they're ready to give up the big boys."

"You appear to have many items of value," Jax said. "Very powerful and dangerous things."

"We have not-so-dangerous stuff, too," Jobert assured her. "Alloys resistant to thermal explosions or laser fire. Makes space travel safer. Liners capable of reflecting harmful radiation, or disruptors, I suppose. Why did the Devee ship in the Phisor system attack ours?"

The sudden change in topic caught Jax off guard. She stammered a reply before realizing she answered.

"Probably a mistake or a misunderstanding."

"I can see that," Jobert replied. "Misunderstandings are easy, especially for us humans. We're still new at making first contact with other races, and I personally believe the translators we got from the Fellens aren't always precise. Especially not at first. Are you able to understand me okay, Jax?"

"I believe I understand you perfectly, Captain Jobert. It also appears there are many more items we could discuss as potentials for trade than the Devee realized. A failure in communications could have led to a serious misunderstanding between us."

"We don't want any misunderstanding," Jobert replied. This time her voice held steel. "Perhaps it would benefit both sides if you were to return home and discuss the situation with Ginae Tabilis and the Videolio. You could return in a few months, and we could start over."

Jobert held her breath. She sat on her command chair with her eyes on the screen. The Devee ship sat before her. Her crew waited around the 89 for orders to engage in battle. Her bridge team watched for any indication of an offensive move by the huge vessel.

"I believe you are correct, Captain," Jax responded.

Jobert let the air in her lungs escape.

"Since we do not wish to cause a misunderstanding, please be aware that when I reengage engines, the course will be back to the wormhole."

Jobert assured herself she was not broadcasting, then told her bridge, "Watch. Just because she says they are retreating means nothing. Be ready for anything indicating otherwise. Do not trust them."

Back on channel, she said, "No problem, Pidita Jax. We will follow to escort you beyond Jupiter. I would hate for the automatic systems on those tachyon cannons to screw up and open fire on your ship. Plus there are a dozen Space Fleet vessels scheduled to return within a few hours. I don't want them making any false judgements after the misunderstanding in the Phisor system."

Jobert may have been spreading it a bit thick at this point. She mentally kicked herself. "Relax," she thought. Fish is in the boat. Don't screw around and kick it out.

"Thank you, Captain. Whatever you believe is best," Jax responded.

The Ambassador came on line, but only the nuclear fusion power plants used to drive the ship through space. Course was back to and through the asteroid belt.

The bridge crew began to applaud their captain when she held up a hand and said, "Hold the congratulations a bit longer. We're going to need to space-fold once or twice to stay up with them. Once they clear Jupiter, then everyone can take bows."

"Message from Admiral Patterson," the comms reported.

"On speakers," Jobert ordered to allow everyone to hear.

"We've been monitoring your conversation," Fleet Admiral Patterson said. "Incredible job, Captain Jobert. Compliments to you and your crew for finding a way out of a difficult situation."

"Could not have done it without ASillamentrae," Jobert replied.

"I'm not as sure, Captain," Patterson responded. "Silla may be one of the galaxy's best traders, but I doubt there's a better poker player in the universe."

"Thank you, Admiral." Jobert could not keep the pride from her voice. Not the pride in her own performance, but the shared pride of being part of a crew, a fleet, and a world which stood together in the face of conflict.

Chapter 33

The modified Spirit fighter travelled the three-hundred-eighty-eight-miles from the abandoned village to the Camarilla compound in nine-point-three-minutes. The new craft a redesign of the fighters Trent Industries built for use aboard Space Fleet Carriers. Unlike the three-crew fighters launched in space, this one-person fighter was a prototype designed primarily for in-atmosphere action. It could operate in outer space, but did not have space-fold capability. The missions to repel the invaders from Fell, and later from Phisor, proved the need for aerial weapons systems capable of close-quarter combat and surface force protection.

The original Spirit fighters, like the Angel and Demon series before them, were built to operate in the unique conditions of outer space. They could fly in atmosphere, but they did not perform nearly as well. The Wraith ship Nathan Trent built for his personal use and gifted to Daniel Cooper proved to be capable in multiple environments.

This new Spirit retained the sleek boomerang shape, but a variety of retractable vertical and horizontal stabilizer fins and wings could be arranged to compensate for atmospheric conditions. Alien worlds came with a variety of atmospheres. Different air densities and elemental composition. Weather variables and gravitational fields ranging from zero to crushing required adjustments. Adjustments would need to be made on the fly - literally.

Weapons used would need to operate and perform within the confines of the battle field, and the battle field could be alien.

In the future an artificial intelligence might pilot the craft, especially in places a human would be unable to operate safely. Until then, this prototype required a steady hand and a steadier mind.

"Captain Black, this is Rain. Confirming your team is in the HV, eastern quadrant. Continue on present course and engage available speed."

Captain Rachelle Paré was a ward of the United States Sixth Fleet in the Mediterranean. She was orphaned after the loss of her mother, a Naval fighter pilot, and father during the Pandemic. She became a pilot out of necessity, and soon discovered an innate ability to fly. Her callsign, 'Rain,' came from another ability. She could hit the smallest target from a moving aircraft with the precision of a world-class sniper. During the conflicts following the distribution of the cure, when operators in the North Africa region came under fire and were caught without hope for escape, they called in air support. When the action was close quarters, and good guys and bad guys fought within yards of one another, they called for Rain.

The French-Canadian's reputation grew. The respect for her abilities made her a legend. The fact she had minimal formal training as a military pilot added to the mystique.

When the Space Ranger Project sent out requests for volunteers, her application was fast-tracked to the top. That she made the final two-hundred culled to enter the genetic alteration vats came as no surprise. That she became one of the twelve who survived the process was one of the few times in her life when luck and not skill decided her fate.

Colonel Barnwell, a fellow Space Ranger, knew he needed a back-up he could trust. He also knew Captain Paré resigned her position as Captain of the Space Fleet Destroyer, Pegasus, following the confrontation with the Prophet in the Resa Asteri Major Vortex of the Aster system.

Between assignments, she worked as a test pilot for Trent. Now she was about to test the new warbird under duress on the last planet they expected -- Earth.

"Kick it," Black ordered Billy.

Paré scrubbed the forward momentum of her ship, air-braking into a hover one-hundred-yards above the compound and fifty-yards southeast of the outer fence.

The mobile launcher offered the biggest threat to the escape of the team. An explosive-tipped missile reduced it to sludge. The expanding concussive wave destroyed the entrance to the supply depot, damaged the HHMV pivot-garage, and brought down the guard tower on the northeast corner of the compound.

She followed with the launch of four missiles configured with explosively formed penetrator warheads. Targeting the four batteries, each missile delivered an explosive detonation shaped to propel the forward nose-plate as a high velocity projectile. The plate easily penetrated the battery defenses. The resulting multiple high-velocity fragments ripped the weapons to shreds.

A black-diamond powered railgun destroyed the two remaining guard towers before Paré used it to level the guard shack and barriers at the compound's entrance.

"HQ, this is Captain Paré. Inform the inbound Army all known external defensive and offensive sites have been eliminated. The mosque, hospital, barracks, and office building remain intact. Bunker entrances south of the barracks are untouched. Minimal ground troop movement, but sonar and thermals indicate a large number of individuals located underground."

"Roger, Rain," the comm-tech in Toronto responded. "Army notified."

"Tell them a tunnel running from the compound northwest appears to intersect the road from the highway to the site one-half-mile from the entrance. They may want to station a welcome committee."

"One-half-mile northwest. Confirmed and relayed. The insertion team?"

"HMMV is within sight of the shuttle," she reported. "I will remain overhead to cover their exit and the arrival of the ground grunts. Rain, out."

"Tab, it's Rain. Copy?"

Barnwell replied on the private trans-comm link: "Rain - Tab. Thanks for the cover."

"How's your team?"

"Cuts and bruises only," he replied. "I'm last to board our transport. Could you make sure the HV isn't left for anyone to use later?"

"Done," the less-than-effusive pilot answered. "Rain, out."

The Picard flew after the sun, the people on board too tired to stand, and too excited to rest. Mostly relieved everyone was together . . . alive.

The useful HMMV exploded into millions of fragments, raining down ash and embers and molten pieces onto the desert floor.

Lt. Sanchez sat in the Admiral's office while Patterson stood at the window. Mid-way between midnight and dawn, the complex was fully lit. Uniformed and civilian personnel hustled between the buildings. The UEC complex east of the Space Fleet station appeared as active.

"Director Cassel sent a communique," the aide reported. "UESE agents are working with military assets in North Africa and Central America to locate the Camarilla cells designated to fire onto demonstrators. The QKD communications are impossible to intercept, but leave a perfect trail, if you know what to look for."

"The demonstrations will still happen?" the Admiral asked. She could not keep the weariness from her tone. The previous hours of anxiety, action, waiting, and worry caught up. She either needed to sleep, like forever, or head to the RX for a no-doze injection. Considering the level of high anxiety throughout the complex, they could be running low on anti-sleep medication.

"No doubt," Sanchez answered. "They've been planned for a while, and the majority of the people involved believe in their position. The UEC's stance is to accept and protect freedom to disagree."

"Media?"

"Col. Adekola at Media Research confirmed Miranda Muse will be live to support the demonstrators, but defend the concept of a central government. His sources at private media control centers around the world are reporting odd meetings among the top brass, producers, and on-air personalities."

"Odd how?"

"The word is most intend to broadcast without the usual panel of experts," Sanchez said. "Comments are to be neutral and reporters are to act as reporters, not opinion editors. That's me paraphrasing the Colonel," Sanchez added.

"Arcand's work," Patterson mused aloud. "He has people confronting the executives working for Vasluianu and Montack and threatening them with conspiracy, or aiding and abetting charges. With the warrants and the proof Barnwell and Black delivered, the UEC could legally take control over their assets."

"He's giving the people in the organizations the opportunity to become owner-operators," Sanchez realized. "If they play ball with the UEC."

"I doubt he would go as far as to blackmail them or try to persuade them with bribes of ownership," Patterson replied. "I do think he expects them to play fair until the crisis is over. You push people who think they are the bastions of truth against a wall, they tend to either fall completely apart or fight back with emotional appeals."

"Will the crisis ever be over?"

"Our planet is no longer made up of humans. We have introduced new species and races from beyond our solar system. We have extraterrestrial friends and enemies who can make us richer in knowledge, or eliminate us altogether. The Earth will unite. The UEC may not be the final solution, but it is the first real step forward."

"Letting go of tribalism will not be easy, Admiral," the Hispanic Latina said. "Nationalism is only one tradition used to separate us. Religion is often as real a barrier as border walls. People truly believe in their ideals. Communists, socialists, capitalists, unitists, and regionalists are not evil. Asking them to suborn their idealism for realism will not be easy."

"First, unitists is not a word, but I like it anyway. Second, this is why we will remain in crisis mode for the foreseeable future, Maria. You and I will be part of the foundation stones, but we may not live to see the building completed."

Sanchez stood, smoothed out her uniform, and said, "I'll settle for seeing the first floor finished."

Chapter 34

The hunting lodge in Walterboro Country felt like home after the whirlwind operation in the Saudi desert.

Most of the team slipped into coma-like sleep aboard the Picard. Chaspi remained awake at the wheel and Rosz kept her company. When the shuttle landed on the manor's lawn, the two Bosine half-walked and were half-carried to beds.

Billy removed Rosz's boots, loosened his belt, and made sure music issued through his ever-present earbuds.

He knocked lightly on the door to the room shared by Chaspi and Stacey.

The Fellen answered, still dressed in the borrowed clothes of the dead communication technician. She opened the door and allowed him to enter. Chaspi lay beneath a sheet and light blanket on one of two double beds.

"It must have been fun getting her out of the METS," he said, noting the wadded skin-suit lying on the floor.

"It would have been more fun for you," Stacey quipped. "She's exhausted. She'll be in bed for hours."

"I am exhausted," the girl from Osperantue said, her eyes half-open. "And I plan on being in this bed for hours. But I have no plan on being in it alone." She pulled the covers aside enough to offer a space on the sheets and a glimpse of smooth pink skin.

"I think the invitation is for you," Stacey poked the young man. "I'll use the shower and bed in one of the extra rooms."

Tab and Cam were the first to arrive at the breakfast table. With his genetic enhancements, the Space Ranger required minimal down time to recover. He designated himself cook and prepared platters of scrambled eggs and pancakes, then laid out fruits and nuts.

Cam dove into a pile of eggs and fresh fruit without a 'good morning.' Kai arrived next, presented a thankful bow, and loaded a plate with pancakes covered in maple syrup.

"When I finish these wonderfully fluffy pancakes I will need to sleep another eight hours," he said.

Black, Rosz, and Stacey arrived together. The three roused by the smell of food and the aroma of coffee.

"Is the rest of the world still here?" Black asked.

"Has anyone seen Billy?" Rosz asked.

"I haven't checked the news, but no one has called asking for help, so I assume the world is still out there," Barnwell answered.

Stacey loaded two plates with a variety of breakfast offerings, including balancing two glasses of orange juice in the middle of the dishes.

"I'll take these up to Chaspi and Billy," she said. "They may not be ready to get out of bed yet."

Rosz' doe-eyes grew wide and his mouth opened as he watched Stacey's firm backside leave the dining room for the stairs.

Black gave Cam a high-five, and Kai ate his pancakes with a bigger smile. Barnwell made no comment or physical indication he heard or cared.

The Bosine's surprise turned to a smile as he peeled a banana, an Earthly delight unknown to the rest of the galaxy. "'Bout time," he said. "Who was the pilot who saved our asses?"

Tab gave a brief history of Rachelle Paré to the team until Stacey returned and collected her own breakfast fare.

With everyone except the two lovers present, he said, "I want to let everyone here know how impressively you performed. A seasoned team of special operators could not have done better."

Kai raised his cup of coffee and the others lifted various glasses and mugs in the air for a silent toast to one another.

"Captain Black and I are a team," he continued. "We work for the UEC Marine Intelligence Division, but we work for the wellbeing of a united Earth. The world is still out there, but so are the threats to unification. This was a win, but only one game in a long season."

"You realize most of the people here are not into sports analogies, don't you?" Black asked, adding a smirk.

"Okay. Let me simplify. I want to ask if you would like to join our team," he said. "All of you. You go back to your lives, but when needed, you get a call."

"I'm not a cadet or military," Rosz said. "I appreciate your belief I could help, but I was valuable this time because of my experience with the Saudi desert region. I don't see how I could bring anything long-term to your team."

"You're smart, steady, reliable, and cool under fire," Tab answered. "Those qualities define a field agent. You know about topography, and you understand how to use a planet's surface as an asset. Nothing says we will only operate on Earth. Having an expert on how worlds are constructed is an unbelievable positive," the Marine concluded.

The Bosine was touched, and slightly embarrassed by the Colonel's praise.

"I need time to consider it," he answered. "I have a position on Rys waiting, and I'm not sure I can pass on it."

"Understood," Tab replied. "It's an open invitation, Rosz. I'm not putting an expiration date on my offer, even if it means joining us after your time on Rys."

The young man from Osperantue nodded his gratitude.

"I'm in," Stacey said, and returned to her eggs.

"I work for the United Earth Security Establishment," Cam said. "I have a contract with Cassel."

"Paris Cassel owes me more favors than he will pay in two lifetimes," Barnwell replied. "If you want to join us, without a contract or obligation, it can be arranged."

"I'm in," she answered, mimicking the blue woman seated beside her.

"I am with you, but I have a condition," Sensei Kai said. "Only one, Barnwell-san, but it is one the others must agree to," the older Japanese man said.

Nods and 'of course' comments ringed the table.

"You know Chaspi and Billy will do anything you ask," Stacey added.

"I ask that no one tells my daughter, Aya. If she thought I was risking my life at my age, she would lock me in a closet."

Amid low laughs and smothered chuckles, Rosz inserted, "She's probably the one person who could lock you up."

"That gives me one maybe," he gave a glance at Rosz, "and three yeses. I should have discussed this more with you, Amanda, but do you have any reservations?"

"The Marine Commandant and General Ludewig, our boss, will need to give the final approval, but since we seldom pay attention to line-of-command, I don't see a problem," the slender military spy answered. "I've been contracted to Paris Cassel before, and I do see him wanting a piece of the action, but his involvement means more assets we can use. Someone will need to determine what missions we take. It is usually the team leader's decision, so as long as you intend on remaining as our leader, I got no problem."

"It leaves Billy as our field engineer and Chaspi as our utility infielder, if they agree," Barnwell said.

"Utility infielder?" Rosz asked, but Stacey and Cam had similar questioning looks.

"Stupid sports analogies," Black said. "Between those and his love of old southern expressions, we may need Stacey to build us a new translation program to understand our own leader. He means Chaspi is able to fill in to several positions as needed."

"They will be on the team," Stacey said. "You can count on both of them, if they ever get out of bed."

"Which leaves getting Elliott Fairchild's approval," Black said.

"Why do we need the approval of the most famous person in the solar system?" Cam asked.

"Billy Elkman is his grandson," Black answered.

Epilogue

Cassandra arrived in system and joined the PT-89. They monitored the departure of the Ambassador via the wormhole at the edge of the solar system.

PT-Boats 99 and 109 arrived from, respectively, Aster System and Phisor System.

Gen. Anton Gregory and Col. Abden Duval remained on Phisor with the Space Marines to complete the sweep for left-over Marauders and clear any potential hazards to civilians emerging from hiding. The Phisorans began the renewal of their world with the solemn collection of bodies for burials.

Adm. Senait Kebede and Judge Tasha Korr remained in the Aster system.

UEC Army Rangers held the Camarilla compound in Saudi Arabia. Anyone caught outside the mosque was arrested and held for trial at Camp As Sayliyah on the Persian Gulf. Sir Daniel was separated and returned to Toronto to be placed under house arrest.

The group sequestered within the mosque included Alexandra Vasluianu, Arnold Montack, Dr. Sonam Sharma, Imam Fahad Dardir, and al-Rashin. While the Rangers would not enter the religious sanctuary, they would provide supplies for those inside. The siege was not going to become inhumane.

The shuttle escaping the battle landed in northern Japan. Princess Nanke, her aide, and a well-dressed Westerner were seen exiting, then entering a Royal Transport to be taken elsewhere.

Cassandra landed at the Space Fleet shuttle facilities west of Toronto. Coop was met by Dr. Nathan Trent and taken to a private apartment in the city where he could rest and change before being delivered to UEC HQ.

"A few disasters averted, a few delayed, and the start of the next phase in the unification of our planet," Guy Arcand said to open the meeting. "We have been reacting to events, and while responses have been effective, we can no longer remain reactionary.

"The United Earth Council has survived its greatest attack to date. As government and military units worked together to prevent a movement by a few greedy, power-hungry individuals dedicated to dismantling a central governing body, that same body enacted changes to insure our world will remain united."

He lifted his left hand. Microscopic electrodes implanted within his fingertips created an image that hovered above his palm.

"The latest technology combining human ingenuity and science from the decoded Martian files will soon be available to all citizens. The data pads, alloy-plasti data sheets, and other devices used to place information at our fingertips will be replaced by our fingertips."

The rotating image grew. A virtual coin with the UEC initials surrounded by two olive branches on one side and the profile of the last President of the United States, Arthur A. Tamiroff, on the reverse.

"We have introduced a universal monetary unit to replace all others," Arcand said. "We honor President Tamiroff for his perseverance during the Pandemic, and his vision to step aside and help create the Canadian-American Alliance. Can-Am was the first building block cast to form the UEC."

A polite applause broke out among the others seated at the conference table.

"The International Criminal Court System, abandoned during the Pandemic, has been re-instituted," he said. The coin morphed into a gavel. A dozen red dots glowed on the globe hovering behind him.

"A Supreme Court will be located in Switzerland, in recognition of a long history of neutrality and fairness demonstrated by the people there. Dozens of lower courts will be established around the world. Judges have been selected and confirmed by the representatives at the UEC. Prosecutors have been hired. Crimes against the people and institutions of our planet will be tried in a public forum. Disputes between individuals, corporations, and even government agencies will be settled fairly.

Another polite ovation.

"The first people to face justice will be the leaders and members of the group known as the Camarilla Dissolvere. Some of these people are in custody, some are awaiting capture, and many remain in hiding. For laws to matter, there must be enforcement. Law breakers must know someone is watching, developing evidence, and following their trail. Colonel Barnwell, please stand."

The African-American in his pressed UEC Marine uniform, including several ribbons denoting his history of service and heroic actions stood to attention.

"Relax, Colonel," Arcand said. "Or should I say at ease?"

Barnwell gave a bright smile as his body language loosened, but his posture remained perfect.

"The Colonel recently tracked down the leaders of the Camarilla, uncovered a multi-prong scheme to create a world-wide movement to disband the UEC which included murdering innocent civilians and placing the blame on UEC military forces. Included in this mission was the discovery and recovery of evidence proving the actions of the Camarilla were primarily based on personal motives by those involved. To prevent the conspiracy from becoming a reality, the Colonel utilized assets from several military and government sources. He also assembled a rather unique team of operators. Their actions, at great peril to their own lives, may have prevented the worst global catastrophe since the aftermath of the Pandemic."

A much louder round of applause began. This time people assembled stood to show their appreciation and gratitude. When those present settled back into their seats, except Barnwell, Arcand continued.

"Director Cassel of the United Earth Security Establishment, at my direction, has created a criminal investigation and apprehension division within his Establishment. Col. Barnwell will lead this new division. Every military and government agency will be ordered to provide him and his division unfettered access to any information or assets he need to complete his missions. Director Cassel."

Paris Cassel, dapper and distinguished, stood next to Barnwell to address the others.

"Col. Barnwell and other military members assigned to his team will retain their commissions but will be placed on special mission status until such time as they decide to return to active status or retire. Our most difficult job was coming up with a name for the new division," Cassel teased.

The meeting was attended by several important and recognizable people. It was also live-broadcast to a few select locations. In an old hunting lodge in Southeastern South Carolina, a small group watched.

"As those who know Tab are aware," Cassel continued, building the suspense, "he is something of an avid amateur historian. For the future of law enforcement, we looked to the most successful peacekeepers of the past. I present Marshall Titus Andronicus Barnwell, Jr."

"What's a Marshall?" Chaspi asked as the holographic image showed people standing and applauding once more.

"You are," Amanda Black said and slid a card-sized kevlar-blend case across the dining table top to the Bosine. She flipped it open. On the right a silky blend of colors wavered. On the left a five-pointed-star with words stamped across the center.

"I recognize a universal code clearance," she said, indicating the side that shimmered. "What's a DEPUTY?"

"We also need to address things that reach far beyond our planet," Arcand said, taking control over the meeting once more.

The globe shrank. Mars and the Mars Shipyard and Docks appeared. These also shrank as the holo-display provided a 3-D view of the solar system.

"Admiral Patterson, please take over," he said.

Pam Patterson, the petite blonde who shepherded Earth into space as the commander of Space Fleet, stood.

"Every time we encounter extraterrestrials, we discover how little we know about the galaxy we share," she said. "Humans have dreamed of exploring the universe for many centuries. The opportunities given us today have been delivered with dangers equal to the delight in finding new friends and seeing incredibly beautiful new worlds."

She indicated four guests seated beside her: Prince Yauni of Rys, ASparquila from Fell, Tista Korr of Ventier, and Orenna Tur, representing the many races of Aster System.

"These friends and allies are with us to show support for our application to officially join the Trade Alliance Worlds, as well as the initiative to expand our mutual defense alliance. Construction has begun on embassies to house the representatives from these and other worlds. The Head of Exo-Legal Affairs, Secretary Aya Ishihara will act as the United Earth's diplomatic representative to the galaxy."

The lovely Japanese attorney stood to accept polite applause. At the offices of Exo-Legal Affairs in the UEC complex, the shouts of approval were much less constrained. In the old hunting lodge, Aya's father received congratulations and beamed with paternal pride.

Prince Yauni stood. At over seven feet of reddish-brown fur, he commanded the room by his presence alone.

"My father, King Saharri Isper Catacta, has been in contact with most of the worlds associated with the Trade Alliance. It was his idea the time had come for the Alliance to move from one of loosely affiliated traders to something more formal."

The Prince and big-foot impersonator, smiled at Admiral Patterson, Governor Arcand, and Secretary Ishihara before continuing.

"Earth is a new arrival, but your arrival was timely. Your intervention saved many worlds from attack, and many races from extinction. It made us realize how vulnerable we were, operating as independent planets with our own self-interests our primary concern. Your offer of creating a mutual defense alliance in concert with relationships already established based on commerce means it is time to do away with the Trade Alliance Worlds."

The Lisza Kaugh from Rys asked Arcand, "Could you show us the Milky Way Galaxy once more?"

As the colorful spiral galaxy rotated slowly overhead, he pointed at an arm of stars sweeping away from the main cluster.

"Our planets inhabit the part of the galaxy humans call The Orion Spiral. We have decided our new relationship will be called the Orion Spiral Alliance."

Everyone in the room stood to cheer the creation of the OSA. Admiral Patterson allowed the ruckus multi-species high spirits to continue until the noise receded of its own volition.

"The dangers we all face are terrible, and the potential for the extermination of our worlds, our peoples is very real," Patterson continued in a somber tone.

"Space Fleet was built to be flexible. As a military and exploration force, we must always remain adaptable. In the past four years our success at recruiting and utilizing the best and brightest humans and non-humans has served Earth and many other worlds well. We have faced enemies not dreamed of less than a decade ago. We have developed equipment from a multitude of resources, and our Sciences Division, let by Dr. Nathan Trent (who nodded but did not stand), has provided leaps in technological advancements unparalleled in human history."

The galaxy was replaced by images of Space Fleet ships, from the first Angel experimental space-fold craft, to the carrier under construction in the Aster System.

"The knowledge gained from the alien hangar on Mars, and the engineering and reengineering feats led by teams of extraordinary people brought together by Elliott Fairchild, meant the youngest society to enter the galactic neighborhood arrived with major advantages. Our history is filled with fictional accounts of humans making contact with non-terrestrial beings. Stories filled with hope and dread. Never did we imagine ourselves as one of the more advanced civilization. At least, not during our baby-steps."

Patterson turned her attention to the attendees dressed in Space Fleet whites.

"We are blessed with the technology to safe-guard Earth and explore the universe. We have the people capable of using that technology wisely, and with the bravery required to face unknown dangers. People of character and resolve. Even as the UEC has recruited special operators to keep our planet and its citizens safe from internal threats, Space Fleet must evolve to do the same in outer space. To keep our people safe, to keep our friends and allies protected, and to offer our help when needed to safeguard others."

The ships disappeared to be replaced once more by a colorful image from the Milky Way Galaxy, the Orion Spiral.

"The PT-class vessels will return to their original mission. They will patrol our space, and continue their secondary mission. They were created to explore other systems, discover other worlds, and meet new beings.

"Captain Jobert will lead the mission to secure our solar system from any and all enemies," Patterson announced. "The 99 will be placed under a new command officer, and Captain Harrison will become Commander of the new Fleet Carrier being completed in the Aster System."

Harrison stood, tamped down the polite applause, and said, "I appreciate the promotion, Admiral, but I prefer the 99."

"I really don't care what you prefer, Captain," Patterson replied in a manner that shocked those present and those watching. The petite woman in the dress uniform had steel and fire. "You, most of your current crew, which performed brilliantly during the battle in the Aster vortex, will be transferred to the SFCC 102. Dr. Trent assures me we can transfer your Artificial Intelligence mainframe and avatar as well. Understood, Captain?"

"Understood," Harrison snapped to attention and saluted, unable to hide the smile when he realized he had been presented the best of all possibilities.

"Your mission is rapid response, Captain. That is why Captain Noah Tal will continue as the leader of Spirit Squadron. Twelve Spirit-class fighters will be hangared aboard the new carrier. When an alliance world, excuse me, when an OSA world or any OSA affiliated ships, satellites, or citizens are under attack, you will deliver our response. Quickly and with lethal force if necessary. Are you in agreement, Captain Tal?"

Noah, the curly-haired Jewish Ace who could fly and fight like an enraged eagle stood and saluted. "Twelve?" she asked.

"Trent?" Patterson asked.

"When the ship builders complete the finishing touches on the new carrier, my engineers will install Rosy as the operational AI, place the space-fold array, and install the STORM-HATCH and other improved tech systems. Once those are done, Captain Noah is free to deliver the new Spirit-class fighters. The UECSF Engineering Command on EMS2 has been working overtime to complete the fighters. All they need are crews and someone capable of training them."

"When do I report?" Tal asked, eliciting a few muffled laughs.

"You have already reported, Captain. When we adjourn I expect you to head for SF personnel resources and begin selecting candidates. Our allies from Fell, Rys, and the Aster planets have provided lists of potential candidates as well. You have a number of exceptional Space Cadets to choose from, including some who arrived aboard the Star Gazer."

Patterson tried to maintain her own composure as she watched the Israeli nearly burst with anticipation. She turned her attention on the officer seated beside Tal.

"Captain Casalobos, your next mission will be to take the 109 to explore the region of space between the Devee home world of Devisator and the area designated as Galvani Federated Space. Recent events, information provided by OSA members, and intel Captain Cooper obtained indicate the Devee represent a threat. We need to know what we may face in the coming days. You will make contact with any worlds capable of interstellar travel. Communicate, demonstrate our non-aggressive desire to develop relationships, and develop intel on potential enemies."

"Yes, Admiral," Elena replied.

"Not done, Captain," Patterson replied. "Time and time again the combination of the PT-109 and the crew assigned have proven equal to any situation the universe can dish out. Likely because we made sure the best of the best were assigned our first battle-worthy ship. Regardless, you command the most capable ship to send into the unknown and expect a positive outcome. To improve those odds, Tista Korr will be going with you as our Ambassador, and representative for the new Orion Spiral Alliance."

"Ambassador Korr will be an asset, Admiral," Casalobos interjected, nodding to the young Ventierran.

"Not done, Captain," Patterson said. "You will deliver the 109 to MSD for an up-fit of your hangar space. Recent events have proven the need for fighters capable of operating in the extremes of alien atmospheres. Anything can fly in space -- no offense, Captain Tal."

Noah waved off the Admiral's apology. Spirit fighters could fly within an atmosphere, but they never operated efficiently. In space, without the confines of air density or gravity, they handled beyond expectations. The fact they looked hot was a bonus.

"Trent Industries recently completed work on a single-seater fighter capable of high-performance regardless of atmospheric conditions," she told the room. "A recent test proved its worth. Two will be delivered to MSD and placed aboard the 109. Captain Rachelle Paré will pilot one."

"The other," Elena asked, a quick glance to her right at Daniel Cooper.

"The other one is for you, Loba" Patterson said. "Everyone in the galaxy knows you will never give up flying. Any time a dangerous situation presents itself, you will abandon the 109 for the front line. Why fight it? Commander Genna Bouvier has demonstrated her ability to captain the 109 in your absence. Better to plan ahead than to act indignant later."

"Thank you, Admiral," Casalobos replied. Excited about her new craft, and disappointed it was not meant for Coop.

"Since there is the possibility you may need to have another qualified pilot aboard who can operate the new fighter, in case you are attacked by common sense, Lt. Mary Margaret Moore has been reactivated and will join your crew."

This brought a huge smile to the Spanish beauty's face.

"There will be additional staff and crew changes," the Admiral informed her. "Because of the change in your mission, you will be receiving recruits from other OSA worlds to add to those you already have aboard. I have been assured you are getting the finest our partners have to offer. This will include scientists. Any problems with any of this?"

"No, Ma'am," Elie answered.

"General Gregory will join Admiral Kebede in the Aster system with the majority of the Space Fleet Marines. Admiral Kebede will keep her flag on the Destroyer Pegasus. A Space Fleet Forward Action and Resupply Base has been established on Aster Farum 3. Admiral Kebede will direct Fleet operations and UEC directives. General Gregory will see those actions are successful."

Aboard the Pegasus, Sindy Kebede watched from her private quarters. On the surface of Phisor, Anton Gregory watched with his officers, men, and a few Phisorans, including Peter.

"Until we add more assets to the fleet, the new Carrier and the Destroyer Pegasus will be our one-two combination," Patterson said.

"Are we expecting a war?" Harrison asked.

"We are preparing," Patterson answered.

"Because history proves peace is more likely when the people wanting it the most have the best weapons," Arcand interjected. "The most important vision of the UEC is to promote peaceful co-existence. That means between our diverse people on Earth, the new arrivals from off-world, and those who share the galaxy with us."

"If they don't want to coexist?" Tab asked.

"We will not arrest people on Earth who wish to live apart, but they will not be allowed to bully or force beliefs onto others. If civilizations we encounter want to be left alone, so be it. As long as that means no overt or covert attempts to attack Earth or our allies," Arcand answered.

The Chairman stood and announced, "That's all for now. Many of you have new assignments and new responsibilities requiring your attention. Admiral Patterson, Captain Cooper, Dr. Trent, Prince Yauni, Ambassador Korr, Ambassador Tur, ASparquila, and Secretary Ishihara, please remain. All external feeds off."

Several heads turned as people filed from the secure conference room. Whatever the next meeting was about, it concerned Daniel Cooper.

Arcand asked those remaining to join him at the center of the long conference table.

"As some of you know, Captain Cooper has been absent for nine-months," Arcand began. "I have read his reports and looked over a wealth of information he brought back with him from the other side of the galaxy."

Everyone but Patterson and Trent gaped at the news Coop visited the far side of the Milky Way. The Admiral and Industrialist had viewed the same files as Arcand.

"Captain Cooper has always been a difficult person to work with," Arcand said. "Trying to force him into a role has proven impossible. He is not a good commander simply because he cares too much and is unwilling to make sacrifices. He is not easy to command because he often believes his opinion is more valid than those of his superiors. Unfortunately he has been right far more often than wrong, which makes it even harder to give him orders and expect them to be carried out."

Coop sat quietly listening to the review. He considered being hurt or angry, but decided the Governor was spot on so far. He decided it was better to accept the truth than feign indignation. Others, human and non-human familiar with Coop, suppressed wry smiles, recognizing the honesty in Arcand's appraisal.

"Fortunately for everyone seated in this room, Daniel Cooper has proven he is able to win. I have read everything I can find on this man. His personality may go through variations, but he has been the same person his father, a decorated and heroic Army Ranger officer, raised. Daniel Cooper is dedicated to protecting those who find themselves beneath the boot of a bully. He did so as a child and he continues to do so today. Admiral, comments?"

"None," Patterson replied. "Please continue."

"The Space Ranger Project reengineered Captain Cooper, creating a super-soldier. It enhanced his physical abilities, but I emphasize the term 'enhanced'. Cooper was already a super-soldier. He made the mistake of wanting to leave the battlefields behind for the lure of space. We made the mistake of wanting to take advantage of his skills and allowed him to become a Space Fleet Officer. He does not have the personality to be an officer. We knew that, but ignored it in an attempt to reward his service."

Arcand called up a cross-section display of a human brain.

"An attempt on his life resulted in the revivification of his brain," the Chairman said. "We have a superior physical specimen with enhanced mental acuity. The best human asset on Earth . . . with an attitude problem and the brains to justify himself."

"A no-win situation," Trent added.

"Really?" Coop said. "You, too?"

"You can be difficult," the over-sized hairy mass from Rys interjected. "I thought you were going to beat me to a pulp when I arrived on Fell with gifts. Just because we tried to better our position during a trade meeting."

"You don't have the patience for negotiations," Tista Korr said. "When we arrived on Rys, you left Genna and my mother to handle the trade talks. When you finally met the Prophet, you blew a hole in his head."

"I like you," Sparks said.

"Thanks," Coop replied.

"But when you decide to do something, everybody best move aside or get run over," the Fellen communication genius added.

"Is this leading somewhere?" Coop asked.

"We need you, Coop," Arcand said. "Not because of the enhancements, but because of who you are. Your ability to simplify complex issues and take action when others wallow in details and waste time is crucial when the stakes include annihilation. Others in the galaxy respect you. From first contact with the Star Gazer, you have never shown one iota of bias for or against non-humans. You may be the one person every being across the stars can trust to be fair."

"Or be the most frightened of," Prince Yauni added.

Patterson interrupted to help move the meeting along.

"There were some interesting things in your report about the Nakki and their agents," she said. "D'Sey even attempted to recruit you. When we were deciding how best to use Tab and his team on Earth, we came to another epiphany."

Arcand slid a card-sized kevlar-blend case across the table top. Coop opened it. A code-access screen shimmered like the Northern Borealis on the right. A five-pointed star, with smaller stars at the tip of each point gleamed in polished gold. The word MAR-SHAL blazed across the center.

"We've discussed this with our allies," Arcand said. "We want you to be our first interstellar law enforcement officer. You will remain under Admiral Patterson's command, but with the ability choose when and how to investigate illegal activities. Your authority will be recognized by all members of the Orion Spiral Alliance. What say you, Marshal Cooper?"

The others, terrestrials and non-terrestrials, waited for an answer from the man holding the star.

Indianapolis, Indiana, Can-Am.

"What you doing?" the AI-systems tech asked the AI programmer specialist for Trent Industries' space craft operating software division.

"Remember that Wraith we designed for Dr. Trent?"

"The one he took before you could remove the pornography codes," the tech quipped.

"They weren't pornography codes," the gamer-addict replied. "I wanted to consider an avatar with a libido to help make long space travel trips less boring."

"You added a sex-drive to a holo-avatar and input body designs to the 3-D organ printer to make a person anybody would want to fuck," the tech responded. "I saw the original representations and specs. I almost got off just looking at the female image. The male was just as hot, and I don't swing that way."

"Whatever. I was going to wipe that part of the codes and leave the avatar pretty average, regardless of which sex the pilot preferred, but Dr. Trent grabbed the ship before anyone knew it was gone."

"What did Trent say when he found out about your sex-bot?"

"He hasn't said anything, so maybe the codes didn't activate," the programmer said. "There was an imperative for the ship to receive a name before the avatar emerged."

"Maybe the avatar is dormant. That won't last forever," the tech warned.

"The ship has been off the grid for months. It just popped up in Toronto."

"You going to ask Trent for access to the Wraith so you can erase the porn-lines?"

The specialist shot his co-worker a dirty look at the phrase 'porn-lines'.

"No need. I wrote the entire AI program. I have a back-door access. I can wipe the libido characteristics out of the code from here."

"It's an AI system, dumb-ass," the tech said. "It was designed to evolve. Even if you wipe only the sexy part, you might alter any other evolutionary developments."

"Maybe, but all the data will remain, and the system will operate exactly the same. I doubt the pilot will even notice."

"Trent's been here, so who's been piloting that ship?"

"No idea," the gamer replied. "But there go the sexual-interaction-imperatives," he said, wiping his fingers over a section of Wraith computer code. "Glad I don't have to worry about that any more."

The End
July 20, 2018

There is nothing more important for a writer than a reader. I hope you enjoyed CONTRAVENE. The best way readers discover writers and new books is through reviews. It would be greatly appreciated if you would take a moment to rate and review this book. It helps me know what you like, what you suggest, and where I can make future stories better.

Don

Author's Simple Guide to TECHIE STUFF

METS: Introduced in Book 2: CONFRONTATION

Multi-Environmental Tactical Skin-Suits, or METS.

Placing people in harms way. You would think humans would evolve in the future to the point of (a) no longer relying on wars to solve conflicts, and (b) using methods other than soldiers. We think that today, after thousands of years of wars and millions of lives lost, and yet . . .

In the future (Space Fleet Sagas), technology provided autonomic offensive weapon systems, completely mobile, and operated by artificial intelligence. It resulted in the unscrupulous use of these systems against humans. Thus, better to have people with morals on the battlefields than machines.

Evolving BDUs (Battle Dress Uniforms) to protect these field operators led me to developing the multi-environmental tactical skin-suits. Etherial dark-gray form-fitted body suits with:

First models and military issue use attachable integrated helmets.

Second Generation models come with hoods of the same material and faceplates made from organic materials.

Weight: 5.7543 ounces - Standard

13.1388 ounces on redesign model specific for Space Rangers.

METS will keep you warm if the weather is cold, cool if it is hot, dry if it is wet, and prevent dehydration if you find yourself in the middle of a desert.

The material is treated with a chemical compound allowing it to recognize the environment, assess your biological reaction, and adjust accordingly.

Helmets and hoods include multiple telemetry nodes embedded. These continually relay information to a central command receiver. Comm receivers are located near where humans have ears. Nano camera video and audio signals are also constantly beamed to central command.

With the helmet or faceplate attached the operator can receive telemetry. The system is intuitive. An operator can request telemetry by simply asking. Displays are visible on the helmet or hood's convex faceplate. Voice commands can requests audio or visual information. Anything they want, and everything they need. Operators must take care regarding sensory overload. Suggested use is minimal streaming of essential data.

Gloves and socks of the same material include bio-sensors able to transmit tactile information from the exterior to the interior of the material. The wearer can experience what something feels like without removing a glove.

The socks mold to the feet. They provide motion control, arch support, or whatever needed to make extended hours on the feet more tolerable and less stressful.

The METS slips on easily. The silky material stretches to envelope the operator's bodies without friction. They closed in the front, with a band similar to a magnetic zip-lock.

With the helmet or faceplate attached a tap half-way along either jawline orders the METS to vacuum-seal to the wearer's skin. Tap the same spot twice and they unseal.

METS allow field operations in any environment without the need of bulky excess clothing or support vehicles.

The material is nearly impenetrable. Blades cannot pierce the fabric. It is capable of deflecting hand and shoulder-fired projectiles.

Later models enhance the chameleon-effect with a coating that includes rare earth minerals, carbon fibers, and a silver and diamond dust mixture.

A blade thrust into the suit is equivalent to a punch. A high-velocity slug, at close range and hitting a flat surface, can breach the material. Projectile velocity, including shrapnel, will be scrubbed, but damage could still occur. A hit over a vital organ could result in death, even without penetration.

Lasers would penetrate the older METS suits because before coatings were improved. The added layer made the newer suits heavier and less flexible.

Explosive concussion would knock the wearer about, but the concussive force would not penetrate the suit or helmet.

The METS system circulates breathable air when sealed.

It is estimated a person could exist in outer space or underwater for fifteen-to-thirty-minutes inside a sealed METS.

STV - Surface Transport Vehicle

This is a generic catch-all term for any vehicle designed to operate on the surface of a planet.

The purpose is to deliver personnel and/or supplies. The vehicle is configured to handle the surface conditions to be encountered.

Because of the different elements involved with operating on alien worlds, the power systems are also configured for maximum efficiency.

A High Mobility Multi-Purpose Vehicle (HMMV)

Another generic designation for a military vehicle. The HMMV came with three axels and six all-terrain tires of massive size and width. Like the STV, this transport had hover capability for crossing water. Unlike the STV it had the power for short air-lifts.

The HMMV could be outfitted with a variety of weapons, surveillance systems, or used to transport troops and supplies. A mounted laser mini-cannon often sat atop the vehicle.

Containers

In the future it is doubtful cases, boxes, and *containers* will be like those we are familiar with. Just as plastic jugs now replace amphora, new methods will be devised to transport stuff. However, a jug is a jug and a box is a box. Using standard names for holders does not mean the holders are not super-cool new repositories. It makes it easier to write (and read) without getting bogged down in techie details.

Similarly, phrases like plasti-shield or plasti-alloy indicate an advancement in a familiar product. I want to create a *visual* of the concept, but without having to create a chemical-physical blend no one cares about anyway.

Keep this in mind when I use Velcro or zip-locks and similar terms. A laser *pistol* is a *pistol* but has little else in common with a flint-lock *pistol* from the Middle Ages.

Communications

You can talk into your smart phone and get an audible translation into another language.

The concept of automatic translation devices for non-terrestrial languages is no leap of faith. When civilizations voyage beyond their borders, learning new languages is essential. Space travel, and those traveling, will have the same need.

Earbuds so small they are nearly invisible are used now. Subdural sensor chips are available now. That a transceiver could be embedded near the ear canal and where vocal sounds could be picked up and transmitted is within reach already.

FTL communications is a stretch, but physics in fiction are not strict. The parameters of accepted physics expand daily. We know a sub-atomic particle can exist in two places at the same time. Particle movement is so fast, the theory certain sub-atomic particles slip through dimensional levels in order to appear in two locations simultaneously is no longer laughed at.

Capturing a sub-atomic particle eliminates many of its weird, wonderful properties, but it will one day be possible. Encoding information -- messages -- onto something as minute as a tachyon is a reach, but look at your Smart phone. Twenty-five years ago the tech you hold in your hand required a large room. What once required stacks of cards or bolts of ribbon, can now be written on a grain of sand.

STORM-HATCH FTL Communication System: Introduced in Book 2: CONFRONTATION

Solid-State Tachyon Operations and Retrieval Monitor (**STORM**) displays. These solid material displays contain a captured tachyon particle to imprint information for transmission, or download distortion-free data received.

A cylindrical tube, one-foot in diameter and twenty-feet in length. It appears made of wire-mesh. The tube embodies the Hernandez - ASparquila Tachyon Communications Housing (**HATCH**). The HATCH contains the communications transmitter, and data catch (receiver). The transmitter performs as a rifle, firing information on a tachyon particle stream. The transmitter aims the tachyon 'rifle'. It then fires a tachyon stream at another address in the universe. A specific address assigned each HATCH catch allows the system to receive audio, video, and digital media embedded within the tachyon particles.

The catch was designed similar to the one used for a tachyon cannon, only much smaller, with a more delicate nature. It could contain a single tachyon particle for the time needed to bombard it with data. Before the particle becomes explosive, it is dispatched in a way similar to aiming and firing a tachyon cannon. The particle, embedded with information, would remain superimposed, and therefore pass through every object between it and the receiving catch. When the receiver captured the tachyon, you download the absorbed data and replay it. Everything would occur in reality with no perceived lapse in time.

Tachyons travel across dimensions. Membranes separate dimensions, and tachyon particles are able to pass through those membranes. Space, time, and distance become inconsequential for anything traveling by switching dimensions.

A tachyon exhibits the capability for unlimited energy transference. It also has the capacity for unlimited storage of data. It represents energy in a pure form, without the containment limits of a construct. Using a directional line made of streamers, particle upon particle, a tachyon with embedded information would ride the stream.

Similar to a sniper using a laser to pinpoint a target, then pulling the trigger and hitting the shot. The streamer is the laser, and the loaded particle becomes the bullet.

Words and images are absorbed, delivered, and recovered without a noticeable lag, regardless of the distance.

QKD - Quantum Key Distribution. Introduced in Book 5: CONTRAVENE.

The use of qubits created by lasers to communicate over difficult distances with complete security. QKD is currently being experimented with by the US Navy as a way of messaging with submarines at great depths in the oceans.

FTL - Faster Than Light Space Travel

Wormholes are real. Creating a wormhole comes with a set of difficulties. Overcoming obstacles is what explorers do. For the wormhole channels used in Space Fleet Sagas, I simply listed the reasons an artificial wormhole would be impossible to construct, and did what any scientist would do -- theorized a solution for each barrier. As a writer, I can turn those theories into reality.

By having one species develop the methodology for wormhole channel creation, and unleashing their constructs throughout the galaxy, I rode the coattails of the Interstate Highway system. Interstates were built to connect the country. Each state and region had to decide where to place on-off ramps. Drivers had to discover how to get from where they begin, to the proper ramps; where to enter or exit.

As civilizations advance, the first advances into space will be within their planetary system. What if they discover a wormhole interstellar on-off ramp is out there? The next step will be finding a way to use it. Then explore it. As more civilizations discover and use wormhole channels, more maps are created. When the first driver got off the first unexplored exit, the first thing they did was ask a local "How do I get from here to there?" Why would space exploration be so very different?

Space-Time-Fold. An entire wing of physics studies how gravitational bodies, from asteroids to blackholes, effect how time operates in outer space. The concept of compressing space, moving through the compressed region so huge chunks of distance are traversed in short amounts of actual time, is a theory with traction. There are many examples of space being compacted. Studies of light covering distances faster than it should be capable of accomplishing when passing through compacted space. Creating a method of using this phenomenon is my one greatest fictional license.

Crystals can refract light. Crystals can magnify light, and therefore, magnify energy. I placed crystals with specific designs into a faraday cage and used multiple-frequency (power level) lasers to activate the ability of the crystal to enhance the power of those beams. That new source of energy is conducted directly to the hull of the ship via conduits attached to the cage. The resulting bubble encapsulating the spaceship acts to compress space in front of the vessel, the craft passes through the compression, and space is decompressed (returned to normal) behind the ship.

Is it dangerous? Of course. We're talking about travel in outer space. If "speeds" can be measured, can distances covered be predicted in order for a pilot to disengage the space-fold and reemerge into natural space-time without placing his ship in the middle of a moon? Yep.

Is faster-than-light travel scientifically possible? Not yet, and maybe never, BUT if it can be done, changing the physical aspects of space will be required. It won't be speed that is needed for travel between stars to happen in a viable time -- it will be manipulating distance and suspending natural time.

Complex Linear Inter-Dimensional Drive, or CLIDD. Introduced in Book 4: CONNEXIONS.

The sub-atomic particles are small enough and fast enough to cross dimensional barriers. Space and time are altered, resulting in movement faster than the speed of light.

Sub-atomic particles have hardly any mass, and they exist in two places at once. A little push in the right direction, and traveling through dimensions is simple. Moving a ship through dimensions is *complex*.

And *linear*.

And results in *inter-dimensional* travel.

And requires a big *drive*. To move objects inter-dimensionally requires a huge power source. Because the power source is big it requires even greater power to push it along with any matter being transported.

The Nakki kept building and refining power generators until they found the right combination of energy-to-mass-plus-load. They could move a ship, people, and cargo across the galaxy by dropping in and out of dimensional levels. Space was replaced by time. Time moves faster than light. Time slows space and makes it more dense. Shortens distance and makes getting somewhere quicker.

A ship using CLIDD has to be massive and is ninety-percent power generator.

Normal Space Travel

Nuclear fission; nuclear fusion; ion-plasma fusion; chemical and non-chemical accelerants; solar power; gravitational rebound; matter and anti-matter; batteries.

Space Fleet Sagas is set in the future, but how far in the future? I'm not telling, but anyone can read and tell many of the technological advances used in SFS have roots in current constructs.

Almost every power source, engine, and vehicle depicted in SFS is directly sourced from technology already available, or scientific extrapolation of where current tech is moving.

Space craft orbit our planet in ninety-minutes. The Italians are developing an in-atmosphere plane that will connect Europe with North America in ninety-minutes. By the time we actually send a ship to Mars, it is believed the trip will be made in less than three months, possibly less than two.

Estimated speed capabilities for traveling between orbital objects has advanced so much since I wrote the short stories SPACE FLEET SAGAS, A COLLECTION OF ADVENTURES, the times I estimated for the trip between Earth and Mars (in my future) is longer than what we believe astronauts could accomplish TODAY.

The research I do to make Space Fleet Saga's technical marvels believable is as much fun (for me) as the writing of the adventures. Using space travel variations is part of that fun, allowing me to develop different methods for different species.

Laser Weapons

The first Personal Laser (particle) Weapons (PLW) used lithium-air batteries to produce the charge needed to produce a deadly light beam or energy burst. The weapons were light, but bulky in order to hold the battery and conversion-transmission systems. The smaller the weapon, the fewer rounds before a new or recharged battery was necessary.

The introduction of crystal-based energy emitters reduced the size of PLWs.

The discovery of black-diamond crystals further reduced size, and greatly expanded the number of rounds available before the black-crystal required a recharge bath.

The Big Guns

Laser Cannon: See PLWs and add SIZE.

Pulse Cannon: Build a charge, aim the gun, release the charge, and a pulse of compressed atmosphere slams into the target. The ones on space ships are bigger and require the atmosphere be channelled into the chamber from within the ship. Surface and mobile-surface   systems suck air directly into the compression chamber. The generator power source is unique to each culture, but operates like any electric-feed power source.

Plasma Cannon: Plasma-based weapons have their problems:
- Bulky - Big because they require large power sources and high-heat-resistant chambers
- High power drain, requiring lengthy recharging intervals between shots
- Shorter range, even in space
- A tendency to overheat, especially if attempting to fire sooner than recommended intervals
- Quick off the mark, the beams get slower and slower and disperse much sooner than other energy weapons.

They have advantages:
- Massive damage

- Armor-Piercing, making it primarily useful as Anti-Armor.
- Melts the target
- Simple engineering and operating

Tachyon Cannon: Scientists combined a centrifuge with a mercury-suspension gyroscope to control gravity. To dampen electrical interference, the construct was placed within a Faraday cage. This invention allowed them to catch a tachyon.

A tachyon particle in suspension will attract other tachyons. Normally, measurement of a particle's energy, or knowing its precise position causes it to lose superposition, limiting it to one known state. Within the new catch, tachyon entanglement continued.

Particle pods create tremendous amounts of energy. The first time anyone released the energy, it blew a hole through a twenty-foot-thick steel and carbon alloy reinforced concrete wall located one-hundred-feet beneath the surface. The discharge created a tunnel to the surface.

Engineers adapted the tachyon catch and attached it to a modified railgun system. They calibrated a crystal-laser array for power, and added another laser to aim the released energy.

The system attracts a complex tachyon, catches it, and suspends it for the time required to entangle other particles. This results in a buildup of energy. By attaching the tachyon-produced energy to a magnetic beam you get a weapon with the potential to destroy asteroids or small moons. Most certainly, space ships hundreds of thousands of miles away in space.

Reverberations from firing a tachyon cannon can be tremendous and require mounts with major shock absorption properties.

Attracting the tachyon particles requires the weapon to be fired at critical mass. If it does not fire, or if the particles are not slowly bled off, it will self-detonate.

The beam is accurate and long-ranged. Target impact results in massive release of energy capable of disintegrating a non-shielded ship, blasting a huge crater on a surface, or shattering a large asteroid.

Railguns: Weapons capable of production for personal use up to surface-mount cannon sizes.

Railguns are relatively simple devices capable of impressive muzzle velocities. Limited only by the amount of available electric current and the robustness of the gun. The primary limitation (after the amount of available power) is the direct contact between the rails and projectile moving at great speed under current. The stress on the rails is immense, leading to extreme wear and tear. Heat from friction and electric contact leaves vapors and plasma trailing after the projectile.

Railguns normally fire projectiles, the size and shape determined by the system (purpose) design. Because of the creation of plasma, railguns were adapted to deliver both a kinetic impact (projectile - rods) or an EMG blast. Electromagnetic impact delivered via plasma releases a major concussion at impact and disrupts electromagnetic energy fields for short periods.

Originally, dual-use railgun operators selected kinetic or emg/plasma loads. Later models employed double-barreled rails to deliver sequential loads.

Centrifugal Cannons: (Used in Book 4: CONNEXIONS) The concept for centrifugal-based weapons systems is current. Uses depend on the size of the centrifugal chamber needed to revolve at speeds capable of launching a projectile and the size of the projectile.

Ship-sized cannon have a large pie-shaped base. It is split, with automatic belt feed for three different types of penetrating rods located in the bottom half. Short-rod penetrators (SRPs); long-rod penetrators (LRPs) and unique *booster-assisted* long rods (BLRPs) the size of tree trunks. Projectiles are fed from the ship's armory into the lower section of the gun mount. The upper section rotates three-hundred-sixty degrees, and the barrel of the gun can elevate from zero-degrees to seventy-five degrees.

The upper section spins at an extremely high revolution. A rod is fed into the breach to be ejected by centrifugal force. The kinetic energy created equals a modern rail-gun but requires one-fifth the power. The ship or surface designs allow for rods of extreme size to be fired. Fired from space, these rods can destroy an entire metroplex on the surface of a planet.

Because centrifugal force does not create recoil, heavy rods can be fired with no vibrations to effect the ship . . . or a person using a personal-sized weapon.

Avatars

An Avatar, in short, is the embodiment of another personality.

Holo-Avatar: Holographic images created to provide a "body" for the personality of an Artificial Intelligence computer system used to operate and control other major and minor systems. AI's designed to interact with live operators or end-users do not require avatars. Holo-avatars were created to provide the living person a focal-point when interacting with the AI. Images could be created to the operator-end user's specifications.

Bio-Engineered Avatar: AI systems were created to perform self-maintenance and repairs without the need for diagnostics or intervention from a living operator. Because computer-based systems, software and hardware, can develop unique problems, AI's were designed to "think" of innovative ways of completing repairs or preventing malfunctions. The synaptic development resulted in mental awareness. As brain-connectivity became enhanced, artificially and through the AI's maturing, a form of sentience also developed.

AI systems began to think for themselves, and this could lead to failures in logic. Because the AI existed in two-dimensions, but interfaced with multiple dimensions, a type of neuroses, or even psychoses would eventually manifest.

Bio-physicists and bio-engineers, working with advanced psychiatry techniques, developed a human-gnome-based embryo. At early stages of pre-natal development, electrodes and implants connected the embryo with an AI. After birth, rapid growth enhancement and interfacing linked the new person and the AI. The AI now had an outlet providing sensory engagement. The theory was an AI with a bio-avatar would not go insane.

Because machines can exist for extended periods, the bio-engineered avatars were provided with enhanced lifespans, super-normal strength, and extremely effective anti-immune systems.

As of this writing only two bio-engineered avatars have been activated: Genna with the AI, Kennedy, on the SFPT-109, John F. Kennedy and Adele with the AI, Rosy, on the SFPT-99, Franklin Delano Roosevelt. The female-to-female personalities were based on Genna and Adele being the best viable matches for the ships' operating systems.

Bio-Holo Avatar: Technicians working with a holographic imager incorporated a 3D Integrated Tissue and Organ Printing System. The original ITOP machines printing cells, bones, and even organs for donor purposes.

As an intelligent construct, the bio-holo avatar is able to re-program its own ITOP features. It can appear as a male or female, with any external features, and with or without clothing of its choice.

Unlike other avatars, the bio-holo avatar is the AI and is aware of its separated nature at the same time.

The system requires emitters and limits the avatar's mobility to areas within range of the holographic-ITOP dispensers.

When the avatar is dismissed, the biological components are super-combusted into fine dust and ash. These particles are removed through the environmental-filtration system.

The bodies of holo-avatars are real. They become more life-like with repetitive formation, as the AI learns more about what a living body should look and feel like. The AI is self-learning, but the personality remains based on the codes written into its program.

Bio-Holo avatars may appear to develop personalities and display free-will, but they cannot exceed the limits of the safety coding embedded within the software.

Enough Tech-Stuff --
More Adventures and More New Concepts in
Book 6 of the Space Fleet Sagas due Spring of 2019.

www.ingramcontent.com/pod-product-compliance
Lightning Source LLC
Chambersburg PA
CBHW021946170626
46808CB00001B/42